BLACK FEATHERS

BLACK
FEATHERS

A NOVEL

Robert J. Wiersema

HarperCollins*PublishersLtd*

Published by HarperCollins Publishers Ltd

First edition

HarperCollins books may be purchased for educational, business,
or sales promotional use through our Special Markets Department.

HarperCollins Publishers Ltd
2 Bloor Street East, 20th Floor
Toronto, Ontario, Canada
M4W 1A8

www.harpercollins.ca

Library and Archives Canada Cataloguing in Publication
information is available upon request

ISBN 978-1-44344-509-2 (ORIGINAL TRADE PAPERBACK)
ISBN 978-1-44341-052-6 (HARDCOVER)

Printed and bound in the United States of America
RRD 9 8 7 6 5 4 3 2 1

For Lex

"*No matter how dreary and gray our homes are, we people of flesh and blood would rather live there than in any other country, be it ever so beautiful. There is no place like home.*"

— L. Frank Baum, *The Wonderful Wizard of Oz*

PROLOGUE

THEN — 1988

"Cassandra."

She woke to the sound of her name in the dark. It wasn't a whisper, but a quiet calling. The voice was familiar, but she couldn't . . .

"Cassandra."

There was a sharp click as her door opened. Light from the hallway fell across her, the bright rectangle broken by the black shadow of the figure in her doorway.

She tried to flinch against the sudden brightness and gasped: she couldn't move.

"Cassandra."

She tried to roll over from her side, tried to push herself to the far side of the bed, but nothing worked.

Roll, she told herself. *Just roll.*

She could feel her arms, her legs, but she was frozen in place, her muscles not numb, not absent, but actively resisting her brain's commands.

All she could do was close her eyes.

"Cassandra."

She knew that voice. Or she knew that she should. The vaguely melodic cadence.

"Cassandra."

Half-whispering, half-singing her name.

Squeezing her eyes tight, she willed herself to roll away, poured all of her heart and soul and focus into the single thought. Once she broke the spell, it would all be all right. Once she had control of her body again, she would be able to roll, to run, to get away.

All she had to do was roll.

She pushed with everything she had, imagining her muscles responding, her body moving.

Nothing happened.

Roll. She tried again.

Her heart was racing, and a choking sob rose in her throat.

Roll.

The shadow man took a step into her bedroom.

"Cassandra."

Roll.

Nothing.

She sobbed again. Her tears were hot on her face as she opened her eyes.

The light spilled through the doorway like a path, leading him to her. She could see it on the carpet, the way the light seemed to push everything else out of its way, clearing a path free of Barbies and books and clothes and Lego. Like the light was guiding him to her, showing him the way.

"Cassandra."

She couldn't see his face, but she didn't need to. She knew there would be nothing there, a blank mask, a doll's face, expressionless, hard and cold.

When he touched her, nothing would change, his face plastic, still.

That's how it always was.

"Cassandra."

She squeezed her eyes shut. It was all she could do, her only resistance. She closed her eyes, and she would keep them closed. She wouldn't look.

She wouldn't see.

In the darkness, there was no sound, save the rough rasp of her breath when she could no longer hold it, the shaky gasp as she breathed in.

She lay there for a long time, trying not to breathe, listening, trying not to hope.

She knew better. She knew he wouldn't just go away. She knew from the stories Daddy read her that monsters and witches and bad things didn't just go away. You had to fight, or wish, or trick, or run.

The monsters didn't just leave.

But she couldn't hear anything. Not a movement, not a sound. Maybe . . . maybe this once . . .

And then she heard it breathe. A long, wet sound, a sound that once heard could never be forgotten.

"Cassandra."

The voice was right beside her, sighing its song, the whisper of her name, and she couldn't help it, her eyes flashed open.

The shadow loomed over her, etched against the brightness from the hallway. She could see its hair, the outline of ears, of shoulders, of hands. It looked like a man, but it wasn't. It was something more, something less. Something . . . else. As if the darkness itself had taken shape, had broken into the sanctity of her dreams.

"Cassandra," it said again, a tone like satisfaction creeping into its voice.

Heart twisting, she turned her eyes to Mr. Monkey, propped up on the pillow next to her head. Mr. Monkey, her oldest friend, close enough to touch. If only she could reach out for him, if only she could hold him, squeeze him tight. Mr. Monkey would protect her. Mr. Monkey would make everything all right.

"Cassandra," the shape breathed, and the sock monkey sharing her pillow turned his head and looked into her eyes with his glistening buttons and said simply, "Scream."

It was like something was knocked loose inside her, and Cassandra screamed with all her strength, breaking the spell, waking the house.

Now — December 1997

PART ONE

Science is wrong, but that's no great surprise.

There are not more than a hundred elements. That's far too simple, far too reductive. As if all of creation could be reduced to parts, like an engine.

In the same way, the mystics were wrong in their time. Earth, Air, Fire and Water: these were mere ways of categorizing the world, of struggling, and failing to understand.

The truth is far more complex, and yet infinitely simpler. It cannot be understood with the rational waking mind.

It must be experienced to be understood. It must be tasted.

There are only two elements, eternally opposed, irreconcilable, irreducible.

Light.

And Darkness.

In the beginning God created the heaven and the earth.

And the earth was without form, and void; and the Darkness was upon the face of the deep.

The notion of God, of course, is a lie, a fiction created by the primitives to help them understand the world around them, within them.

But the primitives did, in their dim, dismissive way, understand a fundamental truth: the Darkness has been here from the beginning. Before form, the Darkness was there.

Light came, to attempt to destroy the Darkness.

Order came, to try to tame it.

Everything that we have built as a species, everything that we have achieved, has been to try to conquer the Darkness, to curb it, to confine it with rules, to control it with morals.

And it has all failed.

The Darkness cannot be conquered. It cannot be vanquished.

It is eternal.

It is everywhere.

"Cassandra."

The knocking at the door was soft, the voice almost a whisper, muffled.

Cassie groaned and burrowed more deeply under the covers, rubbing her head against the pillow, deepening the warm furrow. She tightened her grip around Mr. Monkey, pulled him in closer to her chest.

"Cassandra."

She had no idea how much time had passed. Had she blinked, or had it been five minutes? Or an hour?

"Cassie, honey—you're going to be late."

"Dad." She groaned, nestling more deeply under the comforter.

The knocking at the door was louder this time, more insistent. "Cassandra!"

"All right," she snapped, struggling to wake up. Too bright. Too sunny. Too much morning.

Mr. Monkey looked up at her from the pillow.

She pulled him close, trying to drive away the day.

Something poked roughly at her thigh, and a hard voice was saying, "Hey! Hey!"

Her eyes flashed open; her entire body stiffened.

She held her hand up against the bright light.

Flashlight.

Two people were looking down on her. Hats. Reflective strips on their coats.

Police officers, standing down two steps from the doorway of the bookstore, the woman poking at Cassie's leg with her baton. "Hey," she repeated, her voice firm and unyielding. "Wake up."

"I'm awake." Cassie groaned, sitting up. Every muscle ached, every joint creaked from the concrete stoop and the cold that had etched deep into her bones over the past several days.

"Are you all right?" Was the male officer's voice kinder? It almost seemed like he might actually almost be concerned.

Cassie nodded. She felt like she would never be warm again, and her breath hung grey and crystalline in front of her face.

"You can't sleep here," the female officer said.

Her partner shot her a look.

"She's just a kid," he said to her.

"That doesn't mean she can sleep wherever she wants," the woman said, but it was barely an argument.

"I'll move," Cassie said, pulling on the door handle to rise. "I'll just—"

She stopped. She turned in a tight circle, her eyes darting to every corner of the alcove. "Shit," she muttered. Then she turned all the way around again, more slowly this time, methodically examining the space.

"Shit."

"What is it?" The male cop stepped forward.

"My knapsack," she said. "Someone stole my knapsack."

The woman cop pointed with her baton at the small bag

Cassie had been using for a pillow. "Isn't that it right there?"

Cassie shook her head and spun again, looking around her. "That's not—that's my backpack. Books and stuff. My knapsack, with all my clothes, my—"

She had been going to say "everything," but that wasn't really true. She had lost everything long before.

"Someone stole it."

"Well, that's—" the female cop started, but her partner cut her off with a sharp shake of his head.

He took a step toward Cassie and put his hand on her arm. "Are you sure you're okay?"

He was wearing blue plastic gloves, like a doctor might wear. They both were.

Cassie shook her head. "It had all my—" She stopped herself. She wouldn't have been able to finish that sentence without crying.

"Do you want to come to the station?" the cop asked. "We could fill out a report."

His partner made a snorting sound and took a couple of steps back onto the sidewalk.

"I don't know that it would do any real good," the male cop admitted.

"No," Cassie said. "No, it's okay."

With practised care, she began stuffing the rest of her things into her backpack. She wrapped her blankets around Mr. Monkey as she picked them up, her face burning at what the cops might think if they saw him.

It almost all fit. When the zipper balked, she pulled out her thinnest blanket and draped it over her shoulders; she could pack better later, and at least it would keep her warm.

This time the zipper closed.

"You don't have to sleep out here," the male cop said as Cassie straightened up. "There are shelters—"

"I'm not going back to the shelter," Cassie snapped.

The cop held up his blue-gloved hands in surrender. "Okay," he said. "But listen." He leaned closer, as if not wanting to be overheard. "I know they . . . How old are you?"

Cassie flinched, but she didn't answer.

"That's what I thought," the cop said. "Listen, why don't you come back to the station with me? We can contact the Ministry. They'll have someone for you to talk to, and we can get you out of the cold."

"I'm fine," Cassie said, hefting her backpack onto her shoulder.

The cop nodded. "I know you think you are," he said. "But it's really not safe for a girl out here." He reached into the pocket of his heavy black patrol jacket and drew out a business card. "Listen, take this." He pressed the card into Cassie's hand. "I know you think you're okay, but if you're ever not, call me, okay?"

Cassie looked down at the card; she could barely close her cold fingers around it. *Constable Christopher Harrison.*

"I'm Chris," he said. Then, gesturing at his partner, "That's Jane Farrow. She's not as bad as she pretends to be."

Cassie looked down at the card again. "Cassie. Cassie Weathers."

"Are you going to be all right?" the cop—Constable Harrison—asked. In the dim, Cassie could see a softness in his eyes.

"They took all my stuff," Cassie said quietly, not really able to wrap herself around the full significance of what she was saying.

"I can put you in touch—" Constable Harrison started, but his partner cleared her throat, and he stopped.

"No," Cassie said, shaking her head. "No." It was almost a whisper as she brushed past the officers and hurried down the block.

« »

It was so early Cassie had to wait outside for the McDonald's to open. The sidewalk was clotted with shopping carts and sleeping bags and their owners, uniformly brown and grey, drab in the half light. They smoked and cursed one another, pushing and shoving. A cluster almost dissolved into a fight over money and drugs, the violence only staved off when one of the men stalked away, hurling insults back over his shoulder.

She kept to the shadows, her back to the wall.

A group of boys, young men, not much older than her, were hitting each other, shoving one another into the street. They were laughing, but it sounded mean, menacing.

"Fuck you, asshole," the smallest of them shouted as he staggered back onto the sidewalk.

The tallest, with dreadlocks down to the small of his back, hacked out a laugh and pushed him again. This time, though, he hooked his foot behind the smaller man's legs.

All of them laughed as the smaller man fell into the street.

"Fuck you, motherfucker," he shouted as he pulled himself up.

A chill silence fell as the man with the dreadlocks stepped toward him. "Shut the fuck up, you weaselly little prick, or I'll fucking curb-stomp you, you got it?"

Cassie shrank deeper into the shadows.

When the doors to the restaurant were unlocked, there was a rush for the bathrooms, lines quickly forming outside both doors, and a crowd three deep at the counter.

Cassie stopped at one of the tables off to the side of the door and slumped her backpack from her shoulder. She unzipped the top, her hands stiff and frozen.

Without opening it fully and without taking anything out, she sorted through the bag, checking to see what she had lost. She had been pretty careful to keep anything important in the smaller bag she had been using as a pillow, reserving the larger bag for clothes and her bedding and towels, but she had lost her copy of the first Dragonriders of Pern book, her toothbrush and toothpaste, her deodorant and shampoo. She still had her journal, though, her Discman and Mr. Monkey, and her copy of *The Wonderful Wizard of Oz*. That was something, at least.

Focus, she thought, *on what you have, not what you've lost.*

She zipped up the bag and hefted it onto her shoulder again.

Focus on what you have, and don't let anyone take that away.

She ended up in line behind the group of young men. There were four of them, and their shouts and obscenities echoed off the glass and tile. The one with the dreadlocks seemed to be the leader, his laugh a more confident bark, his punches and pushes not responded to in kind.

Cassie had started to turn away, hoping to find a corner to vanish into to wait them out, when the dreadlocked boy noticed her.

His smile bared his teeth.

"Who's the pretty girl?" His white-blue eyes were cold and unblinking.

Cassie didn't say anything. She looked down at the floor.

"You wanna hang with us, pretty girl?" His friends turned around to look at her, fanning out behind him. "Want me to buy you a hash brown? Egg McMuffin?"

"No, thank you," Cassie said, barely above a whisper. She took a small step backward.

He took a step toward her, closing the distance between them again. "What?" he said loudly, leaning toward her. "I didn't hear you."

Cassie shook her head and took another step back.

"You don't want a hash brown?" the kid asked. "You wanna get right to the good stuff?" He glanced at his friends. "We got some rock. You wanna come with us, have a party?"

His friends were laughing now, nudging each other.

He reached out and took hold of her arm. "Come on, baby. We'll have a good time." His grip was a cold, wiry claw.

Stepping back, she swatted his hand off her arm. "No," she said. She looked up at him, met his eye, held her breath.

Just the way she had been taught in Mrs. Hepnar's guidance class; basically, it boiled down to letting the bully know that you would stand up for yourself, that you wouldn't let yourself be pushed around. "Ninety-nine per cent of the time the bully will leave you alone after that," Mrs. Hepnar had said.

The kid with the dreadlocks met her eyes and didn't look away. His smile widened.

"Another time, then," he said. "I can't wait."

He turned back to the counter, his friends filling in around him.

Cassie's heart was fluttering in her chest, her hands shaking.

When she got to the counter, she ordered a hot chocolate. Her fingers in her half gloves were red and swollen as she emptied her change out of the small Guatemalan pouch she had bought on one of her first days in Victoria, and counted it out to the penny.

Even though she had watched Cassie count it, the girl behind the counter made a deliberate point of recounting each coin into her till before sliding the cup to Cassie.

"Thank you," Cassie said.

The girl behind the till didn't say anything, looking behind Cassie for her next customer.

Cassie took a table in a corner on the main floor. Not too far from the counter, with its crowds and staff. Not too far from the main entrance. Closer to the side door. Her eyes flicked around the room unceasingly. Her hands ached and burned, curled around the hot cup, as they warmed again, at last. She breathed in, counting carefully to four. She breathed out.

« »

The cold weather didn't make for a very full hat.

Cassie spent the first few hours of the morning cross-legged at a downtown corner, her arm looped through the strap of her backpack, her second knit cap on the ground in front of her.

All she had to show for it was a couple of loonies, some silver, and a couple of dozen pennies.

It was the cold. Everyone was in a hurry to get where they were going, scurrying past her with their heads down. With gloves on, they weren't too inclined to stop to fumble for change, even if they noticed her sitting on the cold concrete.

"What the fuck do you think you're doing?"

There were three men standing in front of her. Old men, grey and grizzled.

She had been drifting, not really watching. The cold and her exhaustion had gotten the best of her.

She'd have to be more careful.

"What the fuck are you doing here?" the man in the middle asked, swaying. His face had the sagging look of someone who had lost too many fights, too many teeth. He was holding a drugstore bag; Cassie could see the labels of two bottles of mouthwash through the thin plastic.

Cassie straightened her back up against the wall, gripped the strap of her backpack.

"This is *our* corner!" the man on the right shouted, stumbling. The air around the man was dirty and fetid, but overlaid with the sharp medicinal smell of alcohol-based mouthwash.

"I'm sorry, I didn't—" Cassie started to stand up.

"Is always our corner," the man continued, pointing shakily at Cassie, at the spot where she had been sitting.

"I'll just—"

With neither hesitation nor hurry, the man in the middle reached down and scooped the change out of Cassie's hat.

Cassie started to speak, but the man shook his head and crammed the money into his pocket. "Our corner, our money," he said, and with a measured slowness, he pulled a knife out of his pocket and flicked it open. The blade was dirty, sticky.

"You want money, you get your own fucking corner."

He didn't threaten her, or step toward her, or impose on her. There was no need.

Watching the knife, Cassie picked up her hat and backed away down the street.

« »

"It can't be that bad, can it?"

Cassie started at the voice from the shadows along the dark of the path, leaned forward, struggling to make out who had spoken.

They were the first kind words she had heard all day.

After the men had stolen her money, Cassie had spent the rest of her change on another hot chocolate, huddling in the back corner of the upstairs of the McDonald's on Douglas. She had put on her earphones, flipped through her small folder of CDs and plugged herself into a Nine Inch Nails album.

She had fought the desire to disappear into the music, to close her eyes and let herself go. She needed to stay alert.

She was able to sit there for almost an hour, until the employee cleaning the upstairs bathrooms had pointed at the sign on the wall that warned that occupancy was reserved for customers and limited to twenty minutes.

She had made sure to turn off the Discman to conserve its batteries before stuffing it and the CD case deep in her bag. If anything happened to it, she didn't know what she would do.

After that, she had gone to the mall across the street. She was followed by clerks and shopkeepers in every store she went into. Even when she sat down on one of the benches in the middle of the mall, security guards appeared behind her, talking loudly almost into her ear, until she got up and left.

It was the same everywhere she went. The big bookstore next to the McDonald's was the worst. She had no sooner sat down in one of the armchairs on the second floor than a bright, toothy bookseller was standing in front of her, a security guard a half-step behind, telling her, in no uncertain terms, that "the chairs are for the customers, not . . ."

It was the way she had let the sentence dangle, the way the young woman looked at her, that made Cassie's face burn as she walked back out into the cold.

The cemetery, next to an old church a few blocks from downtown, was calm and quiet, deserted. In the spring and summer it would have been beautiful, but now it was December brown and grey, grass trampled and mud-racked from November storms.

With the black weathered stones and winding pathways, it was sad and peaceful, and she collapsed onto a bench next to a barren flower bed.

Alone.

But that didn't last.

"It can't be that bad, can it?"

It was a girl's voice, which didn't make her feel safe, exactly, but it kept Cassie from bolting right away.

"I'm sorry," the girl said, coming closer. "I didn't mean to scare you."

"You didn't," Cassie said so quietly no one else would have been able to hear her.

"You looked upset."

Cassie's breath had caught in her throat for a moment as the girl came down the path. She reminded Cassie of her sister, Heather, so much she couldn't breathe, but the girl's features resolved themselves, coming into focus. She couldn't have been much older than Cassie, her features sharp and fine, her hair close-cropped.

"I'm Skylark," she said, stopping in front of Cassie. She dropped the knapsack she had been carrying over one shoulder onto the path with a heavy thud.

"I'm Cassie."

Skylark looked at her silently, then sat down next to her on the bench. "I guess it hasn't been very long."

"What?"

"When did you run away?"

The girl seemed so tiny, so fragile, Cassie wasn't expecting such a direct question.

"I'm—" Cassie had no idea what the girl was talking about. "What?"

"Cassie. That's your real name, right?"

Cassie nodded. "Cassandra Weathers."

Skylark nodded. "That's how I knew it couldn't have been very long. You don't have anywhere to go, right? You've been on the street, what, four, five days?"

"Four days," she said. "Three nights." The other girl was clearly out in the cold too; it didn't occur to her to lie.

"That's about what I figured."

"I was at a shelter for a while, but . . ." Cassie shook her head. "Sorry, I still don't get it."

"Out here, nobody uses their real names," Skylark explained. "So when you told me your name right away, I knew you were pretty new."

"Why don't people use their real names?"

"Power. You tell people your name, and they can find out where you came from, what you've done, what you're running from. Names have power."

The girl's words sank heavily to the bottom of Cassie's stomach, and an image of her picture on the side of a milk carton flashed through her mind. "Oh," she said. "Right."

"Yeah," Skylark said. "That's what I thought. So what do you want people to call you?"

Cassie's mind was completely blank.

"Don't rush it," Skylark said. "It's a pretty big deal. You get to *name* yourself. It's kinda cool."

"Why do you call yourself Skylark?" The second the words were out of her mouth, Cassie wanted to take them back. "I'm sorry," she hurried. "That was rude."

"No, it's okay," Skylark said.

Cassie glanced sidelong at Skylark, watched as she lit a cigarette with a plastic lighter. It took her a moment to figure out what was so strange about the other girl: she was clean. Her hair looked light and fluffy, brushed, her face fresh, not streaked with dirt or weathered the way most people's were, out here.

The way hers was.

Looking at Skylark made Cassie uncomfortably aware of how dirty she was. Her scalp tingled and itched, and she shifted slightly away, worried that she might be smelly.

Skylark exhaled a lungful of smoke, looked toward the sky, then back at Cassie.

Cassie turned quickly away.

"What?" Skylark asked.

"Nothing." Cassie shook her head and took a deep breath. "It's been a few days since I had a shower, that's all."

Skylark smiled. "You haven't been down to the Inner Harbour? Down at Ship's Point?"

"No, why?"

"They have showers down there. Public showers." A look must have flashed across Cassie's face. "No, not like that. They're separate showers, with locking doors. But anyone can use them."

Cassie watched Skylark's face as she described where the showers were, how people from the boats moored nearby would leave soap and shampoo. Her eyes were bright, but there was a hardness in the corners of them.

They reminded her of Heather's eyes, the way she had looked at her in the last few months, the way they had sparkled, and then closed up, cutting Cassie out.

It took Cassie a moment to realize that Skylark had fallen silent.

"It's all right," Skylark started, not looking at Cassie, her eyes directed toward the gathering dark. "You don't have to talk about it."

Cassie shifted on the bench, but she didn't say anything.

"Everybody's got a story. Some people put it all out there right away. And other people"—she looked at Cassie—"they hold it close. Maybe they tell a few people. Maybe not."

Cassie nodded, still not really sure what Skylark was talking about.

"I'm not going to ask, okay? Your story's your own, until you choose"—she came down heavily on the word—"to share it."

Cassie felt like she had been holding her breath for days. "Thank you," she said.

When their eyes met, both girls smiled, suddenly shy.

"So, listen," Skylark said, her voice shifting. "You have plans for tonight? Where you're going to sleep, shit like that?"

Somehow, Cassie had managed to put reality out of her mind. "Oh. No, I hadn't thought about it."

"Okay." Skylark turned on the bench so she was facing Cassie full on. "I know these people."

Cassie flinched as her mind filled with images of the girls in miniskirts up the length of Government Street after the stores closed each night, and the headline on that morning's *New Sentinel* at the bookstore: "Prostitute Murdered."

"I'm not—I mean, I'm not that desperate." She took a deep breath. "I'm a . . . I've never . . ."

Skylark shook her head. "No, no. Oh, God, no." She snorted out a laugh. "No, nothing like that. These are just friends. It's where I live."

"Is it like a group home?" Cassie suppressed a shudder at the thought.

"No, it's a family." It seemed as though the words cost Skylark. "But not—"

Cassie nodded. "Not like a real family."

"Better than that." Skylark looked at Cassie as if seeking something in her expression. "It's like a real community, a real home. There's people there from all over the country, and Brother Paul . . ." Her voice drifted off.

Cassie waited a long moment. "Brother Paul?"

"Oh, you have to meet him. He's the leader of the group and"—she shook her head—"he saved me." Skylark looked down at the ground. "That's all."

That's all.

"Okay . . ."

"Do you want to come?" she asked, looking toward the darkening horizon. "Are you hungry?"

Cassie's stomach growled at the thought of food, loudly enough that Skylark smiled. "A little."

Skylark stood up and hefted her knapsack. "Come on," she said. "We're probably still in time for dinner."

Cassie rose slowly, keeping her grip tight on the strap of her backpack.

As they walked out of the park, a single crow watched them from a telephone wire. It followed them down the path with its eyes, hopped in the air and turned around as they passed under it, then watched as they walked onto the sidewalk, waiting until they had disappeared from view before it took flight.

<< >>

Constable Chris Harrison was tempted to put his winter coat back on. He had been inside for more than an hour, but he was still no closer to being warm.

He resisted the urge, though, and left his coat hanging on the hook on the outside edge of the cubicle he was using. He knew the cold would pass.

Harrison had grown up in Victoria: he knew the way winters went. Three or four months of rain, broken occasionally by days so steel grey they hurt the eyes, and only a few days when the thermometer dipped into the negative. The cold never lasted more than a week or so. Maybe, in a rare year, the city would get more than a few scattered flakes of snow, but it would be wiped out by rain almost before it got a chance to settle. The blizzard the previous year had been a once-a-century anomaly.

That was winter in Victoria. That was why people stayed, despite the way the cost of everything kept going up. That was why people came from across the country.

All sorts of people.

Glancing over his shoulder, Harrison took his notepad out of his breast pocket and flipped it open. The name was scrawled on the top of the third page back, behind the scratched details of a domestic disturbance, a public intoxication and a car theft complaint.

Cassie Weathers.

He typed the name into the green search box on the computer screen and waited a few seconds. Nothing.

He tried *Weathers, Cassy*, looking over his shoulder again as he waited.

Nothing.

Weathers, Cassandra brought up a missing persons report.

The paperwork had been filed by the Pressfield detachment of the RCMP on November 15—nearly a month before. Mary Weathers, the girl's mother, had reported her daughter missing from the hospital, where she had been under observation following a house fire. The mother had returned to the hospital the afternoon after the fire to find Cassandra gone.

There was a short description and a school photo.

"Whatcha got there?"

Jane Farrow was almost leaning over his shoulder, looking at his screen.

"That girl from this morning."

"The one we ousted from the doorway of the bookstore?"

Harrison nodded. "She's a runaway."

His partner snorted. "No shit. What did you think she was, a reporter?" He could even hear her smirk.

"No, but I thought we should get some details. The report's about a month old, out of Pressfield."

"Where the fuck is that?"

Harrison shook his head. "In the Interior somewhere?"

Jane straightened and put her hand on the top edge of the cubicle. "We'll pick her up the next time we see her," she said matter-of-factly.

"Not much point," Harrison muttered, reading through the description. "She turned sixteen in October."

Sixteen was right on the line. Legally, a sixteen-year-old wasn't a runaway. Although still minors, they were considered old enough to live on their own, to make their own decisions.

Usually renting an apartment or setting up a hydro account required parental consent at that age, but there was nothing wrong—legally—with a sixteen-year-old living independently.

They could pick her up, try to convince her to go home to her family, but there was nothing they could do to force her, no legal grounds to hold her or send her back.

"Well, good luck to her," Farrow said, somewhere between genuine and bitter.

"Yeah." Still distracted by the computer screen: sixteen years old, a younger sister at home.

It was hard to make the images match up—the smiling girl in the school picture with the groggy, defensive girl in the doorway that morning. It was more than the clothes and the dirt and the unwashed hair that separated them. There was something fundamentally different in her face, something that had shifted and changed the smiling, happy student captured in the photograph into the girl living on the streets.

Harrison scrolled through the notes in the file. An investigation by the Ministry of Children and Families when she was nine. A psychiatric hospitalization when she was twelve. A fire that had destroyed the family home in mid-November, just before she ran away.

Maybe there wasn't that much of a change, after all. There was something there in her eyes in the photo, like her smile didn't quite reach them.

Or maybe he had been looking at the picture too long.

"So listen," Farrow said, and Harrison jumped. He had forgotten that she was there. "A couple of us are going out, getting some beers. You comin'?"

Harrison shook his head. "No. But thanks. I'm gonna finish up here, head for home."

"Another busy night with the wife and kids."

"Yeah."

"All right. Flip side, then."

He was already lost again in the computer screen before she walked away.

« »

The streets were deserted. It was early in the week—Cassie wasn't sure what day—and the moment the offices shut down and the stores closed, downtown cleared out. There were still cars on the streets, racing from point A to point B, but the sidewalks were empty. Their voices seemed to echo in the darkness.

"Here," Skylark said, coming to a stop and slinging her knapsack onto a bench, flopping down beside it.

"Here?" Cassie looked around. She thought she had gotten to know the downtown area, but in the darkness it was unfamiliar. "What's 'here'?"

Skylark gestured at the building behind her. "That's City Hall. And through there"—"there" was a covered breezeway at one side of the building, brightly lit with orange lights, concrete pillars holding up the roof—"is Centennial Square."

Through the breezeway, Cassie could see a flat expanse of concrete with a few raised, empty planters, pools of street light and sharp, deep shadows. In the distance was a dark patch, maybe a lawn, with a huge pine tree in the centre, lit up with Christmas lights blinking blue. Between the breezeway and a building on the opposite side of the square were three stone monoliths in the centre of a low, circular barrier of white concrete. "What's that?" she asked, pointing.

Skylark turned. "That's the fountain," she said. "Well, not right now. They've turned off the water because they're worried about it freezing." She shook her head. "Brother Paul, he told us last night that the temperature when they turn off the fountain is actually five degrees higher than when they open the emergency shelter beds. And they keep the fountain turned off all winter. They only keep the shelter beds open until the temperature goes up a degree or two."

Her expression and her voice were laced with disgust.

Skylark's explanation allowed Cassie to ask the question that had been on her mind their whole walk. "Who's Brother Paul?"

Skylark's face lit up. "Brother Paul—I guess you could say he's . . ." She stumbled over trying to find a description, her eyes taking on that faraway look again. "He's the leader, I guess. But that doesn't really . . . He doesn't . . . You just have to meet him."

Before Cassie could speak, a battered van pulled up in front of the statue in front of City Hall, belching smoke and backfiring. The van was covered in graffiti, layers of bright spray paint, images and words over words and images.

"Right on time," Skylark said, leaning forward on the bench.

Two men and a woman, dressed in jeans and T-shirts despite the cold, hopped out of the van. As they opened the back doors and began to pull out a folding table, the empty sidewalks filled with people. There had been no signal save the arrival of the van, but a crowd quickly formed around the back doors.

Cassie recognized some of them from outside McDonald's that morning. Unlike that pre-dawn crowd, though, everyone waiting around the van was quiet. There was no shouting, no pushing, nothing louder than scattered, hushed conversations. People milled about a little, but they quickly formed into a single line that snaked along the sidewalk to the table. "Come on," Skylark said, standing up as the two men lifted a huge pot onto the table. "We should get in line."

"What is this?" Cassie asked as she followed Skylark, who high-fived a few people as they moved through the crowd.

"The Outreach van," she said as they joined the line. "Soup and bread, sometimes clothes. Condoms if you need them." Skylark shrugged. "They come every night. And hey, if you're here at Christmas? I hear they do turkey." There was a bitterness in Skylark's voice that Cassie hadn't heard before.

But she understood it all too well. Christmas was a week and a half away, but it seemed a lifetime. The thought that she might still be out here, sleeping on the streets, begging for change, made her almost hunch over with pain.

But where else would she be?

≪ ≫

From the cold of the concrete park, he watched.

He stood in the shadow of the fountain, the Darkness watching out of the dark. He wasn't hiding; he didn't need to hide. People would see him, but their glances would slip off him, not really registering him.

He was perfectly camouflaged.

It was all part of the hunt: concealment, observation, tracking.

Watching. Waiting for the perfect specimen.

She was easy to see against the backdrop of the crowd milling around the back of the van. She shone with a strength that was dizzying.

Her inner light separated her from the herd, drew the Darkness to her.

He watched as the girl took her bowl of food, her piece of bread. Her smile, even in the distance, was dazzling.

She led another girl into the breezeway adjoining City Hall, and they both sat down with the group of people already there.

The other people in the breezeway barely registered to him; they were dull, drab things, the little light left within them guttering like pale candles, brighter when they laughed, quickly fading.

The girl, though . . .

He had been watching her for several nights, following her movements. It hadn't been difficult: with a light as bright as that, she could be seen for blocks.

He had watched, and he had waited.

He could have taken her any time, but he was pleased that he had waited. The girl was shining more brightly than he had seen before, arcing white as she leaned against the girl beside her, almost blinding as she laughed.

And the girl she was with . . .

The new girl was like nothing he had ever seen.

There was a rich orange light to her, and it took him a moment to register: This new girl was like a banked fire. She didn't shine—she burned.

A crow descended, arching black against the curve of a street light, and landed on the concrete edge of the fountain.

It too watched the girls.

The bright white of the first girl

—*Skylark*, the crow said—

Skylark, and the slow, deep burn of the new girl . . .

He looked at the crow, but the bird had nothing to say.

The two of them, these two girls.

It was almost too much for him to bear.

"Not yet," he whispered, and the words were like smoke from his mouth.

He drew his collar up tighter around his throat and turned away.

"Not yet," he repeated.

It wasn't just the kill that was important; anyone could kill. It took a special man to hunt.

« »

When Cassie and Skylark reached the front of the line, the man behind the table was scraping the inside of the huge pot with a metal ladle. "I've got enough for one more bowl of soup," he said, shrugging. He was wearing a knit cap and a hoodie over an old concert T-shirt.

"That's okay," Skylark said. "We can share."

"I've got a couple of bagels, though," the man said as he passed the bowl to Skylark. He smiled like it was something he didn't do very often; his teeth were worn brown nubs.

"Thank you," Cassie said quietly as he handed her the bagels.

She followed Skylark through the knots of people slurping soup on the dim sidewalk and into the breezeway.

The space was crowded with people sitting on the ground in small groups, talking as they ate. Their laughter echoed brightly off the concrete and bricks.

It was a sound that Cassie hadn't heard in . . . she didn't actually know. The sound of people talking quietly, just talking. The sound of laughter, honest, heartfelt laughter.

How long had it been?

"Over there," Skylark said, pointing with the soup bowl at a spot along the wall. "Come on."

They threaded through the loose crowd. As Skylark greeted people she knew, Cassie kept her eyes down, not quite staring at the ground, but not looking around.

"And here," Skylark said, setting her knapsack onto the ground by the wall, "we shall stake our claim." A couple of people sitting nearby smiled and slid over a little, widening the space a bit.

"Sit, sit," Skylark said, gesturing.

Cassie set her backpack carefully on the ground, then lowered herself beside it, leaning against the brick wall.

Every part of her ached. It was like being crushed and twisted, minute by minute. The weariness was a physical weight—she was buckling under it with every step. Sitting down should have been a relief, but it was almost worse: every joint screamed, every muscle throbbed.

Now that she was sitting, Cassie worried that she might not be able to get up.

And it was only going to get colder.

Skylark folded herself effortlessly from standing to sitting with her legs crossed, facing Cassie, smiling.

Why was she always smiling?

Cassie realized that she didn't know anything about this girl; she just knew that she was different somehow. Not like most people she had met on the streets. Not like those guys at McDonald's. Or the ones at the shelter.

Cassie glanced around the crowded breezeway, suddenly alert to everyone surrounding her. She had let herself relax: She couldn't do that. She needed to keep aware. She needed to keep safe.

"Who are you looking for?" Skylark asked.

"No one," Cassie said, too quickly.

Skylark didn't say anything, just passed her the soup and

handed her a plastic spoon. A silver ring glinted on her finger, a cat's head with green stones for the eyes.

Cassie cradled the warmth close to her. The soup was thick and rich, with chunks of vegetables and lots of barley.

She took three hurried spoonfuls, then extended the bowl back to Skylark

Skylark took a deliberate bite from her bagel and waved the bowl away. "Have some more," she said, her mouth full.

Cassie forced herself to slow down; she could have emptied the whole bowl without even thinking about it.

"So, are they from a church or—" She looked at the van.

"Sort of," Skylark said, tearing another chunk off her bagel. "I think a church runs the shelter. They make food in the kitchen, bring it out in the van. Breakfast and dinner. I think most of the people working used to be on the street. Now they get training, a place to sleep."

Cassie shook her head.

"What?"

"I don't like shelters." She took another spoonful, like it might prevent her from saying anything else.

Skylark nodded. "Okay," she said. "If you don't want to talk about it, we don't have to talk about it."

Cassie felt her relief as a softening in her chest, a loosening of her spine.

"Thank you," she said, looking down into the soup.

"Our stories are our own," Skylark said. "Like our names." She grinned when Cassie passed her the bowl, now more than half-empty. "That's what Brother Paul says." Her eyes took on a wide, glistening look when she said his name.

Cassie took a bite from her own bagel. It was warm, and the butter coated her fingers. "So, Brother Paul . . ."

Skylark looked around the breezeway. "That's him," she said finally, pointing to the far corner where a man in a long coat was talking with a small group of people. He didn't seem like much to Cassie—not tall, not fat, nothing special about him at all—but as he spoke to one woman, her eyes took on the same faraway look that Skylark had shown. And when he touched the woman on the shoulder, she looked like it was all she could do not to burst into tears.

Cassie turned back, about to speak.

"Come on," Skylark said, bursting to her feet.

"What?"

But Skylark wasn't the only one in motion. All around the sheltered space, people were standing up, shifting to sit in a large, rough circle in the middle of the breezeway, leaving spaces for the pillars that held up the roof. People smiled and greeted one another as they sat down.

Outside the circle, Brother Paul was crouched, talking to an older woman next to one of the pillars. She bowed her head as he spoke, clutched his hand when he reached to touch her shoulder.

Cassie ended up sitting between Skylark and a young man about her age. His hair was long, and his wispy beard made him look a bit like the pictures of Jesus in the storybooks at Sunday school.

They glanced at each other, but they didn't say anything.

Cassie was about to ask Skylark what was going on, but a silence fell over the group before she could speak.

"Happy evening, brothers and sisters," Brother Paul said, stepping into the middle of the circle.

"Happy evening, Brother Paul," the group answered back.

"We've all eaten, I hope," he said, and there was a scattering of responses. "I'd like you to join me in a short offering of thanks."

Brother Paul closed his eyes and held his arms at his sides as he spoke. Cassie glanced around the circle as everyone else followed suit, closing their eyes and bowing their heads.

"Mother Earth," he started, his voice low and echoing in the silence and concrete. "We wish to thank you for the blessings you have graced us with and the people who have come along with them, the sun, the earth, the sky and the sea. We wish to thank you for these blessings and this small place on this earth to call our own. Thank you, Mother. Blessed be."

"Blessed be," the people repeated, and Cassie found herself moving her lips.

As the people around her opened their eyes and raised their heads, the air seemed different somehow: Quieter. Gentler. Warmer.

"Thank you, brothers and sisters," Brother Paul said. His voice had changed too, softened. "Our blessings are truly rich, even as we struggle for a small handful of coins. We join together"—he paused, turning to look around the group—"as a true community, brothers and sisters of the street, brought together to build a better future, not just for ourselves, but for the world around us."

He rocked slightly on his feet. "It brings me such joy to see all of you together here, after so long alone. To see all of you safe in this company, after lives of such danger." He took a small step forward. "The Bible talks about salvation, of finding the path through Christ, a heaven that would take all comers. The sick. The lame. The poor. The hunted. But we have found that paradise together. We have built this community, this family, open to all."

There were mutters of agreement around the circle. It felt like people had been moved to speak, to join their voices.

"I see a few new faces here tonight. First, I'd like to welcome you all." Cassie glanced at Skylark, but the girl was completely focused on Brother Paul. "Perhaps we should go around the circle and introduce ourselves? There are no strangers here."

Brother Paul turned slowly, looking around the entire circle. "Maybe we should start with—" He pointed at an older woman almost directly across the circle from Cassie.

The woman—heavy-set, with a fraying toque over a tangle of red hair—started slightly at the sudden attention. "I'm . . . I'm Sarah," she said, faltering on her name. "I'm from all over, I guess. I came from Edmonton about a month ago. I wasn't expecting it to be so chilly here. Chilly chilly beans."

This drew a small laugh from the crowd and a muted chorus of "Welcome, Sarah."

As it faded, the man next to Sarah—skeletally thin, with a long, wispy black moustache—spoke. "I'm Simon," he said. His voice was low and breathy. "I've lived here all my life. My disability ran out . . ." His voice faded away to nothing.

"Welcome, Simon."

They went around the circle, everyone saying their names, offering glimpses of their stories. Joni, who had lost her job due to PTSD after she was raped. Bill, an alcoholic, who had lost everything when he crashed his car. Stu, who had gone broke when the mill shut down.

Cassie was getting more and more anxious as the introductions got closer to her. What was she going to say? What could she say?

"I'm Ian," said the boy next to her, clearing his throat nervously. "I'm from down East. My dad . . . I had to leave home when I told my dad I was gay." For a moment his voice was thick with sadness. "But I met this guy." He leaned in affectionately into the boy sitting next to him. "And he makes the world an all-right place."

As people oohed and sighed at the sentiment and welcomed him, Cassie felt everyone's eyes shift to her. Everyone was staring, waiting.

"I'm Dorothy," she said slowly, not making eye contact with anyone. "I grew up on the mainland. My family . . . I don't have a family anymore."

She stared hard down at the pavement. She didn't hear the welcome. She didn't even hear what Skylark said, or any of the people on her other side. Her face burned, and she breathed deeply: *in two three four, hold two three four, out two three four.*

"Thank you, brothers and sisters," Brother Paul said when everyone had finished speaking. "Thank you for joining me. Thank you for helping me make this place our place. Our home."

From the inside pocket of his coat he drew out a battered black book, its spine raggedly bound with duct tape.

"For those of you who don't know me, my name is Brother Paul. In another life, I was ordained in the Catholic Church. I gave my life over to God, but he and I . . . stopped seeing eye to eye. Too much ritual, not enough action. Too much piety, not enough wonder." He shook his head heavily, dramatically. "Thankfully, I had this." He lifted the book high in his hand. "The true word. The true teachings." He looked down at the cover of the book. "The people I worked alongside, my superiors at the Church, they said that I had lost my faith. That I had lost my way. They said—" He cut himself off, turned partway around. "They didn't understand. They could no longer see the truth that was right in front of them." He gestured with the book again. "God doesn't believe in earthly riches. He doesn't believe in the Church. He believes in people. His children. And we are all his children." He looked meaningfully around the circle. "God didn't create money. Man created money, and those men, those men who have it, have been using it as a club to beat down everyone else ever since."

A scattering of boos and hisses came from the circle, and Brother Paul shook his head, as if he couldn't understand it himself. "It's a measure of how far we have fallen, how corrupt our world has become. It's all about money, all those buildings, all those people in suits, all those churches." He sneered the word, stretched it out. "They have forgotten that this is our garden." He spread his arms wide, as if to encompass the square, the block, the world. "And that we are all his children."

Around the circle, people applauded.

"We may not have money. We may not have a roof over our heads or one of those fancy condos on the waterfront, but this is our home. This is our home. Anyone is welcome. Everyone is welcome. Living together, we are not poor: we are richer than we have ever been."

This got a cheer that echoed out into the park.

"People, though . . ." He let his words hang in the air, and his eyes swept around the group. When he spoke again, it was with difficulty, as if what he was saying caused him a deep pain. "People don't understand what that means. There are people who would see this community destroyed, stamped out, simply because it's different, because it's something they do not understand." His voice had risen, not angrily, but defiantly. Then it fell. "We're not going to give in to the forces of darkness, of ignorance. This is our place, as God intended. This is our garden. This is our home. We will stand together, and we will protect one another. Alone, we are small, but together . . ." He smiled as cheers rose around him. "Together we are mighty."

When Cassie realized she was cheering, she didn't understand why.

« »

The two girls returned to their spot near the City Hall wall. He watched as the one who shone the brighter laid out a tattered old comforter on the concrete, spreading it wide.

Wide enough for two.

The flame inside the second girl flared at the offer.

They sat together a while on the blanket, the nimbuses of their lights weaving as they talked. The second girl, Dorothy, was showing off her books, passing them to Skylark.

When they stood up to walk across the square together, he moved more deeply into the shadows.

« »

"Hold on," Skylark said, stopping in the middle of the square. "Let's sit." Skylark gestured at the concrete wall that ran the circumference of the fountain.

"Sure."

Cassie sat down uneasily next to her on the ledge.

"So," Skylark said. "That was Brother Paul. Do you see what I mean about him?"

The excitement on her face made her look like a kid.

"I guess," Cassie said.

Skylark pushed her gently on the shoulder. "'Dorothy' seemed to roll off your tongue. Did you think about it, or did it just come to you?"

"It just—" Cassie was distracted by Skylark pulling a joint out of her jacket pocket, dampening it with her lips. "It just came to me. It felt right."

Skylark lit the joint with her disposable lighter, checked the glow of the cherry, then took a deep toke. "Yeah, that makes sense," she said tightly, holding the smoke and extending the joint to Cassie.

Cassie pinched the joint between her thumb and forefinger, careful not to burn her fingers. "It was *The Wizard of Oz*," she said, holding a deep toke. The smoke burned and surged in her throat, but she fought the desire to cough it out. "You know, Judy Garland?" She looked at Skylark as she passed the joint back.

Skylark nodded. "Totally," she said. "I get that. That's perfect." She slapped her palm on her knee. "Strange girl in a strange land, that's perfect. That's awesome."

Cassie shook her head and took the joint back. "No," she said. "It wasn't that. I mean, that's cool. I'm totally going to say that." They both laughed. "No, it was . . . My dad and I used to watch that movie all the time."

But that had been before.

There must have been something in her voice; Skylark draped her arm around Cassie's back. "I'm sorry," she said. "Did your dad—"

She hesitated. "My father's dead," she said, looking out toward the square.

She didn't say anything else.

And Skylark didn't ask.

It was cold enough that Holly's breath was a grey cloud and goosebumps rose unchecked on her bare legs. She would have been wearing stockings, but her last pair had gotten ripped an hour before.

He had apologized profusely.

He had also asked if he could keep the ripped hose.

She had charged him an extra twenty dollars.

Standing on the edge of the sidewalk, she lit another cigarette, revelling in the moment of warmth from her Bic lighter.

She stood with her legs slightly apart, one foot planted on the yellow *No Parking* line along the curb, slightly turned out.

Inviting.

That was the trick: to appear inviting.

So many of the other girls looked so angry, so hard, staring into the cars as they crawled past like they were daring the drivers to stop, like they were looking for a fight.

No one wanted that. If the drivers had wanted a fight, they would have stayed at home.

Oh well. The other girls could spend the whole night on the sidewalk if that's what they wanted. Holly would at least have a warm car or two. Maybe a cheap motel room, if she got really lucky.

She smiled when she saw the minivan coming back toward her; it had already passed her twice.

Third time lucky, she thought as it stopped in front of her.

There was a warm rush of air as the passenger window came down and she leaned closer, taking a careful look at the driver.

"Hey," he said.

He was a little awkward, a little uncertain. A young guy,

not well-dressed, but not a slob. Respectable. Respectful. Plus, minivan. Probably a family man.

"You must be cold."

The sort of thing you might say if you'd never done this before.

"A bit, yeah," she said, leaning on the open window, watching his eyes as they darted to her neckline. She smiled, at him and to herself.

"You . . . you could get in," he said slowly, as if trying to talk himself into it.

"Yeah?" she asked, letting her smile widen. "What did you have in mind?"

"Are—are you . . . ?"

"I'm not a cop," she said. "Are you?"

He smiled and shook his head. "No. God, no. I was just . . ."

"Here," she said, pulling down her top, flashing him her tits. "No cop's gonna do that."

His eyes looked like they were going to pop out of his head. "No," he said. "No, I guess not." He cleared his throat, shifted in the driver's seat. "Are you—You look pretty young."

Sold, she thought.

"You wanna see my ID?" Sassy, but not too sassy.

"No, no. That's okay."

"So." She leaned forward again. "Should I get in?"

He smiled, then looked away and shifted awkwardly. "Um . . . I was just—What do you . . ."

"Are you asking how much?"

He hesitated for a moment, then nodded.

"Why don't I get in and we can talk?" she said, curling her fingers around the door handle.

He took a moment to say, "Sure. Why don't you get in?"

Her skirt rode up as she sat down in the passenger seat. She let it.

Closing the door softly, she pulled the seat belt around her shoulder and clicked it shut. "Better safe than sorry," she said, reaching out and putting her hand on his thigh.

The van pulled away from the curb.

<< >>

Cassandra's eyes opened into a blinding silver light.

There was nothing . . . She was so cold . . . She could feel it eating into her bones, sapping her strength. She couldn't move—

She couldn't move.

She struggled against the invisible bonds, against the nails driven through her elbows and knees, staking her to the bed

—concrete—

as the light from the door fell across her. She tried to blink it away

—there is no door there is no bed—

She waited for the sound of footfalls, but none came. There was only the sound of breathing in the dark

—there's nothing there—

a wet, slavering sound.

Then footfalls. She could picture the running feet, the jump

—it's all in your head—

and the sudden crushing weight on her chest, the pointed knobs of knees crushing her ribs.

A wet, warm, panting breath fell against her face.

"Cassandra."

The wet voice. The smell of garbage and death.

—he's not there he's not there—

She was looking at herself from outside. She could see herself in her bed, the covers messed, the light from the hallway spilling across her.

—I'm not there—

He was crouching on top of her, reaching for her throat. His fingers clenched. They were bony, hard, wiry, clutching at her neck, crushing the wind out of her.

Choking.

—he's not there he can't be—

She tried to move, tried to fight.

All she had to do was arch her back, throw him off.

But her body wouldn't respond.

She was helpless.

—not that never again—

She looked up, trying to meet his eyes as he pressed down on her throat. She looked up, pleading. She looked up, for mercy.

—never never any mercy—

Tears rolled hot down her cheeks, his breath coming fast now, wet.

"Cassandra."

Sparks flared in her eyes, bright white bursts that surged with the beating of her heart.

—not again it can't be I—

"Cassie?"

Her eyes flashed open and she gasped, cold air filling her lungs with an icy, sharp burn.

She didn't know where she was, staring upward into a blinding orange light. Someone was shaking her shoulder, whispering her name.

"Cassie, are you okay?"

It took a moment for everything to come into focus: the light above her, the brick wall behind her, Skylark's face inches from her own, eyes wide, mouth creased with concern.

"Cassie?" Her voice was anxious, tight.

"I'm okay," Cassie gasped, and her body shuddered, all of her muscles releasing at once.

"You were—" Skylark seemed to struggle to find the right words. "You sounded like someone was killing you."

Cassie could still feel the knees pressing into her chest, the fingers around her neck. A sob built in her throat and she couldn't hold it in. Her back heaved as she cried.

"It's okay," Skylark whispered. "It's all right. It was just a dream."

"No," Cassie gasped. But she had no words to explain.

It hadn't been a dream, not at all.

"Shh," Skylark said. "It's all right. Here—" She moved in closer. "Turn over." Cassie looked at her. "Turn over," she repeated.

Hesitating for a moment, Cassie rolled onto her other side, facing away from Skylark.

With a rustling of her sleeping bag, Skylark pulled herself closer, wrapping one arm over Cassie, snuggling in close. "It's okay," she whispered. "It was just a bad dream."

Trying to be subtle, Cassie fumbled under her blanket, looking for Mr. Monkey. She had managed to get him out of her backpack without Skylark noticing. When she found him, she held him close.

She could feel the other girl breathing behind her.

"It was just a bad dream," Skylark repeated, in the soft voice one might use to comfort a child.

"It wasn't," Cassie said, too quietly for even Skylark to hear.

"It was my dad."

And in her last breath before she fell back to sleep, Cassie caught the faintest smell of paint thinner, and smoke.

«»

He pulled the van slowly into the garage, stopping in front of the shelves along the back wall, cutting the engine before he pressed the button to close the garage door.

He sat for a moment in the quiet, both hands on the steering wheel, staring out at the shelves. They were packed, but orderly: A couple of packages of toilet paper, one open. A flat of bottled water, and another of Coke. Soup. Crackers. Cereal. The consolidation of weekly trips to the warehouse store.

Taking the key from the ignition, he stepped out of the van and closed the door behind himself.

Two steps took him to the washer and dryer. He twisted the dial to Cold Wash and Cold Rinse and added detergent as water started to gush into the tub. In the cold of the garage he shucked off his clothes—pants, shirt, all the way down to his underwear—straightening them before folding them into the icy water. He had worn black, but he wasn't worried about staining—the washer would take the blood right out.

Glancing down, he decided to add to the load the sneakers he had kicked off. Better safe than sorry.

After slamming the lid shut, he went back to the van, opening up the back with the fob on the key chain.

He had wrapped the knife in a plastic grocery-store bag; the weight of it in one hand was reassuring as he lowered the back door shut.

He tucked the package in his other hand into the chest

freezer, lifting up several packages of meat wrapped in brown paper and a couple of frozen chickens to add it to the small pile of newspaper-wrapped packages in the far bottom corner of the icy chest. Before closing the lid, he placed everything as it had been.

He was almost at the door into the house when he remembered.

He set the wrapped knife on the shelf by the door and went back down the stairs, popping the sliders on the van.

It took him a minute to put the car seats back in the van, securing them so they'd be ready for the morning.

Then he put the knife into the dishwasher, crammed the bloody plastic bag deep into the garbage can, under the plastic wrap from the hamburger they'd had for dinner, and went upstairs.

A quick shower, and hopefully he wouldn't wake Alice: she needed her sleep.

« »

"You're going to be late," her mother said as she bustled into the kitchen. She was dressed for work, her hair back, a little bit of makeup on her face.

"We're fine," Cassandra said, leaning against the counter as she ate a banana. She had just put her cereal bowl into the sink. Heather was still at the table, lifting a spoonful to her mouth as she stared at the back of the cereal box.

"Not if you don't get out of here," she said, setting her handbag on one of the kitchen chairs. "Heather, please."

"I'm done, Mom," she said, tilting her bowl sideways to show only a faint residue of milk.

"All right, brush your teeth and I'll do your hair. Come on," she urged when Heather was slow at standing up.

Heather started toward the stairs, but stopped when their mother cleared her throat.

Mom nodded toward the table, where Heather had left her cereal bowl and the box, and lifted her eyebrows.

Heather sighed heavily and set the bowl in the sink, tucked the box back into the cupboard.

Cassie smirked. Heather scowled.

"Heather, come on," their mother urged again, fumbling with an earring.

Heather hustled out of the kitchen, turned toward the stairs.

"Whoa, slow down," came a voice from the other room. "Where's the fire?"

Cassandra's right hand, holding the limp banana peel, fell to her side as her father came around the corner, shaking his head, smiling.

"You've got her on the run this morning," he said to their mother, leaning toward her to kiss her cheek. "Good morning." His voice was a warm near-whisper.

"They're going to be late," she said, giving up on her earring and turning to kiss him on the mouth.

"No, they're not," he said, grinning broadly. He looked at the clock above the sink. "They've got plenty of time."

Then he turned to Cassandra. "Good morning, Miss Cassie. How'd you sleep?"

Her words seemed to die in her throat, crushed by the surging of her heart. Her daddy.

"Good," she managed in a gulp. "Good."

<< >>

Cassie woke with a jerk, her heart snapping and racing. The world was a blur of distorted colours and shapes: a flat, brown-red surface, a silver mist, a light that burned her eyes.

And a face, looking down at her.

Skylark put her hand on Cassie's arm. "It's okay. You're okay."

Everything else slipped into focus—the brick wall looming above her, the silver cloud of her breath hanging in the still air, the orange lights in the ceiling high above her.

She nodded uncertainly.

God, it was cold. Her face was on fire. She'd have to start sleeping with her scarf wrapped around her head, the way she'd seen other people do.

"Cassie?"

"I'm okay," she said.

Skylark reached over and Cassie closed her eyes and fought the instinct to flinch as she felt the other girl's fingertips brush across her eyebrows.

"Look," Skylark said.

When Cassie opened her eyes, Skylark was extending her index finger toward her. There were ice crystals on the tip of her finger, glinting in the light even as they melted against her heat. "Your eyebrows are frosty."

It was impossible for Cassie not to smile too.

« »

The camp was awake and packed before the sun was even up.

"Most of us go our own way during the day," Skylark explained as the two girls sat again at the edge of the empty fountain, sipping the bitter, barely hot coffee that the Outreach van had brought, along with the bagels and toast they had already eaten. "It gives people less to complain about. Less for the cops to hold against us."

Cassie nodded, both hands wrapped tightly around the Styrofoam cup. She watched Skylark as she spoke: it was like nothing fazed her, like there was nothing she couldn't handle. "I'm not sure where to go," Cassie said.

Then it all came out in a gush. "I thought I had found a good place yesterday, but this guy came after me with a knife." She shook her head. "That was after the cops—"

Something seemed to flare in Skylark's face. "What about the cops?"

"They were okay, I guess," Cassie said. "I was sleeping on the steps in front of a bookstore, and they woke me up, made me leave. But I guess that's what they have to do, right?" She shrugged her shoulders.

"They didn't bring you in?" Skylark's voice rose in surprise.

"No," Cassie said slowly, uncertainly.

"You don't have a record?"

"What? No. Why?"

Skylark's smile broadened and she bounced to her feet. "Come on," she said, tugging at Cassie's sleeve, practically hauling her back toward the camp.

≪ ≫

Skylark walked so quickly that Cassie almost had to run to keep up.

"Where are we going?" she asked finally as they passed the McDonald's next to the huge bookstore.

"I figured it out," Skylark said. "Everybody else has their turf already, right? And some of them are really protective of it. They've been there for years. But you don't have a police record."

"What does that—"

"It means you've never been there." She gestured at the building at the end of the block, a squat, brown, almost windowless rectangle surrounded by concrete and stairs.

"What's that?" Cassie asked as they walked toward it.

"It's the courthouse," Skylark explained, waiting a beat for Cassie's reaction.

She had none.

Skylark sighed. "If you've got any sort of record at all, you're going to want to avoid the cops, right? Yeah, well, take it from me, the last thing you're going to do is to go where the cops are. So you're not going to go anywhere near the police station, and you're sure as hell not going to put your hat down outside the courthouse, right?"

Cassie smiled.

"It's all yours," Skylark said.

A warm surge of relief rose through her, buttressing her against the cold.

"Come on," Skylark said, taking her arm again. "Let's find you a place to set up."

They walked slowly around the building as Skylark scanned the area. She kept up a steady stream of observations—"There might be all right." "Too far from the doors." "Too windy." "You'll freeze to death there."—and it took Cassie a while to realize that Skylark was nervous. The way she was looking at the building and over her shoulder: she didn't like being there.

Cassie wondered what sort of police record she had.

And she stopped in her tracks.

"What is it?" Skylark asked.

"I don't . . ." She couldn't believe she hadn't thought of it before. "I don't have a record, I don't think. But . . . I'm not . . ."

"You ran away."

Cassie nodded.

"And your parents reported you missing."

Cassie swallowed. "My mom."

Something flashed across Skylark's face, there and gone. She squeezed Cassie's arm. "You don't have to worry about that. If the cops were going to take you in, they'd have done it yesterday. I think you're fine."

The cold wind cut into Cassie's cheeks like a thousand tiny blades on the back of a slap.

"Here, this looks good," Skylark said, pointing to a spot on the sidewalk. "Good traffic from Blanshard, close to the doors, should be out of the wind, but you're not hidden."

Cassie was overwhelmed. There were so many things to consider, so many variables, and Skylark could just rattle them off.

"What do you think?"

"Thank you," Cassie murmured. The words seemed wildly insufficient. "That looks good."

"And look, you've even got something to read." She pointed at the crumpled newspaper on top of the garbage can a short distance away. "Everything a girl could want."

"It's a dream come true."

Skylark smiled. "I'll be back later, all right?" She glanced up at the building. "I've gotta go."

Then the girl was gone, hurrying down the block toward downtown without even a backward glance.

« »

Cassie spread out the blanket from her bag, then double-folded it to give herself a soft cushion and to protect her from the cold concrete.

It didn't make any difference.

With a heavy sigh, she laid out the second knit hat from her bag on the sidewalk, seeded it with a few coins and waited.

And waited.

It was early when she sat down, still well before the morning rush. She figured that once more people were around, on their way to work . . .

But she was wrong. The sidewalks filled with people as the time ticked by, but people rushing to work weren't inclined to stop. Most of them didn't even seem to notice her.

Many of those who did looked at her with such scorn that she wanted to slip between the bars behind her and disappear.

One woman, with tightly styled blond hair and a long red coat, actually stopped and fumbled in her purse, looking at Cassie like something she wanted to scrape off the bottom of her shoe. She dropped a few coins into the hat with an air of imperturbable self-righteousness, and continued along the sidewalk with her nose high in the air.

Cassie checked the hat. The woman had left forty-one cents.

It wasn't all bad, though. One man in a brown suit actually slowed down, bent a bit at the waist to drop a toonie gently into the toque. When Cassie smiled at him, he smiled back, sadly. He shook his head slightly as he turned away.

By late morning, after the coffee breaks and smoke runs, there wasn't even ten dollars in her hat. She had spent a little at McDonald's for a hot chocolate and a breakfast sandwich, and at the drugstore for a new toothbrush and toothpaste, but even with that it wasn't much of a morning.

She considered moving, but the more she thought about it, the more convinced she was that Skylark had been right in her choice: there was something wrong with everywhere else Cassie considered. Too close to the garbage cans. Too hidden. Too exposed to the wind.

And the snow.

As she sat there, her bum frozen, her legs cramping and falling asleep, wispy flakes began to fall, drifting then dancing then zipping past as they got caught by the wind.

She could feel the snow in the tightness of her chest.

She had always loved winter, this time of year. December, with the strings of blinking lights, the nights that seemed to last all day, the first bracing shock of cold as she left the warm house.

She especially loved the first snow every year. It was so wondrous, the ground disappearing under a skiff of white, the snowflakes in the light from the kitchen window.

It was a family tradition: the night of the first snow, she'd have just gotten to sleep when her mom or dad would be shaking her awake, bundling her into her outside clothes while she was still groggy.

Heather would be at the door already, still mostly asleep, and the four of them would wrap up in scarves and mittens before opening the door.

It was magical, walking sleepily through that strange world, the snow cold and stinging a little on their faces, crunching under their boots.

Heather would be holding Mommy's hand, swinging their arms together, singing a song.

And she and her dad would be following behind.

Daddy.

Don't think about it.

Scooping up her hat, the dull rattle of loose change, Cassie stood up, closing her eyes and shaking her head. Keeping her hat tight in her fist, she grabbed the newspaper that someone had left on top of the trash can, stretched a little bit, then sat back down.

Don't think about it.

The newspaper snapped her back into the present.

There was a photograph on the front page, a picture of the breezeway where she had spent the night. It took Cassie a moment to recognize the place; she found the spot near the wall where she and Skylark had slept, and used it to orient herself. Smaller pictures highlighted garbage in the corners and strewn in the square.

The headline read "Squatter Mess at City Hall." The story was short, vicious. The reporter had talked to business owners and people at City Hall, who said, "Homelessness is obviously a problem, but this isn't the solution," and to people who worked or owned businesses downtown, all of whom were "disgusted by the mess," worried that "so many bums and criminals might keep people away from downtown during the Christmas shopping season."

As Cassie read the article, she thought of the speech Brother Paul had given the night before, about the people who didn't understand, who would try to destroy their community.

It seemed he had been right.

There was a small photograph in the corner of the larger image of the breezeway. It was of a young man, hair blowing back in some long-ago breeze, eyes looking into the distance. The caption read "Corbett in 1979."

According to the article, "The squatter camp has been organized by Paul Corbett, who calls himself Brother Paul.

Corbett has a long history of civil disobedience and protest, including the creation of a commune on Quadra Island in the 1970s and involvement with the anti-nuclear movement in the early 1980s. Police have declined to comment on his involvement."

All the police said was that they are "keeping an eye on the situation and will deal with any problems as they develop."

The only other article on the front page was about the murders.

There was a photograph of a group of police officers on a rocky shore, a white plastic sheet at their feet, draped over what was, according to the caption, "the body of 19-year-old Susan Strauss, discovered Monday."

"Police Puzzled, City Afraid," read the headline, but the article was mostly "no comments" and guesses from the reporter. A few things were clear though: the murder had been "brutal" and "savage," the victim had been a prostitute, and police were very carefully not commenting on any possible connection between her death and the murders of "other sex-trade workers this fall."

"It's happening here now."

Cassie jumped at the soft voice.

Standing in front of her, snowflakes whirling around her, was one of the women from the circle the night before. Cassie couldn't remember her name. Bonnie, maybe?

"What?" She lowered the newspaper to the ground.

Without waiting for any sort of invitation, the woman sat down in front of Cassie, making no effort to avoid her hat. "I'm Sarah. Sarah from Edmonton," she said, tugging at her jacket and scarf so they draped around her, seemed to swallow her up. "I saw you last night."

Cassie nodded. "I'm—"

"Dorothy," the woman finished, smiling proudly.

"Dorothy," Cassie agreed.

Sarah's smile broadened. "I'm good with names. Very good. My mom and dad told me that everyone has a gift. I guess that's mine. Names. I'm good with names. Never forget a name."

Cassie felt herself drawing back, and tried not to.

"It's cold out here," Sarah said, crossing her arms to hug herself, to rub her own shoulders. "Cold. Chilly. Chilly beans. Oh, so chilly beans." She giggled.

Cassie forced a smile, wondering what she should do. She didn't want to be rude, but her hat wasn't going to get any fuller with Sarah sitting between her and any people walking by. Should she hint that the other woman should go? Maybe she should find a different place to sit. "It's happening here now," Sarah repeated.

Cassie shook her head. "What is?"

Leaning forward, Sarah smoothed out the newspaper and poked her finger onto the front page, pinning it to the concrete. "That," she said, her voice free of any trace of inflection. "It's happening here now. Like it did before." Sarah nodded deeply, her expression grave.

"What do you mean, 'like before'?"

"Just like before," Sarah repeated, nodding more quickly. "Like the last time." She shifted a little, bounced in place.

"What's happening? What do you mean?"

"It likes the winter," Sarah said. "It likes to hunt in the winter." The head-shaking turned into a faint twitching, and Sarah's body swayed from side to side.

It was scary to watch, and Cassie felt the mania, the fear, starting to infect her. Her heartbeats were coming faster, her breaths shorter; she was starting to get caught up in whatever was affecting Sarah.

"I don't know what you mean," she said. "The murders? They've happened before?"

Sarah's face burst open in a wide smile. "Before," she cried out. "Before. And now here. It's happening here now. It's happening here!"

"What's happening here? Where did it happen? When?" Desperate for any answer, any little bit.

But Sarah was backing up on the pavement, staring at Cassie, backing up on her gloves, crab-walking, pushing herself back with her feet, then jumping up, hurrying away, arms wrapped tight around herself again, weaving. She was talking to herself as she scurried down the sidewalk, but Cassie couldn't make out what she was saying.

She wasn't sure she wanted to.

« »

Cassie couldn't stay there, not after the conversation with Sarah. Even before her heart had slowed, she needed to move, to walk.

She scooped up the few coins from her hat and stuffed them into her pocket as she stood up. The hat itself went into the very top of her bag, crammed and almost bursting it was so full.

Too full, really, for how little was in it.

She needed a new bag. And some new clothes. Especially before she went to the restaurant.

The thought of spending the last of the money she had brought from home caused a defensive pang, but she didn't really have a choice: she couldn't live in one set of clothes for God knows how long.

It wasn't a long walk to the Salvation Army thrift shop; Cassie plugged in her earphones and kept her head bowed against the wind coming straight up the street off the water.

She didn't want to spend any more time in the store than she absolutely had to. The stuffy air was rank with grime and the faint mildew scent of old clothes; the store made her skin itch and feel prickly in her clothes. She wasn't sure if it was the smell, the heat or the chaos.

She went as quickly as she could, moving from rack to rack in a steady, merciless examination, fuelled by the Nine Inch Nails CD playing at high volume in her ears.

A pair of jeans in her size. A couple of shirts. Two white tank tops, a size small, to take the place of her bra, which was practically falling apart. A couple of pairs of wool socks. A black sweater with a hole under the arm but nothing else wrong with it. She winced as she sorted through a beaten-up laundry basket full of underwear, but she didn't really have a choice. When she found a package of two white pairs in her size, still wrapped, with the price tag still on, it felt like she had stumbled across a winning lottery ticket.

Maybe not quite that good.

She paid for the clothes with her last twenty-dollar bill, carefully tucking the change into the front pocket of her backpack before zipping up her coat and stepping back into the wind.

It took her longer than she had expected to find the showers that Skylark had described to her the previous day: the door was concealed in a shadowed recess at Ship's Point on the Inner Harbour, down by the water's edge, between a restaurant and a gift shop.

Inside, there was a wide hallway, with a desk on one side and several doors on the other, all marked *Shower*. Trying not to be conspicuous, she went to the first door, tried the knob.

The door was locked.

"I think the next one's free," came a voice from behind her.

The man behind the desk was standing up, looking at her.

"Oh, I . . ." She had no idea what to say.

"You're looking for a shower, right? I think the next one is available." He pointed to the next door down the corridor. "How are you for shampoo and such?"

Reaching under the desk, he pulled out a small bin packed with plastic bottles. "If you need anything."

She could feel the heat in her face as she stepped over to the desk.

She picked out an almost full bottle of shampoo and a bar of soap.

"You can leave it in there when you're done," he said. "We do a quick clean once an hour this time of year."

"Thank you," she said. "Do I need a key, or . . . ?"

He shook his head. "They lock from the inside. And there are towels in there."

"Thank you," she repeated, and the warm understanding of his smile was so tinged with sadness she had to turn away.

Once she had the door locked behind her and had checked it, pulling hard on the doorknob, Cassie released a heavy breath.

She set her backpack on the chair next to the sink, across from the shower itself, draping her coat over the back. It didn't seem so bad: the room was like a cross between a public washroom and a school shower. With a locked door.

She showered quickly. She would have liked to stand under the water for an hour, letting it run over her, letting the steam fill the room, but she was acutely aware that the only thing separating her from the rest of the world was that door, those locks. Sooner or later, somebody would knock. Somebody would want to get in.

So she washed her hair as quickly as she could, leaving the champoo in while she scrubbed with the tiny bar of soap. She imagined that she could see the dirt lifting off her, layer after layer, like sediment, like time. The small room filled with steam and the smell of green apples from the shampoo.

She dried off as quickly as she could: the towels were small and scratchy, but they did the job. She tore into the package of underwear, then dressed in her new clothes before she even looked at her hair and face. She only gave a passing thought to the clothes that she was putting on. She would have much preferred to have washed them first, but she didn't have that luxury.

Wiping the mirror with the side of her hand, she brushed her hair out, then tied it back into a ponytail with an elastic. She brushed her teeth methodically and for a long time, savouring the burn of the mint in her mouth after more than a day without. She checked her teeth, the corners of her eyes, her skin. She thought about the restaurant, about Ali.

She watched herself blush in the mirror.

When she turned to pack up, she cursed herself: she had forgotten to even look at knapsacks at the Salvation Army. There was no way that everything was going to fit back in.

Then she looked at the clothes she had taken off. Was it worth carrying them around? Were they even salvageable?

She dropped the socks, underwear and shirt in the garbage can.

Her backpack closed, but barely.

She took a hard look at herself in the mirror. It would have to do.

Wait: one last thing.

It took her a long time to find the small, flat container buried deep in her backpack. Unscrewing the cap, she used her right pinkie to apply a bit of gloss to her upper and lower lips, pressing them together to spread it evenly.

It wasn't much, but it was all she had.

She looked at herself in the mirror for a long time, building up her courage.

« »

The wind caught the edge of the door and wrenched it out of Cassie's hand, slamming it against the wall beside the fish tank.

Cassie jumped and felt her face flame, glancing hurriedly into the restaurant to see how many people were looking at her.

But the restaurant was empty, except for Ali, behind the counter at the far end, and one of the other waitresses sitting at a table close by the kitchen door, half-hidden behind a massive plate of food.

"That was quite an entrance," Ali said. She didn't need to raise her voice—the restaurant was tiny, a handful of tables crowded into a shoebox-sized room.

"Sorry," she said, smiling in relief. Her face cooled as she tugged the door closed.

"It happens," Ali said, coming forward, wiping her hands with a white cloth. "This corner is like a wind tunnel. Slightest breeze and—boom!" She clapped her hands with the exclamation and Cassie jumped again.

"I'm sorry," Ali said quickly, taking Cassie's arm. "I didn't mean to startle you."

Cassie shook her head. "That's okay. I'm just a little jumpy, I guess." Ali's hand was warm on her arm. Soft.

"And cold, I'm guessing," Ali said. She squeezed Cassie's arm slightly, then released it. "Let's get you some food. Is up here all right?" She pointed toward the front table, right in the window.

Cassie took a half-step back. "No, that's okay. I can sit in the corner."

"You need to warm up," Ali said, pointing at the grey box tucked into the corner. "And that's where the space heater is. Besides, it's not like we're turning people away."

Cassie didn't move.

"Seriously," Ali said, nudging her. "Sit down. I'll bring you a hot chocolate."

Cassie did the math quickly in her head. "No, no. Just water will be fine."

Ali looked at her for a long moment. "I'll bring it out. Have a seat."

Cassie tucked herself into the corner chair at the front table. The space heater was to her right, and her body began to relax in the warmth.

She felt bad about coming in with barely any money, but the restaurant was one of the only bits of warmth she had found since coming to Victoria the month before.

Well, not just the restaurant.

She looked deeper into the room, at Ali behind the counter, her head down slightly as she focused on what she was doing, her neck taut and pale.

Cassie had found the restaurant on one of her first days in town. She had arrived with virtually nothing, save her CD player and CDs, her wallet, Mr. Monkey, her journal and a few books, everything she had been able to grab in the fire. She had come up the street from the thrift shop, and she had stumbled across the restaurant in Chinatown. She was drawn in by the handwritten sign advertising their lunch special. She was watching every penny, stretching her money while she looked for work, but she had to eat something, right? And a choice of three items from the list for $6.99 was about as good a deal as she was likely to find.

The tall, thin waitress with the short, dark hair, the tiny diamond stud on the left side of her nose, had seated her at a table for two near the back. After taking her order and bringing her food, she left Cassie alone with her book and her Discman, a Sarah McLachlan album lulling her away. When she looked up next, more than an hour had passed. The table had been cleared, and her bill was in front of her, under a plastic-wrapped fortune cookie.

She hurried to the counter, bill in hand. "I'm sorry for taking so long."

The waitress smiled. "You looked like you were really enjoying that book."

It was an Anne McCaffrey Dragonriders book—Cassie had stuffed it hastily into her backpack. She nodded and fished a ten-dollar bill out of her pocket. "I'm sorry, though," she said, handing the bill and the money across the counter. "I shouldn't have taken up your space for so long."

"That's all right," the waitress said, handing back her change. "Anytime you like."

Cassie felt herself starting to blush. "Thanks—" She glanced at the waitress's black T-shirt, looking for a name tag. There wasn't one.

"Ali," the waitress said. "You can call me Ali."

Cassie dumped her change on the empty table and hurried out of the restaurant. But she had come back the next day. And the day after. And the day after that.

Each time Cassie had come, Ali had greeted her with a smile that seemed to brighten the whole room.

"You haven't been in for a while," Ali said as she set the tall glass of ice water on the table and laid a menu in front of Cassie. Her arms were pale and smooth.

Cassie hadn't been into the restaurant since her last day at the hostel, when her money had been running too low for her to afford anything more than day-old bread at the hippie bakery. That was before the shelter. Before the concrete. Before the camp.

"No," Cassie said. "I've been busy."

"Oh yeah?" Ali clearly didn't believe her. "I was worried about you."

Cassie started to say something, but Ali had already turned back toward the kitchen. Cassie watched her walk away, a pale line of skin showing between the bottom of her black T-shirt and the top of her black jeans.

She returned less than a minute later carrying a huge plate of food in one hand and a steaming mug in the other. "Here," she said, and as she lowered the plate, Cassie hurried to move the menu. She set the mug down beside Cassie's water glass: hot chocolate. Full to the brim.

Cassie looked from Ali to the plate and back as the smell and the steam enveloped her face. "I didn't—"

"No," Ali said. "I thought I'd take the liberty. This is what Hong is feeding us girls for lunch."

Cassie thought about the meagre handful of coins in her jeans pocket. "But I can't—"

Ali shook her head. "Don't worry about it."

"No," Cassie said. "I can pay. I just—"

"You don't need to," Ali said. "It's on the house."

"But . . ."

"On the house," Ali repeated. "Now eat up. You look hungry."

She couldn't have known how right she was.

As Ali turned away, Cassie picked up her chopsticks and, after a momentary fumbling, attacked the plate.

The food was like nothing she had ever tasted; she wanted to savour it, but her hunger was too strong to fight, and she devoured mouthful after mouthful.

When she was finished, she pushed the empty plate away from herself and took a long swallow of water. Wiping at the table with her napkin, she pulled her journal out of her backpack and centred it in front of her, where her plate had been.

She had been keeping a journal for as long as she had been able to write. Longer if those old sketchpads with the soft grey newsprint counted.

She still drew. She liked to write and draw in sketchbooks, plain white pages, heavy paper, flat black covers. For her fourteenth birthday, her mother had given her a brown leather cover that slid over the hard backs of the notebooks, so the journals always looked comfortingly the same. Over time the cover had taken on grooves and marks from carrying it in her backpack and school bag. Back home she had made a point of using it every day, even for just a few words or a quick sketch.

But she hadn't opened her journal since she'd left the hostel. She had kept it buried deep in her backpack at the shelter, not wanting anything to happen to it, and she hadn't had a chance to sit with it in front of her for so long.

It felt like she had been missing a part of herself.

It took her a moment of searching in the front pocket of her backpack to find a pencil.

She flipped first to the last partly filled page, but she decided to start on a fresh white sheet.

I haven't written here in so long . . . Too long! So many things have happened . . . I don't know if I'm going to be able to remember everything. I don't think I really want to, but I'll try.

Drawing a line under the words, she started to make a list.

Hostel.

Shelter.

Men in stairwell.

First nights on street.

Friendly cop.

Skylark.

Home?

She looked at the list for a moment. A few days, that was all. Less than a week since the last night in the hostel and everything that had happened since: two nights at the shelter, then the streets. A lifetime.

Using the words as a guide, she began to write.

As the warmth flooded through her, moving down from her belly, up from her legs by the heater, she stopped thinking about what her pencil was doing, lost in the words, in the warmth, in the slow, steady comfort of a full belly.

After a while, she found herself doodling in the margins, so she set the pencil down and took a sip of her hot chocolate, now barely lukewarm. She looked down at the page and felt her face start to burn.

She had scrawled Ali's name in the white space next to the list, the letters tall and dark against the paper.

"Can I take that for you?"

Cassie glanced up and slammed the book shut. Ali was standing at the end of the table, reaching out for the empty plate.

"Sure," she said. "Sure. Yes. Thank you."

How much had the waitress seen of the sketches that edged the pages? The curve of a back, bending over a table, the pale line of skin between T-shirt and jeans. A hand, holding a plate. An eye, sparkling as it looked out from under floppy bangs.

She wondered if Ali had seen her name.

Her face burned even hotter.

Arching her bum off the chair, Cassie dug deep into her front pocket and began pulling out the small handful of change, which she deposited on the table next to her journal. She got most of the change out on the first few tries, but she made one last attempt, twisting slightly to retrieve one last dime that was buried deep.

"I don't think I've got enough," she muttered as she started sorting the coins into stacks of a dollar each.

Ali laid her hand over hers. "What are you doing? I told you—it's on the house."

"But—"

"No, seriously." She let go of Cassie's hand as she pulled one of the other chairs away from the table and sat down across from her.

Cassie forced herself to look away.

"I can't just take—"

"You're not," Ali said. "We're giving. Look, Hong?" She gestured back toward the kitchen, where Cassie got a glimpse of a middle-aged man with a greying hairstyle that reminded her of Elvis in those old movies she had watched with her dad. "He noticed that you were coming in pretty regularly, and when you stopped . . ." Ali looked down at the table. "He asked if I knew what had happened. He thought that maybe"—she took a breath—"things weren't going well."

Cassie shifted in her chair.

Ali looked out the front window as she spoke. "They're not, are they?"

When she turned back, Cassie looked quickly away. For a moment, Cassie was tempted to lie. It was instinctive, a reflex, but for some reason, she couldn't.

"No, they're not." She looked down at her journal.

Ali's hand moved on the table. It was barely noticeable—a slight twitch, a movement toward Cassie, stifled almost before it happened.

"It's nice to be warm," Cassie added. Now that she had broken through that wall, there was no need to pretend. "And full."

Ali nodded slowly. "I was wondering about that. So where are you staying now?"

Cassie looked away. "Here and there," she said, studying the soy sauce container, the scratches on her water glass, the tree outside the window, looking at anything but Ali's face. But Ali saw through it.

"Oh, God," she said, and this time her hand did move, sliding across the table to cover Cassie's again. "That's . . . Have you thought about a shelter?"

Cassie shook her head. "No," she snapped, but she softened at Ali's response. "I'm sorry. I was at a shelter the first couple of nights after I left the hostel." She shook her head again. "This way is better."

Ali started to say something, then stopped, the tip of her tongue pressing against her lower lip like she was frozen in mid-word.

"It's all right," Cassie said, not really sure if it was. "I've met some people. There's this—"

"In Centennial Square."

"—community," she finished, then nodded. "Yes. How—"

"It was in the paper," she said, gesturing toward the back of the restaurant. "Are they all right? Is it okay?"

"It seems okay. I haven't been there long." She picked up her cup, willing her hand not to shake, and drank the last of her hot chocolate. "I only met them yesterday. They're not a cult or anything."

Ali's expression of concern shifted to mild bemusement. "Well, if you say so."

It was nice to have someone worried about her.

"What were you drawing?"

The question seemed to come out of nowhere, but Ali pointed down at Cassie's sketchbook and pencil: "What are you working on?"

"Oh." Cassie felt herself starting to blush again. "It's just my journal. I haven't . . . It's been a while."

"You were pretty focused on it. Like that day with the book."

Blushing more now, hearing that Ali had remembered. "Yeah."

"I tried keeping a diary when I was younger. A few times, actually. But I never stuck with it. Does it help?"

Cassie took a long moment to answer. "Yes. It does."

Ali stood up. "I'll leave you to it, then. I'll be back with some more hot chocolate in a bit. You take all the time you need."

Cassie just smiled. "Thank you."

Leaning back over her journal, she began to flip through the pages, the echo of Ali's question still reverberating in her mind.

Yes, it helped. It helped in so many ways. The journal kept her grounded, reminded her of who she was, her true self, no matter how far things drifted.

It was all her, all right there.

She turned to the first page, the first writing in the new journal she had started in the hospital the month before.

She stared at the words, her truth, her self.

November 15, 1997

I killed Daddy last night.

PART TWO

Scientists believe that light can be both wave and particle. Not that light exists in different states at different times, the way that water can be ice or steam with the application or reduction of heat, but that light exists as both a wave and a particle at the same moment. It is not either/or. It is both/and.

This is also true of the Darkness.

It exists not within paradox, but as a paradox itself.

It is both energy and form.

Both without and within.

It moves within us and outside us. Like a man and like the arc of electricity.

I knew this from the moment the Darkness first came to me.

But even that is wrong. The Darkness was always within me. It is always within all of us. But even though it was within me, it came to me too. I could feel it moving over me, brushing across my face and watching through my eyes as I held the kitten in the kitchen sink, as I turned the water on and let the basin fill.

I could feel the Darkness within me, my Darkness, growing as the kitten struggled, and I could feel the Darkness outside looking on, watching me and watching through my eyes.

The Darkness within me grew with every desperate attempt the kitten made to escape. And the Darkness outside fed off the kitten's death, and from every scratch it inflicted on me, every drop of my blood it spilled in its dying.

The Darkness fed from both of us. And fed. And fed.

As she opened the door from the restaurant, the cold wind was like a slap in the face, stinging and sharp. Cassie took a startled breath that burned all the way down, and stopped short to shift her scarf up over her mouth and nose. It took only seconds for her to feel like she might never be warm again.

And she had been so warm.

It was like waking into a nightmare.

Hunching her shoulders forward, she turned away from the wind, ducking her head. As she scurried past, she caught a glimpse of Ali standing in the window, watching her through the half-steamed glass.

The snow had started to stick, a brittle skiff on the concrete that crunched under her feet. The wind sliced up the gap between her shoes and pants, chilling her lower legs.

The sidewalks were nearly deserted, and none of the people she passed even noticed her. Their own heads were bent, their eyes focused on the snowy ground.

It was getting dark, but unlike the day before, there was already a crowd in the breezeway next to City Hall, small clusters of people hunkered out of the wind, wrapped in threadbare blankets, huddled together for warmth. Standing in the shadows of Centennial Square, Cassie scanned the area slowly for Skylark. She looked again and again, even as the snow whipped around her.

"Why don't you come in?"

The voice was soft, but Cassie jumped and turned.

Brother Paul lowered both his hands slowly, palms down There was something in the simple action that was soothing, and it took Cassie a moment to recognize: it was the same movement the minister at home used to signal the congregation to take their seats.

"You don't have to stand out here in the cold, you know," he said.

"I know," she said. "I was—"

"Waiting for your friend."

"Yes."

"Why don't you come in," he repeated, opening his arms, gesturing toward the camp with his right, lifting his left as if he meant to guide her with a touch on her back.

Cassie took a half-step away.

"The Outreach van will be here soon. And I'm sure Skylark will be back." He paused. "Ah . . ." He nodded toward the breezeway.

The volume of murmuring from the camp rose as Skylark moved from group to group, embracing people, laughing, talking loudly.

"Blessed be, Dorothy," Brother Paul murmured as he drifted away.

Watching Skylark in the distance, Cassie barely heard him.

She looked distracted and kept glancing around. She would look over the shoulder of whoever she was embracing, and between groups she deliberately turned around, scanning the breezeway.

Was she looking for Cassie?

She dismissed the thought—Skylark knew everyone. She was probably looking for Brother Paul, or for a friend.

Cassie drifted slowly toward the camp. She didn't want to seem like she was rushing or trying to make an entrance. She didn't want to look stupid or—

"Dorothy!"

Skylark turned away from the group she was talking to and almost ran across the breezeway toward her, swooping her into a tight hug without another word.

"How did it go?" she bubbled, stepping back slightly. "Was that a good spot? Did you stay warm enough? What about that snow? Oh, I've had a day you wouldn't believe," she said without a breath. "Come on," she said. "We can catch up."

As they turned, the entire camp seemed to stir. Cassie could dimly pick out the sound of a rough engine as everyone started to move toward the loading zone in front of City Hall.

"Dinner first," Skylark said, guiding them into the crowd.

Cassie almost walked into the shadow that stopped in front of her, blocking her path.

"Well, look who it is."

The words stopped her in place.

It was the dreadlocked boy from the McDonald's, with two of his friends.

"I was hoping I would see you again."

Even in the half-light she could see the smirk on the boy's face, the smiles of his friends. "Who's your friend?" he asked, drawing out the word as he turned to Skylark.

"What the fuck is it to you?" Skylark snarled through a wide smile.

One of the boys snorted.

"Skylark," Cassie whispered.

Skylark stayed perfectly still, her smile etched on her face, drawn back over her teeth.

The boy with the dreadlocks grinned.

"So, just 'bitch,' then?"

The other boys laughed; Skylark didn't move.

She didn't flinch when he jerked toward her, snapping his head forward so it was almost touching hers, lingering for a moment before he pulled back and turned away.

"Whatever," he muttered. "Fucking dyke bitches."

The boys were laughing as they drifted toward the food line.

"So, are you hungry?" Skylark asked, turning to Cassie as if nothing had happened.

"Skylark—"

"Because I don't want to get in line with those guys, and if we wait—"

Without thinking, Cassie threw her arms around Skylark, squeezing her tightly. "Oh, God."

"What?" Skylark asked, puzzled.

"Those guys—" Cassie started, but Skylark cut her off.

"Those guys? Those guys are bad news. You can tell just looking at them."

Cassie exhaled heavily.

"The thing with guys like that? They're just bullies. And bullies are usually weak and they use all this bluster and violence to pump themselves up so nobody notices that. Pick on someone else so you don't get picked on, right?"

"I guess."

"So you have to outbluster them. Make them know that you're more confident than they think you are. Stronger. That way they won't pick on you. A predator won't attack something stronger, right?"

She thought of what Mrs. Hepnar had said and how she had tried to stand up to the boys at the McDonald's. "Yeah."

"It's nature. That's how it usually works. Predators prey on the weak. It's all instinct."

Watching the three boys push each other in the line, Cassie wasn't sure she found that comforting at all.

« »

The Darkness watched the girls from the far side of the line that had formed behind the van, another face in a white blur of faces, of grey breath, of scarves and hats.

They were almost close enough to touch.

He had done it on purpose, positioned himself deliberately. Just close enough, just far away enough, teetering on the cusp of possibility. He hungered, and he savoured the hunger, the desire. Wanting to reach out, to sweep them in, to take them— he could feel his heart race at the thought, at the tension in his muscles. It would be so easy.

It was always so easy.

But there was so much pleasure in the yearning. Holding off, letting the hunger build . . . That first bite would be ever so sweet.

The Darkness stopped, looked into the crowd. He could feel a pull, a gentle tug, the inviting breath of a door being opened, a door into another world of warmth, another hunger.

Closing his eyes, the Darkness jumped.

When his eyes opened again, he was in a different place,

inside a different vessel, deeper in the crowd, closer to the van, but farther from the girls.

His first reaction was to scan the crowd, to look for the old host. There, closer to the square, eyes taking in the crowd, but returning, always returning, to the girls. The Darkness could see the hunger, the longing.

The Darkness breathed and grew in the new vessel, expanding to fill the space. He flexed his finger, tapped his toes, turned his head, gradually spun the body in an almost complete circle.

The Darkness smiled.

This was a splendid new development. Not a surprise: doors were always opening for the Darkness, it was human nature. But this, this felt familiar. He had felt these hands, tasted this anger.

Oh, yes, the Darkness had been here before.

And he would return.

But right now . . .

With one last lingering look at the girls, the Darkness jumped again.

《 》

He was surprised when he felt the stirring in the pit of his stomach. Usually it took longer. Usually a night like last night was enough to keep the feelings at bay for a good long time. Weeks, sometimes months even.

But maybe it was like a good meal. You stuff yourself at Christmas dinner to the point where you feel like you might explode, and you swear you'll never eat again, only to wake up on Boxing Day morning hungrier than you've ever been in your entire life.

Yes, it was just like that.

Because last night had been a hell of a feast, satisfying him in ways that he had never even imagined.

And yet, here he was.

It was the television's fault.

The kids had it on while they were playing, some screeching show that set his teeth on edge. And they weren't even watching—they had it on in the background as they built Lego castles and knocked them down. Build, destroy, build, destroy, and all the time that hellish screeching.

And every time he tried to turn it off or change the channel, the kids had pleaded with him like their lives depended on staying tuned in.

So it wasn't his fault.

It was that little slut on the TV, that always-smiling, hair-flipping, head-cocking little slut, her tight little body, her knowing eyes.

That's when the stirring had come back, in one flash of imagination: the way her eyes would widen as he slid the knife into her.

Nothing more than that, and the stirring was back.

He had sat there on the couch as the kids played, as that ridiculous, terrible show screeched on, thinking about the night before, the way that whore had started to scream, the cry bubbling out of her throat in a rush and gout of blood. And that pissy little bitch on the TV—God, he'd leave her throat for the very end, just to hear that screech one last time.

At first, he had hoped for the feeling to go away. No: he actively tried to push it down, to distract himself. He crouched on the floor and started building a castle of his own, laughing as the kids ganged up on him to reduce it to rubble, again and again. He offered to get the kids ready for bed, to take care of storytime and give Alice a chance to get off her feet. He had lingered over the books, laughing with the kids before snugging the covers up to their necks and kissing them good night.

No matter what he did, his stomach roiled. It was impossible to ignore, impossible to push down.

But there was something about it . . .

The realization came to him as he sat on the couch next to Alice, her legs draped over his lap as they watched some crappy rerun: he liked it.

He liked the stirring in his stomach. He liked the way it made him feel.

It was like resisting a snack while waiting for a big dinner: the hunger was satisfying in and of itself.

Though not, he thought to himself, as Alice yawned and started to get ready for bed, *as good as the meal would be*.

She lingered in the living room doorway on her way upstairs.

"Are you coming?" she asked. There was a flirtatious tone to her voice, and she leaned forward a little, a small smile on her lips.

He shook his head, putting on a frown. "Not right now," he said, and her face fell. "I'm sorry," he hurried. "I should put in a couple of hours . . ."

She nodded, her smile replaced with a frown of familiar resignation. "Of course."

"I'm sorry," he repeated, but she shook her head.

"I know," she said wearily. "Work."

"Yeah."

She tilted her head to the left, toward the stairs. "I'm going to read for a little bit."

"I'll be quiet when I come to bed," he said, knowing from years of experience that once she was asleep only the sound of a bomb going off, or one of the kids crying, would wake her.

After that, it was just a matter of waiting. He went down to his office in the basement, spread some papers across his desk, then powered up his computer. The locked file of photos didn't satisfy the hunger, but he had known they wouldn't. It was more a matter of whetting his appetite.

An hour later, he went upstairs. Both the kids were asleep, and Alice had drifted off in her book, the way she did most nights. He marked her place with her bookmark and set the novel on the night table before turning off the light.

In the kitchen, he loaded the dishwasher, but he didn't start it. Instead, he took a knife out of the utensil drawer and set it carefully on the counter, lining it up parallel to the stainless steel edge of the sink.

He took some grocery bags from the basket under the sink and set them next to the knife.

He opened the fridge and took a slow look at the shelves, finally picking up the small container of cream and shaking it. Less than half-full—that would do.

He poured the remaining cream down the drain and ran the cold water over it for several seconds, tossing the container under the sink.

He had his line all worked out: "I went to have a cup of tea, but there was no cream left, so I popped out to the store . . ."

No cream left? Was "but the cream had gone off" better? It didn't matter: he could go either way.

And it wasn't like Alice was going to wake up and wonder where he had driven off to.

Still, he thought, picking up the knife and the plastic bags and heading out to the garage, *it was always good to be prepared.*

Like a Boy Scout.

Cassie wasn't watching the boys, but she was always aware of where they were.

As she and Skylark ate, she knew that the dreadlocked kid and his two friends were sitting at the far side of the breeze-way in a tightly closed knot of crossed legs and raised voices. As people drifted around after dinner, she tracked their movement through the space, out to the square and back.

When the circle formed, they sat down almost directly across from her, laughing and guffawing. She glanced at them as she and Skylark sat down, and the dreadlocked kid met her eye and gave her a tiny, mocking wave, wiggling his fingertips at her across the concrete.

The boys shouldered one another as Brother Paul started the evening, and shifted scornfully as people began to introduce themselves.

When it got to their turn, Cassie leaned forward slightly.

"I'm Bob," the dreadlocked kid said in a tone of mock solemnity. His friends laughed quietly. "I'm here because my dad liked to diddle me."

A quiet murmur rolled through the circle. Cassie and Skylark remained silent.

"But that's all right," Bob said, affecting a slow drawl. "As soon as I got big enough, I put a stop to that. Put him in the hospital right good, and when he got out"—his two friends were laughing openly now, and Brother Paul studied them in silence—"I told him, 'Old man, you keep your hands to your-self or I'll put you right back in there.'" He punched his fist into his palm for effect. "I got outta there as quickly as I could. And that's how I got here."

He leaned back, smirking, and looked across the circle at Cassie with a challenging stare.

She didn't believe any of it.

Neither, clearly, did Brother Paul, who began to pace slowly within the circle, never taking his eyes off the three boys.

Cassie didn't really pay attention to the other two boys and their stories, except to hear that their names were Frank and Joe.

"Don't they look like the Hardy Boys to you?" Skylark whispered.

Cassie was waiting to hear from Sarah from Edmonton, wondering what the woman would say, thinking back to their earlier conversation by the courthouse.

But she didn't say much of anything. Huddled deep in her grey overcoat, scarf wrapped around most of her face, she only mumbled her name and where she was from, staring unflinchingly at the concrete in front of her, worrying the end of her scarf between her fingers.

After the introductions, Brother Paul gave a shortened version of the welcoming speech that Cassie had heard the night before. His voice was tight and clipped, and he kept his side to Bob and his friends all the while, never turning his back on them, never letting them entirely out of his sight.

He saw every eye-roll, every nudge, every barely suppressed laugh.

"Friends, I don't know if you saw the newspaper this morning." Another murmur passed through the circle; clearly almost everyone had.

He nodded. "Good. I'm glad." Reaching into his pocket, he pulled out a piece of the newspaper, folded into a long rectangle. "This is what happens," he said, as he unfolded it and held it up for display. "This is what happens when we confront people's most deeply held beliefs. There are more than twenty of us here. Every shelter bed is full. And the business owners are worried that their Christmas sales are going to suffer! The mayor says that there's a homelessness problem, but that this isn't the answer. Then what is? What solution is the mayor offering to this 'problem'? More shelter beds, but only when the temperature drops?"

He took a deep breath.

"I have seen this before. If you read the article, you know that my name used to be Paul Corbett. That I was a hippie"—a few people in the circle laughed quietly—"and a protester. All of this is true. They try to paint me as some sort of rebel—let them. Even before I joined the church, I lived a life of values and principles. I believed in people. I believed in this earth. Everything I have done has been guided by these beliefs.

"But people do not like being confronted with principles and beliefs. They don't want to see us here because homelessness is something they can't bear to be confronted with. 'Oh,'" he said, putting on a distressed voice, "'those poor people. Oh, heavens, turn the channel!' Well, I'm sorry. There are hundreds of people living on the street in this city. I'm sorry if our community upsets you. I'm sorry if your having to see us disturbs your vision of the world."

All around the circle, people were nodding enthusiastically. A few of them cried out, "Yes!" as Brother Paul made each of his points.

Even Cassie felt herself getting caught up in it, nodding along, unable to take her eyes off him.

"I have said, all along, that if we treated this place and these people with respect, we could expect respect in return." He slumped. "I was wrong."

A ripple of disbelief ran through the circle.

"Look at this picture." He held up the newspaper, turning in a slow, full circle so that everyone would see the photograph of the garbage strewn breezeway. "Look at this." He shook the paper. "This is a lie. This is a lie they tell to tear us apart." He dropped the hand holding the newspaper to his side. "Every morning, I am the last to leave this place. I know what it looks like when we go. We leave only footprints; we don't leave this." He shook the newspaper again. "So where did the garbage come from?" He paused, turned slowly around the circle again. "Where did this 'mess' come from that they're blaming on us?"

Another dramatic pause.

"Why don't we ask the mayor?" A few people in the circle cheered. "Why don't we ask those business owners who are so worried about their Christmas sales?" Bob, the dreadlocked boy, whooped. "Why don't we ask those people who are fine with hundreds of people sleeping on their streets, so long as they can ignore us?"

More cheering now, and Brother Paul let it build for a moment before starting again, his voice quieter, stronger. "We have played by their rules. We have behaved. We have slunk out of here at dawn every morning, gathered by night, all so we wouldn't . . . so they wouldn't be forced to confront their own failings, their own hypocrisies. My father used to have a saying. He used to say, 'Son, you don't rock the boat, especially when you're sitting in it.'" He took a long moment, seeming to think about the words.

"My father was wrong. Sometimes you have to rock the boat."

He drove slowly out of the cul-de-sac, came to a full stop at the corner, signalled his turn. The deliberate care was a combination of not wanting to draw attention to himself and wanting to build the anticipation.

The rumbling in his belly had turned into a burning now, a surging breathlessness that he could feel in his jaw, in his fingers, in his toes. It felt like he was growing too big for his skin, like he was going to burst out of his body, explode in a ball of hot, white light.

Soon. So soon.

He pushed the ZZ Top cassette into the tape player, and sang along.

He drove carefully, attentively, out of Gordon Head, toward downtown. He never broke the speed limit, obeyed every traffic signal, even slowed to let jaywalkers scurry across Shelbourne in the yellow cone of his headlights.

He turned right onto Bay, headed toward Rock Bay.

There were still hookers working the Government Street strip downtown, but more of the girls were around Rock Bay now.

It was almost a hierarchy. The girls downtown were more experienced, higher end, catering to a more genteel crowd of casual gawkers and men who, on a whim, decided to try something new.

The girls who worked Rock Bay generally had no other choice. Maybe it was a drug habit or a criminal record, but there was always a reason to offer themselves in this area of run-down rentals, silent factories, gas stations and dark-cornered, narrow streets.

This was where the real girls hung out, the young ones. Downtown, the police would have picked them up in a second, comparing them to photos in their database of missing kids and runaways. Downtown, there was nowhere for them to hide; up in Rock Bay, they could disappear into the shadows, the stinking alleys, the moment they saw a police car in the distance.

It was ironic, he thought as he turned off Bay. They came up here because they had something to hide, and then they did everything they could to put themselves on display.

He took his first drive down the strip at a regular speed, checking out the situation, but not looking too hard. There were only a few girls out, but he had expected that. With all the news coverage, they were bound to be skittish.

But that would only last until their desperation took hold.

There was no point in rushing; good things come to those who wait.

He drove to a nearby coffee shop and stood in line. There was a sign taped to the front of the counter: *Ladies, be careful. Check your client. Know whose car you're getting into. Keep an eye out for each other. Trust your instincts. Don't take chances. Report any questionable activity.*

What would pass for *questionable activity* in this neighbourhood?

He bought himself a coffee and drank it in the van, leaning back in his seat with his eyes closed, letting the music wash over him.

Pickings were still slim on his next pass down the strip. There were more girls out now, but none that appealed to him. As he drove past, he evaluated each one: Too old. Too strung out. Too hard. Too blond.

It wasn't completely conscious, but he was looking for something, something in particular. He didn't know exactly what, but he knew he would recognize it when he saw it.

He found her on his third trip along the stroll. She was standing back from the edge of the street, almost in the shadows, a tiny redhead in a short black miniskirt with black leather boots to match the black leather jacket she wore open over a silky white top. Was it a camisole?

She couldn't have been more than fifteen, her eyes wide and guileless as they tracked the minivan along the street.

She radiated uncertainty and hesitation. Doing her best to blend into the darkness, she wouldn't have drawn most eyes, but for him, she seemed to glow, a soft white light that he couldn't take his eyes away from.

He pulled up to the curb in front of her on his next trip around the block. He couldn't breathe as he watched her approach him: tentatively, rocking a bit on her boot heels. There was something long and awkward about her, vaguely deer-like, as he unrolled the window.

"You look cold," he said, as friendly as could be. He knew how he looked: the minivan, the haircut, the smile.

He looked like a dad. Not a father: a dad.

She clutched the edge of the window with both hands. "A little, yeah." Up close, he could see that he had been right: she was maybe fifteen, cheeks still slightly rounded with baby fat. Her skin looked like it would be smooth and clear, once he scraped off the heavy makeup.

When she smiled, her teeth were a little crooked, like they didn't fit her mouth. None of her seemed to fit together quite right, like she wasn't quite set yet.

"Why don't you get in, try to warm up a bit?"

She looked at him for a moment, and he thought of the poster in the coffee shop, the warnings and advice.

"Are you a cop?"

"No," he said, shaking his head. "Are you?"

She smiled, as if it were the most ridiculous thing she had ever heard, then opened the door.

He watched her as she climbed into the van, the gawky, awkward angles of her, the paleness of her skin, the way she seemed to glow in the dim light.

≪ ≫

Cassie and Skylark had spent the previous hour listening to music from Cassie's CD player, trading out discs from the dozen in the wallet, sharing Cassie's earphones, one ear each.

It was only when people started unrolling sleeping bags and unfolding blankets that Cassie realized something had changed.

"Are there more people here tonight?" she asked Skylark, making her own bed against the wall.

Our spot, as she had come to think of it.

Skylark took a slow look around the area. "That's what's been happening," she said. "There were only a few people here at the start."

"Were you one of them?"

Skylark shook her head. "No, I didn't get here till later. There were a dozen or so of us then." She spread out the comforter she used as a groundsheet, lining up the edge against Cassie's.

"How long ago was that?"

Skylark thought for a moment. "Last Tuesday?" she said, sounding not entirely sure.

Cassie was sure that she had misunderstood. "Last Tuesday? Like a week ago?"

"That sounds about right." Laying down her blankets, then the ragged sleeping bag over the top.

"Seriously?"

"What?"

Cassie shook her head. "I don't know. Listening to Brother Paul talk, it sounded to me like this place had been around a lot longer."

"Well, that's sort of his thing, right? That this has always been our place." She fluffed the pillow she had pulled from the bottom of her knapsack before placing it at the foot of the wall.

Cassie flattened out her blankets.

"That's not enough."

"What?" Cassie stopped in her tracks, trying to figure out if she had missed something.

Skylark pointed at her bed. "You don't have enough blankets. You're going to freeze."

"I'll keep my gloves on. And I've got a scarf."

But Skylark was already in motion. "Here," she said, taking Cassie's bed apart. "If we put all the blankets together"—she laid Cassie's blankets over the top of her sleeping bag—"we'll probably be toasty. Is that all right? I figure the two of us can keep each other warm."

It was the matter-of-fact way she said it, the complete guilelessness of the comment, that caused Cassie to nod.

"Is it all right? I don't mean anything weird by it or anything. I just figure . . ."

"No, that's fine," Cassie said. "That's a good idea." She glanced around the breezeway, Bob's last taunt ringing in her ears.

They were just keeping warm, that's all. They weren't friends like that.

She thought of Ali, her pale, strong hands, and felt herself starting to blush.

She was about to turn back toward the bed, back toward Skylark, when she saw Sarah.

The old woman was sitting across the breezeway, nestled in the lee of one of the pillars, a shapeless grey lump of jacket and scarf and hat.

The only part of her visible was her eyes.

And she was looking straight at Cassie.

Cassie froze under her gaze, not sure what to do. She tried smiling, but the woman's eyes didn't change. She didn't blink, and her stare never wavered.

Cassie waited, expecting her to say something, or gesture, anything to indicate that she had actually seen Cassie. Instead, she just stared.

It was like she was looking through her.

Pushing down her feelings of unease, Cassie turned back to Skylark, who was unlacing her heavy boots, tucking them away. Rolling slightly, Skylark shimmied under the covers, letting them fall around her lap as she crossed her legs. Cassie watched as she wound the scarf around her neck once, twice, some sort of twist that created a loose width of knit around her throat, then lay down.

"Are you coming?"

"Yeah."

She sat on the foot of the makeshift bed and untied her shoes. It was only when she was putting them under her backpack that she realized she was doing exactly what Skylark had done.

Copying her.

That made sense. Skylark knew how to do things and how things worked. There were worse people to use as examples.

Worse people to have as friends.

Rewrapping her scarf roughly around her neck, Cassie crawled into the bed.

She glanced back out at the breezeway as she settled. There was still no sign of Bob and his friends; Brother Paul was crouched in front of Sarah, talking to her in hushed, gentle tones.

"Is this okay?" Skylark asked again, close enough that Cassie could almost feel every word.

"Yes," Cassie said, though the word didn't seem to be or say enough, as she lay down.

"Good," Skylark said, snuggling closer. "I'm glad."

« »

He washed himself in the icy water.

Balancing precariously on the rocks, he dipped his hands into the waves, rubbing them briskly together, splashing up his arms where the blood had sprayed: it was starting to get tacky, drying too fast.

In the silver snowlight, the blood on his hands had looked black: now he imagined the seafoam tinged pink.

He scrubbed his hands until they gleamed ghostly white. The water burned, but it felt good. Like a cleansing fire.

Clean again. Fresh. New.

She hadn't fought much.

But then, she hadn't had much of a chance.

They had talked a bit while he drove. She was such a cliché:

claiming to be a student at the college, only doing this to get enough money to get home for Christmas.

Poor little girl.

Then they had talked price.

Getting the business out of the way meant there was no delay. He had pulled into a deserted spot close to the water, and the moment he had turned the key in the ignition, her head was in his lap.

She had unzipped him with admirable skill, and he was still partly soft when she had taken him into her mouth.

It seemed like eagerness, but he knew that she just wanted to get it over with.

He luxuriated in the feeling for a moment, closing his eyes as he got hard, then he wrapped his hands around her neck and squeezed, pulling her mouth away and tightening his hands in a single, smooth motion. She jerked, turned to look at him, her eyes wider than he would have thought possible. She tried to scream, but there was no air, and the change in her position meant he could adjust his grip, get his thumbs and fingers just right.

It didn't take long at all.

He had squeezed until she stopped flailing and kicking, until her body sagged heavy against his, until her eyes went red and dull.

Then a little longer.

After a time, he pushed her back into the passenger seat and zipped himself back up. He was fully hard now, his pants almost painfully tight.

Going around the van, he pulled her from the seat and dragged her to the rocky beach. He had to go back for the knife.

He took his time.

He savoured every moment: dabbing tenderly at her cheeks

and around her eyes with the baby wipes from the glove compartment, getting rid of the caked-on makeup. The sighing sound that came from her as he cut across her throat. The puff of steam as he ran the knife up from her belly button to her breastbone. The way the blood oozed onto the rocks as he cut her apart, moved her around, cut into her again.

When it was done, he stood up and stepped back, looking down at what he had done.

She was so beautiful, it almost broke his heart.

He leaned back down, tugged at her jaw to open her mouth. Just one more thing.

As he worked with the knife, there was a sound like metal scraping against metal. A crow had landed on the roof of the minivan. Rocking back and forth, its claws scritched against the paint. Its black eyes gleamed in the dark.

It had all gone so well.

Driving home, though, he felt a niggling sense of regret. It had all been over so quickly. After all that waiting, that joyful, painful anticipation, it had gone by so fast.

Like Christmas. All that preparation and then—he snapped his fingers—it was over.

Had it been everything he had hoped for?

No, it hadn't. There was so much more that he wanted to do.

Next time. He'd do better next time. He'd take his time, not get caught up in the moment. Really enjoy it. Get the most out of the experience.

Wasn't that what life was all about, really? Truly feeling the joy when you experienced it?

Next time.

He turned up the CD player, sang along as he drove home.

Next time.

From out of the shadows, Cassie was watching.

Everything was silent, calm. Everyone was asleep, small clouds of breath hanging in the still, cold air.

No, not everyone.

She wasn't asleep.

"Sarah," she called, her voice high, to carry in the dark.

The grey blankets close to one of the pillars shifted, moved. The older woman emerged, rumpled and grey, and shuffled toward the square.

"Sarah," she murmured, her fingers tightening around the hilt of the knife.

She felt herself moving closer, as if they were drawn together by some strange magnetism. Closer, closer, ever closer.

Her hand began to ache around the knife.

And then she was behind Sarah, following her through the square toward the parkade. She could hear her breathing, the rustle of her movements, the echo of Sarah's footsteps.

Closer. Ever closer.

Close enough now to reach out, grab her by the hair.

Sarah stopped. "I know you're there," she said, without turning, perfectly still.

Cassie circled around her, staying to the shadows.

And then their eyes locked.

"I knew it was you."

Cassie buried the knife in Sarah's throat before she could say anything else, twisting the width of the blade in her windpipe, grinding against the flesh and the bone as blood gushed forth, spilling onto the snow.

The blood steamed and sizzled where it fell.

"I knew it was you," Sarah said again, each word spraying a fine mist of blood.

Cassie twisted the knife again.

« »

Cassie awoke to the sound of her own scream, and sprung upward to a sitting position as it tore her throat raw. She pulled the scarf away from her face, and the sudden sharpness of the air was boiling water against her breath-moist skin.

She gasped and heaved, leaning over and pressing her eyes shut against the bright light on the wall above her.

Oh, God, oh, God, what have I done?

Breath whooped and howled in her throat. All she could think of was the way the knife had felt in her hand as she had twisted it in Sarah's neck, the grinding, gristly vibrations of it—

Oh, God.

And then Skylark was there, rubbing her back, whispering close to her ear, "It's okay. You're all right."

She whooped and gasped.

"Shh, it's okay."

One breath caught, and her lungs filled, the air so cold it burned, but oh so sweet. As she breathed, her heart slowed.

In two three four . . .

"Shh, you're all right."

Someone screamed in the square, and they both turned.

« »

Katherine, one of the younger girls, had found her.

She had been on her way back from the bathroom and had

thought at first that the dark shadow in the fountain was a bag of garbage.

"Oh my God," Skylark muttered, turning back to the camp.

Cassie wouldn't let herself look away.

Sarah had fallen backward into the dry fountain. Her feet were in the air, her legs against the inside of the rim at a right angle to her body. Her arms were spread wide. There was a knife in her right hand. The other was empty. Her head lolled to one side, her eyes staring wide and unseeing into the violet sky, her lips white-blue and slightly parted. There was a deep gash, bloody and gaping, across her throat, a glistening red smile. Her head was framed by a nimbus of blood that pooled around her, copper in the rising light.

There was another pool of blood on the snowy ground outside the fountain.

When she couldn't look any longer, Cassie turned, took several steps and vomited near a garbage can.

It's happening here, she thought.

« »

"She said her name was Sarah." Cassie's voice was barely a whisper: she couldn't seem to take in enough air to form words.

"Okay," Constable Farrow said, writing in her notebook. "Had you known Sarah long?"

Cassie shook her head. "I only met her yesterday. The day before yesterday." Time was starting to blur; it was getting harder and harder to keep track.

"Did she seem troubled to you?"

Cassie looked around the breezeway. Almost everyone was gone. When Brother Paul had said that he was going to call the police, everyone had scattered. Nobody wanted to be around when the police arrived; nobody wanted to answer any questions.

Cassie had stayed.

"Well?"

"Pardon me?" Cassie asked, shaking her head, trying to clear it.

The cop muttered something that Cassie didn't catch. "Did Sarah seem troubled to you?" She spoke slowly and clearly.

Over by the fountain, several police officers were talking with Brother Paul while a group of cops and paramedics milled around, voices hushed, giving wide berth to people in white full-body suits who were examining Sarah's body and the ground around her. From that distance and angle, Cassie couldn't see the blood, but she didn't need to: the images were seared onto her brain.

It's happening here now.

"Jesus Christ," the cop muttered, when Cassie didn't answer. She shook her head and paced a few steps away.

"Hey, cut her some slack," her partner said, stepping toward Cassie. "This has got to be tough."

Farrow waved her hand dismissively.

"Hey, Cassie," Constable Harrison said, leaning slightly forward. "Are you all right? I know this can't be easy."

"I'm all right," she lied.

"Good," Harrison said. "We've only got a couple more questions, then we'll be done, all right?"

Cassie nodded and tried to focus on Harrison. "I'll try."

"Good." He smiled. "Now, did you have any conversations with"—he looked down at his notebook—"Sarah over the last couple of days?"

"One or two."

"Did she seem upset to you?"

I knew it was you.

"Did you have any indication that she might be planning to hurt herself, or do something like this?"

The words didn't make any sense. "Hurt herself?"

Harrison glanced at his partner. "Yes," he said slowly. "I thought someone would have told you."

"She did this to herself?"

He took a deep breath. "I'm sorry. Someone should have told you." Another glance at his partner. "It's too early to be one hundred per cent certain, but, yeah, it looks like your friend . . ."

"So it wasn't the killer? The one from the newspaper?" She tried to picture it: Sarah standing beside the fountain, pressing the knife into her own throat, falling backward into the fountain as the blood gushed out.

It didn't make sense.

Not when she could remember the weight of the knife in her hand so clearly.

Harrison shook his head. "No, there's nothing to suggest there's any connection to that investigation."

"I think that's what she was afraid of," Cassie said falteringly.

"The murders?"

Cassie nodded. "She came up to me yesterday." The constable clicked his pen and started to write. "I was near the courthouse, and I had a newspaper, and she saw . . . She got really upset." Cassie remembered the way she had hurried away, the sound of her voice in the blowing snow.

"Did she say why she was upset? Was there something in particular?"

Cassie took a deep breath. "She said, 'It's happening here now.' Or something like that."

"What's that supposed to mean?" Farrow asked, and Harrison shot her a look.

"You're sure she was talking about the murders?"

Cassie hesitated. "I don't know."

Harrison made a note as Cassie tried to remember the exact details of the conversation. "She seemed to have some problems. Mentally . . ." Her voice trailed off.

Harrison nodded and made another note in his book. "Can you think of anything else?"

In the square one of the paramedics zipped up the black vinyl bag on the stretcher.

Cassie turned away, tried to think of anything she might have forgotten. "I don't think so. She didn't really—" She stopped herself from saying that Sarah hadn't made a whole lot of sense. "She didn't say a lot."

"Okay," Harrison said, as he closed his notebook. "We'll—"

"She was from Edmonton," Cassie said quickly, remembering. "Sarah from Edmonton."

"Thank you," he said. "Everything helps. We want to try to find her family."

He stopped as the stretcher rolled past them, its wheels echoing off the concrete. Cassie stared at the heavy black bag, watched as the paramedics rolled the stretcher into the back of the ambulance on the other side of the breezeway, where the Outreach van usually parked. There was no hurry, no sense of urgency. They took their time, made sure the back door was closed, talking to each other.

When they pulled out a few minutes later, they didn't turn their sirens on. The ambulance blended into the early-morning traffic.

‹‹ ››

She didn't know what to do.

After the ambulance pulled away, it was only the police left, wandering through the breezeway, measuring and photographing the square. The light was hard and cold, especially compared with the warmth of the camp the night before.

Across the breezeway, Brother Paul looked toward her and started to approach. She shook her head. Hefting her backpack onto her shoulder, she walked away from the camp as quickly as she could without breaking into a run.

Skylark had run off as soon as Brother Paul had left to call the police; she had no idea how to find her, no idea where to even start looking.

Cassie ended up at the courthouse because there was nowhere else for her to go. She settled into her spot after grabbing a discarded newspaper from the top of the garbage can.

She didn't read it, just stared at the front page for a long time. The headline was something about the camp, but she couldn't even focus on it, let alone read.

She spent a long time looking at her hands. Her right hand in particular.

The hand that had held the knife.

She could still feel it: the thickness of the hilt, how cold it had been at first, the way it had warmed in her grip.

The way it had felt skating across Sarah's throat, leaving the deep red gash behind. The gristly, grinding resistance as she had twisted it . . .

She turned her hand, watching it in the stark light.

"You don't have your hat out."

She jumped at the sound of the voice, glanced up.

A man was towering above her, the wind blowing his overcoat around his brown suit, tossing his sandy hair.

His clothes, his smile seemed familiar. "What?"

He lifted his hand; he was pinching several coins between his thumb and forefinger. "I was going to make a contribution, but you don't have your hat out." His tone was light, friendly.

"Oh, sorry." She fumbled for her backpack.

"Are you all right?" he asked, crouching slightly to her eye level, his face tightening with concern.

Cassie recognized him then: the man who had dropped the toonie in her hat the day before.

"Hello?"

She shook her head. "Sorry," she said. "I'm okay."

"Okay," he said. But he didn't move. He obviously didn't believe her.

"I'm Cliff," he said. "Cliff Wolcott."

He extended his hand into the silence between them.

Cassie took it carefully, shook it. "Dorothy," she said.

Releasing her hand, he rose to his feet. "Listen," he said. "I was going to just . . ." He lifted his hand again, still holding the coins. "But I was on my way for coffee. Can I bring you anything? Are you hungry?"

Her stomach growled at the question, but she shook her head. "No, that's all right."

"I can bring you a coffee."

She smiled. "That's all right," she said. "I'm okay."

He nodded, mostly to himself. "I'll bring you something. It's no big deal."

She started to protest again, but he said, "I'll be right back."

As he hurried along the sidewalk, her heart jumped in her

chest: Skylark waved from the other side of the street and jaywalked toward her, smiling.

"Can I—" She gestured at the ground next to Cassie. "Just for a minute?"

Skylark folded herself onto the pavement, shifting a little to be sure she was settled just right.

"Pretty quiet out here," she said, looking both ways along the sidewalk as she adjusted her knapsack beside her.

"I think I missed the morning rush." Cassie's breath misted in the air. She folded the newspaper and placed her hat on the concrete.

"I'm sorry about that," Skylark said. "About taking off."

Cassie shrugged. "I know. The police."

"Was it awful?"

"It was fine. They were fine." Better than the last time. "They just wanted to know if I knew anything."

"Do you?"

"I don't think so."

Skylark looked at her, then shouldered her gently. "That was supposed to be a joke."

"Oh." She didn't really get it. Or maybe she wasn't in the mood for joking.

"Sorry," Skylark said, as if suddenly remembering the seriousness of what they were talking about. "So, do they have any leads? Do they think it was the same guy?"

At first, she couldn't understand what Skylark was asking. "Oh. No." She shook her head. "They think she killed herself."

"What?" Skylark's voice rose.

"That's what I said. But the knife was in her hand," Cassie said, as if that explained everything. "They asked me if she had seemed upset."

"And what did you tell them?" There was something brittle about her tone, defensive.

"I said that she had, yeah."

"Why would you tell them that?" Skylark snapped.

"Because she was," Cassie snapped back.

"How would you—"

"Because she sat right there, right where you're sitting. Yesterday. And she *was* upset."

Skylark's eyes widened.

"About what?" Curious now. Not confrontational.

"About the murders." Cassie shook her head to shake off the memory. "I think. I don't know. She was totally freaked out."

"About what?"

It's happening here now.

Cassie told Skylark about the conversation the day before and the way the woman had rushed off, talking to herself, waving her arms.

"And did you notice her last night?"

Skylark looked down at the ground.

"She was sitting there all night long, all wrapped up. Not moving. Staring."

Staring at me, Cassie thought, but she kept that to herself.

Skylark nodded. "Yeah. Sarah had some problems." She blew out a deep, fog-silver breath. "I talked to her a few times. I think she'd been institutionalized . . ." At the thought of the hospital, Cassie looked down at the ground, willing her face not to give anything away.

Two toonies fell into her hat. She glanced up in time to see Cliff Wolcott speeding up again as he passed. He had a cardboard tray with four coffee cups stuck in it, and she thought he was going to stop, but he kept walking.

"Anyway, that's what I told the police. Is that all right?" Unable to keep the hurt from her voice.

Skylark looked away. "Yeah." She nodded. "Yeah, I'm sorry. I overreacted. I get nervous when it comes to the police, and I—"

"I just told them about talking to her. I didn't really have anything else to tell them."

"They just make shit up anyhow."

Cassie had to bite back the questions on her lips. Instead, she gestured toward the courthouse. "Speaking of," she said.

"Yeah." Resting one hand on her knapsack, Skylark rose smoothly to her feet. "Are you going to be okay here?"

Cassie glanced up and down the block, nodded. "Yeah."

"Okay." She lifted the knapsack onto her shoulder. "I'll swing by in a bit, all right? Maybe we can figure out something to eat."

« »

The crash was brutal.

The wanting, the hunger, had so filled him it was like he was high. In the van, on the beach, he knew he could do anything.

And he did.

After, lying in bed next to Alice, he had vibrated, every muscle tingling, every neuron firing. When he closed his eyes, the insides of his eyelids exploded with light and colour.

He had lain in bed for hours savouring the sensations, unable to keep himself from smiling. He didn't need to sleep; he could do anything.

But sometime later, sometime the next day, the crash came. He was sitting at his desk, and the exhaustion hit him, all at once. Every muscle gave out and cried in pain. His head fogged, and he couldn't hold a thought. More than exhaustion; it felt like a complete collapse.

He trudged through the rest of his day like a walking shell, listening to the hum of his computer, counting down the minutes until he could go home.

But there was no respite. With the kids, Alice, there wasn't time to draw a breath, let alone a few moments to rest. He still thought of it as a sanctuary, but in truth home was just another job, just another series of tasks he had to complete, another block of time to count down through.

Sleep, when it came, didn't help.

The only thing that burned through the fog, that woke him up, was the hunger.

It was only with that yearning in his veins that he felt alive.

≪ ≫

Everything was different in the camp that night.

At first, it seemed like no one was going to be there at all. Skylark and Cassie arrived at City Hall shortly after nightfall: the Outreach van was already parked out front, the table set up with its pot of soup and basket of bread, but there was no lineup, no crowd, and the Outreach workers were looking at one another uneasily, shifting from foot to foot in the cold.

People started to arrive after a while, slipping warily out of the dark, but it wasn't the same as previous nights.

"People are scared," Skylark said, finishing off her soup.

They were sitting on the bench in front of City Hall, watching people creep up to the table, get their soup, then retreat into the dark.

"But Sarah—"

"They don't know that she killed herself. They just know that something happened and they had to split before the police came. A lot of people, they won't come back."

Skylark was right: the circle that night was the smallest that Cassie had seen, half the size of the night before.

When Brother Paul stepped into the circle, there was something different about him too. He seemed smaller, somehow, but tensed, like he was trying to hold something in.

When he started to speak, his voice was stronger than Cassie had ever heard it.

He didn't say anything about himself or invite people to introduce themselves.

The air crackled when he said Sarah's name.

"Sarah had only been a part of this community for a short time." He paced slowly in the middle of the circle. "She kept mostly to herself." He was twisting his hands together. "I know that she had a hard life. I know that she was struggling. That she was haunted. But I never expected this."

He stopped and took a long, slow look at everyone in the circle, turning in place to look at every face.

"Something terrible happened here last night," he said. "We lost one of our own."

A low buzz of voices rose from the circle.

"Sarah killed herself this morning, just before dawn."

The voices changed, the tone suddenly questioning, defiant.

Brother Paul raised one hand. "I have spoken to the police," he said. "At length. They say there is no question that Sarah took her own life, in a most terrible fashion." He shook his head at the distant, half-formed questions. "But it was not her hand that held the knife."

Cassie flinched and glanced toward Skylark, hoping that she hadn't noticed.

"Every person who saw her struggling, who walked by instead of lending a kindly hand, they're the ones who killed her. How many more of us have to die before people see us as anything more than animals, more than their dirty little secret?" He raised his head. "I should have done more. I should have seen that Sarah's struggles had started to take her from us. But at least I tried. At least we tried. Society didn't try. Society treated her like trash. Her family, her community, threw her away. Just like they threw all of us away." He stopped and turned, looking around the circle again. "And now they're using her death against us." The whole circle seemed to gasp. "When I spoke to the police this morning, they told me that we would have to move on. That if I didn't disband this camp, if I didn't tear this community apart, I would be arrested. We would all be arrested."

A murmur of voices and a flurry of exchanged glances.

"But this is our land," he almost shouted. "This is our home. This is our community. And no one is going to take that away from us." Someone shouted in agreement. "We will not hide anymore. We will not slink into the shadows so we don't offend their delicate sensibilities. We will stand," he said. "We will fight. All of us. Together." He took a long, slow blink. "And we will do it for Sarah. And for every victim of brutality and neglect. In their names. In their names. Blessed be."

And with that, he stepped out of the circle, into the shadows of the square, leaving everyone silent, watching him as he disappeared into the darkness.

When Cassie looked at Skylark, she was crying.

He couldn't tear his eyes from the two girls. Even in their sadness, they shone and burned. Brighter, it seemed, but perhaps that was because of the dimness around them: the whole ridiculous little encampment shrouded in grey, shadows moving wraithlike through the mist.

There was a beauty to that sadness, a bittersweet flavour he could almost taste.

He knew that no matter how strongly Skylark shone, how brightly Dorothy burned, they could not escape the sadness they were bathing in. It would seep into their pores, work its way into their flesh.

He imagined how their hearts would taste, brined in sadness, but still sweet, still tender.

The thought made him ache.

A black shadow fell from the sky, a crow alighting on the bicycle rack next to where he stood.

Their eyes met, glistening in the dark.

« »

"You wanna get high?"

Cassie didn't know if it was Frank or Joe who called out the question as she and Skylark crossed the square. Bob was silent, occupied with a tiny glass pipe and a lighter that arced with a rich blue flame.

"No thanks," Skylark said. "We're taken care of."

The boys smirked at them, but it was the truth. They had spent the time since Brother Paul's speech sitting on the rooftop level of the parkade, looking out over Chinatown. They hadn't said much of anything, just silently passed Skylark's joint hand to hand.

The boys were standing near the bench close to the door to the parkade. Had they chosen that spot deliberately? Cassie wondered.

"You're such snobs," Bob said slowly, blowing out a cloud of rank, chemically smoke. There was something strange about his voice, though: it wasn't bitter or threatening. His words almost made it seem like he was joking around.

"We had other plans," Skylark said, in the same light tone of voice.

Frank and Joe smirked, but Bob nodded, pondering the idea.

The girls were almost past when Bob said, "Did you know her? That Sarah?"

"Not really," Skylark said, stopping. "She'd been here for a few days, but I never really—"

"She was nuts," Bob said, shaking his head. His body seemed barely under his control, his shoulders giving an occasional jerk, his hands twitching.

"That's not—" Skylark started.

"I'm not being rude," Bob said, oddly defensive. "She was nuts."

"She had some problems."

"She was freaked out. She started talking to me about those murders? You know, the ones in the paper?"

Cassie half-stepped forward.

"She was freakin', man. Like she was worried that the guy was after her, you know? I told her, the guy in the paper, he seemed to like them a lot younger." Frank and Joe laughed, but Bob stared hard at them and they stopped. "And then the next morning, not even twelve hours later." He gestured at the fountain. "It makes you think."

Cassie shivered. "But she wasn't . . . She killed herself."

"That's what the police told us."

"She—"

"Have you ever heard of anyone cutting their own throat?" He looked at Cassie like she was stupid. "They found the knife in her hand—big fucking deal. One minute she's freaked out that someone's after her, next morning she's dead? That doesn't make you think?"

It was exactly what Cassie had been thinking: the police were wrong.

But Bob didn't know about how the knife had felt in her hand, about how it had slid so easily into Sarah's throat.

"Did you tell the police?" Cassie asked, trying to hide her shivering. "That she thought someone was after her?"

Bob snorted. "Are you kidding? I'm not telling the fucking cops nothin'. Fucking Brother Paul calls the five-o and I'm gone, baby, gone."

"Maybe if they—"

"Maybe if they what?" he snapped. "Fucking cops aren't gonna do anything. You think they care? They got this killer in town and it's all doo-dee-doo, 'another dead hooker, makes my job easier.' You think they give a fuck about us? They took pictures, they took the body, 'she must've killed herself.' Case fucking closed."

Cassie took a sharp step back, stunned by the sudden return of his anger.

"It's just us out here and whoever's killing those girls. Whoever killed Sarah. Nobody's gonna do nothin' to protect us; we have to do it for ourselves. Protect this community."

For a moment, he sounded like Brother Paul.

"What do you mean?" Skylark asked.

"You'll see," he said. "There are gonna be some changes made."

His smile was wide and cold.

" "

The square was covered in snow, inches deep, the air heavy and silent. The only sound was the Styrofoam crunch of the snow under her feet.

The world was bright, almost blindingly white.

Sarah was sitting at the edge of the fountain. She smiled when she saw Cassie.

"I knew it was you."

This time, Cassie wasn't surprised. She watched her hand as it brought the knife up, watched the red line across Sarah's throat pulse and widen and burst open like an overripe fruit, blood spilling black down the front of her coat.

Sarah laughed as she fell backward into the fountain, the knife in her hand now.

And then she was standing again. "I knew it was you." The words bubbled the blood at her throat into a pink froth.

Falling.

Laughing.

Standing.

Sarah leaned in close. "What are you going to do now, Cassie?" The words smelled metallic, of rotting meat.

"What are you going to do about her?"

Sarah laughed as she fell backward into the fountain, and Cassie turned slowly.

Skylark was standing behind her.

"You're a mess," she said tenderly, leaning forward to kiss Cassie gently.

When she drew back, there was blood on her mouth. Her tongue was pale pink as she licked her lips, staining her white teeth red.

"I knew it was you," she whispered.

And the knife was in Cassie's hand again somehow, and Sarah laughed as she fell backward into the fountain, and the red line across Skylark's throat burst open like an overripe fruit, and blood sprayed across Cassie's face hot and sweet and she opened her mouth and—

—as she threw her head back, she saw the man standing in the shadows of the parkade, almost completely hidden by the swirling snow, his black coat, his red eyes—

"Daddy?"

—The blood was hot and sweet and Skylark laughed as she fell backward into the snow, a halo of blood spraying around her, arms spread like she was making an angel—

Laughing like a little girl.

<< >>

"Cassie?"

When Cassie opened her eyes, Skylark's face slipping into focus, she jerked away.

"It's all right," Skylark said, but Cassie was already moving.

She fumbled to her knees, grabbed her backpack and started cramming stuff in: her journal, Mr. Monkey, everything she had unpacked the night before.

"Cassie, what's wrong?"

Twisting to sit, she pulled her shoes on, looping the laces into loose knots, not taking the time to tie them tightly.

There wasn't any time: every minute she was there was another minute Skylark was in danger. Her heart pounded, the blood in her temples pulsing and throbbing painfully.

How could she have been so stupid? So selfish? She had run away to keep the people she loved safe; she had to. She couldn't put the people she cared for in danger, so she had run.

And now she was doing it again.

I knew it was you.

The dream words echoed in her head as she struggled to her feet, adjusting her jacket and scarf.

Not just the words: the laughter too.

Sarah laughing as she fell backward into the fountain. Skylark's blood on her face. The taste of it.

"What are you doing?" Skylark was grabbing her arm, trying to turn her, as she whispered, "Cassie, what are you doing?"

"I've gotta go," she muttered, buckling her backpack.

"Cassie, calm down. It was just a dream. You had a bad dream."

"It's not safe." She picked up her backpack. "I'm not safe."

"Cassie." Skylark tightened her grip on Cassie's arm. "Calm down." Tried to turn her around. "Calm down and talk to me."

Cassie jerked her arm away. "I've gotta go."

She knew better than to turn around. Knew better than to look at Skylark's face.

Instead, she rushed into the darkness.

≪ ≫

She wasn't hiding, she was running—there was a difference.

She hadn't known where to go after leaving the camp. She needed to be away from Skylark, so she couldn't go to the courthouse, and nowhere else downtown felt safe. She stayed on Pandora, walking out of downtown farther than she had ever gone. It was still dark, the lights of the occasional cars flashing across her, the dull rasp of their tires echoing in the silence as she stumbled along the sidewalk.

The dream clung to her. She could still hear the sound of Sarah laughing and falling. She could still smell the bloody accusation.

It was so real.

When she found a McDonald's, she locked herself in the bathroom. She ran the water as hot as it would go, scrubbed at her hands until they shone raw and red, scrubbed them more. She could still feel the blood on them, sticky and cold, but no matter how hard she scrubbed, it wouldn't come off.

Catching sight of herself in the mirror over the sink, she jumped back: her face was caked with blood, her mouth a dark, black slash in the rusty gore.

Plunging her hands into the steaming water, she scrubbed at her face: the water ran red, but the blood didn't fade. She scrubbed harder, pumped palmfuls of the frothy soap from the dispenser, scrubbed still harder.

Nothing worked.

She scrubbed as hard as she could, sobbing in frustration. She looked like a deranged clown, sickly and smiling, and no scrubbing would—

There was a knocking at the door, a rattling of the door-knob. Cassie jumped.

She glanced at the door to be sure it was locked.

When she looked back at the mirror, the blood was gone.

She looked terrifying, terrified: her hair was dirty and frizzy, spraying crazily out from under her toque, her eyes wide and frantic and red with tears, but the blood was gone.

Looking down, she saw that her hands were clean too. Not a drop of blood on the counter. Not a trace of pink in the sink.

"Oh God."

She slumped against the counter.

The knocking at the door repeated.

"I'll be right out," she said, quietly, closing her eyes.

She stumbled out of the ladies' room, head low, careful not to make eye contact with the woman who was waiting.

Buying a hot chocolate with a handful of change, she curled herself into a table in the corner. A wall at her back, the window to the children's play area on one side . . . She took a long time just trying to breathe before she opened her journal.

It's happening again. I thought I had it all figured out. I thought it was over. But it's not—

She stopped, set her pen down on the open notebook page and rooted in her pockets, dropping their contents on the table. Picking through the soggy tissues, crumpled receipts and hair elastics, she piled her money aside, counted it.

I have seventeen dollars left. I don't think that's enough to get me anywhere. Maybe over to Vancouver if I hitchhike. But I can't stay here. I can't. I won't.

She leaned back in the chair. The rounded metal bars dug into her back even through all her layers of clothes.

She looked down at her hands. They were pink and puffy, raw from the scrubbing. No blood.

I dreamed I killed Skylark last night. It was so realistic, but when I woke up, she was still alive. Not like last time.

She underlined the word "not" three times.

Seventeen dollars. If I keep everything I make in the next couple of days, maybe I'll have enough to get the bus to Vancouver.

She sighed heavily and wiped her nose with one of the napkins she had taken from the dispenser.

I thought I could run away from it.

"You late for school, little girl?"

Bob slumped down in the chair across from her; Frank and Joe sat at the next table over.

Cassie closed her journal as quickly as she could.

"What are you writing?" he asked, leaning over the table. His pupils were tiny black dots, barely bigger than the tip of her pen.

"Nothing," she said quietly, pulling the book closer to herself with both hands, keeping them protectively over it.

"You got a diary?" His voice was a slow drawl.

She tightened her grip on the book.

Frank and Joe laughed like it was the most hilarious thing they had ever heard.

"What's the matter?" he asked, after a long silence. "You don't want to talk to us?"

"There's not much to talk about," she said, trying to follow Skylark's advice.

"Where's your girlfriend?"

Cassie bit back her protest. "I wanted a hot chocolate," she said, pointing at the cup.

Bob reached across the table and picked up the cup. His hands were shaking and clumsy as he pulled off the plastic lid and raised the cup to his lips. He chugged back several swallows.

The cup rattled when he dropped it back on the table.

"Thanks," he said. "That was just what I needed."

Cassie bit the inside of her lip. If she didn't say anything, didn't protest, he'd leave.

She almost exhaled when he stumbled to his feet a few moments later. She wondered what he was on, the way he teetered and seemed to waver—

Then he reached out and grabbed the stack of money that she had left resting on the table.

"Hey," she said, standing up as he spun away, laughing. Coins sprayed onto the floor.

Frank and Joe laughed after him, and they were gone, out the door, before Cassie could say anything else.

She stood there, just watching, as the door swung shut behind them. Then she knelt on the ground and picked up as many of the coins as she could find.

≪ ≫

This time, she opened the door only a crack, holding it tightly against the tug of the wind as she slipped through to the *Please Wait to Be Seated* sign.

Ali was at the back of the restaurant, at the counter. When she noticed Cassie, she smiled and gestured for her to wait.

Cassie focused on her breathing.

Taking care with the little details, focusing on her breath: that attention was all that was keeping her going.

She had almost collapsed on the floor of the McDonald's that morning. All she had wanted to do was to curl up in a tiny ball on the floor of the restaurant and cry, just cry until everything else stopped. Cry until someone came and took her away again.

That was the thought that had cut through the boiling

flood of grief: not the possibility that they would come and take her away again, but that part of her wanted it so badly.

She did. She wanted to be rescued. She wanted to be taken in somewhere, wanted the cool comfort of the needle under her skin, the sweet weight of the pills on her tongue like candy, the dark, timeless, dreamless sleep.

Part of her wanted that so much.

But she would never let them take her again. She would never be that helpless again.

And it hadn't really made any difference, had it? Daddy was still dead. Sarah was still dead.

Skylark . . .

Skylark was still alive. Cassie had to hold it together long enough to make sure she stayed safe. She had to hold it together long enough to get far, far away.

So she had very carefully picked up every coin, digging against the slick floor with her bitten-down nails for every sliver of silver, then she had sat back down at the table, painstakingly counting out everything she had left.

Once. Twice. Three times.

The small pile of change amounted to $9.71 every time.

She spent a long while just staring at the little pile, counting her way through each breath like they had taught her at the hospital: in two three four, hold two three four, out two three four.

When the manager came to tell her that she had to leave, she didn't say anything. She cleaned up the garbage from her pockets and picked up the empty hot chocolate cup, depositing everything in the garbage can by the front door as she left.

She had spent the rest of the morning on a corner close to the Inner Harbour downtown, far from the courthouse steps where Skylark might find her.

By lunchtime there was a loose scattering of coins that she planned on counting at the restaurant.

Ali waved her over, and Cassie threaded her way through the restaurant. It was busier today, most of the tables full, chairs projecting into the already narrow walkway down the middle.

Ali directed her to the table for two closest to the bar and takeout counter. Cassie set her backpack onto one chair, then sat down in the other, tucked nicely into the corner, with a view of the entire restaurant.

The couple at the table next to her stared at her, their faces wrinkling in distaste before they looked away, shaking their heads as they resumed their conversation.

Cassie focused on her breathing.

"I saw you in the paper this morning," Ali said as she set a hot chocolate on the table. "Here." She reached over the counter and put a tattered front section of the *Sentinel* in front of Cassie. "Right here." She pointed.

The man at the next table glanced between Ali and the newspaper, craning his neck slightly to try to see what the waitress was pointing at.

The photograph on the bottom half of the page had been taken from the corner of the breezeway, close to where the ambulance had been parked. Cassie could see the fountain through the pillars, the small crowd of police officers and technicians and paramedics, all looking toward the fountain itself, a stretcher waiting behind them.

Ali was pointing at the corner of the photo, though, to where, slightly out of focus, a police officer was talking to someone who had her back to the camera.

"That's you, right?" Ali said. "I thought I recognized the backpack."

The man's glance flickered between the newspaper and the bag on the opposite chair.

"Yeah, that's me," Cassie said slowly, still looking at the paper. The article was called "Death at Squatter Camp."

"I thought so."

Ali stood there for a long moment, then said, "I'll get you some food," into the silence.

Cassie only fully realized that Ali had said anything once she was already gone.

As she looked from the door back down to the newspaper, Cassie caught the eye of the woman at the next table. She was staring at her, her lip curled. As she turned back to face the man, she made some comment that Cassie couldn't quite hear.

Cassie unfolded the newspaper, carefully lining it up in front of her.

There was a headline all the way across the top of the page: "Black Day." Below it, in smaller print, was the sentence "Fifth murder and death at squatter camp stretches police resources."

"Are you all right?"

Cassie hadn't heard Ali come back, and she started at the sound of her voice. "Yeah, of course."

She leaned against the table. "No, seriously. You don't seem like yourself today."

The man glanced up at her, then looked back down at the table when Ali caught his eye. The moment she turned her attention back to Cassie, the man and woman began whispering to each other again.

"Can I help you with anything?" Ali asked, turning partway to the next table.

The man shifted. "No, no. We're fine."

"Your food should be right out," she said, smiling broadly in a way that Cassie knew wasn't real. "I'll go check on it now."

There were a couple of people at the counter paying their bills, and Cassie watched as Ali dodged around them on her way to the kitchen before looking back down at the newspaper.

She didn't want to lie to Ali, but Cassie couldn't let anyone get close. She just needed to make it through the next couple of days, then she'd get on a bus and disappear. She had to. And that meant she had to keep people away.

She glanced up reflexively at the sound of the kitchen door swinging, but it was only Hong, carrying a plate in each hand.

He stopped at the far side of the table next to Cassie. "Who's got the beef and broccoli?"

The man lifted his hand slightly and Hong set the plate down in front of him, sliding the other in front of the woman.

"You've got chopsticks there. Do you need anything else?"

The man glanced sharply at the woman, shook his head slightly, and she looked down at her plate.

"Your food should be right out," Ali said, leaning over to refill Cassie's water glass.

Cassie didn't say anything, her face burning under the attention from the couple, who kept glancing at her between mouthfuls.

Ali waited, then turned away.

Cassie watched her as she worked her way around the room, filling glasses, laughing with the customers.

"Here."

Cassie turned. Hong was standing at the other side of the table, supporting a huge bowl with both hands. "I thought maybe some noodles for you today. Lots of vegetables. Some pork. Chicken. Well"—he smiled—"whatever was in the kitchen, really. I just threw it all together."

Cassie's mouth had been watering since the first smell of the steam. "Oh. That sounds . . . Thank you."

Hong slid the bowl in front of her. "You eat. And remember, it's on the house." He looked at the couple at the next table, who were trying to look like they weren't watching. "For you, it's always on the house."

Unable to speak, Cassie watched him as he walked away, as the door to the kitchen swung behind him.

"He means it, you know," Ali said, still holding the pitcher in one hand.

"I know," Cassie said quietly.

Ali put her other hand on Cassie's shoulder and squeezed it gently.

Cassie's first impulse was to lean into the touch or put her hand over the waitress's. But then she thought of Skylark, and of the sound she had made falling into the snow. The shudder of resistance as she had twisted the knife in Sarah's throat.

"Thank you," she said, knowing she would never see Ali, or Hong, again.

« »

It was the warmth of the restaurant, Ali and the way Hong had welcomed her that made Cassie return to the camp that night.

She had planned on avoiding Skylark until she had enough money to leave town, but she knew it would be better if she could talk to her one last time and say goodbye. She took a deep breath, hitched her backpack up and walked into the light.

Skylark was at the far side of the breezeway. As Cassie manoeuvred around people, between groups, muttering, "Excuse me. Sorry. Excuse me," she was met mostly with nods of recognition. That made her feel a bit better.

The crowds seemed to part to usher her through to Skylark.

She had no idea how the other girl would greet her, how she would respond to Cassie's running away that morning without explanation. And she didn't know how she would respond to Skylark if things—

"Oh my God," Skylark cried out, dropping her knapsack to the ground and running toward her.

The force of the girl's hug almost knocked Cassie over, and she had to hold Skylark tightly to keep her balance.

"Are you okay?" she whispered in Cassie's ear, still holding her tight. "God, where did you go? I was so worried about you. Why . . . ?"

"I'm all right," she lied. "I'm okay."

"Where did you go?" Skylark asked, pulling back a little. "Was it something I did? Why did you run away like that? Did I—"

Cassie was stunned to see something she had never seen in Skylark's face before, a wideness around her eyes, a tightness of her cheeks. It was only there for a moment, but Cassie recognized it instantly: Skylark was afraid. Not for Cassie, though: Skylark was afraid she had done something wrong, that Cassie's running away had been somehow her fault.

"It's okay," she said. "It wasn't anything you did, I swear. I just had to go."

"Because you had a bad dream?"

The thought of the dream—of all her dreams—made Cassie feel like she was going to be sick.

"No, it's got nothing to do with the dreams."

« »

Neither of them said much as they waited in line at the Outreach van.

Cassie had to deliberately keep her hands in her pockets to fight the desire to bite her fingernails.

She didn't want to lie to her friend—she knew that if she could tell anyone, it would be Skylark.

But she couldn't tell anyone. Not even Skylark.

But if she was never going to see her again . . .

"So," she started slowly, once they were both finished eating. Cassie, still full from her lunch, had given Skylark her bowl of soup, munching on a dry dinner roll while her friend ate. "I'm sorry for running away this morning," she said. "I should have said something. I'm sorry for worrying you."

Skylark touched her leg. "It's okay," she said, leaning toward her. "I'm just glad that you're all right."

Cassie took a deep breath. "That's the thing, though. I'm not all right. I haven't been all right for a while."

Skylark just looked at her, not saying anything, giving her space to talk.

"I . . ." She didn't really know how to start. She had never had to tell anyone any of this. "I did something. Something terrible."

Skylark leaned closer to her, her face tightening with concern. "Are you okay?"

Cassie shook her head. "It wasn't . . ."

She took another deep breath.

"My father . . ."

She stopped as Skylark squeezed her lips tight, shook her head.

"He died. Last month. In a fire."

She looked down at the ground to avoid Skylark's eyes.

"It was . . ." Another deep breath, a leap into the dark. "I did it," she said quietly. "I killed him."

She couldn't bear to look, couldn't bear to see the reaction on Skylark's face.

"I didn't . . . I didn't mean to do it. Not really. But he . . . I . . ."

She stumbled over the words; there were things that could not be said. Not even to Skylark.

She couldn't tell her what her father had done to her, down in the furnace room in the basement, in front of the wood stove. She couldn't tell her about how the chunk of firewood had felt in her hand as she had brought it down on the back of his head as he had stirred the coals.

She could never tell anyone about the way the kerosene had smelled as she poured it over his body.

Instead, she said, "That's why I have to go. I don't want to hurt anyone else. I don't want to hurt you."

She braced herself, waiting for Skylark's response. Every muscle in her body tensed, ready to launch herself away.

Instead, she felt a tentative touch on her leg.

"Cassie?" Skylark said.

She refused to turn, refused to look.

"Cassie, it's okay. At least . . ." She heard the other girl sniff, and turned to her reflexively.

Tears were streaming down her face.

"I'm not afraid of you," she said. "You don't need to go."

Cassie looked back to the ground. "Yes, I do."

"Cassie, I want to show you something," Skylark said.

Cassie turned to her again.

Biting the tip of a finger, Skylark tugged the glove off her left hand, then pulled the glove from her right. Fumbling with the buttons at her cuff, she rolled her left sleeves up to her elbow.

"Here," she said, extending her arm to Cassie, palm up.

At first, Cassie didn't know what she was looking at, and the lights of the breezeway made it difficult to make out details.

The inside of Skylark's arm was a lattice of scars, criss crossing over the soft flesh. Some of the lines were wider than the others, some longer. Some were so white as to be almost translucent, others were varying shades of pink. Some of the cuts were clearly old, others looked much fresher.

She looked at Skylark, met her eye.

"I tried to tell them that something was wrong, but they wouldn't believe me," Skylark said, rolling her sleeves back down. "They didn't believe me about any of it. About him."

Cassie cleared her throat as Skylark buttoned her cuff again. "Who was it?" she asked, finally.

"My uncle Ted," she said, pulling her gloves back on. "My mom's youngest brother. He was living with us for a while, going to school."

Cassie knew that words wouldn't do any good.

She thought of the insides of her arms, the scars there. Not as many. Deeper. Running the length of her arms from the heels of her hands to the insides of her elbows. Words wouldn't have helped her, either. She knew what it was like to just want the pain to stop.

"Ain't we a pair," Skylark said, and her face broke into a teary smile. "I just wish I had been brave like you . . ."

"You are brave," Cassie said quickly. "You're . . . you're smart and brave . . ."

There was a deep sadness lurking in Skylark's eyes. "That's how I've been trying to live my life. There are some days, though . . ." She shook her head. "Sometimes it's all too much. It feels like I'll never get away from it." She looked at the ground. "The cutting helps me get there, those days."

"Oh, Skylark," Cassie said.

"Laura," she said, snuggling close to Cassie, so quietly no one else could hear. "My name is Laura."

« »

She couldn't leave after that. Not that night, at least.

They stayed close all evening, close enough to touch. Most of the time they leaned together, Skylark's head tucked in the nook of Cassie's shoulder as they listened to Brother Paul's sermon, as they shared Cassie's earphones.

Cassie kept a keen eye out around the camp. She didn't know what she would do when she saw Bob and his friends, but she didn't want to be surprised by them. She was never going to let herself be surprised again.

But they didn't come back. By the end of the evening, she had accepted that they weren't going to return. Of course they wouldn't come back: their whole lives were a hit and run.

The thought of that handful of change stuck with her as she and Skylark made their bed and climbed in. She knew that this was temporary: she couldn't leave that night, not with all that she and Skylark had shared, but she couldn't stay, either. Not if she wanted Skylark to be safe.

Not if she cared.

And she realized, as they slid under the blankets, that she cared very much.

"Here," she said, turning onto her side facing Skylark. When the other girl seemed confused, she said, "It's my turn."

She had spent a long time trying to figure it out. She didn't want to take any chances with Skylark's safety while she slept, so she needed to keep herself as immobilized as she could.

She extended her left arm just under the edge of Skylark's pillow. "Here," she said.

Skylark nestled herself along Cassie's body, curving close against her. One arm snug under her neck and shoulders, Cassie wrapped the other around the girl's waist, tucking her fingertips under her, doing as much as she could to lock both of them in place.

She could feel her friend breathing in her arms.

"Thank you," Skylark whispered, and Cassie buried her face in the back of her neck.

≪ ≫

She didn't want to open the door, but she couldn't help herself.

She watched as her hand reached out, as it unfastened the hook near the top of the door, as her fingers curled around the cold of the doorknob.

She didn't want to do it. Something inside her was making her do these things.

Making her pull the door open.

The stairs to the basement were dark, but the light came on without her having to do anything, illuminating the rough, unpainted wood, the frail railing.

Please no.

Not this.

But she couldn't help herself.

She stepped onto the first stair.

The second.

The door closed behind her.

The wind cut through her like a thousand tiny knives, driving the cold into her so deeply she couldn't catch her breath.

She tried to focus, tried to count her breaths, but the numbers slid away, meaningless and fragmented in her mind.

She could barely see. the blowing snow was thick as fog, the world little more than dark, vague shapes in the distance.

Where was she? She was sure it was Centennial Square, but that wasn't right . . . or was it?

The fountain was to her left, Sarah's body splayed, legs in the air over the edge. As she watched, Sarah's hand came up clutching the knife, seeming to cut a trail through the driving snow.

Sarah's eyes were wide as she plunged the knife into the gaping hole across her throat. She could hear the sound of her twisting the blade over the wind, the ratcheting grind echoing through her hand.

When she looked down, the knife was in her own hand, blood dripping from her fingertips, from the blade, splashing onto the snowy ground with a faint sizzle, tiny puffs of pink steam.

She tried not to turn. Tried not to look. But she was helpless, her body pivoting of its own accord, turning to Skylark—

—falling to the snow, blood gushing in a steaming blast from across her throat—

"Laura!" she cried out, but her voice was stolen by the storm, swallowed up by the snow.

"Laura."

The voice seemed to come from the storm itself, a low, barely audible whisper, deep and cold.

"Laura."

An echo—

She turned to try to find the voice, craning into the storm.

In the distance, a shadow formed, a faint smudge against the white, there and not there. It seemed to pulse like a great black heart, a man, a blur, a shadow—

—and it lifted off the ground with a rush of wings, a whomping against the air that sounded like thunder, a screech that sounded like—

Sirens.

Cassie burst into full wakefulness to the sound of shouting and running feet.

When she opened her eyes, she didn't know what she was seeing, bright red splashes of light bursting into the breezeway like flames, like blood. Shouting voices. Mechanical words.

A megaphone.

"It's the police," someone shouted.

People were running everywhere, flurries of motion, shouts and cries.

Cassie burst up, her heart racing.

She looked for Skylark, but the bed beside her was empty.

Cassie didn't think—she grabbed her shoes and bolted.

The concrete was cold, even through two pairs of socks, but she didn't stop, didn't look back. She just ran as fast and as far as she could.

She didn't stop until she was deep in Chinatown.

She collapsed on the edge of the street planter in front of the restaurant to pull her shoes on, tie the laces.

Red lights flashed in the distance, strobed along the faces of the buildings on the corner.

As her breathing slowed, Cassie felt suddenly faint: her backpack was gone. Skylark was gone.

Everything was gone.

PART THREE

We all carry the Darkness within us.

But we also carry the Light.

And it was through the Darkness I began to see the Light.

Literally.

At first, I wasn't sure what I was seeing. A faint glow around people, a brighter one around the kitten, so it looked like a puff of fluff inside a ball of flame.

When I told my parents, they took me to a doctor, but they couldn't find anything wrong with me.

Of course they couldn't. There was nothing wrong with me.

I had been blessed.

It was a gift. And like all gifts, it grew in value over time, became more complex as I grew to understand it.

There are different Lights. Different strengths, different colours, different consistencies.

Everyone's Light as personal, as identifiable, as fingerprints.

Except there were some who didn't glow at all, whose Light was so dim it may as well have not existed.

I came to realize that these people were like me, their Darkness so strong, so great, it swallowed all Light, even from within themselves.

And there are more of these people—of us—than you might like to believe.

But that understanding came later.

At first, all I knew about the Light was that I wanted it. It drew me to it. Compelled me.

And I knew without knowing that the Light could feed me.

I was right.

As I held the kitten under the water, flinching as its claws dug into me, cut me, I watched as its Light flickered, faded.

But it wasn't merely extinguished.

Science tells us that energy and matter can neither be created nor destroyed.

My fingers crackled as the kitten's Light entered me. I could feel it in my veins, flowing through me. I swallowed the Light like it was a drug, though I didn't make that connection, that metaphor, until much later.

I was only six years old at the time.

"Oh my God."

Eyes slit against the light, Cassie looked up at the voice.

"You must be freezing."

She nodded slightly up at the shadow, the man who had stopped the last couple of days. What was his name again?

"Cliff," he said, fumblingly extending his hand in what must have been a reflexive action. "Cliff Wolcott."

"I remember," Cassie whispered.

"That's—" Looking down at Cassie, curled into a tiny ball, her knees pulled tight to her chest, her arms wrapped tight around her legs, he lowered his hand. "I'm sorry," he said. "Isn't there—"

She knew how the sentence ended; it was the same question she had been asking herself for hours: Wasn't there someplace she could go?

She had thought about it from the moment she had woken to the police attacking the camp, and she wasn't any closer to an answer.

She had walked all night, hunched over against the wind, arms tightly wrapped around herself. There was no place for her to go: everything was closed, and what little money she had was lost in her backpack.

She had left everything.

The thought of it salted her eyes, burned inside her nose, but she refused to cry.

So she had walked.

She shook her head. "No," she whispered, not really caring if he could even hear her.

She couldn't tell him that she was waiting.

She hated being at the courthouse. She hated the way people looked at her, the way they stepped around her like she was a pile of dog shit in their path.

She would rather have been anywhere else, but she knew that when everything calmed down and Skylark tried to find her, this would be the first place she would look.

It had taken Cassie a while that morning to understand that she was looking for Skylark. That was why she hadn't stayed in Chinatown, crouched in the doorway of the restaurant, out of the wind. That was why she had walked all through downtown, criss-crossing her steps.

Not only had she not found Skylark, she hadn't seen anyone. No one from the camp was on the street anywhere. It was like they had all disappeared, melting into the shadows when the police came.

Cliff crouched down in front of her, tilting his head. "Are you all right?" he asked, his voice deliberately gentle.

"I'm okay," she said, trying not to meet his eye.

"But—aren't you cold?"

She stared at him for a long moment.

He shook his head and looked at the ground. "I'm sorry," he said. "That was stupid . . ." His voice trailed off. "I just meant, isn't there a place where you could get a coat? Like a shelter, or a-a-a soup kitchen?"

She couldn't very well tell him that she didn't want to move from that spot, not even to get a coat. What if Skylark came looking for her while she was gone?

"I don't know," Cassie said. "I'll figure it out."

Wolcott shifted on his feet, his hunkering obviously starting to get painful. "Listen," he said. "Why don't I just . . . When I get in, I'll call my wife and she can bring you a coat or something."

"No, that's . . ."

He straightened up. "I'm sure she's got something she's not—"

"No, I'm okay. Really."

"But listen, until then—" Drawing his coat back, he reached into his front pocket and withdrew a slim leather wallet. "Here," he said, extending a twenty-dollar bill toward her. "Take this."

Cassie looked at the bill pinched between his thumb and forefinger. She imagined him losing his grip, the wind catching hold of the bill, blowing it down the block.

"Please," he said.

She shook her head.

"Please," he repeated. "Use it to get yourself something to eat. Warm up."

She stared at the bill, watching it ripple and twist in the wind.

"Please," he said for a third time.

She took a deep breath and reached out for the money. It felt strange to her, taking it. Pocket change was one thing, but this was different.

But she took the money and slipped it into her front pocket.

"Thank you," she said, grateful that he had stood up. There was less chance of accidentally meeting his eye now.

He shook his head. "I just wish there was more I could do."

He stood there for a long moment in the uneasy silence that followed, waiting for her to say something.

But there was nothing for her to say.

"I should get inside," he said finally, making a show of checking his watch. "I've got a meeting."

"Okay," Cassie said.

"But I'll call my wife—" He shook his head as Cassie started to speak. "It'll probably be an hour or so."

"Thank you," she repeated, her voice barely above a whisper.

"Get some food," he said, almost a command. "And I'll see you in a bit, okay?"

He waited.

"Okay."

He smiled before turning away.

He looked back at her as he turned up the main steps into the building. She tried to make it look like she wasn't watching.

Cliff Wolcott seemed like he was genuinely trying to help. You don't give twenty dollars to a stranger unless you really mean it, right? You don't offer to have your wife bring down a coat.

She sighed and leaned back against the railing.

She would wait. She would wait for Skylark, and she would wait for the coat, and she would wait for whatever happened next. She had nowhere else to go, and nothing—

She caught the red out of the corner of her eye. A red-and-black-checked flannel jacket, across the street, farther down the block, coming toward her.

She recognized the coat. She would have recognized it anywhere.

The coat, the hair, the stride, the way he held himself: her breath caught in her throat.

"Daddy?"

She pulled herself to her feet, ignoring the screaming of her legs as they unfolded. Glancing back at the approaching figure, bile burning in the back of her throat, she ran.

« »

She didn't mean to step inside the deli, but she needed to get off the street. She needed to hide, even if only for a moment.

A bell tinkled as she entered.

She stopped in the doorway, almost overwhelmed by the smells and the heat. Steam settled instantly on her cheeks, and her stomach growled.

She looked around to see if anyone had heard, but the only people in the deli were a man in a suit at the counter paying for his coffee and the heavy-set, hair-netted woman taking his money.

Neither of them looked at her.

She walked slowly up and down the narrow aisles, looking at every item on the shelves, studying every label, trying to blend in, pretending to belong. She browsed until she noticed the woman behind the counter looking at her, studying her.

Taking one last breath of the warm air, she turned and pulled the door open again. The bell chimed as the cold wind rushed in and she stepped back outside, looking carefully up and down the sidewalk.

She couldn't spend it. That twenty dollars was all she had in the world, and she wouldn't just squander it on food. It was almost enough to get her away. She could disappear. And this time—

But not before she found Skylark.

She knew it was stupid and wrong.

She should go now, while she had the chance. And the money. Make a clean break of it.

She should just go, like she had done with Mom and Heather. Just walk away.

She pictured the twenty-dollar bill. She could be gone, just gone, across the water before sunset.

But she couldn't do it. There was no way she could go without seeing Skylark.

Just to be sure she was all right. Just to say goodbye.

She had already abandoned one sister without saying goodbye.

She was only beginning to consider what that meant when the minivan pulled up alongside her.

The passenger window slid down as it stopped.

"Hey," the driver said, leaning over the empty passenger seat. "Are you all right?"

Cassie's first instinct was to run. First her father, now this— it was all too much.

No, running would cause a scene. Hurry away as fast as she could, not looking back.

But there was something familiar about the driver. Where had she seen him before? Sometime in the last few days . . .

So many people, all their faces blurring together.

"Yeah," she said, putting on a brave face. "It's not so bad."

"Here," the driver said, and the lock on the passenger door clicked loudly. "Why don't you get in and warm up?"

Cassie stared at him, not quite able to process what she was hearing, what he was asking. Right here? In broad daylight? He expected her to—

"Oh, shit," he said, shaking his head. "I'm sorry. That was . . . Here." He reached into his Gore-Tex jacket and pulled out a leather wallet. He flipped it open as he extended it toward her.

When she saw the police badge, things clicked into place and she nodded, exhaling a misty breath. "Right. Officer Harrison."

"Chris," he said. "And it's Constable." He smiled as he tucked the wallet away. "I'm sorry. I guess I look different out of uniform." He gave a sheepish half shrug. "But good for you, not getting into a car with someone you don't know."

"Yeah, well. Not getting rides from strangers is pretty basic, isn't it?"

"You would think," he said. There was a sharp edge to the words.

The wind cut through Cassie and she shivered despite herself.

Harrison smiled. "Come on," he said. "Hop in. I'll buy you a cup of coffee."

She didn't move. He waited.

Finally, he sighed.

"Well, here," he said, leaning between the seats and reaching into the back. "You should put on a coat, at least."

He passed her a crumpled grey bundle through the window. It took Cassie a moment to process what she was feeling. "Oh my God," she said, letting the coat fall open, holding it tightly as it was caught by the wind. "This—"

"Yeah." His smile was wide and open.

"This is my coat!" All of the tears that she had been holding back almost broke through as she slipped her arms in, as she tugged the coat closed and close around her. "How—"

"It's cold," he said, shrugging again. "And you ran off without your coat, so I thought I'd . . ."

"You were there?"

He nodded. The look on his face told her not to ask anything else about what had happened the night before.

But the thought of the flashlights, the shouting, the voice over the megaphone made her shiver.

"Thank you," she said carefully, remembering her manners. "But won't you get in trouble for giving this back to me?" She kept touching the front of her coat. For a moment, she was so happy she wanted to twirl.

His brow tightened. "Trouble? Why?"

"Well, for taking evidence or whatever?" He started to laugh, but pulled it back in, shaking his head instead. "Evidence of what?" he asked. "You haven't committed any crime." He stopped. "Have you?"

The question made her stomach tumble. "No," she said quickly. "Of course not."

"Well, we're fine, then," he said, and it took her a moment to realize that he was teasing her. "No, they put all the stuff people left behind in the lost and found. I think they're going to bring a van around tonight to see if anyone else wants to claim their stuff." And then, as if remembering: "Oh, I've got this too."

Reaching behind the seat again, he pulled out her backpack.

Cassie felt her knees buckle and reached out to the window frame for support.

"Oh my God," she said, her vision blurred with tears. "Oh, thank you, thank you," she said, reaching in through the window. "I can't—thank you." Reaching for it.

But Harrison held it back from her, just out of reach. "Listen," he said seriously, but still warm. "Why don't you hop in? I'll buy you a coffee. There's some things I want to talk to you about."

She only hesitated a moment before opening the door.

« »

He drove them to a coffee shop a short distance away, and hurried a couple of steps ahead of her to hold the door open.

He didn't give her the backpack. It dangled at his side, where he held it by the loop. He seemed to have forgotten that he had it.

Cassie didn't take her eyes off it.

She stood with him while he ordered a coffee, a hot chocolate and a breakfast sandwich at the counter, despite his suggesting that she should get a table. She went with him to the self-serve bar, watched as he put cream and sugar into the largest coffee she had ever seen.

She didn't let more than a few feet come between her and the backpack. She had lost it once, she wasn't going to lose it again.

But Harrison wasn't letting it go.

When they sat down, he set the bag on the floor, tucked between his feet.

He slid the breakfast sandwich across the table to her.

"Here," he said.

She wanted to argue. Instead, she devoured the sandwich so quickly she barely tasted it.

For a long time, then, neither of them said anything. She stirred the whipped cream slowly into her hot chocolate with the wooden stir stick. He sipped tentatively from his coffee.

"So," he said finally. "Are you all right?"

For some reason, the question struck Cassie as bizarre, if not outright hilarious. She had to hold in the bubble of laughter that rose in her throat.

"Am I all right?" she asked, realizing only as she heard the words that she sounded like Skylark.

Thankfully, he smiled too. "I just meant, after this morning. Is there someplace you can go?"

It took her a moment to connect things, to realize that by "this morning" he was referring to the police attacking the camp. She considered for a moment.

"I've been thinking about going to Vancouver," she said.

He nodded. "That's not a bad idea," he said. "Things are a bit hairy out there right now."

She thought about the stories in the newspaper, and she was about to speak, but then she thought of Sarah, her body in the dry fountain, the blood on the snow.

She could feel the knife in her hand, the stuttering hesitation as it cut into Sarah's throat.

Then she thought of Skylark.

"I don't know, though," she said instead. "I don't want to leave quite yet."

He nodded again, more slowly this time. "Okay," he said, drawing out the syllables. "Did you want me to take you to a shelter? I know—"

"No," she said flatly. "I'm not going back to the shelter."

He wasn't surprised by her words. "You've said. But I know some people—" His face drew in on itself with concern. "Did something happen?" he asked, leaning forward slightly, bridging the distance between the two of them.

"Nothing *happened*," she said, emphasizing the second word. "Exactly."

He didn't say anything. He took a slow sip of his coffee, set the cup carefully on the table, and all the time he just looked at her.

She knew what he was doing: waiting her out, knowing that she would eventually say something, anything, just to fill the silence.

So she took a sip of her hot chocolate and set the mug slowly, carefully, back on the table, all the time looking at him.

"So what," he said, "do you mean by 'nothing happened exactly'?"

She had tried not to think about it. It was what, a week ago, at most? But she had done everything she could to put it in the past.

"Nothing," she said, looking down at the pale wood tabletop.

"Cassandra?" Her name in his voice was startling. "What happened at the shelter?"

She sighed. "Nothing really happened. I just never felt safe. Some of my stuff got stolen, and I reported it, but they didn't do anything, they just told me that I needed to be more careful. And there were these guys . . ."

"Did someone hurt you?" For a moment she had a flash of him in his uniform.

"No one hurt me." She thought of that afternoon, the three men in the stairwell, the animal smell of them as they had closed around her, their hands on her. "Not really." The way the leader, the toothless one, had smiled when he said they knew where to find her, the way they had all laughed when she tried to pull away. "But I never felt safe, you know? I figured that if they didn't do anything when my stuff got stolen, well, what if something else happened? They weren't exactly . . ." She shook her head. "I just didn't feel safe."

He nodded. "There are other shelters," he said, testing. "But yeah, I get that. Listen—" He shifted in his chair. "Cassandra. About your options." Reaching down between his feet, he lifted up her backpack and held it on his lap.

She couldn't help staring—it was so close. She had thought she would never see it again, and here it was, just out of reach.

It was strange: she knew that the bag was hers. She recognized everything about it, from the scuff up the left side to the piece of yarn tied around the handle, but there was a strangeness to it, an unfamiliarity. Perhaps it was because she had given up hope of ever seeing it again, or because she was seeing it now, for the first time, separated from her, with someone else holding it.

But none of that mattered. She just wanted it back.

Harrison held on to it as he asked, "What about going home, Cassandra?"

The question rang like a slammed door, and she leaned back in her chair, putting as much distance as she could between herself and the cop without running out of the coffee shop.

"No," she said.

"I talked to your mom again this morning," he said. "She—"

Cassie jerked forward. "You talked to my mom?"

Harrison nodded and started to reply, but she cut him off. "How could you?"

"Cassandra." He held up a hand.

"I'm not going back there."

"Cassandra."

She shook her head. "I won't. I'll just—"

"Cassandra." Loud enough this time to make people in the coffee shop turn. Loud enough to get her attention.

She leaned back in the chair again, her mouth a tight line.

Harrison turned his head slowly around, meeting people's curious gazes. When he made eye contact, he didn't look away: everyone else broke the stare first, turning back to their tables, their cups, their conversations.

Turning back toward her, he leaned forward, over the table.

"I talked to your mom this morning," he said, his voice pitched low. It was as if her outburst hadn't happened. "They're worried about you."

Cassie didn't say anything, forced her face still to not give anything away.

"And they miss you."

A realization crawled up Cassie's spine, insinuated itself in the back of her mind, whispered to her.

"They'd like you to come home."

It's over, the voice whispered. Her own voice.

"Why did you run away?" Harrison asked, settling back in his chair a bit, giving her space. "Why did you leave the hospital?"

Cassie shook her head.

Harrison sighed. "Cassandra, if you won't tell me, I can't—"

"It doesn't matter now anyways," Cassandra muttered, loud enough for him to hear.

"What do you mean, it doesn't matter?"

"You're gonna send me back," she said. She looked around the café, trying not to meet his eyes. "You've talked to my mom, you're holding my stuff—you're gonna send me back. It doesn't matter why I ran away."

"I'm not sending you back," he said, lifting the bag across the table and handing it to her. "Here. I just wanted to know why you left."

She took the backpack by the handle and held it, staring at him. "You're not?"

He shook his head, and she slowly lowered the bag to the floor, tucking it between her own feet. She kept one hand wrapped around the handle. "But—" The voice in her head was silent, but she was afraid to breathe, in case she had misunderstood.

"I couldn't, even if I wanted to," he said, half-shrugging and lifting one hand in a gesture of helplessness. "You're sixteen years old. Legally, you have the right to decide where you want to live." He leaned forward, planting both elbows on the table. "Besides," he said, his voice lowering, "if I were to put you on a bus, or deliver you myself, you'd just run away again, the first chance you got, right?"

She could feel her face flushing.

She nodded.

"So I want to know why you left."

He left the words hanging in the air as he took another swallow from his coffee.

She tightened her grip around the handle of her bag. She didn't have to tell him anything; she could just walk out. He might try to come after her, but he had already told her that there was nothing he could do. She could just leave.

But she didn't.

"I had to," she said, looking down at the grain of the table. "I had to go."

"Why?"

She didn't want to say too much. She couldn't tell him everything, but she wanted to tell him something. He'd been looking out for her. He had found her and returned her bag. She had to tell him something.

"It wasn't safe," she said, pausing on each word. "I couldn't stay there."

"Did something happen?" he asked. "Did somebody hurt you?"

She shook her head. "No, it wasn't anything like that. I just . . ." The words were bringing tears to her eyes, and she had no idea how to continue. "My father . . ."

Harrison laid both his hands palms-down on the table "Cassandra," he said firmly, but with undertones of understanding. "Cassandra, look at me."

She lifted her head, willing herself not to cry.

"You didn't kill your father."

« »

The crow alighted on one of the weathered, rusting tables along the front window of the café, next to the ashtray and its two cigarette butts.

It hopped across the table, onto the chair back closest to the window.

It craned its head forward.

It watched.

« »

You didn't kill your father.

The words echoed in her head, and she sobbed in a sharp burst.

She leaned forward, rested her forehead on the cool edge of the table and tried to be as quiet as she could. She breathed through her nose with a wet rasp, squeezed her eyes shut, pressed her lips tight.

She couldn't stop, but she didn't want to make a scene. She didn't want anyone looking at her anymore.

"It's okay." Harrison's voice was faint and indistinct against the roaring in her ears. "It's all right."

No, she argued silently. *It's not.*

Everything about that night, everything that she had tried to push down, came rushing back.

It was like she was there again, right there: the cool of the basement, the way her steps creaked on the next-to-bottom stair, the softness of the rags as she piled them, the acrid smell of the turpentine as she poured it into the loose pile of cloth, the sulphur tang of the match as she struck it.

She had dropped it into the pile of rags, watched it pin-wheel in slow motion. The air and the rags had seemed to pop, bursting into a hot blue flame that wavered and roared, licked up the bare wood beams . . .

"It's all right," Harrison said again.

"No," she said, this time out loud. "No, it's not. The fire—"

She lifted her head from the cool table and looked across at him. He was blurry through her tear-muddled eyes, but she saw enough to take the napkin he extended toward her.

He waited in silence while she dabbed her eyes and blew her nose, handed her another napkin without being asked.

"Cassandra," he said. "I talked to your dad."

The world roared in her ears. "You . . . My dad?"

He nodded. "That first morning, after we met you at the bookstore. I called your place."

So dizzy, so suddenly, she felt like she was going to throw up.

"I know that . . . you were seeing a doctor. And what you wrote—"

Then it came to her, all in a rush.

"You read my journal," she snapped. "You . . ." She reeled at the unexpected anger. "What gives you the right?"

He looked at her for a moment as if not understanding the question. "My badge?" he said measuredly.

Cassie snorted.

"Look," he said, elbows on the table again, gesturing with his hands. "Your bag was abandoned property. No ID, no tags, no card saying, 'If found, please call.' Do you know how much stuff I had to go through this morning when we got back to the station? How do you think I knew the bag was yours? From your name inside your journal."

"Oh," she said, sagging.

"I'm a cop. I open a book and the first thing I see is 'I killed my father today,' damn right I'm going to read it. And I have zero issue with that." His face was tight and hard. "Okay?"

Cassie nodded.

"Okay," he said, and the mood started to lift. "And if it's any comfort, I only read enough to make me want to start looking into things." He smiled a strange smile, like the fact that he had read her diary and then started an investigation should be some sort of comfort.

"What do you mean, 'looking into things'?" Her arms still folded over her chest.

"I made some calls. Talked to the RCMP there. That's why I called your place again. I wanted to know if there was anything that wasn't in the reports."

"And?" She bit out the word.

"There wasn't." He shook his head. "It was just an accident."

She wouldn't argue with him. She knew the truth. She had watched the flames pour upward along the beams, she had had the smell of paint thinner on her hands: she knew what had happened that night.

"Is that why you ran away? Because you thought you had—"

She shook her head, blurted the word *no* before she could stop it, then sagged into her chair.

Harrison waited.

"Your mom," he said, after a long silence, "mentioned a Dr. Livingston. Someone that you had been seeing."

"Jesus."

"Was he—"

"She."

"Was she a counsellor?"

"She was a shrink."

He nodded again, and she wondered how much he really knew. How much had her mom told him? Was he testing her, seeing how much she would admit to?

"That's what your mom said."

She exhaled loudly.

"She said you had problems with your sleep. She had a name for it."

"Night terrors. A parasomnia disorder." She almost spat the words out.

"Right," he said. "That was it. Night terrors. Did that start—"

She shook her head. She was done talking.

He waited a long moment in the silence.

"I want to help you, Cassie," he started, carefully measuring each word. "But I don't know how I can help you if you won't talk to me."

She stood up, lifting her backpack with her. "You can't," she said. "Nobody can."

The wind blistered across her face as she opened the door.

<< >>

"He doesn't know," she muttered to herself as she hurried down the sidewalk, head bowed against the wind.

He didn't have any idea what he was talking about. No one did. Except her.

Nobody else had been there in the basement with her the night of the fire. Nobody else had dropped the match. Nobody else had the smell of kerosene on their hands.

"But you were in bed," Dr. Livingston said, inside her head. "Your mom said when she smelled the smoke she had to wake you up to get you out of the house. Did you start the fire and then go back to bed and fall asleep?"

She didn't have an answer for that: she didn't remember going back to bed, but she must have.

"And you thought that you had spilled kerosene on your hands, that you could smell it."

That had always been the way with Dr. Livingston—not letting anything stand. Challenging everything. Making her wrong.

"Yes." Quietly.

"But no one else could smell it. Your mom, the police, the ambulance attendants. No one smelled kerosene."

"They probably just didn't notice."

As she rounded the corner, Cassie let herself speed up. She wanted to put as much distance as she could between herself and the cop and his questions.

He was only trying to make things make sense. That was what the Dr. Livingston in her head was doing too, just trying to figure out the story.

But didn't that mean they should actually listen to her story? Actually pay attention when she told them what had happened?

Wouldn't she know what she had done?

She had started seeing Dr. Livingston when she was six or seven, when the dreams were so bad she would scream and curl into a ball in the corner rather than go anywhere near her bed.

Dr. Livingston had taken her in, had talked her through everything. Had shown her that everything she had experienced had been a dream. That there had been no one outside her door in the dark, calling her name, coming to her bed . . .

She had fought. She had tried to tell her that she was wrong, that the dreams were real.

But after a while, she had stopped fighting. Maybe there was nothing. Maybe, just maybe, it wasn't real.

There had been no more of the waking dreams, the vivid nightmares.

At least there was that.

And then, without warning, she had woken screaming, the memory of a knife in her hand. She had rushed into her sister's room, knowing what she would find: the sheets drenched with blood, her chest ripped open, her eyes wide and red, her mouth frozen in a soundless scream.

Instead, Heather had groaned in her sleep and rolled over, rustling the blankets, not even aware that Cassie was there.

Her sister was safe.

It happened night after night after night. Different, but the same.

Sometimes it was Heather, her chest ripped open, the knife in Cassie's hand.

Sometimes it was her mother, her throat cut into a gaping, gushing smile.

And sometimes it was her father, the smell of kerosene, the sound of the wood crushing his skull.

Always different, always the same.

And then there was the night of the fire, the night her father died.

But her mother was alive. Heather was alive.

That's what had really scared her.

They were safe, but Cassie knew that safety was an illusion. Heather and her mother would never be safe, not while Cassie was around.

So she had run.

She was the only one who knew what had happened, and she was the only one who could keep it from happening again.

So she had run.

And now it was happening again. Here.

The dreams. Sarah. The staircase. Her father . . .

Dr. Livingston didn't believe her. Constable Harrison didn't believe her. Nobody believed her.

It didn't matter. She knew what she had done.

She had dropped the match. She had held the knife.

She had killed her father, burned him alive in the basement.

She had killed Sarah: cut her throat and pushed her into the fountain.

And Skylark.

Skylark.

She knew what she had to do: she had to go, to keep Skylark safe.

But she couldn't leave without seeing for herself that she was okay, that it wasn't already too late.

Pulling her coat tightly around herself, she disappeared into the shadows.

« »

In the distance, she could still hear the screaming, the voice over the megaphone, the heavy crunch of boots. Her breath came ragged and sharp, her chest aching as she ran.

"Come on," Skylark called out, somewhere in front of her. Skylark!

She could almost see the girl in the distant red lights flashing over the buildings, down the deserted streets. Almost.

She followed the sound of her footfalls, echoing faintly in the dark.

"Come on," she called again. "We're nearly there!"

Nearly where? Where were they going?

She almost ran into Skylark.

Her friend had stopped sharply and partially collapsed, hunched over with her hands on her knees, her back shuddering with the exertion of the run as she tried to catch her breath.

Cassie stopped behind her, her chest burning, heaving as she struggled to take in a deep breath.

"We did it," Skylark said, straightening slightly, still gasping. "We got away."

Cassie nodded, unable to speak, and walked in a slow circle to keep from falling over. She didn't recognize where they were—an alley maybe? There was a brick wall, a dumpster, not much of anything else.

"We did it," Skylark repeated.

"We did," Cassie said, stepping behind her.

Wrapping her arms around Skylark from behind, she held her close, buried her face in the nape of her neck. She could feel the kinetic fluttering of Skylark's heart under her hand, the rise and fall of her chest.

"You said," Skylark whispered, her voice almost inside Cassie's head. "You said you'd never hurt me."

The knife in Cassie's right hand slid effortlessly blade skyward through the layers of Skylark's clothes—her coat, her sweater, her shirt—and into the soft flesh of her belly.

"You said," Skylark repeated, and it felt like a kiss.

The knife made a sound like a zipper as Cassie slid it upward through Skylark's body, opening her to the snow and the sky.

"You said."

≪ ≫

Cassie found the camp two days later.

She had spent two nights under an overhang near the parking lot by the Inner Harbour. The walkway above her made the small space seem like a cave, and once it was late there was barely any sound of footsteps above her. She had tucked herself into the shadows in the corner, holding her backpack tight, curling herself around it.

She hadn't expected to sleep; she hadn't wanted to sleep, even, but it was inescapable, and she opened her eyes to a world grey and washed-out with the sunrise.

She had no idea where to go. She had the basics of a plan—find Skylark, get off the island—but no idea how to put that plan in motion. Skylark could be anywhere, and while it made sense to wait for her near the courthouse, the thought of the man across the street in the flannel jacket kept her away.

But she had a little money. She only needed a bit more. It would be easy, she had hoped.

It wasn't.

So few people used the side streets that her hat had stayed resolutely empty. Every few hours, she ducked into the mall or the bookstore to get warm. She didn't even try to sit down;

if she kept moving, they were less likely to throw her out.

The headline in the newspaper the first morning read "Squatter Camp Uproar." There was a large photograph of Brother Paul, and something about an interview, an appeal for help, but she didn't read the article. She had to keep moving.

She used the bathrooms at Ship's Point. She considered having a shower the first morning, but the idea of undressing, of doing all that work only to have to get dressed in the same dirty clothes again, brought on a wave of exhaustion. She settled for washing her face, and she let the water run as she scrubbed her skin, steam billowing around her.

Nobody took the slightest notice of her anyway.

And Skylark was nowhere to be found.

The camp was just around the corner from the Inner Harbour, partway between the museum and the courthouse.

Cassie didn't really know what she was seeing as she came around the block: there was a small park on the corner, overhung by old trees and surrounded by a low chain-link fence.

The park was filled with tents and signs and smoke from several fires. People milled about, drifting between the rough tents, paying no attention to the people watching from the fenced-off safe distance of the sidewalk.

Cassie hunched her head down and scurried along the fence, trying to keep clear of the crowd. The buzzing tension in the air made her want to get away as quickly as she could.

She was almost past the park when she heard her name.

"Dorothy!"

The voice was like something out of a dream.

She jerked to a stop, looked up from the sidewalk. Skylark?

"Dorothy!" Louder this time, and the sound of running.

She turned, and Ian was there at the edge of the sidewalk at a gap in the fence, his smile broad and bright. He was wearing faded grey pants and a thick T-shirt, his eyes bright, his breath coming in fat grey puffs.

"I thought it was you!" He swept her into a hug that almost lifted her from the ground. "It's so good to see you! Where did you go?"

She had to force herself not to struggle free of his embrace, not to push him away. He smelled of smoke and sweat and cold, with a strong tone of some woody perfume, almost like a spice.

"Go?" she asked as he released her and stepped back, still smiling.

"After the police busted up the camp?" He bounced a little on his heels. "Everyone was looking for you."

Cassie felt a surge of warmth. "Is this—" She craned her neck to see past Ian's shoulder into the small park.

He nodded excitedly. "It's ours!" He swept his arms wide, welcoming her.

Her heart raced.

Skylark.

Looking more closely, she recognized a lot of the people wandering around the camp. There were some strangers, but there was Hilary, and Janice was close to one of the fires. Jeff, Ian's boyfriend, was watching them from the end of the path, in the gap in the fence.

"So what do you think?" Ian asked. "Pretty cool, eh?"

Cassie nodded. She wanted to ask about Skylark, wanted to run through the camp calling her name, but she couldn't. "It looks great."

"Come on," he said, touching her shoulder.

She followed him past the fence. Jeff smiled as he joined them.

The air was heavy with smoke from the fires, and here and there Cassie caught traces of marijuana and, almost more surprisingly, roasting meat. It smelled like camping.

"So what's with all the tents?" she asked as they approached the centre of the camp.

"They were donated," Jeff said, in his slow, cautious way.

"Donated?"

"People just gave them to us!" Ian exclaimed.

"But—"

Jeff looked at Ian. "People heard about the police raid or read about Brother Paul in the newspaper," he said, and Cassie was impressed by how carefully he spoke. Ian seemed like a bit of a goofy puppy in comparison. "A lot of people were upset. They didn't think we were doing anything wrong, and they thought that the police were out of line." He shrugged. "So they started bringing us stuff. Clothes. Sleeping bags. Old camping equipment, tents and stoves and lanterns. Food." He smiled broadly at Ian.

"I'm making a stew at our tent," the boy said, obviously pleased with himself. "Are you hungry?"

The thought of food made her stomach growl, but she shook her head. Skylark, then anything else. "Show me the rest first," she asked, not wanting to give too much away.

Ian led her through the twisting, rough paths between the tents, stepping over lines and around piles of stuff.

There were small fires everywhere, and the air stung with smoke.

"People keep bringing us wood," Jeff explained when he saw Cassie squeezing her eyes shut. "Some of it's pretty green, pretty smoky." He sounded apologetic. "It'll dry, though."

"You sound like you know a lot about this sort of stuff."

"I've done a fair bit of camping," Jeff said.

"Jeff's trained as a naturalist," Ian said proudly. "He's working on his doctorate."

"Well, not right now," Jeff deadpanned.

Both of the boys laughed, but Cassie winced: What were they doing there, Ian and Jeff? They were both smart, both friendly, Jeff at least had some education. How did people like that end up living in places like this?

And if they had to, what hope did someone like her have?

"And that's about it," Ian said, wrapping up the short tour as they reached the fence on the far side of the camp. "What do you say to some stew now?" There was definitely a puppy quality to him, a high-energy eagerness to please.

She forced a smile; where was Skylark?

"That sounds good," she said.

Skylark would be here, sooner or later. She would wait, have some stew, maybe ask Ian and Jeff to show her where Skylark's tent was.

She imagined sitting beside Skylark as they ate or falling asleep beside her. She thought of her laugh, the way she would kind of lean against her when they gathered around the circle to listen to Brother Paul.

The thought stopped her.

"Where's the main meeting area?" she asked. Jeff and Ian looked at her blankly. "Where Brother Paul talks? At the evening gatherings?"

Ian and Jeff looked at each other, then turned slowly to face her again. "There aren't any more evening meetings," Jeff said.

"What? Why not?"

"Brother Paul . . ." He looked at Ian like he didn't really know what to say.

"Things are different now," Ian said. "Brother Paul doesn't have time for meetings every night."

Cassie stared at him.

"He's been busy with the newspapers and the TV," Jeff said, stepping forward. "And he spends time with each of the new members of the community."

"But no meetings," she said.

"No," Ian said. "He sees people in his tent."

Cassie followed his gaze across the mess of lines and bundles. "Oh," she said quietly.

She hoped that Frank and Joe hadn't noticed Jeff pointing at them, standing on either side of the entrance to the largest tent in the camp. Bob had, though. He stood up from his folding chair outside the tent and smiled at her across the distance.

≪ ≫

Ian and Jeff fed her. Spicy and hot, the stew filled her in places she hadn't known were hungry.

"What's in this?" she asked as she finished her first bowl.

"Potatoes and rutabaga, carrots, some celery and celery root . . ."

Jeff rattled off the list of ingredients as Ian filled her bowl again without her even asking.

"No meat?" she asked, when he seemed to be finished speaking.

"No," he said, mildly disdainful. "Meat is murder."

She smiled, recognizing the title from an old Smiths album.

Looking into the steaming bowl, not making eye contact, she took a deep breath. "Have you . . . Have either of you seen Skylark?"

"You haven't seen her?" Jeff asked, sitting up to look at her.

"No," she said, shaking her head. "I—"

"We thought . . ." He looked at Ian. "We assumed that she was with you. We didn't want to ask in case something had happened with you guys."

"No," she repeated. "We got separated when the police came. I ran one way, she—" As she spoke, she found herself trying to remember: Had she even seen Skylark that morning? Everything was such a jumble in her mind, all the flashing lights, the shouting, the running. But Skylark had been there, right? She had seen her before she ran, hadn't she?

"We haven't seen her," Ian said, flat, like he was trying to remember something himself.

They all fell silent.

After a few minutes, Cassie stood up. The thought of eating another bite made her feel like she was going to throw up. "I'm just going to . . ." She was hunched over, her head almost brushing the roof of the tent. "I think I need to take a walk."

Both of the boys—not boys, not really, she realized, but that was how she thought of them—nodded gravely. "Sure," Jeff said.

"Can I—" She gestured at the backpack, just inside the zipped door.

"Sure," Jeff said. "No worries. Our *casa* is *su casa*."

Her smile was weak and thin. "Thanks."

"Just come back, okay?" Ian said as she was turning away.

"Okay," she said softly. "I will."

Her emergence from the zipper of the tent woke a dog curled a short distance away. He jumped up and pounced over to her, sniffing her hand, licking her fingers.

The dog kept her company as she walked through the

camp, bouncing against her leg, looking for attention, its tail whipping sharply back and forth. Its presence took the edge off her discomfort, her fear.

A bit of it, anyway.

She stayed in the shadows as much as she could. She had no idea what time it was, but the sun was already setting, and the camp was pools of light thrown by lanterns, the warm glow of fires, the rich smells of cooking. It felt even colder in the dark than it really had a right to.

She did her best to avoid everyone. She recognized some of the voices in the dark, but she didn't want to talk to anyone. Skylark wasn't here, and she just wanted to find a quiet place and try to figure it all out.

"Well, hey, look who's back."

The voice cut through her.

"We were wondering if we were going to see you again. We thought we might have scared you off."

Cassie could barely see them in the dim light. They were clustered at the base of a massive tree, passing their small pipe behind the last tents straggling at the edge of the camp.

"What's the matter? Too scared to talk to us?" The dog thumped against her leg. "Where you been?"

There was a tone in his voice she hadn't heard before, a solidity, a sense of authority similar to that in Harrison's voice.

She shook her head, and she could feel the rumble of the dog growling, not quite silently, against her.

Bile rose in the back of her throat.

She turned into the dark, the dog padding beside her as she hurried away, the boys' laughter echoing in her ears.

"Come on back," Bob called after her, mocking now. "We won't bite."

Cassie spent the night in Jeff and Ian's tent.

Jeff had somehow managed to find a sleeping bag for her while she was walking, and a ratty comforter that he folded lengthwise twice to create a sleeping pad. "That'll keep out a bit of the cold at least," he said as he laid it alongside his and Ian's bed.

"Thank you," she said, still shaking from her confrontation with Bob and the boys. She hadn't told Jeff and Ian about it.

"*De nada*," he said, billowing out the sleeping bag as best he could. "Our *casa* is *su casa*," he repeated.

She had thought at first that it might be hard for her to sleep in such close contact with people she barely knew, but it was warm and comfortable being with them, snuggled close with Mr. Monkey, listening to their whispers and murmurs after Jeff blew out the light.

It made her think of the day she had gone to the pet store with her mom and dad, looking at the puppies in the cage in the middle of the store, all piled up and dozing, shifting and stretching, bright eyes opening and closing.

In the morning, she stumbled sleepily to the small concrete shed in the back corner of the park that the campers were using as a bathroom, trenches dug deep along two of the walls. "Boys on one side, girls on the other," Jeff had told her the day before.

She had gone before bed, but it was different, even in just the pale light of the early morning, to be squatting next to a girl she didn't even recognize.

The smell was acrid, harsh.

As she finished, the girl—who hadn't said anything as she

unbuttoned her pants and squatted down next to her—said, "Be careful."

Cassie started at the voice and at the words. "What?" she asked, half-turning, making sure to keep her eyes on the girl's face.

The girl cocked her head, gesturing toward the edge of the park. "Cops," she said.

Cassie's heart jumped. "Are they coming in?"

The girl shook her head, reached into her jacket pocket for a napkin. "No," she said. "They're just sitting there. Watching." She dropped the napkin into the trench and pulled up her pants, wandering back toward the camp without another word.

Cassie took her time, letting the other girl disappear into the camp before she pulled up her own pants and crept away from the stinking wall.

Zipping the tent seam behind herself, she settled as quietly as she could back into her sleeping bag.

"Dorothy," Ian said, still mostly asleep. "Is everything okay?"

"I had to pee," she whispered, her face warming. Then, a moment later, "There are police outside the fence."

"I wonder what they want," he said, even dozier.

As she listened, his breathing slowed and deepened, a tiny rasp coming on each exhalation as he went back to sleep.

Cassie, though, was wide awake, her mind churning, her body tense. The police raiding the camp kept playing in her mind, the voice of the megaphone echoing in her head.

And the voice telling her to run. Had it been Skylark's voice? Was that the last time she had seen her? Or had she already been gone?

Whose voice had it been?

And where was Skylark? What had happened to her?

Lying in the gloom, listening to the boys breathe, Cassie knew that she wasn't going to be able to fall back asleep. Her heart was racing, and she realized that she was waiting for the police to return, anticipating screaming, the thudding of heavy boots on the narrow pathways between the tents.

Careful not to make a sound, she crept out of the sleeping bag and into the cold morning air. She left the tent zipper partway open as she slipped into her shoes.

Ian and Jeff's tent was close to the edge of the camp; she crept behind it and into the grey blur of the open park.

She kept low as she snuck around the outside of the camp, watching the fenceline. When the police car came into view, she shrank back, made herself even smaller, her breath coming in harsh grey pants.

The police officers weren't in the car. They were standing on the sidewalk, two of them, resting their arms on the top of the chain-link fence.

Faint voices floated in the chill air.

She stopped in the shadow of one of the corner tents, crouching down to watch them.

The cops didn't seem to be doing anything. They were just leaning on the fence, talking. Were they watching the camp? Were they waiting for others to arrive before they invaded?

What were they doing?

"Cassandra?"

At first, she wasn't sure where the voice was coming from. It sounded like someone shouting while whispering.

And the voice itself—had she heard it before? She couldn't be sure . . .

"Cassandra Weathers."

This time a flash of light accompanied her name, a double flicker from the nearest cop's shadowy silhouette.

She crouched lower, tried to force herself to blend into the dark.

The light flashed again.

"Cassandra." The light flashed again "Come here."

There was no hiding; they had seen her. She could run into the camp, but they would follow her. Did she really want to be the cause of the cops coming again?

Her knees popped as she straightened up.

The grass was silver-grey, crunchy under her feet, shimmering in the faint glow of the early morning.

At first, she was almost relieved to see Harrison and his partner; at least it was someone familiar.

But as she got closer, close enough to see the flashlight cradled in his arm, one hand over the lens, close enough to see his breath, her heart clenched again in her chest.

Harrison's face was set and hard, almost featureless. His partner stepped away from the fence.

"Cassandra." He slipped the flashlight into a loop on his belt, across his body from his holster, from his gun.

"We need you to come with us."

≪ ≫

Harrison put his hand gently on the top of her head as she climbed into the back of the police car, pushing down slightly to be sure she wouldn't hit it on the door frame.

He closed the door firmly behind her. There was no handle on the inside. A plate of Plexiglas separated the back seat from the front.

The back of the police car smelled of strong cleaner, almost overpowering, but not powerful enough to completely obscure the smells of booze, urine and vomit. The seat was little more than a plastic bench, ragged and scuffed.

Cassie leaned into the door as close as she could, clinging to it for protection.

In a way, it was a relief: no more waiting, no more worrying. She had known the police would be coming for her as soon as they realized what she had done to Sarah, once Harrison figured out what had really happened to Daddy. It was better this way. No more stress, no more hiding. And now everyone would be safe: Mommy, Heather, Skylark, Ian, Jeff, Brother Paul. With her locked away, they would all be safe.

Harrison's partner opened the driver's-side door, the interior light flashing almost blindingly bright as she slid in behind the wheel, slamming the door.

She didn't look back, didn't even glance at Cassie.

Well, of course not. Not after what she had done.

Cassie jumped as the other back door opened and Harrison slid onto the seat beside her.

He closed the door gently, then turned to her, drawing his leg up partly under himself.

Cassie pulled away farther still, the cold of the door sharp behind her.

"Cassandra—"

"I told you," she said, unable to stop the words. "I told you."

"Cassandra." His voice was calm, soothing. "Cassandra, calm down, please. You haven't done anything wrong."

She forced herself to breathe, to consciously force the air deep into her lungs, and just as important, to not hold it, to push it out. To take another deep breath. Then another.

Harrison watched her breathe, waited.

"I'm okay," she said. "But if you're not—" She closed her eyes, shook her head. "If you're not—"

He took a deep breath. "We need your help." He glanced at his partner.

"What—"

He unzipped his heavy jacket and reached inside. "Farrow," he said to his partner. "Could you—" He cocked his head up toward the light behind the grill in the ceiling.

Cassie snapped her eyes shut at the sudden brightness. When she opened them, Harrison was blinking rapidly. "Sorry," he said.

He was holding something in his right hand, a small card. "Could you take a look at this?"

It was a student card, laminated, but scuffed. She didn't recognize the name of the school in Campbell River, but it took her only a moment to recognize the girl in the picture.

She looked younger, softer somehow, blond hair brushed out and crafted into school-picture waves, but the smile, the brightness in her eyes were unmistakable.

"We think that she might have lived in the camp, and we were wondering—"

Cassie felt all the air go out of her.

The name on the card was Laura Ensley. Division 11A.

"Did you know her?" Farrow asked from the front seat.

Lived. Did.

"Where did you get this?" she asked, gesturing toward Harrison with the card. Her hand was shaking, her mind jumbled with images.

Did. Lived.

Harrison glanced at his partner. "The morning we broke

up the camp, there were some things left behind. Your backpack."

Cassie nodded, her fingertips clenched white around the card.

"There was another bag, close to yours. The ID card was in there."

"Did you know her?" Farrow repeated.

Cassie nodded again, her throat beginning to swell. "Yes."

Harrison glanced at Farrow.

"She called herself Skylark."

Harrison nodded slowly and cleared his throat. "Cassandra—" He reached into his jacket again.

This time, he handed her a photograph.

Cassie knew, even before she had mentally processed the image. She knew, and the world began to spin out of control. She couldn't breathe and she felt like she was going to throw up or pass out.

"Oh my God."

It was a photo of Skylark's face. Her eyes were closed, her skin as white as fresh snow, and as cold. She was lying against a white surface. The photograph had been taken from directly above her, close, unflinching. Her hair was pulled all the way back, her forehead long, a blank, cold plain, unwrinkled, utterly devoid of expression.

Her lips were grey.

Lived. Did.

There was nothing left of her. The brightness, the spark of her was gone. Her lips were slightly parted, but there was no trace of a smile.

"Oh my God."

"Cassandra." Harrison started to reach out, but stopped himself. "I'm sorry," he said.

She shook her head, hunching over as tears gushed forth uncontrollably. Her breath came in great heaves.

After a moment, she felt a hand touch her shoulder. "I'm sorry," Harrison repeated.

"Is she—is she—" She couldn't form the words, but she needed to know. She needed to hear the answer to the question she could not ask.

"Is that your friend?" Farrow asked, in a voice gentler than Cassie had ever heard coming from her.

Cassie shuddered. "Yes. Is she—" She looked up at Harrison.

After a moment, he nodded. "I'm sorry."

Hearing it, hearing what she already knew, brought on another wave, another heaving sob.

She struggled to breathe.

"Cassandra . . ."

"I . . ." She fumbled at the door, but there was no handle, no way to get out. She tried to hold it in, but she couldn't, and half-turning, she threw up on the floor behind the passenger seat.

Farrow said something in the distance, but Cassie's ears were full of a roaring, sucking noise. Her throat and nose burned, and she wiped her chin.

"I'm sorry," she gasped. "I'm sorry." Small shuddering sobs now. She just wanted to go away. She just wanted to disappear.

"It's okay," Harrison said, as Farrow opened the front door and climbed out of the car. "It's not the worst thing to happen back here." He tried a smile, but it didn't work.

"Cassandra," he started, as Farrow opened his door from outside. "Listen—"

"How?" she asked, barely able to speak, watching Farrow's grey shape as she came around the back of the car. "How did she—" She already knew what he was going to say, but she needed to hear the words.

The door behind her opened with a sharp click and a rush of cold air. She tightened, ready to bolt, but she needed to hear.

"Let's—" Harrison mimed a getting-out-of-the-car gesture, started to move, but Cassie didn't budge.

"How did she die?" she asked, completely flat.

He looked at her for a moment. "She was murdered," he said slowly. "A couple of kids found her."

"Where?" she asked.

The question seemed to surprise him.

"Where did they find her?" she asked, the vision of the alley from her dreams filling her head: brick walls, broken concrete. A metallic bin. So vivid, more a memory than anything she had imagined.

Harrison glanced down at the floor behind the passenger seat, then back at Cassie.

"Come on," he said, climbing out of the car.

Cassie pulled herself unsteadily out of the back seat, not trusting her legs to support her, not sure the ground would even be there under her feet.

It felt like a dream, like the world was a movie she was watching, like if she walked in the wrong place she would cast a shadow on the screen, destroy the illusion completely.

But the illusion was already gone.

Shattered.

"Where?" she asked again as Harrison came around the car. The cold air scorched the rawness of her throat, her nose.

"Fernwood," he said. "It's a neighbourhood not far from here." He took a deep breath. "She was found behind a building."

"An alley."

He looked at her. "Yes."

Cassie laughed; she couldn't help herself. It was all so—
She laughed, covered her mouth, but she couldn't stop.

Harrison just looked at her.

"Cassandra—" He leaned toward her, but she stepped away

"I'm all right," she said, the cold cutting into her. "I'm all right."

She could have repeated the words a million times, that wouldn't have made them true. All she wanted to do was collapse on the ground, fall asleep and never wake up. Total oblivion: that was what she wanted.

"We just have a couple of questions."

She shook her head in disbelief. "Sure," she said. "Fine. Whatever."

Harrison flipped open his notebook. "When was the last time you saw Laura Ensley?"

She wanted to hit him. "That night," she said. "The night the police came to the camp."

"That fits with the time of death," Farrow said, coming around the car.

Harrison shot her a look as Cassandra's legs wobbled under her.

"According to her file she had some problems with drugs. Was she involved with anything—"

"Farrow," Harrison said. "We don't—"

He folded his notebook closed as Cassie started crying again. "Okay," he said.

He glanced at Farrow. She shook her head slightly, but he turned back to Cassie.

"Cassie," he said, and the gentleness of his tone was one

of the most terrifying things she had ever heard. "I have to ask you something . . ."

"Oh God," she groaned. "Oh God."

"It's about your father."

A sound came out of her throat, a knife-edged sob.

Harrison glanced at Farrow again.

"Have you seen him?"

The question drove the breath from her. "What?" She gasped.

"Have you seen your father? Here?"

She just looked at him. The question didn't make any sense.

"Your mother called us," Farrow said, stepping forward. "She said that she hadn't seen him. That he had left a few days ago."

Cassie looked between them, trying to make their words make sense.

"She thought he might be coming here."

She surrendered to the sobbing, crumpling to her knees on the cold pavement. "Oh God."

A moment later, she felt a hand on her shoulder. She didn't know whose it was, her eyes pressed shut. Maybe when she opened them, it would all have been a dream.

"Why don't you come with us," Harrison said gently. "We can—"

She pulled herself to her feet, pulled herself away from the touch, from the words. "No," she sobbed. "I can't. I can't."

"Cassie . . ."

"I can't."

"We can get you help."

She bristled at the words, but she tried not to let it show, tried to focus on her breathing.

"I'm serious," he said, his voice tighter now. "It's not safe out here." He glanced into the park. "You need to be careful. Find someone you can trust. You can look out for each other."

She shook her head, wiped her nose on the shoulder of her coat.

"I did," she said.

All the air had been sucked out of the universe.

He looked at her for a long time, like there was something else that he wanted to say, then turned back to the car. "All right, Farrow," he said.

Cassie watched as the two of them got back into the cruiser. Harrison unrolled the passenger window and looked at her as they pulled away from the curb.

She watched as the right-turn indicator flashed at the end of the block, as the car disappeared around the corner.

≪ ≫

She clung to the fence as the sun rose around her, her legs barely able to support her weight, not thinking, not able to think. She cried, and as the tears steamed on her cheeks, she mouthed Skylark's name over and over, no sound, just gentle puffs of grey drifting silently away.

When she couldn't cry anymore, she wiped her face roughly with her sleeve, sniffed decisively, then walked through the gap in the fence and back into the camp.

She wanted to crawl into Ian and Jeff's tent, zip the fly up like she had never been gone, and curl up in the sleeping bag, tug it over her head and let it fill with the warmth of her breath. She didn't want to talk to them, not now—she didn't trust herself to speak—she just wanted to lie there, knowing that she wasn't completely alone.

She stopped short as she rounded the corner.

Bob was standing in the shadows at the head of the path.

"You're up early," he said.

She just nodded, afraid to try to speak.

"Have a good chat with your friends in the five-o?" He looked at her like he actually expected her to say something, but then he shook his head. "Come on," he said. "Brother Paul wants to see you."

"Now?" she managed to croak.

"When else?"

For a moment she thought about saying no, about returning to Ian and Jeff's tent, hiding herself away. But it wouldn't do her any good. And she didn't want to think about what Bob and his friends might do if she refused.

She followed the dreadlocked boy down the path.

≪ ≫

Brother Paul's tent shimmered in the dim light, the flickering of several lanterns causing her to squint as Bob held the flap open for her and she stepped inside.

Brother Paul was pulling on his jacket, head slightly hunched under the ceiling of the tent. He stopped when she came in.

"Dorothy," he said, stepping toward her. "Oh, I am so happy to see you back with us."

As he opened his arms, Cassie realized there wasn't enough room in the tent for her to step away. She had no choice but to allow him to wrap his arms around her, to pull her into the smoky, musky smell of him.

"We were all so worried about you girls," he murmured in her ear as his hands rubbed up and down her back.

Cassie didn't say anything, didn't move, stayed frozen in place, trying not to breathe.

"You just disappeared," he continued. "We thought—"

He was cut off by a scratching at the front flap of the tent behind Cassie, and Bob's voice. "Brother Paul?"

He stepped back from Cassie. "Yes, send her in," he said, loudly enough to be heard outside.

The flap of the tent parted, and a girl entered, carefully balancing a mug between her hands.

"Thank you for this, Charity," Brother Paul said as he took the mug from her.

It took Cassie a moment to recognize the girl who had been next to her at the wall; it seemed like it had been a lifetime ago. Charity looked like she was a little younger than Cassie, her face smooth, her hair clean and pulled back into a blond ponytail. She looked at Brother Paul with an openness to her expression, eyes wide and focused on him.

The way Skylark had looked at him.

He took a sip from his mug. "That's perfect," he said, exhaling contentedly. "Thank you so much."

He brushed the girl's cheek with his hand, and she turned away, blushing, disappearing back out through the flap without speaking.

"She's very special," he said, watching her go. "Poor child."

He took another sip from his mug. "Tea," he said. "Should I have her bring you a cup?"

Cassie shook her head. "No. No, that's fine." The words were all she could muster.

He nodded. "All right," he said. "Would you like to sit

down?" He pointed at his bed, a mess of blankets and a sleeping bag on top of an air mattress.

"No," Cassie said. "No thank you."

"All right," he repeated. "Well, then." He took another sip from the mug, pursing his lips like the tea was too hot. "So I am told you had an encounter with the local police this morning."

Cassie didn't know if the chill running up her back was from his voice or from the draft blowing through the tent flap.

It felt like there was glass in her throat when she swallowed. "They . . . they wanted . . . Skylark . . ."

He looked at her for a long moment, and his face fell. Tea sloshed from the top of his mug, splashing with a crackle on the plastic floor.

"Oh my God," he said. "She . . . ?"

Cassie nodded.

"Oh my God." He turned, first to the left, then to the right, like he was looking for somewhere to go, something to do. Stepping toward the far end of the bed, he set his mug down on the overturned milk crate, next to the black book he always carried, then turned back to Cassie. "Did they . . ." He stopped himself. "Oh, Dorothy. I'm so sorry."

He stepped toward her, his arms open again.

This time, Cassie stepped back, buckling the plastic wall of the tent.

Brother Paul lowered his arms, nodded. "Yes. Yes, of course." He shook his head. "She was so lovely," he said. "Such a lovely person. Did the police . . . Did they tell you what happened?"

She shook her head, barely able to speak, not sure that she wanted to. To tell him—to say the words out loud, to describe what Harrison and Farrow had told her, to hear it, in her own voice—would make it all real. It would mean that Skylark was truly gone.

Laura.

"Are you all right, dear?" Brother Paul asked, leaning toward her, his voice lowering. "This must be so hard for you . . ."

Cassie bit her lip and nodded. She knew that if she made the slightest sound, she would start crying again, and this time, she probably wouldn't stop. Ever.

"Are you sure you don't want to sit down?" He gestured again at the bed.

She shook her head.

"All right," he said, nodding slowly. "But know," he said, staring at her, his eyes locking on her own, "that we are all here for you. This loss, it lessens all of us. She was such a . . . presence. We're all here to support you, to give you what you need. We're a family, you know that." He gestured toward the front of the tent. "I'll have Bob find you a good tent—"

"No," she said, her voice louder than she intended. "Thank you. I can't. I just . . ."

"You can't be thinking of going back out there?" Brother Paul's voice was incredulous. "By yourself?"

She shook her head. "I don't want to," she said.

"Then don't." He didn't give her time to finish what she was going to say.

"I—" She started to argue with him. She wanted to explain, to make him understand why she couldn't stay. But there was nothing she could say that would make any sense, even to herself. "I'll be all right," she said, instead, knowing that it was a lie.

"Dorothy—" But she was already turning away, out through the zipper, into the cold.

The wind blew cold and hard down Douglas Street, cutting through Cassie's layers, driving tiny snowflakes like needles into the exposed skin of her face. She staggered headlong into the wind, lashed and beaten with every step.

That she had run away again—not able to face Brother Paul, not able to even speak to Ian and Jeff when she had gone for her bag—that she had no place to go, didn't really register for her. The tears that blistered on her cheeks in the driving snow were for Skylark.

Laura. Laura Ensley.

She had been so beautiful, so full of life. It had made Cassie feel better just to be near her.

And now she was gone.

She had been in grade eleven, the same grade as Cassie. In another world, in other lives, they might have been friends. Out here, sleeping on the frozen concrete, begging for change, they had been something else, something more.

Skylark had given her a home, a community, a shoulder to lean on. Cassie hadn't realized how much she had been missing all of those things. And now she was gone.

She would never hear the sound of her laugh again. Never hear the sound of her voice. Never share a meal, a bed, a smile.

She was gone.

And the last thing Cassie would remember of her was the way the knife had slid into her stomach, almost without a sound, the way her eyes had widened in sudden surprise and the sound, almost like a zipper, as she had drawn the knife upward, splitting Skylark's belly open, like unzipping another layer of clothes, the real Skylark spilling onto the ground as she cried out.

« »

This was his favourite part.

Watching the girl, bent-backed, as she slumped down the sidewalk, bouncing around people as they bumped into her without noticing, as they passed her without even realizing she was there.

The sidewalks were crowded with Christmas shoppers, but none of them really saw the girl. She had become invisible.

She was nothing. And she knew it.

That was the best part: she was fully, consciously aware that she had been stripped of everything. Her family, her home, her friends, the new home she had found, all gone. Nothing left.

She was a smear on the pavement, a cigarette butt in the gutter, a hamburger wrapper caught in the skeletal twigs of a wintering shrub, discarded and forgotten.

He felt a wild rush of thrumming pleasure.

In her despair, she was beautiful. The red around her eyes and at the base of her nose, the silver trails of tears on her wind-rough cheeks, the small gasp at the back of her throat with every breath.

So lovely.

Soon, now. So soon.

But not yet.

There was no need to rush, no call to hurry.

He could linger, savour that torment and pain, let the meat marinate in its own seasoning a little longer.

She would be so tender when it was time.

« »

Cassie walked until the streets were mostly empty. The stores had closed hours before, the last few customers hurrying away, blinking into the light snow that rimed their hats and collars. She walked slowly past the crowded restaurants, the small clusters of smokers out front laughing grey clouds into the night.

When it was just the bars and nightclubs open, music echoing down the narrow streets, she slipped into the doorway of the bookstore where the police had woken her the week before.

Had it only been a week? Less? She had no idea; it felt like a lifetime since that day. The day she had met Skylark. The first day she had visited the camp.

A lifetime ago. All gone now.

She settled herself uncomfortably into the corner, slipping her arms through the straps of her backpack as it sat on her lap, securing it to her.

It was still cold, well below freezing, but she was out of the wind and the snow, hidden in the shadows.

She wondered what it would be like when the cold took her. She hoped it would be like falling into a dreamless sleep, never having to wake up.

Dreamless.

She bowed her head against the rough fabric of her backpack. When she closed her eyes, tears leaked from them; she no longer even knew that she was crying.

"Cassandra?"

The voice came to her as if out of a dream, distant and detached, but warm in its familiarity.

"Cassandra."

PART FOUR

Metaphors.

Always metaphors.

I hate them for their vagueness. Their imprecision.

Trying to describe the Darkness is impossible. It slips from your analysis like quicksilver.

But none of the metaphors are right either.

Is the Darkness transmitted or absorbed?

Is it like a fog, draping over everything, infusing with every breath, or is it like a cancer, spreading under the skin of the world?

Does it move from person to person like a virus or like electricity?

In many ways, the old metaphors are better. Sometimes the Darkness does feel like a demon, living inside me, looking through my eyes, taking leathery wing to another host. Sometimes I do feel like a monster, strewing carnage in my wake.

But . . .

Wouldn't the nature of the Darkness, its true nature, mean that we are all monsters? That the world is populated with demons, all around us?

That sounds right.

The Darkness IS all of us, everywhere, always.

But you can't really understand it until you have fully embraced it.

When you have tasted blood, you have no further need of metaphor.

When you have fed on the Light, you understand the Darkness.

"You're going to be late," her mother said as she bustled into the kitchen. She was already dressed for work, her hair back, a little bit of makeup on her face.

"We're fine," Cassandra said, leaning against the counter as she ate a banana. She had just put her cereal bowl into the sink. Heather was still at the table, slowly lifting a spoonful to her mouth as she stared at the back of the cereal box.

"Not if you don't get ready," her mother said, setting her handbag on one of the kitchen chairs. "Heather, please."

"I'm done, Mom," she said, tilting her bowl sideways to show only a faint residue of milk.

"All right, brush your teeth and I'll do your hair. Come on," she urged when Heather was a bit too slow at standing up.

Heather started toward the stairs, but stopped when their mother cleared her throat.

Mom nodded toward the table, where Heather had left her cereal bowl and the box, and lifted her eyebrows.

Heather sighed heavily and set the bowl in the sink, tucked the box back into the cupboard.

Cassie smirked. Heather scowled.

"Come on, you two," their mother urged again, fumbling with an earring.

Heather hustled out of the kitchen, turned toward the stairs.

"Whoa, slow down," came a voice from the other room. "Where's the fire?"

Cassandra's right hand, holding the limp banana peel, fell to her side as her father came around the corner, shaking his head, smiling.

"You've got her on the run this morning," he said to their mother, leaning toward her to kiss her cheek. Good morning." His voice was a warm near-whisper.

"We're all going to be late," she said, giving up on her earring and turning to kiss him on the mouth.

"No, you're not," he said, grinning broadly. He looked at the clock above the sink. "You've got plenty of time."

His smile widened when he met Cassandra's eye. "Good morning, Miss Cassie. How'd you sleep?"

Her words seemed to die in her throat, crushed by the surging of her heart. Her daddy.

"Good," she managed in a gulp. "Good."

Truth was, she couldn't be entirely sure. She had dreamed something, she was sure of it, but the memory of it was just out of reach.

"Good," he affirmed. "And what about that algebra? Did it stick?"

It took her a moment to remember, then everything slipped into focus: the two of them at the kitchen table, working over math problems while Heather and Mom had watched TV in the family room; his patient, supportive voice as she worked through function after function; the warm sound of the television and laughter in the distance; the way he had tousled her hair and kissed her on the forehead when they were done. "You should sleep on that," he had said. "Let your subconscious work on it. In the morning, it'll all be there."

"I think so," she said. "I guess I'll find out later." Algebra quiz, fourth period.

"I bet you dreamed of functions."

He smiled, and Heather appeared in the doorway, clutching a hairbrush.

No, she hadn't dreamed of functions. What had she dreamed of?

It was right there, like something she should remember, but the harder she tried, the farther away it seemed to be. All she had were strange fragments: a city, a group of people sitting in a circle, a girl looking at her.

And cold. She remembered the cold.

"Are you all right?"

She turned, and her mother was leaning toward her, eyes wide, head tilted slightly to one side.

"I'm okay," she said, not really sure. "Just tired, I think." She let her eyes wander around the room, looking for something to change the subject.

The clock, over the sink.

"We should get going, Heather," she said, turning. "Are you—"

Her sister was already at the back door, jacket zipped, shoes on. "Ready," she said.

Cassandra smiled and then, without thinking about it, half-turned to kiss her mother on the cheek.

Her mother seemed to jump.

"I love you, Mom," she said, turning away and starting for the door. "Come on, kid. Let's not miss the bus again, all right?"

She turned back to the room as she slipped her shoes on. Her mother was touching her cheek where Cassandra had kissed her, looking at her with a hint of a question in her eyes. Her father was standing at the table, smiling.

His back was to the door to the basement.

"You girls have a good day," he said as Cassie lifted her backpack to her shoulder.

"Love you, Daddy," Heather said as she opened the back door.

"Love you, Heather," he said.

Then he turned to Cassie.

The words stuck in her throat.

He tilted his head slightly, waiting.

"I love you, Daddy," she said quietly.

The expression on his face stopped her in the doorway.

She waited, one hand wrapped around the doorknob, fingers tight.

In the end, all he said was, "Love you too."

She closed the door firmly, unable to shake the feeling that something was wrong, that there was something bad, just waiting, just out of sight.

« »

The girl was stepping toward the curb before the minivan had come to a complete stop.

He smiled to himself as he reached over and turned down the music. This was getting easier. Almost too easy. They were coming to him, offering themselves up to him without his even having to try.

The hunger roiled inside him as he rolled down the passenger-side window.

"It's cold out there tonight," he said, loading his voice with warmth.

The girl shivered. "A bit, yeah." She was chewing gum, her deep-red lips wide and wet looking.

He smiled at her. She was a little older than he liked; he could see it around her eyes, around her mouth. Twenty, maybe? Twenty-one?

"Why don't you get in?" he asked, popping the lock with the button on his door. "You can warm up a bit."

"What did you have in mind?"

The question threw him for a moment. They weren't usually so forward. Usually those sorts of questions didn't come until they were already inside, the seat belts snug around them, the door locked behind them.

He smiled. "Why? Are you a cop?"

She rolled her eyes and snapped her gum. "Do I look like a cop to you?"

"No," he said. "I just thought . . ."

"There's some heavy shit going on these days," she said, turning her head to try to look into the back of the van. "A girl needs to know what she's getting into."

The hunger burned inside him like acid rising in his throat.

"Why don't you hop in and we can talk about it in private?"

She looked at him more closely. "Why? Are you a cop?"

He shook his head. "No, no," he said, trying not to let his anger show in his voice. "I just thought—"

She took a full step back from the door, shaking her head. "I don't think so," she said.

What? What was happening? This bitch, this whore, who the fuck did she think she was?

He wanted to shout at her, to force her into the van, but

she was already turning away, tottering up the block on her towering heels, toward a small crowd of girls.

"Fuck," he muttered, putting the van into drive.

His heart was racing as he pulled away, watching her in the rear-view mirror as she watched him driving away. "Fuck, fuck, fuck."

He had been so close. She wasn't perfect, but she would have been good enough. Better, once he got done with her. Once she was clean and silent and cool.

He took several deep, calming breaths and turned the music back up.

It was better this way. She wasn't the one, that much was clear. The one was still out there; it was just a matter of finding her.

Flicking on his turn signal, he turned toward downtown.

He would wait. He would get a cup of coffee and wait. It was still early.

He would find her.

≪ ≫

Heather was curiously quiet as they walked along the lane. The leaves in the trees lining the gravel path were in full green, and the air was heavy, warm and rich with the smell of new growth, gilded with birdsong.

Heather had been swinging her bag and smiling as they left the house, but as soon as they had turned the corner to the lane, the bag had slowed and fallen motionless to her side.

It took Cassie—who usually tuned out her younger sister's endless chattering—a few moments to realize that something was wrong.

"What's up, bub?"

Heather didn't answer at first. She was staring at the ground as she walked, her face knit tight.

"Bub?"

She hesitated. "Just tired, I guess." Not lifting her eyes from the ground. "I had some . . . strange dreams. Last night."

The tightness of her expression, the set of her mouth, stopped Cassandra in her tracks.

Heather took another couple of steps before she realized that Cassie was no longer with her. She turned.

"Nightmares?" asked Cassie.

Her sister fumbled to answer. "I guess. They seemed so real."

For a moment, Cassie was back inside her own dream, sitting next to a brick wall, looking through a cloud of her own breath at people sitting around a circle.

"Do you remember them?"

Heather opened her mouth, then closed it, shook her head.

Cassie took two steps toward her, crouched down slightly to bring her gaze level with her sister's. "Heather, you can tell me. I know what it's like."

Her sister flushed. When she spoke, her voice was almost a sob. "I don't know," she said, an edge of desperation to the words. "I can't—"

Both of them jumped and turned to the sharp bark of a horn in the distance.

"The bus," Heather cried, starting down the lane.

"Heather," Cassie called after her.

"We're gonna miss the bus," Heather called, without looking back.

"Heather!" Cassie had to run to catch up to her.

As they rounded the bend, the bus was idling at the side of the road, its door open, steam rising from its tailpipe.

She caught up with Heather as she slowed to a walk just before reaching the bus. Cassie swept her hand across her sister's arm, and Heather turned to face her.

"What is it?" Cassie asked. "What are you dreaming?"

Heather shook her head, then glanced at the bus. Mrs. Cormack was watching them expectantly from the driver's seat.

"There's someone there," Heather said finally. "I don't know if I'm asleep or awake, and it's like there's someone in my room." She twisted, brushing Cassie's hand off her arm, and leapt up the steps inside the bus. "There's someone calling my name."

Cassie stared at the open doorway, frozen in place by her sister's words. She couldn't move . . .

Mrs. Cormack honked the bus horn, and a flock of crows lifted from the bristled field across the road, blackening the sky.

« »

He had made the right decision.

Walking toward the minivan from the coffee shop, he felt invigorated in the bracing cold. All of the anger from the encounter with that bitch earlier had left him, dissipated by the anticipation, the hunger.

It was good. She was still out there, waiting for him, and she would come to him like it was meant to be, like they had been waiting their whole lives for this meeting, for this one moment, for what they would do together.

It was all perfect.

He hadn't really wanted that bitch anyway: she was too old,

too hard. The hunger had almost driven him to doing something that he would have regretted later. Her retreat from the van was the best thing that could have happened to him.

He was glad he had waited. With the music and the sound of the motor, the warm air blowing on him from the vents, it felt like he was alone in the universe.

No—it felt like the universe was his, and his alone.

He turned up the music.

His good feelings began to fade, though, as he took his first slow drive through Rock Bay.

Where were the girls?

There were a few of the old-timers under the street lights at the corners, as much a fixture as the street signs themselves, but where were all the other girls, the younger ones, the ones who stayed closer to the shadows?

He took another turn around the block, slower this time, craning his neck to see into the dark. Was it too cold? Had there been a bust?

His disappointment churned within him, the coffee spilling acid into his throat as the hunger cried out to be fed.

He took one more turn around the block.

Where was she?

He squeezed the steering wheel with both hands as the cold truth sank in: it wasn't going to happen tonight.

He had left it too long. It was all that bitch's fault. If it hadn't been for her—

He took a deep breath, tried to talk it through in his mind.

If it wasn't meant to be, it wasn't meant to be.

Better he wait, better he let the hunger build, than spend it all on the wrong girl.

He would come back. He would always come back.

There would be other nights.

He almost smiled to himself, and he turned up the music as he cut across to Hillside. It was time to go home, to dream of nights to come.

<< >>

Cassie could barely breathe as she climbed the high steps onto the bus, Heather's words echoing ceaselessly in her head.

There's someone there.

Mrs. Cormack said something about leaving them behind the next time they were late, but Cassie barely heard the words.

Calling my name.

Heather scurried up the narrow aisle, stepping deftly around bags and outstretched legs. Cassie imagined sliding into a seat next to her, trying to talk to her, but with a glance over her shoulder at her sister, Heather slipped into a seat next to Nicky Adams, pulling her bag onto her lap and pressing her knees resolutely into the seatback in front of her.

Cassie shook her head as she passed. Heather looked away.

Calling my name.

"Are you okay?" Laura asked as Cassie slid into the seat next to her. Her eyes were inquisitive, partially hidden behind her blond bangs.

Cassie nodded. "Yeah, I'm fine." She tried to shake it off, tried to clamp down the echoing sentences.

"You don't look fine."

"Thanks." She elbowed her friend lightly, trying to make a joke out of the whole situation, even as she craned her head slightly to see several rows ahead. All she could make out was the back of Heather's head.

"So, did you get the algebra done?" Laura had her math text open on her lap, mostly obscured by her binder.

The top sheet of paper was blank.

"Yeah. My dad had to help me, though."

"Nice," Laura said. "Do you mind if I—"

Cassie rolled her eyes. "Do I ever mind?" she asked, fumbling with the zipper of her backpack. "Maybe you can figure it out." She wrestled her binder out of her bag, managed to balance everything while she clicked out the homework page. "Here."

As Laura reached for the sheet of lined paper, the stark winter light caught the ring on her finger, flashing off the green eyes of the cat.

"Thanks," she said, laying the page next to her own. "I'll give it right back."

"Sure."

Cassie slouched against the seat, her gaze wandering from her sister's head to Laura's hand holding the homework sheet steady, then out the window at the cold, grey world passing by.

<< >>

Aside from the single car behind him, the streets were almost deserted all the way home. The farther he got from Rock Bay, the better he felt. The hunger didn't go away exactly, but instead of overwhelming him, it seemed to be giving him strength, growling within him, rumbling like a force of nature all to itself.

As he slowed to turn into his cul-de-sac, the car behind him slowed as well. As he turned, he felt almost like waving; there was a surge of comfortable happiness rising in him that he didn't really understand but that he wasn't about to argue with.

Turning into his driveway, pressing the button for the garage door, he glanced out the passenger window. The car that had been behind him had stopped right in front of the entrance to the cul-de-sac, completely blocking it.

He turned as the garage door rose, as the light flashed on, revealing the four police officers standing inside the garage, their guns drawn, facing the van.

Spotlights in the rear-view mirror blinded him, and as he cut the engine, he heard running footsteps and shouting.

<< >>

Their bus had the earliest drop-off, so the school was mostly empty when they arrived. The busload of kids disappeared into the echoing void and it swallowed them up. Within moments, it was as if Cassie and Laura were the only people in the whole building.

Even Heather had disappeared, blurring into the crowd and vanishing into the school without a backward glance.

Cassie could hardly blame her. She knew all too well how powerful dreams could be, the way everything started to bleed together, until she could no longer tell if she was asleep or awake.

She had never been sure . . . What if it wasn't a dream? What if the voice, the shadow, the weight on her, the sound of her name, what if she hadn't dreamed all that? What if it really was—

She shrieked and jumped as the boom of Laura's bookbag hitting the floor echoed up the deserted hall.

Laura laughed. "Jesus. Why are you such a spaz today?"

Her heart thrummed like a tiny bird.

"Are you going to be okay? You look like you're having a heart attack." She was still smiling, but there was genuine concern in her eyes.

Cassie swallowed, nodded. "I'm okay."

Laura looked at her. "No, really."

"Really."

Another long, studying look. "Okay."

Laura opened her binder on her lap, took a pencil out of her bag and continued copying Cassie's homework. Cassie waited, then pulled her journal from her backpack and started to write, the metal of the locker doors cold against her back.

« »

That evening, Cassie tried to talk to her sister, but she never got a chance. Heather helped their mother with dinner, something that she never did, leaving Cassie and their father with the dishes afterwards. Rather than doing her homework in her room, the way she always did, Heather brought her books downstairs and spread them out on the table in the dining room, one open doorway from where their parents were sitting in the family room watching TV. When she was done, she went into the family room and sat with them.

Cassie watched for a moment from the doorway, plainly within Heather's line of sight, but her sister pretended not to notice her.

At bedtime, Cassie decided to make one last attempt. She waited in her room until she heard Heather next door, then she vaulted off her bed and into the hallway. She closed Heather's bedroom door behind herself and blocked it with her body.

Heather snapped around to face her, slamming the dresser

drawer shut, clean pyjamas dangling in her hand. Her eyes flashed with fear.

"I know you don't want to talk about it," Cassie rushed, before Heather had a chance to say anything.

Heather scowled at her, but as quickly as it had come, the expression vanished, replaced with a tired heaviness.

"There's nothing to talk about," she said, turning to putter with things on the top of her dresser: hair elastics, bottles of nail polish, a brush.

"I know—" Cassie started.

"It was just a bad dream," she said. "I was just a bit freaked out about it, that's all. I shouldn't have said anything. I knew you'd freak out."

Cassie drew a sharp breath, felt her face burning.

"You—"

The expression on her sister's face stopped her: Heather looked scared. No: terrified. And she was striking out the only way that she could.

Cassie counted her breath. "It's okay," she said, biting back that first flare of anger. "I didn't freak out. I'm just—"

Heather's face was hard, her jaw set. But her eyes were wide.

"I just wanted you to know . . ." Cassie took a deep, steadying breath. "If you ever want to talk, about anything—"

Heather's jaw relaxed, her eyes softened, but Cassie saw her flinch just the tiniest bit.

"—you know where to find me."

She didn't give Heather a chance to answer. She turned quickly, pulled the door open and slipped into the hall.

She replayed the scene over and over in her head as she got ready for bed, thinking of other things that she could have said, better things that she should have said. Her lips moved silently as she washed her face, tried out lines in the mirror that she would never speak.

Pulling the blankets up high around her neck, she turned off the lamp on her bedside table. The room descended into complete darkness for a moment, then light started to reassert itself: the red glow of her clock radio, the faint aura through the curtains.

In the darkness, she could hear faint music, the sound of Heather's radio next door. Cassie couldn't sleep with music on: she needed to be able to hear. The distant sounds of movement downstairs, her mom and dad, the breeze outside, the light rattling of her window.

She had spent so many nights lying here, listening, waiting. Dreading the soft creak of the floorboard just outside her door, that singsong whisper of her name. She needed the quiet before she went to sleep, to know that there was nothing out there waiting for her to doze off.

But this time it wasn't her name she was waiting to hear.

She lay in the dark, eyes wide, listening.

« »

The Darkness waited inside him as the police officers stepped toward the van, the headlights casting long shadows against the garage wall behind them.

He breathed heavily, almost panting, each breath frail and shaky. The red and blue lights behind the minivan arced and sprayed across the dashboard, swirling and dancing almost hypnotically, almost nauseatingly.

But he didn't break.

Not even when the cop stood outside the driver's-side door,

his feet wide apart, both hands on the pistol that was pointed directly at his head.

Not even when a second cop yelled at him to put his hands on the dashboard, not to move, just put his hands in front of him in plain sight.

His breath even slowed when the cop used his name

He almost smiled. They knew his name. They knew everything.

Of course they did.

Inside, the Darkness smiled. The Darkness fed.

« »

When the floorboard creaked, it wasn't outside of Heather's room.

Cassie's eyes snapped open. She hadn't heard the sound in years, but it all came flooding back to her in a merciless rush.

"No," she sobbed silently.

She couldn't move her mouth to cry out. She couldn't move at all. Hot tears spilled down her cheeks, and her chest shuddered. A pool of warmth formed under her hips, between her legs.

"No."

She couldn't breathe through the terror, her throat closed up in fear.

Not again.

Please, God, not again.

"No."

But yes, it was happening again. And she lay there listening, waiting, the silence like a rope around her throat, pulling tighter, tighter.

"Please."

Waiting.

Waiting until it felt like her heart might shred.

And then—

"Cassandra . . ."

The singsong voice was almost a relief.

Her doorknob rattled.

The door swung slowly, silently open.

≪ ≫

"Cassandra."

Cassie's eyes flashed open, her mouth opening in a scream as she glanced sharply around—too bright, too cold.

Cold.

The ground hard, unforgiving, the light high above her almost blinding.

"Are you—"

That voice.

She pulled herself back. She could move!

She pushed herself deeper into a corner.

"It's okay."

She choked back a sob, glanced around again. Metal. Brass. Almost above her head. Cold ground. Bright light. A face—

"Cassie, it's me."

—creased in concern.

She should know. The dislocation, the confusion. She should know.

Where was she? What—

"Cassie, it's okay."

It all came back to her in a rush. Concrete steps, bright light, handrail.

Doorway.

Victoria.

That face . . .

She dragged herself out of sleep like a swimmer too far from shore, her brain leaden, starved for air.

Victoria. Doorway. Face.

"Ali?"

"It's me, Cassie. It's me."

Every moment of wakefulness brought more pain. Her back was tied into a tight throbbing knot by the cold concrete and all of her muscles ached. Her hands—

She looked down.

Her hands were mottled pink and white. When she flexed her fingers, they roared in pain, waves of burning travelling up her arms.

Ali's eyes followed her gaze down to her hands, and when Cassie gasped, Ali's eyes widened.

"Come on," she said, leaning in clumsily and wrapping an arm around Cassie's back. "We have to get you warm."

Her touch inflamed a new burst of pain and Cassie pulled away, scrambling backward into the corner again, bracing herself against the wall next to the door, hands pulled tight to her body.

Ali jumped back. "I'm sorry. I'm—"

Cassie shook her head; she didn't stop. "It's not real. It's not real. It's not real," she whispered, over and over again. "It's not real."

"Cassie, I'm not going to hurt you."

"It's not real. It's not real."

"Cassie, we need to get you warmed up. You've got frostbite on your hands, and I'm worried about hypo—"

"It's not real. It's not real."

"Cassie." A thin, high sound of desperation threaded into Ali's voice. "Cassie, please."

She leaned forward again, slowly this time, with the careful caution one might use in trying to reach a scared kitten. "I'm not going to hurt you."

Cassie watched the shadow looming over her, coming closer, closer. "It's not real," she whispered, her voice breaking. "It's not real."

"Let me help you."

She flinched at Ali's first touch, but she didn't pull away. There was no place left for her to go.

"It's okay," Ali whispered. "I'm not going to hurt you."

She wrapped her arm over Cassie's shoulders and helped her slowly to her feet. Cassie's body screamed with pain, every muscle, every joint aching and burning. When her hand brushed the cold brass handrail, she gasped sharply.

"Here," Ali said, gently taking Cassie's forearm and raising it across Cassie's body. "Tuck your hands under your arms. Try to warm them up a little."

Cassie let Ali move her, manipulate her body. She felt like a doll being posed. She could move herself now, not like before, but she didn't have the strength to do more than breathe.

"Can you walk?" Ali asked, stepping down to the lower step. "Cassie?"

She didn't answer.

"Okay," Ali said. "You can lean on me." She guided Cassie toward her, pulling her close along her side, her arm, her shoulder. "Is that okay?"

Cassie lowered her head to rest it against Ali's shoulder. "Are you real?" she whispered.

But Ali didn't hear. "Okay," Ali said. "Let's get you warmed up."

« »

They staggered together through the downtown core. The streets were silent, the only people faint shadows picking at garbage cans or wheeling overloaded shopping carts or slumped in doorways. When a car passed, Cassie would flinch at the sudden roar, the blinding flash of lights, and Ali would pull her closer, whisper encouragement.

"What time is it?" she asked finally, her first words since leaving the doorway of the bookstore. The lights on the Legislature building were reflected in the surface of the Inner Harbour.

"Around seven, I think," Ali said, not sounding at all certain.

"In the morning?"

Ali smiled. "Yes, in the morning." Her voice was soft and kind.

Cassie looked at her. "Why . . . why are you out so early?"

Ali looked at her as if the question made no sense.

"I was looking for you."

« »

About fifteen minutes later, past the white-light outline of the Legislature and through the narrow streets on the other side of the Inner Harbour, Ali guided Cassie down the driveway of a three-storey house.

Rather than going up the front steps, Ali led Cassie to a door around the side, down two steps and flanked with two narrow windows, overhung with a small awning.

The lock popped open and Ali switched on the light.

Cassie's first impression was of warmth, not just the heat that enveloped her as Ali closed the door, but of the apartment itself.

"This is your place?"

"Home sweet home," she said, leading Cassie to a chair at the table, setting her down before pulling off her own coat and draping it over the chair next to her. Ali tugged off her boots and left them crumpled beside the table.

"Let's get you warmed up."

Stepping into the kitchen area, Ali took a clean towel out of a lower drawer and soaked it under the faucet. After wringing it dry, she refolded it and placed it in the microwave, which she set for one minute.

As the microwave roared, she stepped back to Cassie. "How are your hands feeling?"

"They hurt."

"They're probably going to hurt a lot more," she said, her voice soft but firm. "Here—" Taking Cassie's sleeves, she gently unfolded the girl's arms. "Try not to move your hands." With the gentlest of touches, she helped Cassie back to her feet.

She reached for the top of the zipper of Cassie's coat, but stopped. "Can I?"

Cassie hesitated, nodded.

Ali unzipped the coat and gently guided it off Cassie's shoulders, coaxing each arm out of its sleeve, careful to slip the cuffs wide around Cassie's hands, trying to avoid touching them as much as possible.

As Ali draped the coat over her own, Cassie shivered and reflexively folded her arms again, tucking her hands back into her armpits.

She couldn't stop shivering.

"Oh God," Ali said, turning in place to look at the timer on the microwave. "Let me get you a blanket. Here." And she guided Cassie back down into the chair. "I'll be right back," she said, touching Cassie gently on the shoulder before she raced away.

Cassie closed her eyes, tried to breathe through the waves of pain, but even her lungs were shivering, and her breath came in harsh, brittle jolts. She had thought that teeth chattering was just something you saw in movies or read about in books—the reality was far worse than she had imagined.

The darkness inside her eyelids burst with red and white spirals, orbs and shadows of colour and light that spun and twisted around one another. It was almost hypnotic, and Cassie felt herself starting to spin and turn. She had to open her eyes to keep from throwing up.

"Here we go," Ali said. "I've got a blanket for you."

She almost dropped the blanket as she reached out for the newspaper on the table beside Cassie, flipping it over and pushing it to the far side of the table almost in a single motion. "Sorry, that's just—"

But Cassie had already seen the front page, Skylark's school picture blown up and blurry under the headline "Runaway Murdered." She had just had time to read part of the next line, the words "police helpless," before Ali pulled the newspaper away.

It's not real.

"This should help," Ali said, as she draped the blanket over Cassie's shoulders, drew it tight around itself, around her. "I'm sorry about that," she said quietly as she tucked everything together around Cassie. "I didn't mean to leave that out."

"It's okay," Cassie said, feeling helpless herself. "The police—"

Slipping her arm out from the cocoon, she stretched across the table and pulled the newspaper toward herself, clumsily flipping it over without bending her fingers. The sight of Skylark twisted her heart. She had been so beautiful, so happy.

"She was my friend," she said, looking at the picture.

"I was wondering," Ali said, fixing the blanket again.

Cassie looked at her.

"When I saw the article—that's why I went looking for you this morning."

The microwave finished with three long beeps.

Ali turned back into the kitchen.

"To tell me?" Cassie asked, half-turning in the chair. "The police—"

Ali shook her head as she popped open the door to the microwave. "No," she said, fumbling with the hot towel, passing it quickly from hand to hand before dropping it on a plastic cutting board that had been leaning against the microwave. "I was worried about you."

Cassie wasn't sure if she had heard the words or imagined them.

"Here," Ali said, setting the cutting board on the table and picking up the steaming towel between the thumb and forefinger of each hand. "This is going to be hot. Hopefully not too hot."

She crouched in front of Cassie, delicately balancing the hot towel between her two hands. "Give me your hands," she said, lowering the blanket again.

Cassie considered for a moment before allowing her hands to emerge from within the safety of the blanket like two small, half-blind animals.

"I'm sorry," Ali said, cupping the towel and reaching for Cassie's hands. "This is going to hurt."

Cassie choked back a scream, inhaling sharply and clenching her jaw shut.

Ali glanced up at her face as she wrapped the length of the hot towel over Cassie's hands, snugging it firmly, but not too tightly around them.

"Sorry," she repeated. "We need to bring your skin temperature up fast, though, to minimize any damage."

"It's okay," Cassie managed, struggling to breathe through the pain. As the heat seeped into her hands, the pins and needles burned, searing, so much worse than the frostbite had been. She closed her eyes to focus on every breath.

"Okay," Ali said, mostly to herself. "Let me just—" She turned the water on, letting it run as she fumbled in the drawer beside the sink. "Can you take Advil?"

As Cassie nodded, her body was racked with an all-over shudder.

Ali filled a water glass from the tap; Cassie could see thin wisps of steam rising from it as she brought it back to her.

"Oh." Ali stood awkwardly in front of her, pills in one hand, the glass in the other. "How are we—"

Cassie opened her mouth, touched her tongue to the inside of her lower lip.

Ali looked as if she were about to speak. Instead, she placed the pills carefully on Cassie's tongue, then held the glass of warm water close to her mouth.

"It shouldn't be too hot," she warned.

Cassie took a small, careful sip. "It's all right," she said.

"Come on," Ali said, setting the glass on the table. "Let's get you lying down."

Without even thinking, Cassie rose slowly to her feet, guided and supported by Ali's soft touch on her back. She started toward the couch, but a soft pressure from Ali's hand shifted her toward the door at the end of the room.

"You might as well be comfortable," Ali said. "Here, sit." She directed Cassie toward the edge of the bed. "Let's get your shoes off."

Ali knelt at her feet, and struggled with the shoelaces. Through the haze of the pain, Cassie felt a flash of shame, imagining how her feet must smell, picturing the expression about to come over Ali's face.

But all Ali did was unlace her shoes and set them at the foot of the bed. "Come on," she said again, and she helped Cassie down onto the bed, unwrapping the blanket as she turned.

"You should tuck your hands under here," Ali said, lifting the edge of the pillow. "It's gonna hurt a bit."

Cassie didn't even notice.

The pillow was soft and warm, and smelled faintly of soap and shampoo. The thought of how long it had been since she had slept in a bed, the softness and warmth under her, was enough to make her cry.

"Let's just—" Ali laid the blanket over Cassie, then draped the covers gently over her, tucking them close under her chin.

Cassie could feel tears leaking from her eyes, spilling down her cheeks, soaking into the pillow.

"Is that all right?" Ali asked, stepping back from the bed.

Cassie nodded against the pillow, her eyelids suddenly, unexpectedly heavy.

"That'll help you warm up," Ali said, and then her voice softened even more. "You sleep for a bit. I'll be—"

"No," Cassie groaned, and Ali stopped.

"Could you—" The words were hard to form, harder to speak. "Could you please stay with me?"

Ali looked down at her for a moment. "Of course," she said quietly.

She crawled into the bed from the other side and nestled herself against Cassie's back. Her arm over her was a comfortable weight, and comfortingly weightless.

Cassie's eyelids barely responded to her attempt to hold them open. She blinked heavily, slowly, and wished all of this could be real.

She blinked again.

She blinked—

« »

The bus was noisy, the kids were shrieking, running up and down the aisle, ripping the air with high-pitched squeals and laughter.

"Jesus," Cassie muttered, rubbing her temples. "What the hell—"

Laura touched Cassie's leg comfortingly. "It's just the snow. Little kids always flip out on the first day it snows."

Snow? That didn't seem—

But Laura was right: all the kids were in snowsuits and toques, mittens hanging from strings. The aisle was a slurried muck of melting snow and mud. Outside the bus windows, the landscape was white, vaguely unfamiliar.

"What's up with you?" Laura asked. "You look like you're—"

"Just a headache," she said. "I didn't really sleep . . ." She could barely remember the dream, let alone talk about it.

"Did you take something for it?"

Cassie almost laughed. "What, you're a doctor now?"

Laura shoved her with her shoulder. "Screw you."

Cassie flinched at the jostling, pulled away.

"Sorry," Laura said, as if she had been reprimanded, and she slid farther away on the seat, closer to the window.

"It's okay," Cassie said. "I'm just not feeling good."

Laura nodded. "You can lie down in the nurse's room if you're—"

That hadn't even occurred to her. "I might do that."

She had never been in the nurse's room. Some kids did it all the time: kids who wanted to get out of class, girls with cramps who didn't want to run laps, kids waiting for their parents to pick them up.

But her mom didn't send them to school sick. If she or Heather wasn't feeling well, Mom would make them soup or cinnamon toast sticks, build a nest for them on the couch.

So why hadn't she—

"You can put your coat and shoes in the cubby," the nurse was saying, pointing to the shelves on the wall. "Do you want some water?"

"Yes, please," Cassie said, sitting down at the edge of the bed to pull her boots off. It was an automatic process, pull and tug, but she stopped. There was something wrong with her right boot.

Slipping her hand along her shin, she slid her fingers into the top of her boot.

There was something there, something hard. It took a bit of stretching before she could pinch it between her fingertips, pull it up far enough that she could wrap her fingers around the cool thickness and pull it out.

She knew what it was. She had always known.

The kitchen knife felt comfortable in her hand, warming and welcome. It caught the light, and there was a reflection of her eyes in the blade.

At first, she couldn't identify the sound, a distant, vaguely metallic blur of voices and noise. As soon as she realized "television," though, the voices came into focus, and it filled her with warmth. TV. She'd just lie there a little longer, then go downstairs to see Mom and Dad and Heather.

But . . .

Her heart began to speed up.

This wasn't her room.

The winter light through the blue curtains made the whole space seem to glow: the walls, with paintings and posters. The dresser, glossy white. The books along the windowsill.

She had never seen any of it before, but somehow it felt familiar.

A towel was crumpled into a damp spot beside the pillow.

She sat up and looked at her hands. They were pink and tender, but there were no blisters, no angry white patches anymore. The screaming pins and needles were gone, but . . . Taking a deep breath, she bent her fingers, slowly at first. No pain. There was a dull, throbbing ache, like a tired muscle, but no real pain, not even when she clenched her fists.

She smiled and stood up, eager to tell Ali the good news.

It was only as she stepped toward the door that everything came flooding back to her: Ali's place.

Ali had come looking for her, in the dark.

How do you thank someone for that? What do you even say?

Ali had said that she had come looking for her because she was worried after reading about Skylark in the paper.

No, not Skylark. Laura.

But . . .

Laura wasn't dead.

Cassie had just seen her. They had been on the bus, and Laura had gone with her to the office to ask for the nurse . . .

It was just a dream.

Blood vessels started to throb behind her temples, the first distant thunder of a headache coming on.

Coming back.

It felt like the headache from her dream. She should talk to the nurse . . .

Cassie shook her head, trying to clear it.

It was just a dream.

How many times had she said that?

How often had it actually been true?

Don't think about it.

She could tell the difference now. That was the main thing that Dr. Livingston had taught her, the first thing: how to tell dreams from real life.

The doctor's goal had been to have Cassie learn two things. First, dreams are not true. And second, dreams cannot hurt you.

That was what had saved her.

It was just a dream.

And dreams cannot hurt me.

Taking a deep breath, she turned back to the bed and lifted the blanket that Ali had first wrapped around her. How long ago had that been?

The blanket was thick cotton, with a pattern of what looked like storybook characters on it. *Anne of Green Gables? The Wizard of Oz?* It was too faded for her to really tell. The blanket was old—maybe it had been Ali's when she was little.

She lifted the corner of the blanket to her cheek and rubbed it gently against her skin. She closed her eyes and held the cloth to her face.

At the sound of a throat clearing in the other room, she opened her eyes. Draping the blanket over her shoulders like a cape, and with no idea what she was going to say, she stepped out of the bedroom.

Ali was sprawled on the couch, her legs extended over the coffee table, next to a stack of books. Dressed head to toe in black—T-shirt, jeans, socks—she looked like a shadow on the pale couch.

"Hi," Cassie said awkwardly from the bedroom doorway.

Ali straightened up and turned to her. "Oh, hey. I was just going to come wake you." She patted the couch next to her. "Come here, sit down. How are you doing?"

Cassie shuffled over and nestled into the couch next to Ali. "I'm okay, I guess. Strange dreams. I'm sorry I slept so long." Though she had no idea how long she had been asleep.

Ali smiled. "You should sleep as much as you can. Get your strength back."

"Oh." Cassie wondered what she had missed. "I thought I'd slept too much. I thought you said you were going to wake me up."

"Oh, no," Ali said, smiling and shaking her head. "No, I was going to get you up to see this." She pointed at the TV.

"What is it?"

Ali picked up the remote control and turned up the volume. "Breaking news. They think they've caught the guy."

On the television, a heavy-set man was talking to a crowd of reporters. "What guy?"

"The killer," Ali said, nodding toward the television. "That's the police spokesman there."

Cassie's throat closed and she struggled to breathe.

Between the news and Ali's answers to what she had missed, Cassie was able to piece together a very sketchy sense of what was going on. There weren't many details: the police had apprehended a suspect (but they weren't releasing a name), there was compelling physical evidence (but they weren't saying what), and they felt confident (but there would be more information later in the afternoon). It wasn't much, but when Ali was finished, Cassie could only sag into the couch, shaking her head.

"Wow," was all she could say.

"I know, right?" Ali said, not skeptically, but somehow incredulous.

"When did this happen?"

Ali pointed at the screen. "Right now," she said, and Cassie noticed for the first time the word "Live" in the upper corner of the picture.

They watched the rest of the press conference in silence, then Ali reached up with the remote control and turned off the TV. They both sat there, staring at the dark screen.

"Well, that's good news," Ali said finally, looking at Cassie for a reaction.

"Yeah," Cassie said absently, wondering who the police had picked up, thinking back to her dreams. She knew what was real now, and what wasn't; Dr. Livingston had taught her that.

And she remembered the way the knife had felt, slipping into Sarah's throat, the way her blood had hissed as it hit the cold ground, the way Skylark's eyes had gone wide, the look of shock and betrayal there before they went dark.

"I wonder who they arrested?" she thought aloud.

"Well, he was probably the nicest guy. Polite to the neighbours but kept to himself. Spent a lot of time in the basement." There was a strange half smile on Ali's face, and it took Cassie a moment to realize that she was making a joke. "Sorry," Ali said, her face reddening. "Sometimes I make jokes when I'm—"

Cassie shook her head. "You're probably right."

Ali frowned. "Yeah," she said. "Hey!" She reached toward Cassie's hands, then stopped herself. "Can I—"

"Sure."

"How do they feel?" she asked as she lifted Cassie's right hand gently from her lap, looking at it in the light.

"Good," Cassie said, nodding, and Ali repeated the examination with her left hand. "A little achy, like a muscle cramp, but that's it."

"Oh good," Ali said, setting Cassie's hand back down and turning herself slightly on the couch so she was facing Cassie. "I'm glad. I was worried."

There was that word again: "worried." She still didn't know how to respond to it.

"How long was I asleep for?" she asked, trying to change the subject without being too obvious about it.

Ali glanced at the clock on the kitchen wall. "A few hours," she said. "I'm surprised you're up so soon."

"I don't sleep very much."

Ali looked at her like she had a question, but she didn't ask it. "I was going to leave you a note when I went to work," she said. "And just let you sleep. You know, 'food in fridge, help yourself. The shower faucets are backward, so don't scald yourself.' That sort of thing."

Cassie straightened up, found herself looking at the clock as well. "Oh. You have to go to work."

Ali nodded, started to rise. "And I'd better get a move on.

I got distracted by the news." She smiled and stepped around the coffee table.

Cassie struggled to her feet. "I'll just—" She gestured toward the bedroom. "I think my shoes are—"

"You don't—"

"Is it okay if "

"Cassie, you don't have to—"

"—brush my teeth real quick before—"

"Cassie."

The flat force of her name on Ali's lips stopped her short.

Ali smiled at her. "You can stay here when I go to work."

"But I—"

Ali shook her head. "It's ugly outside—there's no reason for you to be out there if you don't have to be." She leaned her head forward, waiting for a response. "Okay?" she prompted.

"Okay," Cassie said, nodding slowly.

Ali smiled widely, all the way to her eyes. "Good." She sounded almost excited by the idea. "Now," she said, looking at the clock again, "I'm going to be late if I don't haul ass. But you make yourself at home, okay? There's food in the fridge, fruit on the table. There's stuff for you on the bathroom counter. It's a great tub if you want to have a long bath." Her words were speeding up as she bustled around the apartment, pulling on her jacket and boots, picking up her purse, tucking her keys into her pocket.

She paused. "Are you all right?" she asked. "I could—"

Cassie shook her head, struggled to find words. "No, I'm okay. It's just . . . It's all a bit . . ."

Ali nodded, frowning sympathetically. "Yeah," she said. "I can't even imagine." She wrinkled her face into a smile that couldn't quite hide her concern. "You just take it easy, all right?

Have some breakfast, have a bath, maybe sleep a bit more?" She pulled open the door and a wave of cold broke over the kitchen, stole Cassie's breath.

Cassie nodded and Ali stepped into the winter bright, pulling the door closed behind her. A few seconds later there was a faint jangling of keys and a solid thunk as the lock turned.

« »

In the warm, enveloping silence, Cassie released a breath she hadn't known she had been holding. It was all too much to process, almost too much to bear.

She had no idea what to do. She felt frozen to the spot.

She looked around the room. Pictures hung on every wall. Paintings. A small row of cookbooks ran along a ledge on the kitchen wall; a larger bookshelf and a desk, cluttered with books, were at the end of the room, past the point where the kitchen gave way to the living room area with the couch and TV. There were small sculptures on every surface and mixed in with the books on the shelves.

Taking a deep breath, she padded over to the kitchen table and sat down in the same chair she had sat in earlier that morning. Pulling the newspaper toward her, she started to read the story about Skylark on the front page.

What she hadn't known before was buried deep in the article, almost at the end. Two paragraphs about how Laura Ensley had grown up in Campbell River, how she had been a good student, popular with other students and liked by her teachers. How her parents—who were coming to Victoria to "claim their daughter's remains"—had no insight into why she had run away, but an unidentified police source had suggested there had been an open Ministry investigation into possible abuse at the time she left.

She dropped the paper back onto the table, wondering if Harrison might be the unidentified source. She thought he might be: it was the sort of thing she could see him doing.

But what was she going to do? She considered taking a bath, like Ali had suggested, but the thought of having to get back into her grungy clothes was too much. There was a washer and dryer in the corner by the door; she could wash her clothes, but what would she wear while they were drying? She could eat, but it felt wrong to be going through someone's cupboards while they weren't home, even if she had been told to. She was still bone-tired: she could lie back down again, but that didn't seem right either.

And she didn't want to risk going back to sleep.

The more she thought about it, the smaller the room seemed. It felt like it was shrinking around her, the walls tightening in, the ceiling lowering, pressing down on her. She could feel it in her chest, a tightness in her ribs that was making it hard to breathe, and she realized she was bouncing one leg, the vibrations travelling all the way up through her, a hum in her teeth, in the clenched muscles of her jaw.

She stood up, turned in a full circle trying to catch her breath. Ali had put her shoes neatly by the door; she hopped as she pulled them on. Then her coat, doing it up tight to her throat. Her backpack was there, her scarf crumpled on top of it. Without thinking, she grabbed a pair of the stretchy gloves out of the basket by the door as she looped the scarf around her neck. Hefting her backpack onto her shoulder, she pulled open the door, taking one last warm breath before the cold rolled in.

«»

It took Cassie a while to find her way back downtown; the streets of James Bay were a maze of blind corners and tiny alleys, narrow lanes and sharp turns. The weight and sense of confinement she had been feeling in Ali's apartment followed her. The whole world was closing in. She walked faster and faster, then started running, her breath ragged, rough silver clouds that broke against her face. The dampness steamed and froze in the cold, the bitter wind coming off the water cutting through her clothes, chilling her again.

She let herself stop when she got to the Legislature, collapsing onto the bench inside a bus shelter, panting, out of the wind.

The feeling of imprisonment slowly dissipated: through the glass shelter wall, she could see the world opening up, the Harbour on one side of the road, the silvered lawns of the Empress Hotel on the other.

Her breathing slowed.

She never would have guessed that she would ever find downtown Victoria—this miserable place, these sidewalks and street corners—comforting, but she did. It was home, these hidden corners, these doorways. These streets.

Home.

It was almost a full minute before the truth of the previous days collapsed on her: Skylark was gone.

She couldn't go back to the camp.

She couldn't stay at Ali's.

She couldn't put anyone else at risk.

But she had nowhere to go.

She was completely alone.

Glancing from side to side, Cassie pulled her knees to her chest, hid her face.

You could call home. You could go home.

The thought came in Harrison's voice, like a punch to the stomach.

She cursed the cop: she had been doing so well, pushing down any thought of home, and now it was all she could think about: her mother's face, Heather's beseeching, uncomprehending look.

She shook her head. Going home just wasn't an option. It never had been.

Tears stung at the corners of her eyes.

"No," she whispered firmly. "No, no, no."

She thought of how worried they would be, how scared for her.

"No."

She could call. She could go home.

"No."

They would know what she had done to her father. And what she might do next.

"No."

She struggled with a sob as the force of that single thought crushed all of the other memories, destroyed any doubt.

She couldn't go home.

She stood up, stepped back into the wind.

« »

She kept the change in the hat in front of her to exactly five dollars, a mixture of coins to give the illusion that other people were generous, a subtle hint to those passing on their way into the courthouse.

It wasn't really working.

She scooped any new coins out of the hat as soon as the person who threw them in was out of sight; keeping the change to exactly five dollars made it easy to keep track of how much people were putting in. After two hours, she had only a couple of dollars to show for the time.

That, and a frozen bum and a chill that ached all the way up her spine and spread to her kidneys.

She had looked for someplace to sit on one of the main streets as she walked through downtown. The sidewalks were clotted with Christmas shoppers, smiling, bustling along with bags. The courthouse, she knew, was too far away from most of the crowds, and people going into the building—or coming out—likely had their own reasons not to be generous.

But anywhere she looked on Government and Douglas, anywhere that looked remotely promising, already had someone sitting there, hat brimming with silver and scattered bills. A few of them, people who recognized her from the camp, smiled at her as they saw her slowing down, but she kept moving. The others just looked at her warily, not releasing their gaze until she sped up and moved on.

So she had ended up back at the courthouse. Safe, quiet. Far from the drama of the busier streets. And the spot that Skylark had found for her was mostly sheltered from the wind.

Mostly.

A darkness seemed to hover over her: this spot would always feel like Skylark to her. She spent the hours there half-expecting her to suddenly appear, to drop to the ground next to her, smiling and laughing.

But then, was there anywhere in the city that didn't feel like that?

"Thank you," she called out after a woman in a business suit who had thrown what sounded like a good handful of coins into her hat without really looking at her, hustling away before the change even landed.

Cassie knew better than to get her hopes up, but she was still disappointed to find—after sifting out the new change—that the noisy handful amounted to exactly thirty-eight cents.

She tucked the money into her pocket; it was better than nothing.

"Hey."

She glanced up sharply at the voice, bile rising in her throat. A short ways down the block, Harrison and his partner had seen her.

Cassie shaded her eyes with her hand. The grey sky was surprisingly bright, like sunlight on metal. She wondered how long it had been like that. She wondered how long it had been since she had actually looked up.

"Come on," Harrison said. "We'll buy you a hot chocolate."

She looked at them warily, swallowed thickly.

Harrison extended his hand to help her to her feet.

"We need to talk to you," Farrow said. There was a faint look of discomfort on her face as she spoke. "About your friend."

Of course. She had known they would be coming.

She looked at them for a moment, then lowered the hand from her eyes. "All right," she said. "Sure."

She ignored Harrison's hand, carefully pocketing her change and stashing the hat into the top of her backpack before creaking to her feet.

It took her a moment to straighten up fully—her bum and

back crackled with pins and needles, and she could almost hear a popping sound as she unbent.

"So where should we go?" Farrow asked.

"What about the place where—"

"There's a little deli around the corner," Harrison interrupted, giving her a look. Clearly she wasn't supposed to talk about seeing him off-duty a few days earlier.

"Is that all right?" Farrow asked Cassie, in a tone that suggested her answer didn't really matter either way.

Neither of the officers spoke as they walked toward the deli. Partway along the block, Cassie noticed that they had shifted so they were walking on either side of her, boxing her in. They both just stared straight ahead, jaws firm, faces set.

Clearly they didn't want her to run.

In the deli, she sat down across the table from Harrison while Farrow went to the counter for their drinks.

She didn't know if she should say anything; the ice seemed too thick for mere words to break.

"We've got a picture we would like you to look at," Harrison said as he stirred sugar into his coffee. Farrow had pulled a third chair up to the table.

"Jesus," Cassie muttered, shaking her head. "There's always pictures." Thinking of how clean Skylark had looked on her school ID. The grey chill of her skin in the other photo.

Farrow's face wrinkled. "Sorry about that."

"Hopefully this is the last time," Harrison said, setting his spoon on a napkin on the table and reaching into his jacket.

He slid the photograph across the table to her. "Do you know this man?"

Gorge surged to the top of her throat, and Cassie had to swallow quickly to keep from throwing up.

She nodded. "Yes," she said, carefully, staring down at the picture.

Harrison glanced at Farrow, then back to Cassie.

"Are you sure?"

Cassie nodded, then looked up at Harrison. "Yes, I'm sure. Why?" she asked slowly, already knowing the answer, still fighting not to throw up.

Harrison seemed about to speak, but Farrow cut in. "How do you know him?"

Cassie glanced between them, then back to the photograph. "I think he works in the courthouse," she said carefully. "He said his name was Cliff Wolcott."

It was the first time she had ever seen him not dressed in a coat and tie: in the picture, he was wearing a black T-shirt, and his hair was messy. His face, though. His eyes. His eyes were cold, sharp, staring directly into the camera lens, directly at her.

On the white wall behind him, black lines and numbers. Measurements.

"Is that him? Is that the guy?"

Another glance between the cops, and Harrison nodded. "He was arrested at about 2:30 this morning. He's the main suspect in—"

It sounded like he was reading from a script. He broke off, shaking his head. "Yeah, it's him. We arrested him at home. In his driveway."

"What?"

Harrison nodded. "He tried to pick up a girl, and she says she got a weird vibe off him, so she refused to go. He apparently got threatening, and the girl called in his plates. The vehicle matched the partial description in witness testimony from a couple of the murders. So we staked out his place, waited for him to get home."

He shook his head, inhaled a ragged breath.

"Chris," Farrow said, and Cassie thought she heard a note of warning in her voice.

"We had to get his family out of the house before he got home," he said, staring at the table. Farrow shook her head, sighed and leaned back in her chair. "Two little kids. Girls. His wife. We were worried that he might—"

"He's exhausted," Farrow said, and it took Cassie a beat to realize that she was talking about Harrison, not Wolcott.

"We were worried that this guy might use his wife and kids as hostages if we didn't get them out of there." Harrison sagged in his chair.

Cassie had no idea how to react. It wasn't Wolcott, she knew that.

So why did they think it was?

"But his family is okay?" she ventured.

Harrison nodded. "His wife is pretty freaked out."

"You would be too," Farrow said. "Woke up in the middle of the night, whisked out of your house, told that this person you love is probably a murderer."

Cassie tried to push down the bile she felt rising again, thinking of how her mother had been, after.

"'Probably'?" She seized on the word.

Farrow glanced at Harrison, sipping now from his coffee. "We have to say that," she explained. "Probably. Allegedly. Guardedly. All the legal bull—" She cut herself off. "He's our guy."

Harrison was almost the same white as his coffee cup.

"How . . . ," she started, not even really sure of what she wanted to ask. "How do you know for sure?"

"There was evidence in the vehicle that suggested—"
Harrison cut Farrow off.

"He had a kill room in the back of the van," he said quickly, anger biting through the raggedness in his voice. "He had a plastic drop cloth, like you buy in the hardware store, with the paintbrushes. He had it taped up to the walls of the van. The van. The fucking minivan."

"Chris," Farrow said sharply, but Harrison didn't stop. "He was killing girls in his minivan. With two car seats in the garage—"

"Chris!" Farrow said again, in a tone so sharp that Harrison stopped in mid-sentence. His eyes were bright, darting from side to side, sunk into deep, dark hollows.

"You need to go," Farrow said firmly, half-rising from her chair. "Walk around the block. Splash some water on your face. Take up smoking. I don't care. But you need to pull yourself together, or I'm going to have to file a report, okay?" Her voice softened as she spoke, the caring starting to show. "And you know how much I hate paperwork, right?" She looked like she was forcing a smile.

His face twisted into a grimace that bore only a passing resemblance to a smile. "Yeah," he said, nodding, his eyes still haunted, furtive. "Gotcha, boss. I know how much you hate reports."

He rose to his feet, bracing himself against the back of his chair as he looked around the restaurant, his gaze finally stopping at a doorway at the far end of the counter from the cashier. "I'll just—"

Farrow nodded. "Take your time. Us girls will be fine."

They both watched him as he shambled across the deli. He seemed smaller than Cassie remembered. Older. Like an old house, starting to fall in on itself.

"He's not usually like this," Farrow said, turning back to the table. "This whole thing has taken a lot out of him."

The woman's voice was stripped of her usual brusqueness.

"Yeah," Cassie said, sipping at the hot chocolate.

"He'll be okay. It's just . . . we all have cases that get to us. You never know when it's going to happen, but sometimes it gets under your skin, and . . ." She shook her head helplessly. "He'll be fine, though." She sounded like she was trying to convince herself.

"What was it that—"

"Set him off?"

Cassie nodded.

"Well, he hasn't been sleeping. Night shifts are bad at the best of times, and everything's messed up with Christmas coming, so there's that already. He's exhausted. And I think the kids were the last straw for him. He's having trouble wrapping himself around the idea that a father could do something like that." She sipped her coffee, scowled at it. "Which is ridiculous, considering some of the things we've seen. But—he's tired. And he's been worried the last while." She took another sip of her coffee. "About you."

The words landed on the table between them and exploded like a firecracker in Cassie's face.

"Me? What?" She shook her head. "That doesn't—"

Farrow shrugged. "I know. It makes no sense. No offence, but it's not like there's not a couple of dozen other teenage girls on the street at any given time."

It didn't even occur to Cassie to be offended: it was a statement of fact, nothing more.

"He's a dad. I think he imagines his daughters in a few years when he sees you. And these murders—" She glanced at the doorway that Harrison had disappeared into. "All young girls. Like you. Like his daughters in a few years." She shrugged. "I guess it's hard to be a father."

Cassie dropped her gaze to the table, refusing to meet Farrow's eye.

But that didn't stop her. "Cassie, your dad—"

She shook her head sharply.

"Cassie."

"I don't want to talk about him."

The officer took a deep breath.

"Fine," she said. "All right. This isn't about you anyhow."

Cassie almost snorted in disbelief.

Farrow shrugged. "I think he sees something in you. That's all." She took another swallow of coffee. "It's all over now, though. Hopefully he'll be able to get some sleep, enjoy his Christmas."

"Is it?" Cassie asked, before she could stop herself. "Is it really over?"

"Oh yeah," Farrow said, as if there wasn't a doubt in her mind. "This guy . . ." She shook her head. "We went through his office. Crown Counsel's office, can you believe that? That's gonna make for a nightmare when it comes to trial. Anyway, not my problem. So we go through this guy's office . . . We've got him. He's the guy."

Cassie looked down at the photograph again.

"He was always . . ." She shifted in the chair, thought about the folded bill in her pocket. "He was kind to me."

Farrow blinked slowly and her jaw twitched.

"Yeah," she muttered.

"That doesn't happen very much."

Farrow shook her head and turned the photograph to face her on the table.

"Your friend Laura. Did she ever mention him?" She tapped the picture. "Do you think their paths ever crossed?"

Cassie started to speak, stopped herself. No, Skylark had never mentioned Cliff Wolcott.

And she knew, as sure as she could taste the blood in her mouth, that their paths had never crossed. Not even at the end.

"I don't think so," she said carefully. "I mean, he might have seen her, but she never said anything."

"So what are we talking about?"

Cassie jumped at the sound of Harrison's voice, at the sudden shadow he cast over the table.

His face was slightly pink now, and he looked a bit fresher, like he had taken to heart Farrow's advice to splash some water on his face. His eyes were calmer, less frantic looking, but they were still ringed with deep grey, almost black circles. Cassie could see the exhaustion that Farrow had been talking about.

"About Skylark. She never . . . ," she started, only to discover that she had no idea how to finish that sentence. She wanted to say something comforting, something to let him know that he didn't need to worry about her. "So, it's over."

He nodded slowly and picked up the photograph. "So it would seem," he said quietly, staring at Cliff Wolcott's face.

Then nothing else.

Cassie glanced at Farrow. The cop shrugged slightly.

"So . . . ," Cassie started, trying to draw him out.

"Tell me what you know about Cliff Wolcott," he said, laying the photograph back on the table. His voice was cool and calm: he sounded like a cop again, like a switch had been flicked. "When did you first encounter him?"

He pulled his notebook and pen out of his pocket and waited for Cassie to speak.

« »

By the time Cassie left the deli, it was already getting dark, the sky fading to the colour of a ripe bruise. Harrison and Farrow had offered her a ride, but she'd turned them down.

She had left them in the doorway to the deli without really saying goodbye. She slipped on the stretchy gloves she had taken from Ali's basket and willed herself not to look back.

When she did dare a glance, as she turned the next corner, they were both still looking at her, watching her walk away.

The temperature had fallen as the sun dropped below the horizon, but the wind had stilled, so it wasn't as blindingly cold as it had been earlier. It wasn't exactly warm, but it was certainly better.

As she walked, she mentally cursed the two cops. She had missed the afternoon rush out of the courthouse. When she got back to her spot, the sidewalk was deserted.

Ah, well. It hadn't been a particularly lucrative day, even when the sun had been up.

She changed direction, turned toward downtown.

No money, or not enough to make a difference.

She thought for a moment of going to the restaurant. To Ali. But she couldn't.

Or could she?

It was all so confusing—she remembered what had happened so vividly. It couldn't have been a dream. If she thought about it, even for a moment, she could smell the rusty, metallic tang of Skylark's blood, taste it in the back of her throat.

How could she have dreamed that?

How could her mind have invented something that horrible?

But the police had caught the killer. Cliff Wolcott had killed all those girls. They had arrested him; they had proof.

And that meant she hadn't killed Skylark.

It meant that Sarah had really killed herself.

It all came back to the dreams again.

It always came back to the dreams.

But she could remember so much, the tiniest of details. The way the blood hissed on the cold concrete, the steam rising from her hands . . .

She stopped in the middle of the sidewalk, facing the brightly cluttered window of a games store, and tried not to scream.

She took several deep breaths, counting, trying to calm herself down. People passed around her, cutting large arcs in their paths to avoid the crazy girl on the sidewalk.

Breathe. Breathe.

Breathe through the confusion. Slow down.

She knew how to deal with it. She had gone through it all with Dr. Livingston.

Breathe.

Think it through.

Cassie struggled to remember exactly what she had said.

"Permeable." That was the word Dr. Livingston had used.

The subconscious is permeable.

She had explained what she meant using the example of a screen that sifted materials as it allowed them in, but Cassie couldn't shake the image of a sponge, a sponge that soaked everything up, everything Cassie saw or touched or tasted, even things she wasn't aware of. It sucked everything up.

And dreaming was what happened when the sponge was squeezed. All this stuff came pouring out, all mixed together.

When she had told the doctor about the sponge, Livingston

had leaned forward excitedly. "That's excellent, Cassandra. That really gives us something to work with."

That had made sense.

Together they had explored how Cassie's mind worked, how the night terrors happened when her mind was moving from one level of sleep to another. She wasn't really paralyzed; her body was just shut down while she slept. No matter how realistic it seemed, it was just a dream.

That was why there had never been any blood on her sheets when she woke up. Why the bruises and welts never showed up in the daylight.

But that hadn't answered all of her questions: that had only been the beginning.

Over a period of months, years, they had broken down Cassie's dreams second by excruciating second. At first, she had been terrified to live those dreams over and over, no matter how safe Dr. Livingston's office felt.

But the doctor had held her hand—literally, sometimes— as they had talked through her dreams. For each image, the two of them developed lengthy analyses.

Fear of the dark is mankind's oldest fear was how the explanations started.

Cassie didn't always understand everything that Dr. Livingston said, but the fact that there was some sort of explanation, some rational process behind them, seemed to rob the dreams of much of their power.

She had even talked to Cassie about lucid dreaming, about people who could actually control their dreams and not just get dragged along by them, but Cassie had never quite figured out how to make that work.

As she walked past the Eaton Centre, she imagined talking

through everything that had happened with Dr. Livingston.

She hadn't killed Skylark. Realistic or not, it was just a dream.

The police had arrested a man for killing young girls—girls about the same age as Skylark. As her.

She had read about the murders in the papers. They had talked about it at the camp. Sarah had been freaked out about it.

She pictured the sponge sucking it all up: the killings, the victims, their ages, how they were killed, all absorbed. The fear that seemed to be hovering over everything. The helplessness that she had been feeling.

All absorbed.

And then squeezed back out as dreams: A girl killed. A girl she knew, dead. And herself, not helpless anymore. Guilty, but in control.

It all made a sick kind of sense.

Without even realizing it, she had been walking north along Government. The dragons on the gate marking the entrance to Chinatown surprised her when she looked up, but not really.

That was probably her subconscious too.

She almost smiled as she walked down the block toward the restaurant, skirting the bins of fruits and vegetables spilling out of shops, dodging Christmas shoppers too focused on getting home to veer even momentarily from their paths.

Ali was sitting at the table closest to the counter at the back of the restaurant. She smiled widely and started to rise as Cassie opened the door.

« »

On their way back to Ali's apartment, they walked close enough that their hands occasionally brushed.

"Have you lived here all your life?" They were walking so quickly that Cassie's lungs were starting to ache. It seemed odd to her: she had done nothing but walk around for weeks, but clearly there was a difference when there was actually a destination involved. It had been a long time since she had had somewhere to go.

"Born and raised," she said, and Cassie was oddly pleased to hear a hint of roughness in Ali's voice now too. "In that very house, actually."

"Really?" Cassie tried to picture a family living in Ali's place. It wasn't overly small, but it didn't seem big enough for a mother and father and a little girl.

"Yeah. My parents still own it, but they've got a place at Shawnigan now. We did some renos, broke the house up into three suites." Cassie nodded. That made more sense. "They're letting me stay in the basement suite while I'm in school. I don't have to pay rent so long as I look after the place."

"School?" Cassie asked. "You mean like university?"

Ali nodded. "Visual arts up at UVic. Painting and sculpture mainly."

Cassie thought about the art on the walls of the apartment, the tiny sculptures on every surface. It was like a light going on in her head. "The paintings at your place. Are they—"

"Some of them," she said. "Some of them are from friends. We all look out for one another, support each other when we can." She paused, and when she spoke again there was a different tone to her voice. "You can meet them," she said. "Tomorrow night."

"What's tomorrow night?"

"The beggars' banquet," Ali said.

"Is that—" Cassie started. She didn't want to seem like an idiot, but she didn't think she had ever heard of a beggars' banquet, aside from on an old record in her father's collection. "I don't know what that is."

Ali smiled. "It's not really a thing. It's just something that my friends and I came up with. Every year between the solstice and Christmas, we have a big dinner, like a potluck." Cassie nodded. "It's really nice."

Cassie tried to picture a houseful of friends hanging out and laughing.

In her mind, she saw Laura grinning and laughing.

She shook her head sharply, trying to make the thought go away. No—that had been a dream.

She pictured the sponge in her mind.

Just a dream.

"Are you all right?" Ali was looking at her.

"Yeah," she said, too quickly. "I'm just cold."

Ali smiled. "We're almost there."

They walked in silence along the Inner Harbour, the lights of the Legislature floating in the still black water, shimmering like a Christmas tree. It was hard to believe that the camp was just a block or two away, a different world.

"Listen," Ali said finally, slowly. "I know that they've arrested that guy."

Cassie thought back to her conversation with Harrison and Farrow, the look of haunted, exhausted desperation in Harrison's eyes. "Yeah."

"But—"

Cassie waited.

"I just wanted to tell you that, even so, if you wanted to

crash at my place for a while . . ." She didn't look at Cassie as she spoke, and her words were measured, almost to the point of awkwardness.

"I—"

"Don't say no right away, okay?" Ali said quickly, cutting her off. This time she looked at Cassie, a sidelong stare that she held as she continued. "I'm worried about you. That's really it. And it's not just that your friend . . ." She shook her head, turned her attention back to the sidewalk. "When I found you this morning, I thought you had frozen to death. Or had hypothermia. You weren't even . . ." Another head shake. "The thought of you sleeping in a doorway . . ."

The worry in Ali's voice warmed her more than the towel wrapped around her hands that morning had.

She wouldn't hurt Ali. She wouldn't. It had been the dreams, nothing more.

"I can sleep on the couch," Ali continued. "And you can have the bedroom . . ."

"I can take the couch," Cassie blurted. Her cheeks began to warm.

Ali turned to her. "Really?"

Cassie shrugged. "It'll be a lot more comfortable than a lot of places I've slept."

Ali laughed. "No, I mean, really, you'll stay?"

"I'd like to," Cassie said, hoping Ali couldn't hear just how much. "If it's not too much trouble."

Ali reached over and touched Cassie's forearm, squeezed it slightly. "It's no trouble at all. The place isn't very big, though."

"That's all right," Cassie said, a smile starting to form at the corners of her mouth. "I don't have a lot of stuff."

Their laughter echoed over the water, into the dark.

"You can go home, you know."

Harrison jumped at the voice behind him. His first instinct was to cover up the papers on his desk, to change his screen over to something more banal, but it was too late: Farrow would have already seen.

"I know," he said. He gestured helplessly at the files and reports on his desk, knowing that she, of all people—the one who did the bulk of their reports—wouldn't be convinced.

"Chris," she said, her voice low, somewhere between concerned and warning.

She had already changed out of her uniform, and her winter coat was zipped at the bottom. "It's just the arrest report," he said, as if that made any difference.

She nodded.

"I just wanted—"

"We got him," she said.

"I know," he said.

"Then what are you doing? They've got a whole crew upstairs going over this stuff. It's gonna stick. There's not a chance he walks on this. Not after—"

He nodded. "I know," he repeated. The stories had been making the rounds of the station all day, rumours of just what they had found in the freezer. None of the detectives were saying anything, but that didn't do anything to slow the rumours down. "I just—"

"Go home," she said.

She took a step forward and crouched in front of him, putting one hand on his knee. "Seriously," she said. "Go home. See your family. Have a drink or six. Or more." She squeezed his knee. "God knows you could use a good black-out drunk right about now."

He forced a smile. "That sounds good," he said.

She rose to her feet, but she didn't step back. Looming over him, she said, "Come on, then. I'll wait while you change and walk you out."

He started to speak, but his eyes returned to the desk, to the computer screen.

She saw the look.

"Yeah," she said. She shook her head.

"I won't be long," he said. "I just want to . . ."

He wasn't sure what came at the end of that sentence. She was right: it was all sewn up. They had the guy.

There was something about the reports, though, something that bothered him; he just wasn't sure what.

But Farrow wasn't waiting for his answer. She was already turning away.

≪ ≫

"Jesus," Ali said, pulling the door shut behind the two of them, turning the latch. "It's brutal out there."

Cassie didn't say anything. Without the wind, she had barely noticed the cold.

"Should I give you the formal tour?" Ali asked, leaning over to unbuckle her boots. "Or is that redundant at this point?"

Cassie smiled, not quite sure how to respond. She pulled off her gloves and dropped them in the basket by the door. Ali noticed and smiled.

Compared to Ali's leather jacket, which looked snug and went just to her waist, Cassie's coat was like a sack. Taking it off felt like climbing out of something, rather than just removing a garment.

Ali took the coat from her and hung it up as Cassie pulled off her shoes. She set them next to Ali's—even, toes to the wall, heels together. Tidy.

That was the word that went through Cassie's mind as Ali guided her through the apartment. Everything was tidy, clean.

Everything in the apartment had its place, and everything belonged.

It made Cassie wonder what possible place there could be for her here. She was chaos personified.

She didn't belong anywhere.

"You didn't have a bath this morning?" Ali asked, noting the still-folded towels on the bathroom counter.

"Um . . . no," Cassie said, looking down at the floor. "I didn't . . . I didn't have any clothes . . ."

"Oh, shit," Ali said, miming hitting herself on the forehead with the palm of her hand. "I'm sorry. I meant to get you some clothes from the bedroom, but I didn't want to wake you."

"I don't think—" Cassie looked pointedly at Ali, then down at herself. "I don't think we're the same size." She tried to make it sound like a joke, but Ali was so skinny, there was no chance she'd be able to squeeze into her clothes.

Ali looked at her disbelievingly. "I guess it's been a while since you looked in the mirror."

Ali pulled Cassie to the bathroom counter.

Cassie looked at Ali's reflection first, her short hair, the slightness of her, the muscles of her arms, the edge of the tattoo peeking out from under her sleeve.

She didn't recognize the girl beside her.

She had blond hair, dirty and stringy, hanging into her red, blotchy face. But aside from the difference in colouring, the two girls in the mirror were equally slight, fine-boned, sharp featured, almost the same height even.

"I'm guessing that's a bit of a change?" Ali said as Cassie watched the other girl's reflection in the mirror turn toward her own.

"Yeah." Cassie reached up, tentatively touching her fingertip to her cheek, verifying that the reflection was really her. She traced her fingers along her cheekbone, the line of her jaw.

It took her a moment to realize that Ali was watching her, and as their eyes met in the mirror, she had to fight the reflex to jerk her hand away, gently lowering it to her waist instead.

"So, you're welcome to anything in the closet," Ali said, turning away from the mirror.

Cassie's gaze lingered there a little longer. She couldn't get over how different she looked. And how dirty.

≪ ≫

After her bath, Cassie dressed in the clothes that Ali had brought in from her bedroom.

When she opened the bathroom door, steam spilled out around her into the main room. It wasn't cold in the apartment by any means, but Cassie shivered slightly at the sudden difference in temperature.

"Is that better?" Ali asked. She was sitting on the couch, tucked into the far corner of it, her legs folded under herself, a glass of wine in her hand.

"So much better," Cassie answered, smiling and half-closing her eyes at the thought. She settled herself on the couch on the opposite end from Ali, sitting facing her. "You can't imagine."

Ali shook her head and looked down at her wineglass as a wave of sadness seemed to spread across her face. "No, I really can't."

Cassie had no idea what to say. "Thank you," she said, hesitating. "For the bath. And the clothes. And the toothbrush." She smiled, and Ali smiled too. "And the food at the restaurant. And the couch."

"You don't have to thank me," Ali said. "I mean, you're welcome. But really, you are welcome. Here."

"I really appreciate it."

"I like to think that's just what people do for each other."

Cassie thought of the past few weeks. "No," she said. "Not most people."

Ali looked down at her wineglass again and unfolded herself from the couch. "I'm sorry," she said. "I'm being an awful host. I'm drinking away"—she lifted her wineglass in a half-toasting gesture—"and I haven't offered you anything." She stood up and edged past Cassie, setting her wineglass on the table next to a magazine. "What would you like?"

Cassie turned on the couch so she was facing into the kitchen.

"I'll have whatever you're having," Cassie said.

Ali nodded, reached into her cupboard and set a wineglass on the counter. "Red okay for you?"

"Sure." Cassie had no idea. Her experience with wine was limited to small glasses at Christmas and New Year's, and the couple of times that Laura had broken into her parents' wine rack and they had split the—

No.

She shook her head. *Heather.* She and Heather had stolen a bottle from their parents' wine rack. They had taken it out to the woods to drink it. Heather had thrown up.

Why had she thought of Laura?

Why had the memory been so vivid? It was like it had really happened: she could remember them in the hayloft of Sullivan's barn, leaning back against the bales, prickly and rough, passing the bottle back and forth.

But that had never happened.

She had only met Skylark in Victoria; why was she dreaming of her in Pressfield?

"It's not just what people do, no," Ali said, jarring Cassie from her thoughts.

She looked into the kitchen; Ali was looking back at her.

"I had a friend," Ali said, looking down at the wine bottle. "In junior high. A good friend. She . . ." Ali shook her head, still looking away. "She didn't get in trouble, but that's what everyone at school said. It was easier than saying that she had come out to her parents, and they had thrown her out."

She looked up at Cassie, then quickly away again.

"I didn't . . . I was fourteen, maybe fifteen. I had no idea what to do." She twisted the cork, pulled it out of the bottle. "So I didn't do anything. I didn't say anything." She shrugged. "What could I say?"

It seemed like she might be expecting Cassie to answer, but she didn't leave her any time.

"She dropped out of school. Just disappeared. I didn't see her again for, I don't know, months." She tilted the bottle toward the two glasses on the counter in front of her. "Then, I was downtown, and I saw her."

She set the bottle on the counter. She had filled only one glass.

"She was panhandling. Begging. She didn't . . ." She shook her head again, clutching the neck of the bottle as if for support. "I pretended I didn't recognize her. I was with some friends, and I just—"

"Pretended she wasn't there." Cassie hadn't intended the words to sting, but Ali flinched.

"I pretended I didn't hear her when she called after me." Lifting the bottle, she filled the second glass. She took a sip, set it down on the counter and filled it again.

"I went back downtown, by myself, to look for her. But she was gone." She forced the cork back into the bottle. "I never saw her again."

Cassie started to speak, but Ali shook her head. "Anyway," she said. "That's— No, people don't always do right by each other, but . . . I'm trying."

A hot wetness filled Cassie's eyes. "You've always done right by me."

"Well, thank you for saying that," Ali said, picking up both of the glasses.

"No," Cassie said. "Thank you."

Ali shook her head sharply, wiped the corner of each eye by leaning in to the shoulders of her T-shirt.

"Here," Ali said, passing her the wineglass by the stem as she shuffled past. With her own, she settled back into the far end of the couch.

The bowl of the wineglass was half-full: the wine caught the light, glowing red and warm.

"I guess we should have a toast," Ali said, leaning toward Cassie. "What should we toast to?"

"I—" Cassie tried to think of something. She wanted to be profound, or at least thoughtful. Or funny. Funny would be good too. Especially now.

"How about 'to winter'?" Ali suggested.

"To warm houses," Cassie countered without thinking. "To warm houses in winter."

She held her breath, hoping she hadn't said something stupid.

Ali smiled. "I like that," she said, and Cassie exhaled.

"To warm houses in winter," Ali said, extending her glass.

Their wineglasses tinging together brought Cassie a small shiver.

The mere act of holding a wineglass, of sipping from it, made her feel grown-up. She could picture her parents, toasting in front of the fire . . .

She had to suppress a shudder.

"How's that?" Ali asked.

"It's good," Cassie said, taking another sip.

"Good," Ali said. "I'm glad." She shifted on the couch, drawing her legs up to her chest. "Can I get you anything else?" she asked. "Is there anything you need?"

"I don't think so," Cassie said, looking at the glow of the light in the wine. "I'm okay. I'm liking just . . . being here." She didn't know if the words sounded as significant as they felt.

"It must be so strange," Ali said thoughtfully. "Never knowing . . . well, like, never knowing where you're going to sleep . . ."

Cassie flinched at the thought of the concrete, the cold, her heart thrumming suddenly in her chest.

There was a rush of heat where Ali touched Cassie's arm. "I'm sorry," she said. "I didn't mean—"

Cassie hurried to shake her head. "No, it's all right."

"It's just . . . I can't even imagine what it must have been like."

Cassie sipped her wine.

"It's a world I just—"

"No," Cassie said. "I can't even really explain what it's like."

Ali's lips parted as if she were about to speak.

"So many things to remember, places you can go, places you can't go, people to keep away from. So many rules."

"Rules?"

Cassie nodded, took another swallow of wine.

"Yeah," she said. "That friend of mine, Skylark? One of the first things she ever told me was to keep my name to myself. Not to tell anyone. That if they didn't know my name, they couldn't hurt me."

She should have been expecting it, but she wasn't: the thought of Skylark, that first day in the park, brought tears burning in the corners of her eyes.

"Oh, Cassie," Ali said gently, touching her knee. "I'm sorry."

Cassie tried to smile. "I just miss her."

"Of course you do."

Cassie could hear the kitchen clock echoing through the small apartment.

Ali broke the awkward silence. "So, all the people living . . . out there." She stumbled, clearly uncomfortable saying things like "living on the street" or "homeless." "They all use different names?"

Cassie nodded. "Street names," she said.

Ali stretched her arm out along the back of the couch, lowered her head into the crook of her own shoulder. "Did you have one?"

Cassie nodded.

"What was it?"

Cassie leaned against the back of the couch, her face just inches from Ali's fingertips. "Dorothy." She tried to make it sound exotic, mysterious.

Ali smiled. "Dorothy? Why Dorothy?"

Cassie felt the heat rising in her cheeks; it was almost too silly to say out loud. "From *The Wizard of Oz?*"

A huge grin spread over Ali's face. "That's one of my favourite movies," she said, an excited, girlish trill in her voice.

"Mine too," Cassie said, a strange sort of excitement bubbling up from her belly. "My dad and I . . ."

The bottom fell out of the world, and she was suddenly tumbling into the darkness. She straightened up, cleared her throat, as it all came rushing back in: The smell of kerosene. The fire. The basement.

Daddy.

The basement.

She shook her head. "My dad and I used to watch it," she said, forcing herself to speak. "It's one of my favourites."

The air in the room was suddenly still.

Ali tilted her head slightly to one side. "Are you all right?" she asked.

"Sure," Cassie said, and swallowed the rest of her wine. "Why?"

Ali's eyes tightened: she wasn't just looking at her, she was scrutinizing her. "You just . . . When you started talking about your dad . . ."

Cassie shrugged and shook her head. "I think I'm just tired," she said.

Ali nodded slowly, clearly not believing her. "Cassie," she said, her voice serious and slow. "Did something happen with your father?"

"My father's dead," she said.

« »

The day filled Cassie with a sense of grim foreboding. It wasn't anything outside: even early, the sun was high and warm, the corn rising and green in the fields along the lane.

But inside Cassie it was grey, all grey.

Heather had left early. She had waited until Cassie had gone upstairs to brush her teeth and get her stuff, and she had left, without a word to her.

Cassie didn't run, didn't call after her, didn't try to catch up. She knew what was happening; she knew there wasn't anything she would be able to say to make it better.

Nothing made it better.

When she came around the corner, Heather was already at the bus stop, standing with the Harkin kids from up the road.

"You got ahead of me," Cassie said, dropping her backpack to the ground with a heavy, satisfying thud.

"Yeah," Heather said.

There was a wall up between them. Heather didn't say anything else, didn't meet her eye. As the Harkin kids pushed each other around, shrieked and laughed, neither of the sisters said anything. Cassie looked off into the distance at the fields across the road, the small mountain just on the other side of the railroad tracks.

When the bus came, a flock of crows lifted from the field, blackening the sky.

"Hey," Laura said, shuffling over in the seat to allow Cassie to sit down.

"Hey." Cassie was focused on the back of Heather's head, her hair bobbing six or seven rows ahead.

Laura waited. "So . . . ," she said slowly, drawing out the word, trying to get her attention.

"The algebra?" Cassie asked.

"Did you finish it? I had problems"—Cassie was already opening her bag—"with a few. Aw, thanks, C, you're the best."

Cassie turned her attention back to Heather as Laura started to fumble through her binder. One of the Harkin girls was talking to Heather, but Heather seemed to be staring straight ahead. Her head wasn't moving at all.

Cassie could remember those days all too well.

"Cassie?" Laura said, and Cassie turned at the confusion in her voice. She was flipping through Cassie's binder, glancing between her and the papers. "Where'd you put the homework?" The bus lurched as it turned onto the highway.

"What do you mean? It's right at the end—" Cassie broke off as Laura tilted a blank page in her direction. "No, before that."

"That's yesterday's," Laura said, angling the page of problems toward her.

"Maybe I missed a page," Cassie said, reaching for the binder.

Laura held on to it, flipping slowly through the pages. "I've gone all through," she said.

"Here, let me." Cassie grabbed the binder and started at the beginning, looking carefully at each page as she flipped past.

All of the pages were carefully marked and dated, all in order. She flipped through to the last sheets, but the homework wasn't there. The notebook ended with the work from the day before.

"Shit," she muttered.

"What?"

She tried to piece it together: she had done her homework at the kitchen table while Mom got dinner ready. Dad had come in partway through, hanging his jacket on the back of the chair next to hers.

She could picture it all so clearly: the pages of the textbook, the numbers she had written on the page . . .

"Did you leave it at home?"

"I don't think so," Cassie said slowly. "I mean, I wouldn't have taken it out of my binder, right?"

She took a deep breath.

"I'll redo it at lunch," she said, trying to seem calmer than she was feeling. "No big deal. I did it once, I can do it again."

When she saw how Laura was looking at her, she wondered what sort of questions she must be thinking to give her that strange expression.

"No, really. I'll just do it at lunch."

The strange expression on Laura's face didn't fade.

It continued through the morning. Cassie would look at her in class or pass her a note or roll her eyes at something Miss Purser said, and Laura would respond the same way she always did, but there seemed to be a moment of hesitation, the slightest, stuttering gap before the response, and Cassie could see that look of puzzled confusion.

By the end of third period, just before lunch, she forced herself to stop looking at Laura. She stared straight ahead at the blackboard, wrote notes in her social studies binder and kept her head down when Mr. Phillips asked for answers, waiting for the bell to ring.

"So, Lakeview?" Laura asked, as if nothing was wrong.

Cassie shelved her binder in her locker. "What?"

"Are we going to the Lakeview for lunch?"

There seemed to be something missing. Had they talked about going out for lunch? Had she forgotten? "I don't—"

"I figured you wouldn't want to get busted, us doing homework in the library or the caf."

The pieces tumbled into place. "Oh," she said, grabbing her algebra text. "You mean, you copying my homework?" She tried to make it sound like a joke, and when she closed her locker and turned to face Laura, her friend was smiling.

"I'll buy you some fries," Laura said.

Cassie shook her head. "Do you really think I'm that cheap?"

Laura's smile was huge. "Most days, you do it for free." She smirked. "Come on."

No one really knew why it was called the Lakeview Diner. There was no lake. The closest body of water was little more than a pond, a slough, miles away, nowhere near the restaurant.

In fact, all you could see from the cracked vinyl booth where Cassie and Laura sat down was the four-way stop, the thrift shop and one corner of the school field.

They were less than a block from the school, but eating at the Lakeview still felt like a big deal. Only juniors and seniors were allowed to leave the school grounds at lunch, so it had only been—

Cassie froze. How long had it been?

She couldn't remember. What was happening to her? How could she not know what month it was? It had been cold, but not too cold. Warm, but not too warm.

She took a deep breath, struggled to answer.

She just needed to sleep, that was all. Too many nights, too many dreams: of course she was exhausted.

She took another deep breath.

"Do you want menus?"

There was acid in the waitress's voice, and she was looking at the two girls with unveiled contempt.

Laura glanced at Cassie. "No, I don't think so."

"Right," the waitress said. "Of course you don't. You know you're supposed to wait to be seated, right?"

"There wasn't anyone sitting here," Laura said innocently, though they both knew the rule.

"Not right now," the waitress said. "But we'd rather give real customers the best seats, not kids." The waitress tucked her dark hair behind her ear and stood there like she was daring them to argue with her.

"Well," Laura said, a trace of haughtiness creeping into her voice, "we're going to order, okay?"

The waitress pursed her lips, pulled her order pad out of the pocket of her apron. "All right," she said. "What'll you have?"

"I . . . I'd like a hot chocolate," Cassie said.

"And a coffee," Laura added.

The waitress looked at them over the order pad. "Food?"

"Fries," Laura said, nodding her head as if she had just won some sort of victory. "And gravy."

The waitress didn't even bother writing it down. "So, a hot chocolate, a coffee, two orders of fries and gravy."

"No," Laura said quickly. "Just one order of fries and gravy. We're going to share."

The waitress looked at them for a moment, then shook her head and turned away before she said anything. Cassie watched her as she walked back toward the kitchen, the narrow flash of white skin between the top of her black jeans and the bottom of her black T-shirt, the very edge of a tattoo.

Something opened up inside her, and the world jittered, blurred, shifted out of focus. She could only hear Laura like she was at the far end of a tunnel, laughing lightly.

"Alicia Felder, working at the Lakeview," she said. "Wait till I tell Cheryl that I ran into her big sister."

Alicia.

Cassie fell into the black.

Cassie's breath tore at her throat. The covers fell away from her as she sat bolt upright on the couch.

Everything snapped back into focus: the couch, the coffee table, the grey square of light over the kitchen window.

But none of it seemed real.

Or it seemed too real.

She didn't know.

Her heart was thundering in her chest, and her breaths were ragged, short.

Focus on your breathing. In two three four. Hold two three four. Out two three four.

In two three four.

Twisting at the waist, she turned on the lamp on the end table. It took her three tries, and something fell over on the table in the dark.

Blinking against the sudden light, she righted the small sculpture that she had knocked over. It was heavier than she had expected, a solid piece of metal in the shape of an owl.

It teetered a bit unsteadily on its base, and it looked at her, unblinkingly, with its wide eyes.

Hold two three four.

It was all too real. Too sharp. The owl, looking at her: she could trace every line and crease in the metal with her eyes, every burr, every scratch. There was no detail too small for her to notice.

The scratches on the tabletop. The faint ring where a glass had stood. No, not a glass—a coffee cup. She could picture it there, steam rising from it.

Out two three four.

Too real. So real, she knew it couldn't possibly be. She would pick up the owl and it would turn to a snake in her hands, and that would be okay. It was just a dream.

It was just a dream.

In two three four.

The whole room, the whole world, seemed bright and angular and sharp, perfect in every way, but she knew she could put her hand through it, that it was only the thinnest of membranes, a mask over the real world.

She smiled.

Dr. Livingston would be so proud of her.

Hold two three four.

It was just a dream, and dreams couldn't hurt her.

More than that: she could control them. If she focused, she could change the dream itself.

If she focused, she could even—

Turning on the couch, she lowered her feet to the floor. Faintly cold, another perfect detail.

Out two three four.

She stood up. She was standing. She was doing it!

She thought of the expression Dr. Livingston would have on her face when she told her.

She shuffled between the couch and the coffee table and allowed herself to smile. Doctor Livingston had been right: once you took control of the dream, it was easy. She could stand up, she could move, and she didn't even really need to think about it.

In two three four.

She padded across the living room and ran her fingers along the top edge of the television, faintly rough to the touch.

Hold two three four.

She had been so busy with her own breathing she hadn't noticed the sound of the steady, deep breaths coming from the bedroom.

She followed the sound, stopping at the door.

The covers were up to Ali's neck, her head turned into the room, away from Cassie. One leg wasn't under the covers; long and bent, it curled away from the doorway, glowing pale in the faint light.

Out two three four.

She didn't need to think about moving. It just happened. But not in the helpless way of her old dreams. This time, she knew that she was moving, deliberately, mindfully.

In two three four.

As gently as she could, she lifted Ali's covers just enough to slide under, lowered them to cover both of them again.

Ali stirred, groaned, but she didn't wake.

Hold two three four.

« »

Cassie spread her math books out on the table: algebra text farthest away from her, binder right in front of her. She wrote the new date at the top of the first clean page.

She sighed and leaned forward over the table.

Laura didn't say anything, just shifted a little on the vinyl bench.

Her pencil hovered above the first blank blue line of her notebook.

"So which one of you had the coffee?"

Alicia Felder was standing at the edge of the table, a steaming mug in each hand.

Laura raised her right hand off the table slightly. "Here," she said.

"Of course," Alicia said, as she slid the mug of coffee along the table to Laura. "So that means—"

Cassie could see it happening before it happened: Alicia's hand extending toward her, over the books on the table; the drooping angle of the mug, the sudden stutter in the motion of her arm, the sloshing of the hot chocolate, the long spill of the steaming liquid, the way it splashed down on the textbook, the binder, the spray of heat over her hand and arm where she had been waiting to write—

She flinched back against the seat, and Alicia lost her grip on the mug entirely, the cup splashing down on the Algebra 11 text, spraying hot chocolate over the table, soaking the pages of the textbook and her notebook.

For a moment, everything seemed to freeze—

Then just as quickly, Alicia was stepping back from the table.

"Shit!"

For some reason, the word stung more than the hot chocolate soaking into her T-shirt, dripping off her arms and face.

"God, I am so sick of you kids coming in here like you own the place. Throwing stuff around. Making a mess."

Cassie glanced across the table at Laura, looking for support, waiting for her to put the waitress in her place.

"What the hell, Cassie?" she asked, her eyes flashing at her. "Why are you—"

"Get out," Alicia said. "God, that's it. Just get out. And don't bother coming back."

The world spun and swam around her. "But . . . what . . . ?"

"Just get out. You're done here." Alicia spun on her heel,

stalking back to the kitchen.

Cassie looked at Laura, who was shaking her head.

She reached for a napkin, wiping her face. The hot chocolate hid the silent tears.

"Jesus, Cassie," Laura said, standing up. "Why do you have to be such a freak?"

She stomped off. Somewhere in the distance, Cassie could hear the bell over the front door.

She wiped her hands, mopped as much of the hot chocolate as she could off the textbook and the pages of her notebook. It was no good, though: the paper was soaked, inflated, already sticky. There was nothing she could do.

"You need to go," Alicia said.

« »

Cassie woke up without moving, fully asleep to fully awake in an instant.

She knew exactly where she was—knew it was Ali's wall and dresser in the soft, dawn-blue light, knew it was Ali's arm curled around her, at once light, almost weightless, and reassuringly heavy over her, curled over her side, her hand resting against Cassie's stomach.

Ali's breath, warm and damp, at the back of her neck, the warm press of her body along her back.

It all felt so real.

PART FIVE

Free will is a myth.

It's another of those lies designed to impose order, to hedge against chaos.

Yes, we are free to make choices, but none of them matter. Only the Darkness matters.

The Light fades from everyone. Everyone.

The aged live with the faintest of sparks within them, their lives swallowed, daily inch by daily inch, by the Darkness until finally they wheeze to black.

The sick fight, they flare, they burn brightest in those last moments before the Darkness takes them.

And all around me, I see people rushing and fighting, getting and spending, laying waste their powers, eking out what passes for an existence as the Light within them is ground away.

Your choices do not matter.

Free will is the most insidious of lies.

The Darkness takes us all. It is up to you, though, to determine how.

Do you feed, or do you eat?

Do you die slowly, as a sheep, or do you make your life extraordinary?

The Darkness takes us all.

"Dorothy?"

She jumped at the sound of the voice, almost bumping into . . .

Was that Brother Paul?

She took a step back.

He wasn't the same man she had known at the camp. Brother Paul was taller now somehow, a tracery of stubble around his cheeks. He looked stronger, bigger than he had before. "I thought it was you."

His eyes were blue, and shone in the grey light.

She nodded slowly. "It is."

Seeing him, the sudden memories of Skylark almost broke her heart. It was a feeling she was getting used to, that she would never get used to.

He nodded deeply. "I was calling," he said, taking a large step toward her. "Across the square. I guess you didn't hear."

"No," she said. Looking around, she realized that she had absolutely no idea where she was. She had been drifting, deep inside her head, with no idea where her feet were taking her. "I didn't hear."

But there was something familiar about the place. It took her a moment: the buildings on all sides, the park, the fountain . . .

It all seemed so familiar.

Like something out of a dream.

Then she knew. City Hall. The square. The fountain. If she turned, she'd be facing the breezeway, the pillars, the camp.

What used to be.

She forced herself not to look.

Something in her expression must have given her away. Brother Paul nodded again. "That's right. Where it all started, right there." He pointed, and Cassie couldn't help but turn.

"I thought I should see the old place again," he said. "I can't say I was expecting to see you here, though."

"I didn't—" She took another step back.

"Are you all right?" he asked, taking another step toward her. "I know how devastated you must be, but . . . it's not safe out here."

Cassie took another step back.

"You know that better than anyone."

Another step toward her.

"You're welcome back at the camp, Dorothy. I know that everyone—"

"I—"

Neither of them saw the hand coming from behind him, slamming firmly down on his shoulder with enough force to buckle his knees. Brother Paul staggered under its force, twisted to get away.

"Is there a problem here?" Constable Harrison asked from behind Brother Paul, his hand still firm on his shoulder. He wasn't in his uniform, but his voice carried its own authority.

"Not until now, Officer," Brother Paul said, twisting again, trying to get away from Harrison's hand.

"Why don't I believe you, Paul?" The words coiled and

seethed. "Is there a problem, Cassie?" Looking her directly in the eye.

"I don't—"

Harrison nodded slowly. "I think it's time for you to take a walk, Paul," he said, releasing his grip on the man's shoulder. Paul stumbled, stepped away.

"Officer Harrison—" he started, rubbing his shoulder.

"You need to leave this young lady alone."

"Oh, it's not her with the problem," Brother Paul said, straightening back up to his full height. "Just another bit of police brutality."

"There are no reporters here, Paul. And you know the rules. If you hang around here, I can bust you for loitering." He took a step toward him. "You want to go back to jail, Paul?"

Brother Paul shook his head. "No. Sir." He said it slowly, drawing out the words. Harrison nodded, his face stony. "That's right, Paul. You just head on out, and there's not going to be any problem."

Brother Paul's mouth formed a tight, sharp smile. "All right, Officer," he said. He looked at Cassie, met her eye. "I'm sorry for bothering you, Cassie."

He smiled, and lingered over her name.

Her real name.

As Paul moved toward the breezeway, Harrison started in the opposite direction, toward the street at the far side of the square. "Are you all right?" he asked, forcing her to walk with him in order to answer.

"Yes," she said. "I think so."

"He didn't . . . ?" Harrison said, glancing over his shoulder at Brother Paul.

She forced herself not to look back, shook her head.

Harrison took a long look at her. "Something's happened," he said. "Clean clothes, clean hands, clean hair. You look better."

"You don't," she said, quickly bringing her hand up to cover her mouth. "Sorry," she added.

She wasn't wrong, though. Harrison's face was even greyer, thinner than it had been the day before, his eyes burrowed deep in black sockets. He looked like he was sick.

But he smiled at least. "That's all right," he said. "I know I'm not at my best. I haven't been sleeping."

She knew better than to ask why not, but he responded as if she had spoken: "Work," he said. "Just work."

"Okay," she said quietly.

"You've got someplace to stay? Someplace warm? Someplace safe?"

The words echoed in her head: "warm," "safe."

"It's supposed to get really cold out tonight," he continued.

"I've got a place," she said. "I'll be all right."

"Are you sure?"

The urgency in his tone almost stopped her cold. "What's going on?" she asked. "Is there something you're not telling me?"

The way he shook his head as he said, "Nothing," made it sound like a lie.

There was something going on that he couldn't talk about. Something that he wanted to say, but couldn't.

"Okay," she said, her disbelief plain.

"I just want you to be safe," he said, his voice softer now. And even less reassuring. "Don't take any chances, all right? It's—"

"I know," she said. "It's not safe out here."

"Don't be glib," he snapped. "I'm serious."

"Okay," she said, lowering her gaze to the ground, still suspicious, but unwilling to risk saying anything else.

"I'm sorry," he said, crouching slightly to meet her eyes. "I'm just worried."

"I'll be all right. I've got a place to go."

"Good," he said, but he didn't sound convinced. "Listen, can I drop you off? My car is—"

"I'm okay walking," she said, too quickly.

"Okay," he said, his voice clipped. He looked at his watch, then at the sky. "You should get going then. It'll be getting dark soon."

She shook her head and turned away. She had taken a couple of steps when she stopped and turned back around. "You should get some sleep," she called to him. "You're going to drive yourself crazy."

It was what her mother used to tell her.

"I'll take that under advisement," he said.

They both turned away.

≪ ≫

On her walk back to Ali's apartment, Cassie stopped at the mall on Government Street. She dodged through the crowds into the department store, bracing herself against the heat, the Christmas carols, the lights, as she worked her way into the housewares department. No one gave her a second glance as she looked at the display cabinets. No security guard appeared at her shoulder. It was like she was a different person.

She bought a paring knife from the kitchenwares section. The cashier wrapped the blade in layers of brown paper, and Cassie slipped it into the pocket of her coat.

"Hey, Larry—you got a minute?"

The detective—Lawrence Donofrio—looked up from the table in the second conference room to where Harrison was leaning against the doorway. He waved him in. "Sure. I'm just—" He glanced at the table, a mess of papers and files, a storm searching for order. "You getting off shift?"

"Nah," Harrison said. "I was out Christmas shopping, thought I'd drop in before it got too late. You the last one here?"

Donofrio nodded. "Fucking Christmas," he muttered.

"Is that Wolcott?" Harrison gestured at the mess. "How's it looking?"

Donofrio shrugged. "It's a mess. But it's coming together." He leaned back in his chair, his shirt stretching over his belly.

"Slam dunk, though, right? Given the evidence?"

Donofrio rubbed his eyes. "You mean the tongues?"

Harrison flinched, mostly from the detective's matter-of-fact tone. "Yeah. That seems fairly conclusive."

"We're taking a cursory look at the wife too, while the ME does his thing. She had access to the freezer, so it could be her . . ."

"It's not her, though."

"You lookin' to make detective, Harrison?"

Harrison let himself smile. "Maybe," he said, playing along. "Down the road, though."

Donofrio nodded. "I thought so. You've got the look."

"There's a look?"

"Yeah. I've seen it dozens of times. Big case comes up, and all of a sudden it's a circus. Half the guys are just curious, want to be in the loop, get the scoop, you know? Most of the others"—he shrugged—"they're looking to be seen interested. They're the ones who volunteer for task forces and shit like that. Working the system, bucking for promotion."

Harrison knew the type. Hell, Farrow was the type.

"Yeah. A few, though, you can see it in their eyes. They want to understand. They look at this"—he gestured at the table—"and they figure that if they can just sort it out, it'll all make sense."

He ran his tongue between his top front teeth and his lip, making a quiet smacking sound. "Those guys make good detectives." He nodded. "That's the look you've got right now."

Harrison hesitated. "It doesn't make sense."

Donofrio leaned forward. "Well, that's the thing. I used to have that look. And I did exactly that: made detective, figured I'd be able to make it all make sense. And you know what?"

Harrison shook his head. "What?"

"It never fucking does." He leaned back in the chair again. "Guy kills these girls, cuts out their tongues and keeps them in the fucking freezer, right next to a fucking Sunday-dinner chicken? How does that make sense? Yeah, we can make a case, but that shit's never gonna make sense. Fact is, I'm not sure I even want to understand it anymore. I don't think I want to know. I don't think we're wired to handle that kind of darkness."

He rubbed his eyes.

"And this fucker just sits down there, not saying anything."

"He's still here?"

"Yeah." Donofrio reached toward the monitor in the corner of the table. "He's got his hearing first thing in the morning." He pressed the power button and the screen flashed to life, showing the inside of one of the holding cells in the basement.

Cliff Wolcott was sitting on the bed, his knees drawn up to his chest, his socked feet resting on the bare mattress. "He just sits there, staring off into space. I had to turn it off—he was creeping me out."

He didn't seem like much, just a normal guy, sitting on a bed.

Harrison leaned toward the monitor. "So, you've talked to him?"

"A few times. It's funny—" His eyes made it clear that it wasn't funny at all. "Talking to him, he's the nicest guy. Comes across a little bit shy. Kinda nerdy, I guess. But nice." He shrugged. "But that's what they always say, right? The neighbours? 'He seemed like such a nice young man.' 'Who would have thought he'd do such awful things? Six tongues in his freezer? He didn't seem—'"

"Wait," Harrison said sharply, turning to face the detective. "Six tongues?"

Donofrio nodded slowly. "Yeah. Six. Welcome to the shit." He shook his head. "That's why I'm here so late."

"But there were seven . . ." A wave of nausea rolled up from Harrison's belly.

"*Were* seven victims," Donofrio said, emphasizing the past tense. "Not anymore. I'm just waiting on the ME's report on"—he sifted through the files, picking one up to read the name on the tab—"Laura Ensley." He dropped the file back onto the table. "The last one."

Harrison's legs wobbled.

"She still has her tongue."

The temperature in the room dropped ten degrees.

Donofrio lifted his hand. "Don't jump to any conclusions. The ME's report should tell us more about the knife, the strokes. Similarities, differences."

"But what do you think?"

He knew what he was asking, so he wasn't surprised when Donofrio replied, "Between you and me?"

"Of course."

"I think there's going to be a press conference tomorrow morning about Mr. Clifford Wolcott here being charged with the murder of six prostitutes, while police still look for the killer of—" He reached for the file again.

"Laura Ensley," Harrison said quietly.

"Yeah." He stretched the word out like a sigh.

"So . . ." Harrison started to pace along the end of the table. "There's a copycat out there."

"That's not a word you'll hear come out of this building," Donofrio said, straightening in his chair.

"But someone's still out there."

"That's the working theory right now. We've been keeping it under wraps, hoping he'd screw up, thinking he was safe with this fucker behind bars." He pointed at the monitor; Cliff Wolcott hadn't moved. "But with the hearing—" He shrugged helplessly. "We put it off as long as we could."

"So you knew—"

"We suspected. When we found the girl's body. There were too many differences."

"The body wasn't found near water," Harrison said, thinking it through out loud.

"She wasn't a prostitute."

Harrison nodded, thinking of Cassandra Weathers. He needed to find her. He needed to warn her.

"And there was the crime itself." The words were flat, almost clinical.

"There were differences?"

Donofrio picked up the file, handed it to Harrison. "He didn't cut out her tongue," he said.

Harrison took the file, was opening it when Donofrio spoke again.

"This fucker cut out her heart."

« »

"There you are." Ali's voice came from somewhere inside the apartment as Cassie pushed the door open.

"Here I am," she said awkwardly, not sure how to respond.

"I was starting to worry," Ali said, unfolding herself from the corner of the couch and setting a magazine on the coffee table.

Cassie bent over to unlace her shoes enough to wiggle them off. "Why?" she asked as she slipped the shoes next to Ali's.

Ali shrugged as she came into the kitchen area. "Just because," she said, taking a sip from the glass of wine she held. "I worry about you. That's all."

"I'm all right," she said as she took off her coat.

"I know," Ali said, and she smiled. "And you will be too."

"How do you know?" Cassie asked, not even sure where the question came from.

"I just have this feeling," she said. "I think you're probably strong enough to make it through anything the world can throw at you."

What world? Cassie wanted to ask, but she bit back the words, smiling instead.

"So how was your afternoon?"

It seemed like such a natural question, like it was just a normal day, like they were just normal people.

"Okay, I guess." She didn't mention meeting Brother Paul in the square or her conversation with the cop. She didn't tell her about buying the knife at the department store or stopping near the camp on her way back to the apartment, standing in the shadows outside the fence, watching, just watching.

A grey silence rose between them. "What about yours?" she asked a moment later, attempting to drive it away.

This was what normal people did, right? They asked each other about their days?

"It was all right," Ali said, her voice brightening a little. "It was pretty dead at the restaurant, but Hong and I spent the day working on food for tonight anyway, so that was all right."

"Right. Tonight." She glanced around the room. "When—"

Ali looked at the clock. "People'll start arriving in a half hour or so. Most of them are coming from work, so they'll trickle in. It doesn't usually get rolling till about seven or so."

"Half an hour?" Cassie looked in vain around the apartment for signs of preparation, for any indication that people would be coming to the door so soon. "Shouldn't we—"

"Oh, no," Ali said, shaking her head. "It's not here." Cassie's brow pinched. "It's upstairs, at Collette's. Her place is bigger, so we all get together up there. Plus," she added, as if it were the most important part, "she's got a great stereo."

Cassie nodded slowly, absorbing the information. "So, do we need to—" She cocked her head upward, at the apartment above them. "Should we go up there and help her get ready or anything?"

"That's sweet," Ali said, and Cassie flinched at the words before she realized that Ali wasn't making fun of her. "No, Collette's got all that taken care of. We just need to show up. Oh, and bring the wine." Ali started toward the door like she had just remembered something. "Which I will end up forgetting."

With the side of her foot, she pushed a cardboard box out from under the coat hooks. Bottles tinged and shifted inside as the box rasped heavily along the floor. "My friend Erin and I made this at one of those you brew places this summer," she explained as she slid the box over so it was partially blocking the door. "There," she said. "Now we won't forget it." She smiled in satisfaction. "Now it's just a matter of us getting ready."

Cassie looked at Ali, and her chest tightened.

"What's wrong?" Ali asked.

Cassie shook her head. "Nothing," she said. "Just nervous."

Ali reached toward her, and Cassie forgot how to breathe as Ali brushed her hair off her forehead, tucking it behind her right ear. "It's all right," she said. "There's nothing to be nervous about. Just some friends."

Cassie wanted to lean in to Ali's hand, to nestle her cheek against Ali's palm, to close her eyes. "I know," she said instead.

"You'll fit right in."

She wanted to believe her.

"Come on," Ali said, taking her hand and leading her toward the bedroom. "Let's find you something to wear."

Cassie couldn't help but smile at Ali's excitement. "You really like this," she said.

"I do," Ali said, turning to her. "I always loved this time of year when I was a kid. There was something so magical about it. I remember this one time, we actually had a white Christmas. We woke up and the whole world was changed." She sighed deeply, remembering. "It was so magical. It only happened the once."

That stopped Cassie. "Really? You only ever had one white Christmas when you were a kid?"

Ali nodded and shrugged. "Victoria doesn't really do the white-Christmas thing." She hesitated, then, "Things were different for you? Where you grew up?"

Cassie smiled. There was something very sweet about the way Ali was asking about her without actually asking. It was the clumsiness that made her smile, that allowed her to answer.

"Pressfield," she said, looking into Ali's closet so she wouldn't have to risk meeting her eyes. "I grew up in Pressfield, in the Interior. And yeah, we had a lot of white Christmases when I was growing up. Most of them, I think." She touched the edges of the hanging dresses. "Along with white Valentine's Days. White Easters, some years. It pretty much snowed November through March, every year."

"What do you think of this one?" Ali asked, pulling out a blue dress, holding it in front of herself.

Cassie looked, nodded.

"It's a bit short on me, so it should be good . . ." Ali turned the dress, held it up in front of Cassie. "Pressfield," she said, almost to herself, as she evaluated the dress, angling her head slightly. "How did you end up in Victoria?" she asked with a deliberate casualness, not meeting Cassie's eyes.

"It's a long story," she said.

"You don't have to tell me," Ali said, and when their eyes met, there was a crackle like electricity between them. "I mean, I'd like for you to. I know you might . . ." She shook her head. "Whenever you want to," she said. "Tell me, I mean. I'll listen."

Cassie took a shallow breath, then another.

"I like it," she said, taking a half-step forward so the dress draped over her. "Do you think it'll look all right?"

Ali looked at her for a moment, then nodded. "I think it'll be fantastic," she said.

<< >>

The locker room was quiet, deserted—he had known it would be. It was close to the middle of the shift, right around dinnertime: Harrison had the whole place to himself.

He needed it, the privacy, the quiet. The last thing he wanted right now was small talk—he'd probably punch the first person to bring up the hockey game.

In the bathroom, he splashed cold water on his face and braced himself against the counter. He forced himself not to look into the mirror, fighting a lifetime of automatic action: he knew what he would see there, and he didn't want to look at himself. Couldn't bear the thought of it.

He didn't feel sick. He had just about thrown up in the conference room, but he didn't feel sick anymore. His heart wasn't racing, his guts weren't heaving.

He just felt cold. Clear.

Calm.

He knew what he had to do.

He turned off the faucet and dried his face with paper towel from the dispenser. He trailed his fingers along the wall as he walked into the locker room itself, then sat on the bench in front of his locker.

He took his notebook out of his pocket, flipped it open, balanced it on his knee and began to write.

It didn't take long. There wasn't much to say.

When he was done, he tore the sheet out of his notebook and folded it in half.

He wrote her name on the front of the fold, then slipped the note through the vent slot of Farrow's locker door.

For a moment, he remembered high school: slipping notes into Cindy Galloway's locker, the way the cut grass smelled on the ball diamond, laughing on the bus with the rest of the team.

Ancient history.

Slipping his service revolver into the back of his waistband, he straightened his jacket, stood tall.

« »

Cassie floated through the evening in a blur. The wine warmed her, a warmth deeper than she had felt in months, and softened the edges of the rooms, the lights on the Charlie Brown Christmas tree blurring and swimming soothingly. Voices bubbled around her, and she smiled and laughed and talked.

Hong had introduced her proudly to his wife as they were setting out the food for the feast.

"This is May," he had said, draping his arm around her shoulders.

May had smiled shyly, and Cassie had been the first to extend her hand.

"It's the sweetest story," Ali said a few minutes later.

Every seat in the living room was taken, so they were sitting on the floor under the window.

"They met in a camp in Vietnam. They were both kids. Well, teenagers, I guess." Ali's voice was slow and deep, a little slurred and uncertain. "Anyway, they fell in love, but they got separated and sent to different parts of Canada. They thought they'd never see each other again, but one day, about ten years ago, Hong was at work and she walked in. He knew it was her right away. It turns out she'd been looking for him." She sighed happily, a warm, faraway look on her face.

"And?" Cassie felt the expectation of the rest of the story pushing her forward with an almost physical force.

"And nothing," Ali said, looking toward the kitchen door. Through the crowd, Cassie could see Hong and May at the table, serving up plates of food. "Happily ever after," she said.

Part of Cassie wanted to tell her that there was no such thing, but the other part of her, the part that was warm and safe and happy, wasn't so sure anymore.

"Everybody's got a past, Cassie," she said. "Everyone's got a history." She smiled as she said it, a warm, happy, safe smile. The lights of the tree flashed against her cheek.

For the first time, it felt a bit like Christmas. Looking up at the world from the floor, Cassie remembered being a little girl, sitting at the kids' table when all of her relatives got together, being sure to eat everything on her plate on Christmas Eve so she wouldn't upset Santa at the last minute. The blinking lights on the tree, the carols on the stereo, the loud, confusing hum of voices in conversations that she couldn't follow: she winced against the pang that arced through her chest.

"What's wrong?" Ali asked in a whisper.

Cassie just shook her head.

Ali put her hand on Cassie's leg, squeezing it gently. "It's all right," she said.

It was almost overwhelming, but she could tell, looking at Ali's face, that she knew exactly what was going on in her head. She hadn't said anything, but Ali understood.

She laid her hand on Ali's and squeezed.

Harrison began to feel his exhaustion near the bottom of the stairs to the basement. He had to cling to the railing as his ragged breath echoed off the concrete stairwell, sweat stinging in his eyes. The faces of the murdered girls swam in his mind.

His jacket was only making it worse. He wished he could have left it in his locker, but that wasn't really an option.

He knocked on the heavy door at the base of the stairs, peering through the wire-reinforced window, waiting to be recognized.

There was a faint buzz and the clicking of the lock. Harrison turned the handle and opened the door to the holding cells.

Boris, working the desk, looked up from a magazine at Harrison, his back to the bank of video monitors, one for each cell.

"You draw the short straw?" Harrison asked as lightly as he could. He knew Boris well enough to joke with him.

Boris looked him up and down, taking in his boots, his winter jacket. "Hey, at least I get to be inside tonight, if you want to talk about drawing the short straw."

Harrison grinned and leaned on the ledge at the top of the desk. "True that," he said, trying to keep his tone light. "Busy in here?" Harrison cocked his head toward the second heavy door, the end of the hallway to the holding cells.

Boris turned slightly to check the monitors. Harrison's eyes followed, focusing on Cliff Wolcott, still sitting on his bed.

"Nah, it's pretty quiet. Couple of drunks. Crackhead seeing visions. Usual stuff."

"Folks taking time off for the holidays, you figure?"

"Wouldn't that be nice? Not likely, though. We'll get a

pretty heavy run of domestics and public disturbances, starting tomorrow afternoon."

"Right around the time folks get home to spend the holidays with their families, right?" Harrison knew the answer: he had worked enough Christmases to know what it was like.

"Fa la la la la," Boris said drily. "So, you down here 'cause you don't have anything better to do or what?"

"Actually, I was just up talking to Donofrio—"

Boris rolled his eyes at the name.

"And he suggested I might want to have a word with his Mr. Wolcott."

Boris turned back to the monitors. "This guy?" he asked, tapping the screen on Cliff Wolcott's head. "Fucking freak."

"That's what I hear."

Boris took a closer look at Harrison, studying him. "Are you on the task force?" Harrison shook his head. "Nobody's supposed to see him except task force members and his counsel. Looks to me like they're trying to keep something quiet." He looked guilelessly at Harrison, as if hoping he might have information to share.

"Donofrio didn't say anything about that," Harrison said, watching every word. "He just suggested I come down and talk to him." He started to turn away. "But if you've been told that it's task force only—"

"Jesus," Boris muttered, and Harrison stopped, stifling the smile he felt coming on before turning back around.

"What the fuck do I care who sees him, right?"

Harrison hesitated. "Are you sure?"

Boris shrugged. "It's nothing to me," he said, dropping a clipboard on the desk. "You sign in, it's your problem. You and—" He raised his eyes toward the third floor, where Donofrio was probably still sitting in the conference room. "Here," he said, tapping the clipboard. "It's all on you."

Harrison took his pen out of his pocket and filled out the line on the sign-in sheet. He checked the clock on the wall behind him for the time.

As he tucked the pen back into his pocket, Boris stood up, hitched up his pants. "You'll need to check your side arm," he said, going through the steps exactly as the policies and procedures dictated.

Harrison forced a smile. "This ain't my first rodeo, Boris," he said. He held his breath as he held his jacket open so Boris could see he wasn't wearing his gun belt. "Left it locked up," he said. "Figured I'd save you the hassle." Prayed silently that he wouldn't be asked to turn around.

When Boris nodded, he lowered his jacket, waited.

Harrison tried not to breathe a sigh of relief. He wasn't going to come around the desk. He wasn't going to ask him to turn around or lift his coat.

Instead, Boris spun the clipboard to face himself, checked it carefully and nodded, initialling the line.

"All right," he said, tucking the clipboard back down behind the ledge. "He's in three. I'll buzz you through."

"Thanks, Boris," he said, as he stepped toward the door to the cellblock.

"Pfft," he grunted, and the door buzzed and clicked.

Harrison pulled it open and stepped through, waiting for it to shut and lock behind him before he stepped forward.

It was almost like a hospital corridor: wide and white and bright, smelling of heavy antiseptic cleaners. Doors lined both sides of the corridor, each with a small window at face height, all the glass wire-reinforced.

As he walked along the hallway, Harrison glanced behind himself and up at the video camera mounted above the door he had just stepped through, a red light solid and unblinking at its base.

When he stopped in front of the door to holding cell number three, he nodded at the camera.

A moment later, there was a buzz, and the lock clicked free.

Wolcott didn't even look up as he walked into the cell, as the door closed behind him.

Sitting on the bed, he reminded Harrison of those statues of Buddha in the windows in Chinatown. Not the laughing ones, the serene ones, the ones where he was just sitting there, utterly still.

The difference was striking, though. Those Buddha statues had a calming effect. Hell, he had even bought one for Farrow, as a bit of a joke; she still had it in her locker.

Cliff Wolcott's stillness made the hair on the back of his neck stand up.

"Wolcott," he said.

He didn't move.

The older cops always talked about how they could tell if a suspect was guilty just by watching them in holding. The thinking went that innocent suspects would be stressed and anxious, pacing, working themselves up to a good, distraught frenzy within a matter of hours at most. The guilty ones, though, they were calm, unruffled, like they were protected inside a shell.

Over time, Harrison had come to realize that the theory was bullshit; looking at Cliff Wolcott, he wondered if there might be something to it after all.

"Wolcott," he said again, a little louder, taking a step forward. Nothing.

The collar of his uniform pinched his neck, cut off his breath. He tried to calm down: it wouldn't do to be angry, but he couldn't help it. There was something about this fucker, just sitting there, calm as could fucking be, like he didn't have the blood of those girls on his hands, like he hadn't—

The fingers of his right hand tightened and relaxed, tightened and relaxed.

The gun was heavy at the small of his back.

He crossed the room in four steps. "Hey," he almost shouted, kicking at one of the legs of the bed. "Wolcott."

His eyes opened languidly as he lifted his head. "Hello, Officer," he said, fixing his gaze on Harrison.

The temperature dropped in the room, and a shudder ran through him.

« »

"This is unbelievably sexist," Collette called back into the living room. "I just thought you men should know that." As she turned back into the kitchen, she barked out a laugh. Her pale skin was pink and flushed, her red ringlets limp and sticking to her forehead.

"Men," she said. "Why do we keep them around?"

"That's always been my feeling," Ali said, turning off the water. The sink was full and steaming, bubbles high over the edge. "But you can't seem to keep away." She shook her head in mock sadness.

Collette opened her eyes wide, twisted the dishtowel she was holding and snapped it toward Ali.

Ali jumped out of the way, bumping into Cassie. Her eyes were bright, shining.

"That's enough of that," Erin said, grinning just as widely despite the mock sternness in her voice. "Don't make me put you in time out."

When Collette stuck her tongue out at Erin, both Cassie and Ali had to turn away to keep from cracking up.

Ali started washing the dishes, placing them in the rack in the second sink. Cassie tried to keep up, drying each piece as it came and passing it to Erin to put away, but she quickly fell behind, and the rack began to fill.

"I'm just saying, could it be any more sexist?" Collette asked no one in particular, draining her wineglass. "The menfolk in the living room, burping and farting, while the womenfolk do the dishes?"

Cassie half-turned. "That'd be a lot more convincing if you were actually doing anything."

Her heart thudded to the pit of her stomach as soon as the words left her lips and she waited for Collette's reaction. She had meant it to be funny, but it wasn't funny, was it? She had just insulted Ali's friend and their host and—

Collette cocked her head, her eyes going wide. "Oh yeah?" she said, as she began to twist her dishtowel again, but a smile was breaking over her mouth.

Cassie wasn't quick enough to get out of the way, and the towel caught her on the hip with a stinging snap. "Hey!"

Collette looked at her with mock defiance, a come-and-get-me look that she only managed to hold for a moment before she stuck her tongue out.

Even May, putting leftover food into storage containers at the table, laughed.

With all of them working, they made short work of the

dishes. As Ali pulled the plug, the water beginning to drain with a roaring gurgle, Collette stepped back into the living room, her wineglass in one hand, a bottle in the other.

"Oh, not fair," she called out a moment later. "They started without us!"

Cassie looked at Ali to see if she knew what was going on, and then the smell of pot smoke tickled at the base of her nose.

"Yeah," Ali said, then took a concerned second look at Cassie. "Oh. Is that—"

"I grew up in a small town," she said. "Not a convent."

"So you're okay with—" She gestured toward the living room. In the corner of her eye, Cassie saw Erin hanging her dishtowel on the handle of the oven door and stepping into the other room.

"Sure," Cassie said. "Why wouldn't I be?"

Ali shrugged and shook her head, smiling a little. "Sorry," she said. "I'm just being overly careful."

"Why?" Cassie asked, and Ali hunched over the sink, scrubbing the metal walls as the water drained, not looking up.

"Ali?" She touched her at the small of the back, let her hand linger there. "You don't have to be careful," she said quietly.

"You don't either," Ali said, and the look that she gave Cassie melted her legs. When Ali reached up and brushed Cassie's hair back from her forehead, tucking it loosely behind her ear again, Cassie trembled.

She glanced toward the living room. "So," she said. "What happens now?"

≪ ≫

A few steps away from the man on the bed, Harrison straight-ened, feet shoulder-width apart, balanced and firm in place, his training coming back without him even realizing it.

Bracing himself for a shot.

"Cliff Wolcott?" he asked, now that he had the man's attention.

Wolcott looked from side to side, checking if there was anyone else in the cell. "Yes, Officer?"

"I'm Constable Harrison. I'd like to ask you a few ques-tions." He reached into his pocket for his notebook and pen, trying to make it appear as professional as possible.

The back of his jacket brushed against the gun.

"Really?" Wolcott asked. As he unfolded his legs, Harrison fought an instinct to take a step back. "Is that how it usually works?"

The question seemed to come out of nowhere.

Wolcott ran his fingers through his short, thinning hair. "The last few times someone wanted to talk to me, they brought me upstairs into one of those little rooms. You know, the ones with the table and the three chairs and the mirror along one wall? It was like I was in an episode of *Law & Order*."

Harrison nodded. "Usually. But we're going to talk here." He gestured over his right shoulder at the video camera in the upper left corner of the room. "If that's all right with you."

Wolcott shrugged. "Sure."

Harrison nodded, clicked his pen. "I wanted to talk to you about those girls."

"The ones I killed?"

Harrison couldn't move his hand to write.

Wolcott smiled, a harmless, friendly smile. "You don't need to dance around it. I figure you guys have been all through the house, the freezer." He paused, watching Harrison's face. "So you found my packages. What's the point in mincing words now, right?" He shrugged again. "You've got me. What do you want to know?"

Harrison was completely unprepared for a full confession, and the line of questioning he had devised, all the feints to draw him out, all the little tricks to trip him up, fell apart. "Well," he said. "Start at the beginning, I guess."

Wolcott smiled. "Constable Harrison. How far back do you want me to go?" He chuckled. "Do you want me to tell you about Janet Colburn, back in the seventh grade? She was a year older, fourteen, and one day, in the storage room off the music room at school, she lifted up her skirt and showed me her pussy. She told me I could touch it if I wanted to. And I did. Is that what you had in mind?"

Harrison shook his head, even as he scrawled across the lines in his notebook.

"No," Wolcott said. "I don't think that's it, is it? That's all ancient history. You want to know why I did it, right?"

Wolcott shuffled off the bed, stretching as he stood up.

"Of course you do," he said.

Wolcott cracked his knuckles, swivelled his head in a deep, slow circle, like he was working out a kink.

It would be so easy to reach behind his back, right now, to draw the pistol. To fire.

"But you already know," Wolcott said. "I can see it in your eyes."

Harrison took a step back, cursed himself immediately. "No, I don't," he said, forcing his voice to remain calm and level. "Why don't you tell me?"

Wolcott smiled. "There's something in us," he said. "Inside

all of us. We all feel it, every day. It's not sadness or depression . . . Well, it's part of those things, I guess, but . . . It's something different. You know that. You've felt it. I can see it."

Harrison took another step back.

Wolcott stepped toward him. "What is it for you, Constable Harrison? Do you cheat on your wife? Or your taxes? Drive too fast?" He backed off. "No, that's not it."

"Why did you kill them, Cliff?" he asked, trying to take control of the conversation again. "Those girls . . ."

Wolcott pivoted on his heel, stopped.

"Because I could," he said, his voice flat, uninflected. "Because I wanted to."

Harrison swallowed hard, pushed the bile back down, glanced behind himself again and up at the unblinking red light on the video camera.

"That's not an answer."

"It's the only answer, Constable. It's the only reason any of us do anything. Dress it up however you like."

"This is a waste of time," Harrison muttered, snapping his notebook shut.

Wolcott smiled. "I'm answering your questions, Constable. You just don't like what you're hearing."

"No, you're not," Harrison said. "You're handing me this lukewarm Psych 101 crap that reads like a textbook diminished-capacity defence. You can practise that with your lawyer. I'm not going to help you set it up." Harrison turned toward the door.

Wolcott laughed. "Is that what you think? A diminished-capacity defence? Constable, I'm going to plead guilty in the morning."

Harrison stopped, turned around.

"Why?" It was all Harrison could think to ask.

"Because I did it. I killed those girls." It sounded like he was describing any other event in the course of a typical day: *I got up, I went to work, I killed those girls.*

"But why?"

"Have you ever known a fat girl on a diet, Constable?" Wolcott asked. "My sister, she was a big girl. Solid, my mother called her. Anyway, when we were growing up, my sister was always on a diet. Always. And do you know what always happened?"

Harrison nodded, hating the fact that he had been drawn in.

"She became obsessed. All that food she couldn't eat? She couldn't think about anything else. The more she resisted, the worse it got."

Wolcott shook his head, looked toward the ground.

"That's how it works. That's how we work, Constable. Isn't it?"

He looked like he was genuinely waiting for a response.

"The darkness is going to have you, no matter what you do. If you fight it, it gets stronger. You're on a diet, and all you can think about is cake. Until you give in. The hunger"—he took a deep breath—"it wins, either way."

"So that's it?" Harrison asked, his voice tight, bristling. "You killed those girls because you, what? Got obsessed? Because you couldn't think about anything else?" He snorted derisively. "That's the lamest defence I've ever heard."

"It wasn't intended as a defence, Constable," Wolcott said, and Harrison had to fight against the way the anger rose in him every time Wolcott used the word "constable." "It was an explanation, that's all. I thought you would understand."

And Cliff Wolcott smiled, a cold, flat smile that showed his teeth. "I thought you'd be able to relate."

Harrison's hand dropped to his waist, within easy reach of the gun.

He shook his head.

"Can I ask you a question, Constable? How old is your daughter?"

Harrison's breath caught in his throat. "How—how did you—"

Wolcott smiled again. "I knew it. You look at me and you see the bodies of those girls, and you see your daughter . . . She's what, ten? Eleven?"

He couldn't reply.

Wolcott nodded. "You can't stop thinking about it, can you? Those bodies. Your little girl. Me. They just keep"—he made a ratcheting motion near his right ear—"ticking and ticking and ticking, and you can't sleep, and you can't think about anything else but what you would do . . ." Wolcott raised an eyebrow. "'If I ever get my hands on that son of a bitch,'" he mocked, slowing his voice, putting on a bit of a drawl.

He looked up, and Harrison followed his gaze to the camera in the corner of the room. "So what are you going to do, Constable?" he asked, his lips working back into a smile. "You've got me right here, all to yourself."

Harrison's fingers twitched, but he didn't notice.

"It's not going to bring those girls back. It's not going to keep your daughter safe." The pity in Wolcott's voice was almost mocking. "But you want to do it. It's not really about them at all, is it?"

Wolcott smiled.

"What will you do, Constable?"

Harrison stopped his right hand as it started to slide into

his jacket, and turned toward the camera. Looking directly at the lens, he made a circling motion with his index finger at the level of his right ear. "Wrap it up," he mouthed.

He tucked his notebook and pen back into his pocket. He let his hands fall to his waist.

The lock on the door clicked almost immediately.

When he looked back at Wolcott, there was an expression somewhere between disappointment and confusion on the killer's face.

Harrison turned the knob and opened the door. "I don't do things just because I want to."

He didn't breathe again until the door closed behind him, until he was watching Wolcott through the wired glass.

He shivered in the chill air; he was soaked with sweat.

<< >>

Cassie turned the CD case over in her hand, closely studying the song titles as the music pulsed and flowed out of the speakers.

"It's good, isn't it?"

Ali's friend Murray looked at her expectantly over his wire-framed glasses. His eyes were green and bright.

"They're from the UK. Manchester, I think."

"Bristol," she said. "They're named after a town close by."

A smile twitched at the corners of his mouth.

"What?" she asked. "I read about them in *Rolling Stone* or somewhere."

"So, are you a big Portishead fan?" He pointed at the CD case.

"No, this is the first time I've heard it. It was on my list, though."

"Your list?"

"I used to keep a list of records to look for the next time I got to the city."

"No record store where you're from?"

She stopped herself from reflexively answering.

He smiled kindly as her face flushed.

"Okay, I'll quit prying," he said. "But I have to admit, we're all pretty curious. We all love Ali, and she shows up here tonight with someone we've never even heard about, let alone met. And you're"—he paused—"a bit younger. You know Hong, so you've been to the restaurant. Ali says you met there . . ." He nodded slowly, then smiled again. "I'm sorry," he said. "I'm a bit of a writer . . . . I'm always looking for the story. Imagining things." He shrugged. "Mostly we just want Ali to be happy."

He took a sip of his wine. "You do have a story, though, don't you?"

Cassie shook her head. "No, no story. Nothing important."

He looked at her. "I don't believe that."

"It's true," she said, unable to keep her voice from catching.

The room fell silent around them, and he reached past her and pressed the button to restart the CD.

"It is a great album, though, isn't it?" he said.

« »

Harrison wiped the sweat from his sleeve as the door to the holding corridor clicked unlocked.

He turned the handle, opened the door, breathing only when it had closed behind him.

Boris was standing at the desk, watching him.

"I told you he was a piece of work, didn't I?"

Harrison nodded. "You did," he said, trying to control the shaking in his voice, in his hands.

"I'm impressed, though," Boris said, the grudging tone making it seem like the words only came with difficulty. "The Crown's gonna love the full confession." His face wrinkled into a smile. "Nice job," he said. "That'll go a long way if you're looking to make detective."

Harrison shook his head slowly. "No," he said. "I don't think so."

Boris cocked his head slightly to the left, looking at Harrison curiously.

"I'm sorry to do this to you, Boris," Harrison said. "There's gonna be some paperwork." He stepped toward the desk.

"Paperwork?"

He broke off when Harrison reached around to the small of his back and laid his side arm on the desk between them.

Both of them took a step back from the gun.

"It's loaded," Harrison clarified. "So you know."

Boris's face had gone white as he looked between the gun and Harrison, and back to the gun. "You were strapped? Harrison, what the fuck?"

Harrison didn't answer. His hand was shaking as he laid his badge down on the desk next to his gun.

Boris shook his head. "Take it back," he said, meeting Harrison's eyes. "There's no need to make a career decision out of this. Nothing happened. You don't need to—"

Harrison shook his head. "I'm sorry about the shit that's gonna rain down, Boris. But I need you to call this in. I'm gonna go upstairs and make some calls."

He was starting to turn when Boris spoke. "Nothing happened in there. This can be just between us. It doesn't have to—"

"Yes, it does," Harrison said, turning back. "I brought a concealed weapon into a holding cell." He cocked his head toward the monitor, which showed Wolcott sitting back down on his cot. "I had every intention of putting a bullet into him. Do you really think I should be wearing a badge right now, let alone carrying a gun?"

He didn't wait for Boris to answer. Harrison turned and walked toward the stairs.

« »

Cassie and Ali stumbled along the walk in front of the house, clinging together, holding each other up for the quick jaunt between the front door that led from Colette's suite to the side door into the basement. Neither of them noticed the cold at first.

At the end of the walk, Ali stopped and turned toward the street, shouting, "Merry Christmas!" at Hong and May pulling away in their car, at Erin and George walking away down the sidewalk, his arm around her shoulders.

They were almost the last to leave: Murray was still upstairs at Collette's, but it didn't look like he was going anywhere.

Cassie smiled and blushed at the thought.

Her breath hung silver in the moonlight.

It was only then that she realized she was holding Ali's hand.

As if she could read her mind, Ali tugged on Cassie's hand. "Come on," she cried, turning and dragging Cassie. "Let's get inside before we freeze to death."

Their heels clattered along the driveway, echoing in the cold stillness.

Ali flung the door open and practically pushed Cassie inside, slamming the door behind them. The air was a cushion of heat they seemed to fall into the moment the door was closed.

"Oh my God," Ali said, shaking herself, running her hands up and down along her bare arms.

Her skin was shimmering with goosebumps. Even in the half-light, Cassie could see every fine hair, every raised bump.

A dream.

No.

She shook her head, trying to push out the thought. Not a dream. This was real. This was real.

"Are you all right?"

Ali was looking at her, her head partially cocked, her eyes concerned and curious.

"Yeah," Cassie said, nodding for emphasis. "Better than."

"Are you sure? You looked—"

Without letting herself think, Cassie kissed her. Her lips lingered on Ali's, feeling the cool of her mouth, the warmth of her breath.

Not a dream, Cassie told herself, forcing the thought away. Not a dream. Not a dream.

"That—" Ali said, as Cassie withdrew. "Um. Okay."

Cassie looked away.

"I . . ." Ali struggled to find words. "I'm not really sure—I don't know what to do right now."

"Do you want to dance?" She could feel the heat of a blush on her face, but she wasn't sure what it was from: The wine? The warmth? Ali?

Ali smiled and touched the tip of her tongue to her lower lip. "There isn't any music," she said, taking a step toward Cassie.

"No?" Cassie said, heat lightning crackling in the air between them. "Are you sure?"

"No," Ali said, opening her arms.

At least it's not too cold, Cassie thought, kicking at a skid of snow at the edge of the sidewalk, the last dregs from the storm a few days before.

She stopped, watched the chunk of brown-tinged snow slither away along the pavement.

When had it snowed?

It was spring, wasn't it?

For a moment, she didn't know where she was. She looked around: the familiar buildings against the backdrop of mountains, the corner. She could have drawn the scene from memory, right down to the heavy grey clouds, almost black, looming over everything.

But something didn't feel right. It was clearly winter—she wasn't imagining the wind cutting through her—so why couldn't she remember the snowstorm?

She knew it had happened. She could see the proof. So why couldn't she remember?

Why had she thought it was spring?

Something tickled her nose, and she half-turned. It was starting to snow, tiny flakes dancing and spinning in the air.

Definitely not spring.

Bundling her jacket tightly around herself and hoisting her backpack more securely onto her shoulder, she walked toward downtown.

The wind screamed down the sidewalk, a howling gale that twisted the bare trees, that sliced into her flesh.

She stopped in front of the window of the Lakeview. She thought maybe she would go in, sit at the counter and order a hot chocolate, but then Alicia Felder came into view, her hair pulled back, her order pad in her hand.

She stopped at the front window, flipped the pad open and took the pen out from behind her ear. She was smiling, laughing, leaning forward to talk to whoever was sitting at the table. She was like a completely different person, and Cassie was surprised to feel a strange warmth in her chest as she looked at her.

When Ali looked up from her pad, though, she curled her lip into a silent snarl and shook her head slightly at the window before turning away.

Cassie was shaking as she walked away.

She walked past the pool hall, with the legendary arcade in the back, edging past the crowd of boys out front, pushing and shoving one another in a cloud of cigarette smoke and cologne, past the girls with their hairspray and perfume, who seemed to cling to the wall, who watched her warily as she passed.

When she got too cold, she ducked into Schmidt's, just across from the bank.

She spent a long time walking up and down the aisles, not really looking at anything, but letting everything wash over her, like the shimmering heat from the boxy unit near the back of the store.

It was so warm inside, she had to undo her jacket.

Schmidt's wasn't very big, but it had a little bit of everything: clothes and curtains, books and tools, a magazine rack and a small bin of CDs and cassettes, hardware and toothpaste. It was like a relic from another age.

The cash desk was a raised platform in the middle of the store, offering Mr. Schmidt clear sightlines over most of the cluttered space.

She knew better than to linger near the magazine rack. Mr. Schmidt watched the area like a hawk. Cassie kept her head down, tried to make herself as small and inconspicuous as possible, and kept to what she thought might be safer areas of the store.

She was flipping lazily through a clearance rack in womens wear when she felt the prickle of someone watching her.

Mr. Schmidt was staring right at her from the cash desk.

She took a sharp breath, her heart jumping. She tried smiling at him, but his grim, suspicious focus didn't falter.

She looked back at the rack, pretended to be engrossed in the clothes, scrunched her brow like she was concentrating.

When she looked up, he was still staring.

She drifted over to the kitchen section, keenly aware of his gaze tracking her.

She tried to concentrate on a display of pots and pans, tried to make it look like she was actually interested in—

"What are you doing here?" The voice at her elbow made her jump.

Mr. Schmidt was standing right there, staring at her, daring her to speak.

"Shouldn't you be in school?" he snapped, the words coming out in a sharp, accented bark.

"I'm—"

He waited, his face twisted, about to speak, just waiting for her to say something that would allow his words to come.

"I'm looking for something for my mother," she said, tripping over the words in her hurry to get them out. "For Christmas."

She wasn't sure where the lie had come from—the Christmas tree in the front window maybe or the carols playing faintly—but the old man's face brightened, and he took a step back. "Oh, of course," he said. "Such a sweet thought."

Cassie felt a flare of anger at the man's sudden change. One minute he was looking at her like she was a criminal, like she was lower than dirt, and the next he was being as sweet as could be, all because she had told him that she wanted to buy something.

It made her feel like she was going to throw up.

"Did you have anything in mind?" he asked wetly, spraying a little with each word.

"A knife," Cassie said. "For cooking."

As soon as she spoke the words she knew that they were right: she needed to buy a knife.

The old man smiled, revealing yellow, cigarette-stained teeth.

"Such a good daughter," he said. "Let me show you."

He opened a small display to show her a variety of knives, all the time keeping an eye on the front door in case anyone else came in.

"Do you see something you like?" He looked at her expectantly.

"I think so," she said. "How much is that one?" As she pointed at the knife—just a little larger than a paring knife—she glanced surreptitiously at her watch. She smiled. Time enough to get back to the school for the bus.

When he told her the price, she nodded. "That sounds great."

"Excellent," he said. "Excellent. I wrap it for you, yes?"

He was already several steps toward the checkout before she was able to say, "No."

He stopped and turned back to her. "No?"

"No, thank you," she said. "I'll wrap it when I get home."

He turned away, leaving Cassie to wonder how this had all happened. Why was she buying a knife? Why had she told him not to wrap it?

She didn't have an answer, but when he handed her the bag, the blade of the knife wrapped in brown paper, Cassie almost jumped back, like the bag had given her a shock. Holding the knife, it felt like she had always held it, like her hand was expecting it somehow.

When she slipped it into the pocket of her jacket, it felt like it belonged there.

Stepping out of the store was like stepping into another world: entirely white, snow against a black sky, the wind whipping around her. "Jesus," she muttered, bracing herself to step out of the doorway. The snow was almost up to her knees.

How was that possible? She hadn't been in Schmidt's that long, and it had barely been snowing out when she went in. This was like it was in the mornings, when it had snowed through most of the night. This was—

In the distance, she heard an electronic buzzer.

The school bell.

"Shit," she muttered. She had to get back, and with the snow like this . . .

Her foot cracked through the icy crust and plunged into the snow. Her ankle burned with the cold as the snow went up her pant leg, over her sock. "Shit," she cried out again, but she took another freezing step. And another. No time to hesitate, no time to delay, or she would be walking all the way home in this.

Every footstep seemed to echo.

There was no one else around as she trudged through the snow. The sidewalk was completely empty, the snow unbroken except for her steps. The street was empty, no cars, and no tracks or ruts in the white. It was just her, the sound of the wind and the roughness of her breath as she hurried back to the school.

A crow alighted on the stop sign at the corner, its talons scritching against the metal.

As she passed, the crow followed her with its eyes.

It's like a dream, she thought. *It's like—*

Rounding the corner closest to the school was like waking up. Without warning, the sun was bright, reflecting off the dark, high clouds. There wasn't a trace of snow on the ground, and the warm air was full of the sound of laughing and shouting. A member of the basketball team shouldered past her with barely a glance, wearing shorts and a hoodie with the school logo.

She froze in place, unable to will her legs to move.

Her legs . . .

She looked down to her feet. Her shoes were dry, her pants completely dry. No trace of snow, no hint of wetness.

But she could still feel the cold.

"What the—"

"Cassandra!"

She almost dropped her backpack at the sound of her name.

Mrs. Murrow was standing on the sidewalk between her and the school, her hands firmly on her hips. "I trust you have a good reason for missing class this afternoon?"

She barely registered the words, turning, looking over her shoulder, looking back—

"Cassandra!"

Cassie snapped around to face her, but she didn't really see the teacher as she struggled to process what she had just seen.

The street behind her, the street that she had struggled through in the wind and the snow only seconds before, was now bright and clear. Not a trace of snow. Cars parked on both sides. People passing on the sidewalk.

"Miss Weathers, is there something wrong?" She wielded the question like it was a stick. "Miss Weathers—"

She had skipped class?

What was going on?

"I'm sorry," she blurted. "I was at the doctor." Survival instincts kicking in, Cassie fell back on the familiar.

Mrs. Murrow smiled a thin, watery smile. "That's what Laura Ensley told me when I asked."

Good for Laura, Cassie thought.

"You have a note from your parents, then?" Mrs. Murrow asked, knowing very well that she didn't. "Or from the doctor?"

"I do," she said, too quickly. "It's just—" Behind Mrs. Murrow, the first school bus pulled out of the parking lot. "It's in my locker, but—" Cassie gestured helplessly toward the school. "I'm going to miss my bus."

She seized on it, she knew she could use the bus as her escape.

"Miss Weathers, that doesn't—"

"I'll bring you the note in the morning," she said, already starting to edge past the teacher. "I just can't miss my bus."

"Miss Weathers!" Mrs. Murrow barked out her name and Cassie stopped in place, obeying an instinct so deep she couldn't resist it.

Mrs. Murrow took a single step toward her. "You will bring me that note before school tomorrow, along with your missing assignments, or I'll have you in detention after school for the next week." She smiled that thin smile again. "And I will be talking to your parents and letting them know about your behaviour."

Missing assignments?

The words chilled Cassie as she glanced between her teacher and the school driveway. She could almost hear the clock ticking away.

"Are we clear, Miss Weathers?" It wasn't so much a question as a demand.

Cassie nodded. She had no idea how she was going to get a note, but that mattered less at the moment than the seconds ticking past.

"Yes, Mrs. Murrow," she said, rocking on her feet. "Before school."

Mrs. Murrow's smile was poisonous. "Don't miss your bus," she said, like she would like nothing better.

Cassie ran for it, dodging the crowds on the sidewalk and in the bus pickup area. She made it to the bus just as Mrs. Cormack was about to close the doors.

"Cutting it pretty close," Mrs. Cormack said with a smile that seemed almost genuine.

"Yeah," she gasped, breathless.

The bus lurched as it departed, and Cassie had to hold on to the seatbacks to keep from falling as she swayed back to the empty seat next to Laura.

"Where were you?" Laura whispered, twisting in her seat and pulling herself close, so her head was almost tucked against Cassie's.

That was really the question, wasn't it?

"Just in town. I went to Schmidt's, got a Christmas present for my mom."

Laura looked at her curiously.

"What?" Cassie asked.

"Isn't it a little early for Christmas?"

"I—" What? Was it? She had no idea when it was. It looked almost like spring outside the bus windows, but downtown had been . . .

She scrambled. "I was hanging out in Schmidt's. You know how he gets. I had to buy something." It was the best that she could do.

Laura seemed to accept the explanation. "Yeah. He's such an asshole." She rolled her eyes, and Cassie forced herself to laugh along with her friend.

They didn't say anything for the rest of the trip, and when the bus pulled up to Cassie's stop, all Laura said was, "So, are you going to be there tomorrow?"

Cassie thought about the doctor's note, and the two, now three, algebra assignments. "Yeah," she said, not really sure how she was going to make it work.

Laura smiled. "Cool," she said. "I thought maybe you had decided to disappear or something."

Disappear. The word sent a pang through her, but she didn't know why.

"No, I'm not going anywhere."

"Okay," Laura said.

The air was positively warm as she got off the bus. There was no trace of cold, not even a hint of winter in the gentle breeze that blew through the trees along the side of the road, all of them verdant and full. The whole world was green, as far as Cassie could see, leafy and in bloom, the corn in the field across the road almost knee-high, the air thick and sweet smelling.

She was going insane.

Was that it? Was this what it felt like to go crazy?

That's what it had to be—there wasn't any other explanation.

Or was there?

She looked up from the dusty verge as the bus roared away. Heather was already far along the lane, her pace quick, her body hunched.

Cassie trudged along toward the house, watching her feet, the tiny puffs of dust they raised with every step. The sun on her shoulders was almost hot; it felt like May, with the end of school in sight, summer lurking just over the fields.

So what had happened in town?

She wasn't going crazy.

She didn't know if that was true or not, but that was the assumption she had to make. To consider anything else was too terrifying.

So if she wasn't going crazy, what was happening?

Then it came to her. The memory of the street, how loud her footsteps had sounded, how sharp the world had seemed when she had stepped out of the store: it had all been like a dream.

Had she been dreaming?

She knew that reality wasn't to be trusted, that her mind could do strange things without her even really being aware of it. Was that what had happened? Had she fallen asleep, some- how, somewhere?

She reached into her jacket pocket. The knife was there, its weight a vaguely comforting pressure, so she knew that she had been in Schmidt's. Had the rest of it been some sort of sleep- walking, a waking dream that she hadn't even known she had been having until Mrs. Murrow had woken her?

The explanation made at least a little sense. She would talk to Mom and Dad about it tonight, maybe see about making an appointment with Dr. Livingston.

She could even tell them that she had fallen asleep in the library, and that was why she had missed class.

She was almost smiling as she turned into the front yard. She hadn't really solved anything, but having a theory and a possible plan made it less overwhelming.

When she got to the house, Mom and Heather were talking in the kitchen and Cassie took one look at the two of them, leaning together, and kept walking. There would be other time, better times, to talk to her mom.

But there weren't. First it was making dinner, then doing the dishes, then helping Heather with her homework, then watching TV with Dad: there was no time Cassie could get her mother alone, no opportunity to take her aside without it seeming like a major issue. And then it was bedtime, and she hadn't said anything.

In the morning, then. She'd talk to her in the morning, get her to make an appointment with Dr. Livingston and ask her for a note for Mrs. Murrow. Yes, that would work.

Cassie finished brushing her teeth, tapped her toothbrush on the edge of the sink and turned off the bathroom light.

She could hear music from Heather's room as she pulled the blankets to her chin, but she didn't let it bother her. Nothing bothered her; she was exhausted, and it would all be better in the morning. Mom would know what to do, what to say, how to deal with it all. In the morning. In the morning.

"Cassandra."

Her eyes flashed open at the voice from the hallway. Her bedroom was dark, a faint silver light glowing behind her curtains, too weak to actually penetrate the room.

"Cassandra."

She prayed that she was dreaming, but when the voice

came again, there was no doubt, no denial. She stifled a sob, trembled. All she wanted to do was curl into a ball—

She curled into a ball.

She gasped.

She stretched her arm out, just to prove that she could. She balled her hand into a fist. She wiggled her foot, just a little bit, trying to be silent.

She could move.

"Cassandra."

The doorknob rattled, and the door opened with a creak. The sound cut through her.

She tried to slow her breathing, tried not to pee the bed or throw up. She braced herself, getting ready to scream.

But it didn't come in.

As the door swung open, she could see it there, a black shadow in the glare of the hall light, unmoving, staring.

But it didn't come in.

Maybe it knows, she thought. *Maybe I'm too old. Maybe it knows that I can move, that I'm not helpless.*

"Cassandra."

The voice was like fingernails on a chalkboard, and she clenched her eyes shut, tried to shut it all out.

"Cassandra."

When she opened her eyes again, the figure was stepping away. One step. Two. Then it stopped again.

Waiting.

She didn't know how she knew, but she was sure that the shadow was waiting for her.

"Cassandra."

Was that a beckoning tone in the voice now? Did it want her to follow?

She wouldn't. She just wouldn't. She would fight. She would—

She stood up, dropping the covers to the floor with a soft thud.

"Cassandra."

The thing seemed to float in front of her, a black hole in the world, a darkness in the bright hallway.

And she followed.

She didn't want to, but she had no choice.

And what terrified her, more than anything, was knowing that if she turned around, if she looked back, she would see herself still in bed, staring back.

"Cassandra."

She followed the shape down the stairs. She could hear her own footfalls on the carpet, soft thuds, but no sound from in front of her.

Light seemed to follow them through the house. All the lights were off except the single faint bulb over the kitchen sink, but the shape always seemed to have light around it, in front of it.

Then she realized: the shape needed the light. Without light to create it, the darkness didn't exist.

The darkness.

The words echoed in Cassie's head as the figure stepped through the open door at the top of the basement stairs.

She froze in place in the middle of the kitchen.

No no no. I won't. Not there. I won't.

But she didn't have any choice: her feet followed of their own accord.

With each step down, each rough, unpainted stair, her heartbeat quickened, her breath coming in shorter and shorter gasps.

No no no.

But the figure didn't stop, didn't slow as it led her down the stairs, into the basement. The concrete floor was blisteringly cold under her feet, but she barely noticed.

All she could feel was the heat of the fire on her face, coming from the doorway on the far side of the room.

The doorway seemed to glow orange as the figure moved toward it.

No no no.

She couldn't resist the figure's pull, couldn't fight the power driving her to follow.

No, Daddy.

The figure turned to her as she stepped into the room. It smiled at her with her father's face, twisted almost unrecognizably, his mouth wide, a gaping black hole under his burning red eyes.

It was the face she only saw here, in this room, when it was just the two of them.

But this time he wasn't alone.

There were other people in the room, standing in a rough semicircle around the wood stove, its door open to reveal an orange, hungry maw of jumping, roaring flames.

Her mother was there, standing behind the stove, Heather standing beside her, both of them staring at Cassie. Laura was standing next to Heather, holding her hand.

On the other side of her mother, Alicia, the waitress from the Lakeview, and beside her, Mrs. Murrow.

"Hey, little girl."

Bob and his friends appeared in the wavering light, the cold of his eyes bright sparks in the heat.

No one moved. All of them just stared at her, the only sound the roaring crackle of the fire.

Until Laura laughed.

Raising her free hand, she pointed directly at Cassie and laughed.

Cassie's heart stopped.

Then her mother laughed, a low, guttural laugh.

Mrs. Murrow snorted, then everyone joined in, the tiny room ringing with laughter, everyone pointing at Cassie.

Her knees faltered, almost gave out, and she just about fell, catching herself on the woodpile closest to the door.

That was when she caught a glimpse of herself, realized with a sudden clarity that she was naked.

But—

As she fumbled to cover herself, everyone was laughing louder, Alicia pointing at her emphatically.

Bob just looked at her, his grin widening, showing his teeth.

"Cassandra."

"Cassandra."

She woke with a start, the sound of laughter echoing in her ears, a cold shiver running through her.

It took her a moment to understand where she was, and as the picture came into focus she shuddered and swayed. Only grabbing the doorknob kept her from falling.

Doorknob. Ali's doorknob.

She was standing in Ali's bedroom, at the head of her bed.

Ali was asleep, on her side, facing Cassie, facing the room, her face soft, relaxed, calm, one bare shoulder showing above the edge of the blankets.

The bed beside her looked rumpled, tousled, as if someone had just gotten up.

She couldn't remember going to sleep, but she must have.

And she had gotten up. Why? To go to the bathroom maybe? To get a drink of water?

No.

It came back to her with a shocking clarity, an immediacy that she knew had to be true.

But she looked down, just to be sure.

She looked down at her right hand, the hand closest to Ali. The hand that she hadn't used to grab the doorknob.

The hand that held the knife she had bought that afternoon.

Unable to help herself, she looked from the blade to Ali, still curled on the bed, the covers rising and falling with each breath.

She pictured taking hold of her hair, tugging her head back on the pillow, felt the way the knife would slip so easily into the skin of her throat. That was why her thumb was at the base of the blade—to give it a little more stability, to give a little more focus to the pressure.

First the blade would slip into her skin, then, with the slightest resistance, a small pop she would feel in her hand, it would sever her carotid.

The blood would spray like a hot rain—

The knife fell from her hand, clattering against the patch of bare floor between the rug and the bed. Ali stirred in her sleep, groaned, nuzzled her head against the pillow.

And Cassie ran.

PART SIX

There are Dead Places in this world.

Even those who have no true understanding of the Darkness recognize them. There are houses, long abandoned, that seem to watch you, even as you instinctively avoid them, crossing the street to put as much distance between you and that Dark cold.

There are forests and fields where bodies have fallen, where the earth has tasted blood, where the sun itself seems to dim.

Corners and rooms that raise goosebumps on the skin.

Cold Places. Dead Places. Haunted Places.

Dark Places.

But there are also Darkening Places. Dying Places.

Places where the pall thickens like smoke from a slow fire.

Not battlefields, or cities under siege.

Not just those.

But places—neighbourhoods, houses, rooms, cities—caught up in the Dark.

And they quickly become vortexes, widening gyres, as the Darkening Places call out to the Dark, drawing us in. They wake the Darkness in those who have not yet seen the Truth of the Way. And they call out to those of us who walk now, always, in the Darkness.

And we come.

We come to tear the guts of these Darkening Places with our teeth.

We come to feed.

The sidewalks beside the courthouse were a sprawling emptiness, wind blowing scattered leaves and a few errant snowflakes with an unburdened abandon.

There was a crowd near the front doors, news vans and cameras and screaming people, but none of them came near Cassie.

There was no money in her hat, but it didn't matter. None of it mattered. Cassie wasn't really trying, not anymore. She hadn't even bothered to seed her hat with change, and she slumped against the iron railing, eyes half-shut, breath limp and grey in front of her mouth.

It had still been dark when she'd sat down; she had watched the world gradually brighten to the harsh, steel grey of a winter morning. At first she had been cold, shivering, but that feeling had passed. Now, she didn't feel anything.

The few people who went by seemed to go out of their way to not see her. Their strides didn't break, they didn't slow or vary their voices. It was like she wasn't even there.

Maybe she wasn't. Maybe she had been swallowed up by the world of grey, just another featureless lump in the gutter, something to be swept up by the street cleaners after the holidays.

Maybe that was for the best.

At least that way she couldn't hurt anyone else.

When the police cruiser pulled up to the curb and turned off its engine, she barely registered it. Doors opening, closing, footsteps: none of it mattered. It all seemed to be happening in a different world.

It was only when a pair of heavy leather shoes came to a stop in front of her, their toes pointed directly at her, that Cassie looked up.

Farrow was looking down at her; the cop's face broke from something that looked like anger into an expression of concern.

"Jesus, you look awful. Are you all right?"

Cassie nodded and tried to answer; her lips burned as she tried to move them.

"Yes," she managed.

"Let's get you up." Farrow took a step forward, kicking Cassie's hat out of the way, and leaned over. Cassie felt the woman's hands under her arms, felt herself being lifted to her feet. Cassie was only able to stay on her feet by leaning against the railing.

"I'm all right," she said, the burning in her lips dulling as she used them. She nodded, as if this might somehow strengthen her point.

"Jesus Christ," the cop said, taking a step back. "Are you trying to freeze to death?"

When Cassie didn't answer, Farrow cocked her head. "I need to ask you a few questions. Have you taken anything? Drunk anything?"

Cassie shook her head.

"No drugs? No booze?"

"No," Cassie said carefully.

"Can you tell me what year it is?"

"I'm all right," Cassie said.

"Can you tell me what year it is, please?" Farrow was still using that loud, almost shouting voice.

"It's 1997. December. Christmas Eve."

Farrow nodded. "And do you know where you are?"

Cassie almost smiled at how ridiculous the question was, but she stopped herself. "Victoria," she said. "At the court-house." Not that she could really be sure anymore.

The answers seemed to satisfy Farrow. "What are you doing out here?" she asked, a tone of genuine concern in her voice. "I thought Chris told me that you had found a place."

"Chris?"

"Constable Harrison."

"Oh. Right."

She craned her neck around Farrow. All she saw was a man-shaped shadow in the driver's seat of the cruiser.

"He's not there," Farrow said.

"What?" She'd never seen Farrow without Harrison.

Farrow shook her head. "Here," she said, stepping toward the cruiser. "Let's get you something to drink," she said, as she opened the passenger door and reached in.

"No, I—" Cassie took two steps toward the car, tried to see inside. He had to be there.

"It's got so much cream and sugar in it, it probably doesn't even count as coffee anymore." Farrow pushed the door of the cruiser shut with one hand, holding a metal Thermos in the other.

"Here." She unscrewed the cup from the top of the Thermos and handed it to Cassie. "It'll warm you up." She poured the cup half-full.

Cassie looked between Farrow and the police car.

"What's going on?" she asked. "Where's Constable Harrison?"

Farrow sighed heavily. "Drink first."

Cassie raised the cup to her lips, took a gentle sip. Sweet, hot; just what she needed.

Farrow nodded. "Good girl," she said. "Now listen." She took a half-step forward, leaned toward her. "Chris got himself in a little trouble last night."

A kaleidoscope of images filled her head. "What happened?"

Farrow shook her head. "He was questioning a suspect." She paused, blinked quickly a few times. "And there was a breach of protocol."

Cassie rocked back. "What? Is he—"

"I haven't seen him. I don't think anyone's seen him." Farrow took a deep breath, shook her head. "He's on administrative leave. Indefinitely."

"What happened?" It was like her whole body woke up at once, like an electrical current was running through her.

"I shouldn't be telling you this," she said. "But Chris asked me to." She glanced back at the car, and toward the courthouse itself.

"It was Cliff Wolcott."

Cassie's stomach plummeted.

"Chris went down to holding to talk to him, and when he left, he revealed that he had taken his side arm in with him."

Cassie had to force herself to breathe. "Did he—"

"He surrendered his weapon and his badge to the officer on duty, and requested emergency leave. It looks like some sort of breakdown."

"Did you know? Did he say anything?"

"I had no idea." Her voice was almost disappointed. "But

you saw him," she said. "He wasn't sleeping. He was just—"
She motioned with her hand beside her head.

"But why—"

"That's why I'm here," Farrow said, cutting her off.

Cassie brought the cup to her lips and was surprised to discover that it was almost empty.

Farrow started speaking as she poured her more. Steam billowed from the mouth of the Thermos. "Chris left me a note. He asked me to find you." She screwed the lid back on the Thermos. "He wanted me to tell you that it isn't safe for you."

Cassie stopped with the cup at her lips. "I thought—I mean, Cliff Wolcott is the guy, right? He killed all those girls, right?"

"Not all of them."

Cassie flinched. Almost dropped the cup. "What?"

Farrow shook her head slightly. "Your friend Laura?"

Cassie nodded.

"Cliff Wolcott didn't kill her." She held up her hand as Cassie started to speak. "I know," she said. "But we're sure. The MO doesn't match. And"—she bit her lip—"there are other . . . pieces of evidence."

The coffee started to slosh ominously in Cassie's stomach.

"Chris wanted me to tell you that you need to be careful."

Cassie tightened her grip on the cup; it was the only thing anchoring her to the sidewalk.

It all made sense now.

Of course Cliff Wolcott hadn't killed Skylark.

She had known it all along, but she had let everything else push it out of the way.

She had killed her. Just like she had been about to kill Ali this morning.

It was all she could do to hold herself together.

"Are you okay?" Farrow leaned forward, touched her arm. "I know this is a lot to take in."

Cassie nodded slowly, her head spinning, but not for the reason that Farrow thought.

She couldn't believe that she had been so stupid, that she had let herself believe that everything might actually be all right. Skylark was dead and her father was dead and Ali was in danger and it was all her.

It had always been her.

But that stopped now. Today she would figure out a way to end it. It was all that she could do. No amount of running would be enough: it needed to end.

"I'm okay," she said finally.

"I don't mean to be intrusive, but is there somewhere you can go? Someplace safe?"

Cassie rocked at the sound of concern in the cop's voice. "I'll figure something out," she said. "I'll be all right."

"Listen—" Farrow started, but she cut herself off. "I know that there might be issues but . . . Why don't you at least think about going home? I'm sure—"

"No," she said, taking a step away. "I can't." She shook her head furiously. "I can't."

"Cassandra," she said, moving toward her, reaching again for her arm. "I know it's hard. Your mom told me about the dreams and the fire, and Chris mentioned the investigation—"

"What?" She took two steps away from Farrow, ramming her back into the top of the railing so hard it took her breath away. "What are you talking about?"

Farrow bit her lips. "The investigation." She took a deep breath. "When you told your doctor that your father was abusing you."

Cassie glanced both ways up and down the sidewalk, fought to keep from putting her hands over her ears. "That was a mistake," she said quickly. "I was just dreaming."

"Were you?" There was a challenge in Farrow's voice, but a warmth too. It was like Dr. Livingston all over again, arguing with her about what she knew to be true. "What about when you were in the hospital, when you were twelve?"

"I didn't—"

"You tried to kill yourself."

"No." The word trailed off into a high-pitched whine, and Cassie shrank into herself.

"Cassie," Farrow said, taking a step toward her.

Cassie pulled back, turned her shoulder to the police officer.

"Cassie," she said, and Cassie felt a hand on her shoulder. "I understand."

Cassie sniffed.

"I believe you."

For a moment, Cassie's legs wouldn't hold her and she slipped back against the railing. It was like the world had opened up under her feet, like she was tumbling into a bottomless darkness.

"What?"

"I believe you."

Hearing the words for a second time didn't make them make any more sense.

"I know that other people . . . maybe they didn't. Maybe they . . . couldn't. But, Cassie . . ."

She shook her head. "I can't," she said, and shook her head harder. "I can't."

"Cassie, I—"

Cassie pulled away from the woman, spinning away, spinning free, falling into the darkness.

The coffee arced out of the cup in a brown parabola as it fell to the ground.

<< >>

He knew that waiting would bear fruit.

He watched from across the street as she talked to the police officer, as she scurried crying down the block.

The police officer had started after her, but stopped after only a few steps, shaking her head and turning back to the car, picking up the cup from the Thermos.

He waited until she had gotten back into the car, until she drove off, before he slipped out of the shadows to follow the girl downtown.

He wasn't worried about losing her. There were only so many places she would go.

She went to the most obvious.

When he found her again, she was sitting on the edge of the dry fountain in Centennial Square, on the opposite side from where that woman's body had been found.

That woman. How quickly the names disappeared.

But this one . . . this one would be remembered. Watching her in the square was a sharp reminder of what had drawn him to her from the start.

The flame still burned within her, but it had changed from orange-gold to blue. She was running on desperation now, fear, anger, sadness.

Despair.

In the absence of fuel, the fire burned itself, blazing hot, but short-lived.

He would need to take her soon; the way she was burning, she wouldn't last long.

While it still burned, though, she would be the rarest of delicacies.

The burning called to him, fed the darkness within him.

Tonight. It would be tonight.

But then something happened that he had not foreseen: a woman entered the square, tall and slim, scarf pulled up to her face, knit cap pulled down tight on her head.

She went directly to the girl at the fountain, and when she touched her shoulder, the girl's blue flame flared, almost exploded, then turned the blinding white of burning magnesium. Tendrils of white trailed up the girl's arm and into the woman's hand.

He stepped back as the white flame seared down the woman's arm and met the flame burning at the heart of her, turning the steady red glow to a vibrant, pulsing orange.

At the same time, the woman's red flame coursed up her own arm and leapt to the girl's body. The white flame wavered, then burst into rich orange life.

He frowned, then smiled.

It was beautiful, in its own way, how the flames fed each other, how they burned without consuming themselves, or their hosts.

It was sad; that blue flame would have been so sweet.

But now there were two.

He would wait.

He would watch.

He would feed.

Tonight.

"I'm sorry," Cassie said, snuffling and brushing the tears from her cheeks with her sleeve.

"For what?" Drawing her coat around herself, Ali sat down on the edge of the fountain next to Cassie.

Cassie shook her head, wrinkled her face in a disgusted smile. "Everything," she said.

"You don't have anything to be sorry for." She reached out to brush an errant lock of hair from Cassie's face, but she seemd to catch herself and withdrew her hand. "I should probably be the one apologizing."

"What? Why?"

Ali shook her head and looked away. "All of it," she said. "My part in all of it." She turned back to Cassie, and met her eye. "I really like you," she said. "So I think . . . it wasn't fair. I maybe pressured you into something you weren't . . . that maybe you didn't want. Don't want." She shrugged again and turned away. "Anyway. I'm sorry. I won't . . ."

When Cassie touched her leg, Ali turned back.

"You don't have anything to be sorry for," Cassie said. Leaning forward, she kissed her, softly but firmly. "You didn't do anything wrong," she whispered, without pulling away. She smiled sadly. "I think you're the only right thing that's ever happened to me."

"Then what is it?" she asked. "What's—"

Cassie shook her head and pulled away.

"Don't," Ali said, and Cassie started. "Don't run away. Please don't."

"I . . ." She felt so small.

"I don't like . . ." Ali cleared her throat, thick with emotion.

"I didn't like waking up and finding you gone. I worry about you. I want to help."

"You can't." It wasn't an accusation, just a sad statement of fact.

"Cassie—"

"I don't know what's real anymore," Cassie blurted. She needed to get the words out as quickly as she could.

Ali looked confused. "What?"

Cassie shook her head, already regretting saying the words, bringing up something that she couldn't understand, let alone explain.

"Tell me, please."

Cassie shook her head. "I thought I had it all figured out. I thought . . ." She took a deep, steeling breath. "When I was little, I had these dreams. Night terrors. I couldn't"—she sniffed—"I couldn't tell what was real and what wasn't. My dad—"

"Oh, Cassie . . ."

"But I thought, it couldn't be real, right? What he did to me? God!" She clenched her fists and her eyes shut. "How do I know this isn't a dream?" she asked, the tears streaking silver on her face. "It feels real—" She looked directly, openly, at Ali. "But when I'm asleep, it feels just as real. I'm back home, and it's just as real as this. And this feels like a dream, then." She took a deep breath. "And I'm worried that I'm going to do something. Something terrible." She looked at the curve of Ali's throat.

Ali nodded slowly. "I don't . . ."

Cassie shuddered into sobbing. Ali leaned forward and held her as she cried, rubbing her back gently, whispering soothing words in her ear.

"My father," Cassie said, sniffling, wiping her face. "He's alive."

"What?"

Cassie nodded and told her about Harrison and Farrow, what they had told her, about Farrow finding her at the courthouse, about what Harrison had done.

"Oh my God," Ali whispered. "That's—"

Cassie nodded, wiping her nose on her sleeve.

"But . . ." She spoke slowly, carefully. "I don't understand."

Cassie smiled sadly. "That's what I mean."

Ali thought for a moment, absently rubbing Cassie's back. "So . . ." Again: slowly, carefully. "You dreamed that your father was dead?"

"Maybe," Cassie said, just as slowly and carefully.

"Or?"

"That's what I mean," Cassie said, her back shuddering again as she fought back tears. "I don't know what's real anymore. I don't know what's been real my whole life. I don't—" She looked at Ali desperately. "What if this is just a dream? What if . . . Alicia?" She sobbed. "I don't know what's real."

"I'm real," Ali said. "I'm right here."

Cassie's smile was wide, a mask over fear. "Well," she said, her words dry, "you would say that, wouldn't you?" She almost laughed. "This could all be . . ." She swept her arm around the square. "I can't trust any of it, can I?" She stared at Ali, half-defiant, half-hopeful, desperate that she might have an answer. "Can I?"

"No," Ali said.

"Right."

"You can't trust anything. It could all be a dream. I could . . ." Ali shook her head. "You can't trust anything."

Cassie looked at her, stunned.

"Except yourself."

Cassie met Ali's eyes, and neither of them looked away.

She felt a weight starting to lift from her, a looseness in her chest that let her breathe.

A small smile played at the corners of Ali's mouth. "Trust yourself. You're not crazy, you're just dreaming." She paused. "You're not crazy, are you?" she asked with a sly smile.

Cassie smiled back. "I don't think so," she said. "I don't know."

She leaned in to Ali, let herself breathe. *In two three four.*

Ali squeezed her hand again. "You're going to be okay," she said. "We'll figure it out."

Cassie loved the way she said it, as if nothing could stop them, as if it was only a matter of figuring it out, that it would be all right in the end.

We.

She smiled, but the smile quickly faded from her face.

"What is it?" Ali asked.

"What—" Cassie said, and stopped, her voice thick again with tears. "What if this is a dream?"

Ali reached out and, with the gentlest of touches, wiped away the tears from her cheeks.

"It's not," she said. "This is real."

≪ ≫

In the dark of the bedroom, in the quiet of the night, it seemed natural to whisper.

"I'm scared," Cassie said, in a voice even softer than a whisper. So soft, she was sure that Ali wouldn't hear.

But she did.

"Oh, Cassie," she said, turning over to face her. "It'll be okay. I'm right here."

Cassie couldn't tell her that her being right there was one of the things that she was afraid of. She hadn't told her about how she had woken up that morning, standing beside the bed, looking down at her.

It wasn't the sort of thing you could just tell someone, was it?

And, to be honest, she had expected Ali to ask her about it, to ask why there had been a knife on her bedroom floor that morning. All evening, that thought, that inevitability, had lurked at the back of her mind. What could she possibly say?

But Ali hadn't asked, hadn't even hinted at it, and it was only when they were in the bedroom, getting ready for bed, that Cassie understood why.

The knife she had dropped that morning was still on the floor, right where it had fallen: just under the edge of the bed, half-concealed by the fall of the covers. She never would have seen it if she hadn't been looking for it.

While Ali's back was turned, she had nudged the knife farther under the bed with her toe.

Now, in bed, Ali draped her arm loosely over Cassie's midsection: the warmth of her skin crackled against her.

"Thank you," Cassie said, even more quietly, after a moment.

"For what?" Cassie could hear the sleep in Ali's voice.

She wasn't really sure how to answer the question; it all seemed so clear, so self-evident. "For coming after me. For finding me," she said, finally.

The arm around her belly tightened. "I'll always come after you," Ali said. "I'll always find you."

The words were warmer than the blanket over her, warmer than the breath that carried them.

In the dark, she listened as Ali's breathing slowed and deepened, the arm around her loosening, growing heavy.

The room brightened by degrees, the squares of the windows taking on a faint silver glow. Not much light, but enough.

Slowly, and with as much stillness as she could manage, Cassie rolled out from under Ali's arm and out of the bed, gently setting both feet on the floor and waiting. When there was no sign of Ali waking, Cassie rose slowly to her feet.

She didn't need any light: it was only a few careful steps to the corner of the room where her backpack stood. Crouching down, ignoring the hint of cold in the air, Cassie lifted the flap of the bag and reached inside.

When she had what she was looking for, Cassie padded slowly back to the bed. Careful not to make any sharp movements, she crawled back under the covers, shimmying under Ali's arm and nestling it around herself. Ali's breathing caught, and Cassie used the moment to shift position to snuggle in beside her, her back to the woman's front, wrapped in her sleeping arms.

When Ali—still asleep—sensed her there, she pulled Cassie close, until Cassie could feel the whole warm length of her against her back, her breath soft and regular at the back of her neck.

It was only then, safe in her embrace, her own arms wrapped tightly around Mr. Monkey, pulling him close, that Cassie let herself drift off to sleep.

« »

Outside, the world was quiet. The wind had died off, and the snow that had been threatening for days was finally falling, a thick wall of pasty, heavy flakes shrouding the house from view.

No need now to hide in the shadows. He watched the house from the sidewalk across the street. It was Christmas Eve, and anyone tempted to be out on that night of lights had been driven indoors by the snow.

The night belonged to the Darkness.

≪ ≫

"Miss Weathers."

Mrs. Murrow had a way of saying her name that sounded like curdled milk in her mouth.

She clutched her binder to her chest and stepped into the otherwise empty classroom.

The teacher was writing on the chalkboard, and she turned her back on the girl as she approached.

"You have your assignments?" she asked, without looking at her.

Cassie nodded, then, realizing that the teacher couldn't see her, said, "Yes. Yes I do."

She hated the way her voice came out, thin and weak.

"Leave them on my desk." The chalk screeched on the board as the teacher sketched out a sample problem.

Cassie set her binder on a desk in the front row and clicked it open. Retrieving the three sheets of loose-leaf, she snapped it shut again.

Picking up the binder, she placed the sheets on Mrs. Murrow's desk.

"And the note?" the teacher asked. She hadn't turned around, but Cassie felt like she was watching nonetheless.

Cassie felt her stomach and legs turn to water.

Mrs. Murrow turned slowly to face her. "Miss Weathers? Do you, or do you not, have a note to explain your absence yesterday afternoon?" There was a smug, satisfied tone to the teacher's voice.

"I . . . I just . . ."

"Miss. Weathers." She broke Cassie's name sharply in the middle, like breaking a bone.

"I'm sorry," Cassie said. "I—"

"You don't," Mrs. Murrow said, her voice clear and cold.

Cassie shook her head.

"No." The teacher's thin lips curled around the word. "Of course you don't."

As she spoke, Cassie realized that she had reached into her jacket pocket, curled her fingers around the knife that she had bought at Schmidt's.

"And what," Mrs. Murrow started, "are we going to do about that?"

Cassie's lips parted as she slid the knife from her pocket—

"No," she said, quietly but firmly.

"I. Beg. Your. Pardon."

But Cassie hadn't spoken to her.

"Miss Weathers," Mrs. Murrow said, stepping toward her desk, her hands on her hips. "I asked you: What are we going to do about this?"

But Cassie wasn't listening. She recognized that voice. Why was she having so much trouble placing it?

When she thought about it, a chill ran through her, a memory of a cold deeper than she had ever felt.

But she had felt it.

And then she remembered.

Victoria. The camp.

Chilly beans.

"Nothing," she said decisively.

"I beg your —"

"Nothing," she repeated. "There's nothing to do anything about. There's nothing here."

"Miss Weathers—"

"You're nothing," she said, and as soon as she said the words, she knew they were true, and that awareness was like steel in her blood. "You're a dream. A memory of a woman I met."

"A woman you killed."

The words were like a slap, and Cassie took a step backward to keep from falling over.

Mrs. Murrow advanced on her desk, bending toward Cassie. "You cut her throat. You cut her throat and you left her in the snow." Cassie cowered, tried to protect herself, clutched her binder tightly.

"You liked it, didn't you? The power, the strength. You've always been such a pathetic little whelp, always mewling and whining. 'Oh, I have bad dreams. Make them stop. Make them stop.'" Mrs. Murrow came around the desk, her face twisted. "You liked killing that old woman."

"I didn't—"

"The way the blood sprayed into the snow? The way it sizzled when it hit?"

"No, I—" Cassie backed up as the teacher towered over, bumping her thighs on the front desk.

"Did you taste it?" Mrs. Murrow hissed, close enough for Cassie to feel her breath on her face, to smell it, a rank, rotting smell, like garbage, like meat gone bad. "Did you lick her blood off your fingers?"

Cassie could taste it in the back of her throat, the rich, metallic, musky tang.

But she shook her head.

"No," she gasped.

Then she stopped.

She straightened up.

"No, I didn't." Her voice was cold. Calm.

"You pathetic little bitch."

"Shut up," she said, not breaking down, even as Mrs. Murrow's face loomed into hers, close enough to kiss.

That face flashed a deep red. "You can't talk to me like that. I'll—"

"You'll what? Punish me? Send me to the principal's office?" She took a step forward, and the teacher stepped back. "Nothing. That's what. You'll do nothing."

"You can't—"

"I can do whatever I want," Cassie said, looking down at the binder against her chest. "Everything here"—she lifted the binder toward the teacher—"is mine."

She was holding Mr. Monkey in her hands between herself and the teacher. His button eyes stared sightlessly at the old woman.

"Just go," Cassie said.

And the classroom was empty, an algebra problem half-completed on the blackboard.

« »

In the bed, Cassie stirred. Ali's arm tightened around her, and she slipped back into full sleep.

Footfalls crunched in the fresh snow outside the window.

« »

Cassie exhaled a long breath and let her body relax.

She hadn't been sure that that would work. She hadn't even been sure what she was doing. But when she recognized Sarah from Edmonton, it had all come rushing back: the camp, the cold, the body in the snow.

Pieces began to fall into place.

She had dreamed that she had killed Sarah: that part hadn't been real. But everything else: Brother Paul and the restaurant and Skylark—

"Of course I'm real."

The voice from the doorway made her jump, but that was purely a reaction to the silence being broken: Cassie had been expecting her.

"So what should I call you?" she asked as she turned. "Skylark? Laura?"

The girl shrugged, smiled. "That's up to you, isn't it?" She took a step into the room. "It's your dream, right?"

She smiled, and Cassie's heart swelled despite herself.

"I'm sorry for what happened to you," she said gently, stepping toward her.

Skylark's smile showed her teeth. "What you did, you mean?"

It was like the world stopped. The walls of the classroom seemed to close in on her. Everything seemed to narrow to a single point, a single focus: Her. Skylark. Laura.

Cassie shook her head. "I didn't," she said.

"They never found the knife that killed me, did they? The knife that you used?"

"I didn't—"

Skylark smiled. It was warm, inviting, the Skylark she remembered. "It's okay," she said. "I mean, there's nothing we can do about it now."

"But I—" She shook her head: it couldn't be, she couldn't have.

Skylark wrinkled her lip in an empathetic frown.

"You don't remember, do you? That morning? What happened?" She looked sadly at Cassie. "I woke you up, and we ran away from the camp, remember? From the police."

Cassie shook her head. That morning was a blur of lights and shouting. And then running.

Oh, God.

The running.

Skylark nodded slowly. "I know this is hard," she said, her voice gentle.

The cold, the echoes of running footsteps, shouting in the distance, red lights flashing against the brick fronts of buildings even blocks away.

"We ran until we couldn't run anymore," Skylark said, taking a step toward her. "We hid in that alley—"

"No." Tears flowed out of her eyes, left corrosive streaks down her cheeks. "That's not—"

"You came up behind me," Skylark said, like she was describing waiting in the cafeteria line. "I was bent over, out of breath, and you grabbed my hair and pulled me back—" She tilted her head back, stretching her throat taut, pale and fragile. "And then—"

As she drew her finger across her throat in a slow slitting

motion, the skin opened as if cut, the flesh gaping like a wide, obscene mouth. "You killed me, Cassie." The words bubbled out of her throat in a froth of blood, but Cassie heard the accusation as plain as day.

Skylark relaxed her neck. The wound had vanished, the blood disappeared, all without leaving a trace. "I'm sorry, Cassie," she said, and her face radiated a warm sadness. "I know this is hard, but it's better if you know, right? Before you hurt anyone else?"

Cassie thought of Ali, curled on her side in her bed. Looking down at the white plane of her neck, the ridge of her jugular.

Skylark nodded, slowly. "You don't want to hurt Ali. She's been so kind to you."

Cassie nodded. Ali. A blur of sensations, of memories: the one crooked tooth in the bottom of her smile, the gleam of sweat on her when she brought food out from the kitchen of the restaurant, the way her eyes had shone in the twinkling lights of the Christmas tree—

"No," she said slowly, a realization beginning to form.

"I'm sorry, Cassie, but you—"

"No," she said firmly. "I didn't."

Skylark smiled sadly, pityingly. "Oh, Cassie."

"I never would have killed you," she said, more sure than she had ever been of anything.

"You did," Skylark said. "I know you didn't want to—"

"I didn't," she said, clutching Mr. Monkey. "I couldn't. I would never have hurt you."

"But you did," she said, and Cassie heard the faintest hint of desperation in her voice. "Just like you killed your father. Just like you almost killed Ali." Her voice rose slightly.

"I didn't kill my father," she said. "I know the difference

between what I dreamed and what really happened. I didn't kill him." She took a step toward Skylark.

"But what about—" Skylark shrank back.

"What about Ali?" She knew exactly what Skylark was going to ask: of course she did. "I didn't hurt her. Even when I was fast asleep. Even when I was dreaming. I couldn't. I wouldn't. I woke up before anything happened."

"This time."

Cassie smiled, suddenly calm, suddenly sure. "Every time. Always."

"Because you love her." She tried to make it sound mocking, her voice rising in a sardonic screech.

"Yes."

Skylark seemed to deflate, to shrink.

"I really am sorry for what happened to you," Cassie said. It seemed so little to say. "But I can't stay here. I need to go." The door behind Skylark seemed to beckon her, draw her in. "Right through there."

As she walked past her, Cassie expected Skylark to touch her, to brush her arm or her shoulder. When she didn't, she had to fight back a sob: she was really gone. The immense reality of Skylark's death, the sheer weight of loss, pressed down on her.

Gone.

"There's something you haven't thought of," Skylark said, behind her, her voice hushed.

Cassie tried to resist, but she had to turn, had to look at the shade of her friend.

Skylark smiled, somewhere between sadness and glee.

"If you didn't kill me," Skylark asked, "who did?"

As the snow began to blanket the world, he descended upon the house.

The girls were in the basement, that much was clear. The rest of the house was dark, while the bottom floor had throbbed with light and life as soon as they had returned.

He had waited, had watched, through the evening, and then the lights had begun to blink out, one by one, until the entire house seemed to be asleep.

And still, he had waited.

Yes, there were plans to be made, precautions to be taken, but mostly it was the deliciousness of the anticipation that filled the time. The hunt was always something special, but this hunt, this hunt promised to be extraordinary.

And then it was time.

A slow, careful inspection around the house revealed several weak points: the window over the kitchen sink was open a crack, with no lock and nothing to block it sliding. The bedroom window was hidden from prying eyes by a shrub, already sagging under the weight of the snow.

But most promising was the area around the door itself. The lock was a deadbolt, but the window to the left . . .

« »

Cassie took one last look back into the classroom as she reached the doorway. Skylark was gone, and the room was empty.

It was eerie: too calm, too quiet. Some places were made for people, and when they were empty, they seemed wrong somehow.

Taking a deep breath, she turned back to the door.

And stopped.

The doorway looked the same as it always did, the door the same brown metal with the small window near the top that she saw every day. But outside, where there should have been a corridor lined with lockers, there was a dark stairway, going down.

She recognized it immediately: the rough, raw wood stairs, the unfinished wall along one side, the shaky railing along the other. She had seen it almost every day of her life.

It was the stairs from the house, down to the basement. Down to the storage room. Down to the furnace room, with the woodpiles, and the stove.

Down.

At the base of the stairs, there was a click, and the single bare light bulb burst into sudden, blinding life.

Cassie gasped and took a step back.

There was someone down there, waiting for her.

Someone, or something.

She took a deep breath. Of course there was.

There was always going to be someone waiting at the bottom of those stairs; it was always going to come down to this.

Clutching Mr. Monkey close with her right arm, she stepped carefully down on the first stair, resting her hand lightly on the railing.

Down to the second stair: the air was colder, and her breath hung in front of her mouth like a still, grey cloud.

Third stair.

With a creak, the door at the top of the stairs slammed shut.

≪ ≫

He slipped the corner of a black credit card into the narrow seam between the window and the frame, wiggling it and shifting it slightly so the entire edge of the card slid through.

As the card began to slide down toward the latch, he straightened, a prickling along the back of his neck, a crackling in his ears.

Had it been the wind? The sound of the falling snow? Something . . .

Reaching under his coat with his right hand, he curled his fingers around the hilt of the hunting knife on his belt.

There was something behind him.

He started to turn as the hand fell onto his shoulder.

"Don't. Move."

The voice was rough, a breathy snarl through clenched teeth, but he recognized it immediately.

His fingers tightened around the knife.

"Turn around. Slowly."

As he turned, he slipped the knife out from under his coat, tucked it behind his back, holding it loosely in his right hand, just out of sight.

The police officer from the morning that woman had died at the camp looked like he was on his last legs. Dressed in a heavy winter coat, a black toque tight over his ears, he looked pale and drawn, his eyes twitching and frantic.

"Step away from the door." His voice shook as he spoke.

The cop was standing less than three feet from him, close enough to cut off any avenue of escape with a single step.

He looked at him carefully. There was something wrong with this picture, something out of place. Something missing.

"I've got you for breaking and entering. Don't make it worse. Step away from the door."

It was the voice that gave him away, the stressed firmness of it, the sound of authority coming apart, much though he tried to conceal it.

"Constable Harrison," he said, drawing his lips back in a smile. "Shouldn't you be at home with your family?"

"Step away from the door."

"And if you're going to be out on a night like this—"

"I'm not going to tell you—"

"Shouldn't you be armed?"

Taking a single step forward, he planted his right foot firmly on the snowy ground and used the momentum to drive the knife deep into the constable's midsection, bringing his left hand up in the same motion to cover the man's mouth.

He could feel the scream against his gloved palm, could see the cop's eyes widen as he struggled against the pain, against falling backward into the snow.

Pulling the knife from the constable's body, he took hold of the shoulders of the man's jacket and dragged him behind the corner of the house. He didn't do anything else to conceal the body. No one would find it tonight, and by morning he would be gone.

He wiped the blade against the cop's legs, held it up to the silvery light.

It was time.

It took only a few, silent moments with the edge of the credit card, a small, almost inaudible click, and the window swung open.

Pushing it slightly, carefully, listening for creaks, he reached through and turned the deadbolt.

« »

Cassie silently counted each of the stairs as she descended into the basement: nine, ten.

Her hand was loose on the rickety railing; she knew better than to trust it with any of her weight.

Eleven.

The stairs themselves were brightly lit, but outside of that pool of light, the basement was pitch-dark. Cassie tried not to think of what might be lurking in that darkness, afraid that anything she imagined in this place might come to life.

The phrase "It's all in your head" had never been so terrifying.

Twelve.

Not far to go now.

Thirteen.

It had been so cold at the top of the stairs, and now it was sweltering. Sweat dripped down her back and pooled at the base of her spine. Her shirt was soaked.

Fourteen.

One more step.

As her feet touched the concrete floor of the basement, there was an echoing click, and the light flashed out.

Cassie stumbled in the sudden dark, crashing into the wall with her shoulder. Her breath was ripped from her and it took her a moment to be able to breathe again.

Her heart racing, she leaned against the wall, willing her eyes to adjust to the dark, counting her breaths.

In the distance, she could hear the roaring crackle of the fire.

And footsteps.

She froze in place and held her breath.

Nothing.

No sound save the distant flames.

But there had been something. She was sure of it.

"Hello?" she called out, willing her voice not to shake. "Who's there?"

There was a slight shuffle, an almost silent rasp that might have been a footfall, or it might have been her imagination.

It's all in your head.

"Hello?" She tried again, louder this time. "Is someone—"

Her skin prickled and she shivered. Someone was there. She couldn't see them, but they were close enough for her to sense.

Close enough to touch.

She turned and took a single, careful step toward the furnace room.

"Hello?" She called out. "Hello?"

She heard the sound of a breath a fraction of a second before two hands wrapped around her throat in the dark. Mr. Monkey fell to the floor as the fingers tightened.

"You selfish bitch," a whisper hissed, close to her ear.

She brought her hands up, tried to pull the fingers away, but they were too tight, and they tightened even more as she struggled.

"How could you do this?"

Bright flashes of light exploded in her eyes and a low buzzing started in her ears.

"Heather," she gasped, struggling with her sister's fingers at her throat. "Please—"

"You ruined everything."

The buzzing grew louder and Cassie dug her fingernails into her sister's hands, trying to wrench them away. There was a sharp cry, a flinch, but her fingers didn't release.

"Heather."

"This is what you—"

With the last of her strength, Cassie kicked out as hard as she could and reached toward the sound of the voice. She caught her sister in the leg with the kick, and as she stumbled forward, Cassie dug her fingernails into Heather's face, clawing and scratching.

Heather screamed, and her grip released. Cassie fell to the floor, pulling herself away as she gasped for breath.

"You fucking bitch," Heather shrieked. "Why can't you just die?"

"Heather, I'm—" She cut herself off and scrambled away from where she had been attacked. In the dark, Heather would only be able to find her if she said anything, made any noise. Otherwise, her sister was just as blind as she was.

She hoped.

"Heather I, Heather I, Heather I." Heather put on a whiny baby voice, parroting her own words back to her. "It's always about you, isn't it? You don't care about anybody else. It's all Cassie's world to you, isn't it?"

Shuffling, almost silent footsteps in the dark. Faltering. Searching.

Cassie crouched down, trying to make herself small, trying to calm her breathing, trying to be silent.

"I can hear you," Heather said. "You can't hide forever."

More shuffling, then a crash as something fell over. Cassie jumped, forced herself not to scream. Heather was searching for her, working her way through the dark.

"And when I find you, I'm going to—"

"Girls!" The basement light flashed on overhead, and Cassie slammed her eyes shut and ducked her head at the sudden brightness. "What's going on in here?"

« »

With the door closed, he stood stock-still in the kitchen, not breathing, not making a sound. Listening.

After a long moment, the usual night noises of the house faded away, and there were only the two girls, breathing. Deep, regular, soft breaths. Sleeping breaths. Unbroken. Undisturbed.

He smiled. No need to rush. No need to squander such an opportunity with undue haste. On this night, the lightest of nights, there was a feast waiting to be savoured, long undisturbed hours of pleasure ahead.

The smile widened.

There was time, and space, to do it right this time. To prepare.

Shoes went beside the door, jacket hung on a hook, pockets emptied onto the counter: a package of cigarettes, a lighter, a handful of change, a receipt from a coffee shop, a battered black journal, duct-taped along the spine.

The knife was already warm in his hand.

He smiled. All was ready.

« »

After a long moment, Cassie risked opening her eyes.

Heather was standing a few feet away, eyes clenched tightly shut, blood dripping onto her pyjamas from the scratches on her cheeks.

Cassie shivered: she had backed herself into a corner. It would have been only seconds before her sister found her.

"Are you two fighting again?"

Their father was standing in the doorway of the furnace room, dressed in his usual at-home clothes: a pair of jeans and a checkered flannel shirt.

Again? But they never fought. She and Heather had always been so close. It wasn't until—

Cassie had to shake her head to remind herself that she was dreaming. It all seemed so real: the world, the people, the memories. It was hard to keep it all straight.

"She started it," Heather cried, taking a few steps toward him, gesturing at her face. "Look at what she did to me!"

"Let me take a look at you," their father said, and Heather stepped in front of him, tilting her head back and closing her eyes. "Yeah, that looks pretty bad."

Cassie rose slowly to her feet. Mr. Monkey was on the floor a few feet away, and she picked him up and held him close.

"I don't think there's going to be any scars, though." Taking Heather's head in his hands, he turned it gently, angling it toward the light so he could see better. "Yeah, I think it's going to be okay."

"Thank you, Daddy."

She tried to lower her head, but her father held it fast.

"What did you do to your sister to make her do this to you?"

Even from across the room, Cassie could see the way his hands were pressing tighter and tighter around Heather's head, holding her fast. She took a step forward.

"I didn't—" Heather's words gurgled out of her mouth on a wave of tears and snot. Her body churned and twisted as she tried to pull herself away. "I didn't do anything."

"Don't lie to me, baby," he said, half-lifting her from the ground by her head, her neck stretching. "You know what I do to lying little girls."

"She didn't do anything," Cassie said, stepping into the middle of the room.

Her father turned to her without easing his grip on Heather. Her sister flailed and twisted, but it wasn't doing any good. Her face was getting redder and redder, covered in a wet sheen.

"It was an accident—"

Her father smiled like he had been waiting for that answer.

"I think it's really sweet," he said, his voice dripping. "How you'll stand here and lie to me, all to save someone who was trying to kill you not five minutes ago." Heather was making a gurgling, gasping noise, her feet kicking useless pinwheels in the air.

"She's not 'someone,'" Cassie said. "She's my sister."

"She's nothing," Cassie's father said, and there was a cracking noise and one final scream from Heather as her head burst, spraying blood against the wall, collapsing into a red-grey mush of bone and flesh.

Her father dropped Heather's body. It landed on the floor with a wet thud.

He wiped his hands on the front of his shirt.

"But you—" He turned to face her fully. "You're less than nothing."

Cassie had to fight not to throw up, had to force herself not to look at the crumpled heap on the floor that had once been her sister.

Had to remind herself, over and over, that it was only a dream.

"I know what you're thinking," her father said, and suddenly they were standing in the furnace room, the wood stove glowing with heat.

Cassie blinked, shook her head, clung more tightly to Mr. Monkey. But it didn't change: Furnace room. Stove.

She knew there was a blanket on the shelf behind her, red and soft. He kept it folded with an even-creased precision.

"You're thinking, 'This is just a dream,'" he said. "You're thinking that you can do anything here. That you're in control. That nothing can hurt you. Right?"

Cassie had never thought that she couldn't be hurt here—the pain in her neck, her shoulder, the burning in her lungs seemed to make a lie of that—but ultimately, yes, he was right about what she was thinking.

Of course he was right: he was part of the same dream.

"And now you're thinking, 'Well, of course he knows what I'm thinking,' right? He's part of my psyche, just another bundle of bad thoughts, of course he knows."

Cassie didn't speak, didn't move.

Her father took a step toward her and smiled.

She flinched: the smile looked like something out of a nightmare, wide and wet and reptilian. Like a snake or an alligator.

It looked hungry.

"But Cassie, my love my dove my dear little girl . . ." And the smile widened. "If this is all a dream"—he took a step closer—"why can't you wake up?"

≪ ≫

He stopped in the doorway to the bedroom, willed himself silent and still.

The girl was stirring in the bed, twitching and thrashing in her sleep. A mewling cry rose from deep in her throat, a primal sound beyond conscious fear, beyond rational expression.

It was a sound he loved.

Had something startled her? The closing of the kitchen drawer? Strange footsteps? Was she just so attuned that she was aware, even deep in sleep, of a presence in the apartment?

No—this was something else.

The other girl shifted, seemed to fold herself even more snugly, drawing her arm even more tightly around her friend, nuzzling into the back of her neck.

"Shh," she half-moaned. "It's okay."

And, gradually, the girl calmed and stilled. Her breathing slowed, grew even and deep.

It was possibly the most beautiful moment he had ever experienced. The knife trembled with anticipation.

« »

Her father smiled as she screamed, as she shredded her throat, as she struggled against the world around her. She had to wake up. It was just a dream. It was just a dream. She could wake up.

She had to wake up.

"When you realize you're dreaming, don't you wake up?" Her father spoke into her screaming, slow and thoughtful. "Isn't that how it usually works?"

All of Cassie's strength left her at once, as if all of the energy, all of the momentum that her certainty had created all fled.

She sagged. Almost fell.

"Oh, I'm sorry," he said. "I forgot. You've never had a normal dream, have you?"

"What—" She struggled to speak against the waves of exhaustion.

"That's a good girl," he said. "My sleepy, sleepy girl. Here." He reached past her, drew the red blanket off the shelf and spread it on the floor between them. "Why don't you lie down?" His eyes flickered; his smile yawned.

"No." She shook her head. "No." She took a step back.

"Be a good girl," he said. "Be Daddy's good little girl."

A rush of sad desperation rose inside her; it felt like the world breaking, like she was being shredded, split in two.

Tears rolled down her face, and she didn't even notice them.

"That's a good girl," Daddy said, and he crouched beside the blanket. "Why don't you come lie down?" He patted the blanket, stroked it, showing her how warm and soft it was. "You can bring Mr. Monkey if you like."

Cassie nodded, stepped toward the blanket.

"Are you cold, baby? Do you want me to build up the fire?" He turned toward the stove, opened the heavy iron door.

When Cassie looked down, there was a chunk of wood in her hand where Mr. Monkey had been seconds before, cut for the stove. Heavy. Solid.

She raised it over her head.

She knew what she had to do. She had done it before.

The wood fell with a deep, crushing thud.

This time, though, her father didn't fall into the stove.

This time, he straightened, and he turned to her.

"You little bitch," he said, but he was smiling.

He was smiling as she slammed the chunk of wood into the side of his head, knocking him sideways to the ground.

He was smiling as she swung the chunk of wood into his face, crushing his cheekbones, breaking his jaw. He smiled as she beat his face bloody, as she shattered his teeth, broke his nose. He smiled as his breath bubbled out of him in a thick, red slurry.

He smiled until he wasn't her daddy anymore. Until there was nothing left that she recognized.

Until she dropped the chunk of wood on the floor.

She slumped down onto the blanket, between Mr. Monkey and the thing that had pretended to be her father. The fire crackled in the stove, but the heat wasn't overwhelming anymore, just a gentle warmth that seemed to enfold her, to comfort and cozy her.

She couldn't move. She couldn't stand. More than anything in the world she wanted to cry, but she didn't even have the strength to do that.

She lay there in silence for a long time, hard on the ground, looking over the landscape of her father's body toward the orange glow of flames in the stove.

It took her a long time to realize that she was waiting.

She had done it. She had confronted the dream, taken control. Shouldn't something be happening? Wasn't this supposed to bring it all to an end?

Shouldn't she be waking up?

If this was all a dream, shouldn't it be over now?

"You're wrong," whispered the voice, so close to her ear it was almost as if it was coming from inside her own head. "You've always been wrong."

She turned with a start, looking for the source of the voice, her heart racing in her chest again.

But there was no one there.

"It's not a dream," the voice said. "It was never a dream."

She looked into the shadows, trying to discern a shape. She looked at the doorway, expecting someone to be there, looking in at her.

But she was alone.

"Who—"

"This is your life," the voice said. "This is your world."

She looked down.

Mr. Monkey was looking at her, his button eyes reflecting the orange glow of the flames.

He blinked.

"This is our place," the monkey said. "There's no way out."

≪ ≫

As the girl stirred again, he stepped back from the bed, into the shadow of the open bedroom door. She moved helplessly, a tiny sobbing sound deep in her throat.

The dreams she must be having, to trouble her so.

The other girl woke up slightly, leaned over and whispered in her ear.

"It's all right, Cassandra. It's all right."

Her words were like music, the most pleasing of lullabies. There was love there, and passion, but a deep caring as well.

He knew that those things did not always come together, no matter what the greeting cards claimed.

At the sound of the other girl's voice, Cassandra—Cassie, like that cop had said—settled again. Her body collapsed into the bed, her head heavy on the pillow, her breathing growing thick and slow.

It took the other girl longer to settle. She adjusted her pillow, pulled up the blankets and as she curled herself again around Cassandra, she took her hand, interlacing their fingers.

It was only then that she too went back to sleep.

≪ ≫

Mr. Monkey pushed himself up on his front paws and swung across the blanket. As he moved, he began to grow, to change: his movement was a constantly shifting blur, a wavering between states of being.

When he swung off the blanket and turned to face her again, Cassie flinched. He was the height of a small child, his features wavering between his familiar stitching and the face of a real monkey, with matted brown fur, loose, snarling lips and yellowing fangs.

"Stop it," she said quietly, her voice quavering.

"You don't like it?" He danced a few steps, and when he stopped to tip his hat—

—his hat—when had he gotten a hat?—

—she recognized him. He looked like one of the flying monkeys from *The Wizard of Oz*. They had terrified her the first time she'd watched it; she had cried so hard she had thrown up.

"Why . . . why are you doing this?"

The monkey was still growing, his features still wavering. It wasn't that the two faces were alternating or shifting; he was both of them at the same time, like those puzzles in the books where the picture is an old lady and a young woman, depending on how you look at it.

A vase or two faces.

Two monkeys. One that had been her best friend for as long as she could remember, and one that was one of her oldest memories, the first thing she knew that could terrify her.

"Doing what?" Mr. Monkey asked, dancing again. Grinning.

"Stop it."

"Stop what?" Dancing. Tipping his hat. Mocking her.

"I can't—" She broke off, not able to go any further. It was all too much. She could feel parts of herself shutting down, going to sleep.

"No," the monkey snapped, leaning toward her, his freakishly long body seeming to stretch even farther. "You can't, can you?" He spat the words, tendrils of thick drool hanging off his fangs. "You can't do anything."

"It's all too much."

The monkey stopped stock-still and cocked its head, studying her with its yellow eyes.

"I'm sorry," it said, and Cassie couldn't be sure if it was still mocking her. "Is this better?"

The room was gone. It didn't vanish, it was just gone, all of it—the rows of stacked wood, the stove, the blanket, her father's body, her father's blood, gone. Like they had never existed.

Cassie was standing outside. Snow was falling in huge white flakes, and there were several inches on the ground between her and the monkey. But there was nothing else: no light, no dark, nothing hinted at in the distance, no distance. Just endless grey, and the snow, and the monkey, and her.

"Is this better?" The politeness, the concern, they had to be a show.

"What is this place?" She looked around herself, trying to get her bearings, but there was nothing. There was snow on the ground, but she didn't even know if there was really ground under it. The snow was falling, but it didn't seem like there was any sky for it to fall from.

"This?" The monkey gestured around. He was as tall as she was now, but he seemed to have stopped growing. "What, you don't like it?" His every word seemed to have the edge of a taunt, of a joke at her expense.

Cassie shook her head. "It's awful."

"That's too bad," the monkey chattered, dancing a bit in place. "You don't recognize it?"

Cassie hesitated. It was something she was supposed to know. "No," she said carefully.

"It's you!" the monkey shrieked, turning a hands-free back-flip. "It's all you!"

Cassie took a step back.

"We're in your heart!" the monkey screamed. "Look around! Don't you recognize it? Cold and grey. Empty. This is the very heart of you. This is where you live, no matter how far you run!"

≪ ≫

The snow burned against his face, melted against the blood soaking the front of his coat.

It was all Harrison could do to open his eyes, to pull himself onto his side. There was no hope of standing up. The way the world was swimming around him, shapes twisting and distending, it was almost impossible even to orient himself.

It wasn't until he saw the tracks in the snow, the long streak where he had been dragged, that he knew: the door. The door was that way.

Pressing his left hand as hard as he could against the wound in his belly, he began to follow the footsteps, planting his right elbow in the snow, pulling himself forward, almost collapsing each time.

He had to get inside. He had to stop him.

≪ ≫

"No," Cassie said, her voice little more than the bubble of a thought, powerless.

The monkey leaned in close, close enough for her to smell the rankness of its breath. "Yes," it whispered.

"No," she repeated. "It can't be. There are people—"

"What people?" the monkey asked, stepping back.

Tapping both paws to his chest, the monkey seemed to explode, black fragments spraying into the air, taking wing, a flock of crows, hundreds, thousands, wheeling and arcing and cawing against the white sky, swooping over Cassie, close enough she could feel the breath of their wings, coiling back together, taking on form again.

"People who love you?" her father asked, standing where the monkey had been a blink before.

She took a sharp step back.

"Why do you think anybody would love you?" her father asked, stepping toward her. "You've pushed away anyone who's ever cared for you." He looked at her sternly. "You told such terrible lies about me, and then you ran away. You left your family to worry about you."

"You didn't even try to help me," Sarah said, standing where her father had been, her body odour sharp and biting in the empty space. "You left me to die alone in the cold." Every word she spoke spilled a fresh gout of blood from the slash across her throat, down the front of her drab grey clothes.

"You said you'd always be there for me," Heather said.

Cassie stepped back.

"You left me to die," Skylark said, and the look of pain on her face made Cassie's heart ache. "You ran away, and you left me with him."

"Who?" Cassie asked, in a whispered gasp of tears. "Who did this to you?"

But all Skylark did was smile. "You did," she said, the sadness at odds with her smile. "If you had stayed . . . That's not what you do to someone you love. You fight for them." She shook her head. "But you ran away."

"You ran away," Heather said.

Her father.

Sarah.

"Stop it," she cried out, covering her eyes with her hands, trying to block out the images.

But the voices still drifted around her, echoing her failings in the dark, fathomless void.

"You tried to kill me."

The words were an accusation, but they were spoken gently, sadly.

When Cassie took her hands from her eyes, Ali was standing in front of her. Ali the way she had first seen her, in the restaurant, her dark hair sleek, her black jeans, the T-shirt that rode up a little when she moved, revealing the pale line of her stomach, the small of her back.

"I took you into my home, into my life," Ali said. "I came looking for you, and you tried to kill me."

She lifted her hand to Cassie's gaze—she was holding the knife. The knife that she had bought at the department store downtown. The knife that she had bought at Schmidt's.

Cassie took another step back, shaking her head. "No," she whispered, knowing what was about to happen, but unable to stop it, unable to look away.

"Is this what you wanted?"

Ali lifted the knife to her throat. Tilting her head back, she slid the point into the side of her neck. Blood sprayed on the snow as she tugged the knife across her throat, pushing it in deeply, jugular, trachea, carotid, severed in a slow series of dull pops.

Blood rained from the not-sky, hot and bitter as it splattered on Cassie's face, in her mouth, in her eyes, soaking her almost instantly, drenching her red.

Then snow, and Ali speaking in a low, burbling singsong.

"This is what you wanted, right?" Her head lolled loosely, still tilted back. Her voice came from the wet, red gash across her throat, the blood-rimmed second mouth she had carved into herself.

Cassie cowered back. "I didn't," she said. "I didn't."

Opening her hand, Ali let the knife fall. Cassie watched it spin slowly down, down, until it disappeared in the snow.

"No," Ali said, her head flopping loosely. "But you wanted to. You dreamed about it."

"But I didn't—"

"It was only a matter of time."

Ali raised her hands to her neck, gingerly touched the edges of the gash in her throat with her fingertips. "It doesn't even hurt," she said quietly.

More firmly, she ran the fingertips of her right hand along the top edge of the cut, tracing the full length of it from just under her left ear to just under her right.

With her left hand, she did the same thing along the bottom edge of the cut. Both her arms were quickly soaked, blood dripping from her elbows onto the snow.

She slipped the four fingers of each hand into the wound, pressing them in when they met resistance. Past the first knuckles. The second.

Then, curling her fingers, she tugged. With her right hand pulling up, and her left pulling down, Ali tore the remaining flesh of her neck, a crunching, shredding sound as the wound widened, blood spraying upward as she wrenched back on her own head.

One final, brutal rip, and a snap echoed through the snowy air as she broke her own neck.

Cassie tried to hide her eyes, but she couldn't look away, not even as Ali tore her own head off. Not even as she held it at her side for a moment, fingers clenched deep in its throat, before dropping it into the snow.

There was a dull thud.

Cassie doubled over at the waist, gorge rising in her throat, spilling out of her mouth with a sulphurous burning.

Feathers.

Black feathers spilling wetly into the snow, steaming yellow in the still air.

Ali's sightless eyes stared at her from the snow across the null space, blood soaking the white under the ragged edge of her neck.

Cassie heaved again. Nothing came up but feathers.

Ali's body was still standing, like gravity didn't exist: the body didn't waver, didn't move, simply stood. Snow fell on the bloody stump of her neck, sizzling against the blood.

All else was still. Silent.

The snow swirled.

And then Ali's hands reached up, began to dig at the bloody meat of her neck, fingers working with wet, squelching noises, pulling at the flesh, tugging at it, yanking it down.

As she pulled, something seemed to be pushing up, a bubble of what almost looked like skin slowly pushing at the stump,

Ali's hands seeming to guide its rise, pulling down on the flesh.

It looked like her mother helping Heather pull on a sweater, the collar tight, the head pushing up through the hole—

Not a head.

The membrane split, and there was the monkey's little hat. The hands kept pulling, and the monkey's head slithered up the bloody remnants of Ali's neck like it was putting on her body.

And then it was just the monkey, grinning at Cassie from both its faces at once.

"You see," it said, every word a laugh. "This is all you. This is your world. You made it."

Cassie didn't move, didn't speak. She stood helplessly as the monkey danced, as it drew back and kicked Ali's head, which arced into the non-distance and disappeared.

"You've been building it your whole life. This place"—the monkey stopped dancing, straightened up into a show of respectability and stepped toward her—"is yours." He leaned in, like he was going to try to kiss her. "And you"—he touched her under the chin with a finger that felt like soft leather—"are mine."

She cringed away, tried to pull into herself.

"No," said a voice from beside her. "She's not."

Ali took her hand.

《 》

In the bedroom, he watched as the flames roared between the two girls, building from red to orange to blue to a pure white, a fire that lit the room, a heat that warmed even the cold of him.

Bathing in the heat, the light, he moved toward the bed.

It was time.

The world had disappeared. Harrison no longer even registered the falling snow, the bitter cold. Everything had contracted to a single point of focus: the door at the side of the house. Getting there. Getting inside.

Plant the elbow. Pull.

Every stretch, every tug pulled at the wound at his side, forced another hot jet of blood against his hand. His vision swam and flickered as he fought against passing out.

Plant the elbow. Pull.

The snow looked so welcoming, so warm. He wanted to lower his head to his arm, nestle down in the soft white comfort, let himself float away. But he wouldn't. He couldn't.

He just needed to make it to the door. He needed to make it inside.

Plant the elbow. Pull.

He thought of Cassandra Weathers, helpless in the dark, not knowing what evil was lurking just outside her dreams.

He thought of Laura Ensley, her body splayed open on the garbage-strewn ground in that alley, the way her eyes had stared sightlessly toward the sky as the snow fell on them.

He thought of his daughters, tucked into their beds, thinking of nothing more than their stockings in the morning, full of wishes and dreams.

Plant the elbow. Pull.

The door wavered in his awareness. So close.

Three more stretches.

Two.

One.

Pulling himself down the two short steps to the door, he twisted and stretched, biting back a scream as the knife wound gaped and bled into his hand. He pulled himself so he was partially sitting, leaning against the door frame.

His hand shook as he reached for the doorknob.

Please let it be unlocked. Please let it be unlocked.

The door swung open almost silently, and Harrison allowed himself to fall into the apartment.

≪ ≫

The monkey stared at the two girls.

For a long moment, it was silent.

Then: "You . . . you can't be here!" Its voice was a petulant squawk.

Cassie felt Ali squeeze her hand. "But here I am."

"How—" The monkey did a backflip, landed and glared at Ali. "This is *my* place!" The monkey's voice had no trace of mockery now. Instead, there was anger, frustration. And something else, something it took Cassie a moment to recognize it was so alien, so unexpected.

Fear.

"No," she said slowly, realization only gradually building in her. "This is my place. You just told me."

"But this, this—" The monkey stepped toward Cassie. "You're mine," he snarled.

"No, I'm not," Cassie said, calmly stepping between them. "You stole me when I was a little girl. I was never yours."

Ali looked at Cassie and brought her other hand around to cup their two joined hands. Cassie felt a rush of heat, a slow, sure warmth. Ali.

The monkey's eyes widened. "You can't. You can't."

And something began to happen to its face. Its features blurred, flickered, like a television trying to find a distant station, shapes and images shimmering and swimming, never resolving, never settling.

Lifting her head, Cassie stared directly into the monkey's eyes. "I was so scared, and you were there. You took me away. You made me think I was safe. But it was you all along. You stole me, and you kept me a prisoner of my own fears. Of things I didn't understand. You built this place." She looked around the void. "But it's not going to work on me anymore."

She turned to Ali. "We all have our own darkness," she said. "We all fight it, every day."

And then she turned back to the monkey. "The only power you've ever had is what I've given you and what you stole from me. And that's gone."

She turned back to Ali again, opened her mouth to speak, but the other girl was gone, the snow swirling like she had never been there at all.

There was a long moment of silence, then the monkey howled. "You see?" he said, his voice frenetic. "You see what I can do? She's gone. Just like everyone who ever loved you is gone."

But Cassie had seen the look of confusion on the monkey's face, could hear the frantic edge under its words.

"No," she said, and a stark certainty rose in her. "You didn't do that. You couldn't."

The monkey stared at her. "I made her go away. It's just you and—"

"No," Cassie said again, feeling herself straighten, feeling herself grow strong. "You couldn't. You didn't." She took a step toward the monkey, and the monkey stepped back. "You can't."

The strength vibrated through her, like blood flowing back into a foot that had fallen asleep. She tingled, and it felt like she was expanding. Growing. Already the monkey seemed smaller, weaker.

"I thought you were my friend," she said. "And this whole time it was you. You kept me afraid. You made me doubt every thing. Even myself."

The monkey was small now, no bigger than he had been when she had kept him so close, had clung to him every night.

Then even smaller.

"You kept me weak."

She was towering over the monkey now, standing between two worlds, inside both the null space that the monkey had built inside her, and the furnace room, the fire crackling nearby.

She shook her head. "You have no power over me." She bit her lower lip with the sadness of the realization. "You never did."

The monkey looked at the snowy ground, eyes wide and sad.

Then: buttons.

The sock monkey had fallen on the red blanket next to the wood stove. Next to it was her battered copy of *The Wonderful Wizard of Oz*, a slip of construction paper marking her place.

She had always loved the basement; it was always so safe, so warm. She would spend hours down here, reading or drawing pictures. Mom would bring her snacks, and when Dad came down to tend the fire, he would sit with her, read her stories, and they would laugh and talk, and it was the most wonderful thing she could imagine.

Cassie smiled even as the tears stained her cheeks. That had all changed. Her favourite place in the world had turned into a nightmare. A dream that she had lived through, over and over again, on that blanket, in front of the stove.

A dream that she had survived.

She sniffed deeply, suddenly aware of the tears coursing down her cheeks.

When she left the furnace room, she left the monkey on the blanket, button eyes staring unseeing as she climbed the stairs, her eyes fixed on the rectangle of light at the top.

She would never come back here again.

"Cassandra."

She stopped, convinced that she was imagining the sound, the singsong cadences of her name.

"Cassandra."

She clutched the railing, knowing better than to trust it with any of her weight as she climbed the stairs.

"Cassandra."

She shook her head, tried to will the sound away. "No, no, no," she muttered.

She knew that if she reached the light, it would be okay. If she could just get to the light . . .

"Cassandra."

She climbed faster and faster, counting the stairs as she went, the old habit still there, even in her dreams.

Nineteen, twenty-three, twenty-eight.

"Cassandra."

Thirty-one, thirty-seven, forty.

The rectangle of light wasn't getting any closer, no matter how far she climbed, no matter how fast.

"Cassandra!"

Finally, she burst through the doorway at the top of the stairs into—

≪ ≫

For a moment she didn't know where she was.

No—she recognized Ali's pillows, the bedroom, the shelf beside the bed with the alarm clock. It was Ali's room, she knew that, but something was wrong. The room was too bright. Something was—

And then her heart stopped.

Ali was standing in the corner, her eyes wide with fear, staring wordlessly at Cassie.

Tears rolled down her cheeks, but she didn't make a sound.

Someone was standing behind her, holding the blade of a knife to her throat.

"I thought you'd never wake up, Cassandra," Brother Paul said, stretching out the syllables of her name like they were a prize, almost singing them. "Or is it Dorothy?" He smiled, revealing his teeth. "It doesn't matter."

Cassie shook her head, tried to make the image go away, tried to force herself to wake up.

"Oh, you're not dreaming," Brother Paul said. "God knows it was hard enough to wake you."

Cassie struggled to rise, but Brother Paul shook his head. "No, no, no," he said, almost clucking his tongue. He tugged back on Ali's hair, pressed the knife harder against her throat, drawing a fine line of blood.

Cassie froze. She held up her hands to reassure him and slowly raised herself to a sitting position.

"I'm not moving."

And then nobody said anything.

"What . . . what are you going to do?" Ali said finally. "There's nothing. Take whatever you want."

Brother Paul smiled again.

"You killed Skylark." Cassie's voice echoed into the silence. Ali flinched, and Brother Paul blinked.

"Your friend," he said.

Cassie's breath burned in her throat.

"Did you know that wasn't even her real name?" He looked as if Cassie should be surprised by this revelation. "It took some convincing, but she eventually told me. Laura . . . something." He seemed to be savouring the memory.

Cassie could imagine Skylark's last moments: scared and begging for her life, crying, cowering, but still holding fast to her deepest of secrets.

What had he done to get her to tell him her name?

"Why?" she asked softly, unable to help herself, knowing that he wouldn't answer.

But he did. "Why did I kill her, your little friend?"

Cassie hesitated, then nodded. "She loved you. She trusted you."

Brother Paul nodded deeply. "I know," he said, his grin growing impossibly wide. "That made it so much better."

Ali gasped, and the knife slid against her throat, opening another fine cut.

The pain stilled her, but large tears slid from her eyes. She looked desperately at Cassie.

Her eyes flickered, the tiniest of motions. Cassie tried to look like she wasn't looking, kept her gaze fast on Brother Paul as he spoke.

"But . . . why?" Cassie had no ideas, no plan. She just knew that as long as he was talking, he couldn't do anything else.

Ali's eyes flicked again, first to Cassie, then to the open bedroom door, then back to Cassie.

"Because I wanted to," he said. "No, I'm sorry. That was flip." He drew the knife along the side of Ali's throat again, drawing another line of blood, another suppressed shriek. "Because I needed to."

Ali's eyes flickered toward the doorway, back to Cassie, her face tightening with an expression of urgency.

"I was never much into safaris," he said, retightening his grip on Ali's hair. "I had friends in school who would summer in Africa with their parents. I never really saw the point. Until I realized how brilliant it was."

Ali's eyes—to the door, back to Cassie, to the door. When Cassie finally figured out what she was trying to communicate, she had to fight to keep her face still, to not respond.

Ali wanted her to run.

"A world, just for hunting," Brother Paul said, oblivious to everything passing between Cassie and Ali. "So every so often I build myself a wildlife preserve." He smiled and licked his lips. "You have to go where the wildlife is, of course. So I watch the news. I see reports of unsolved murders, like Victoria, a few months ago. Cliff Wolcott." He shook his head. "You use the natural terrain, the camouflage. Once you've found the right place, though, you wouldn't believe how easy it is." He shook his head slightly, and in that moment of distraction, Cassie shook her head at Ali, the slightest of motions, barely a twitch, but firm enough to show that she was sure: she wouldn't leave Ali.

Ali responded with a stern set of her jaw, a lingering stare at the door, then a glare at Cassie, but Cassie wasn't going to be swayed. She wasn't going to run.

"Those people, they're all looking so desperately for something to believe in. If you give them food, and give them a sense of belonging, they'll follow you anywhere." He shrugged, and Ali glanced again at the door. "Look at history. Look at Hitler. Look at Jesus. It's all the same."

"Sure, you have to deal with all the riff-raff, all the shit, but it's worth it when someone like your friend Skylark comes along. And you know what?" He looked seriously at Cassie, as if the question was more than rhetorical. "There's always someone like Skylark." His eyes shone as he thought about her. "So young. So . . . idealistic. So broken." He looked almost wistful. "Girls like her," he said, his voice sounding far away. "They taste so sweet."

Cassie shuddered, and Brother Paul noticed. "But you," he said. "You're something special. I've never seen a girl like you. So fiery, so full of love, so shattered." She could feel his hunger. "I've watched you for a long time."

"So you just . . . you find a place where someone is killing people, you create these communities, you attract people, then you—" She struggled to keep the conversation going, even though the words tasted like copper in her mouth.

"I go home," he said, with a note of pride.

"Home?"

"Toronto," he said. "I've got a nice place in Rosedale. Well, it was my parents' place, but I like it."

"So . . ." Cassie struggled with what he was saying. "You're rich?"

His smile was smug. "I'm not like you," he said.

"So you create these places, you find these girls and then you just . . ."

"Disappear," he said, waving his knife hand like a bird in flight.

Then it clicked. "Edmonton," she said. "That's what Sarah meant."

He looked like he was going to laugh. "Oh, she told you, did she? I thought I got to her before she had a chance to say anything."

She could still hear the fear in the woman's voice. "You killed her?"

"Well," he said. "I helped." He tilted his head, tugged on Ali's hair. "The wonderful thing about paranoid schizophrenics is that they're so suggestible if they're off their meds. In fairness, though, she did a far better job of it than I would have."

The full significance of what he was saying was only beginning to resolve itself in Cassie's mind. How many girls had there been? How many murders? How many cities?

"I honestly didn't expect her to recognize me," he said. "She was pretty nutted out. Hmm." It was a puzzled sound. "I guess it's nice that people can still surprise you."

He tightened his grip in Ali's hair, pulled her taller, taut. "Enough talking," he said. "I want to be on the first flight home, and I don't want to rush anything."

He smiled lasciviously at Cassie as he lifted the knife away from Ali's neck and slipped it, blade up, into the neckline of the T-shirt she had put on to sleep in.

"First your girlfriend," he said. "Then you." He slid the knife downward, the fabric parting with a barely audible hiss against the blade. "Saving the best for last."

Every muscle in Cassie's body tensed, coiled.

As the knife slipped through the fabric, Ali's T-shirt fell open, and Brother Paul glanced down.

Just as Cassie had known he would.

She sprang from the bed, planted one foot on the floor, and bounded for the door.

Brother Paul was fast, but not faster than she had imagined.

Throwing Ali out of the way, he reached her before she got to the door, grabbed her hair and pulled her off her feet, back into the room.

She tumbled to the floor beside the bed, the wind pushed out of her, her head screaming where he had yanked her hair. Her shoulder flashed with pain where it had taken the weight of her falling body.

But she was right where she wanted to be.

"You little bitch," Brother Paul screamed, kicking her so hard in the side she almost threw up. "You little whore."

As he started to drag her across the room by her hair, she forced herself to roll toward him, her hand coming up from under the edge of the bed, the knife flashing in the light as she drove it into his calf.

The point of the blade caught on his jeans, then sliced through, plunging deep into the tight ball of muscle and tendon.

Brother Paul screamed, started to turn, and Cassie forced the knife back and forth in the back of his leg, the blade tearing more than cutting. Blood soaked her hand, the handle of the knife suddenly slick, hard to hold, but Cassie tightened her grip, kept sawing at Brother Paul's calf until, with one final pop and a long scream, he dropped.

He fell partially atop her, crushing her arm, forcing her to lose her grip on the knife. But he lost his as well, and it clattered to the floor.

Not far enough away, though. Cassie watched helplessly as he scrambled for the knife. She struggled against his weight, but she was pinned, powerless, as his fingers curled around the handle of the blade.

There was a scream, and Ali was towering over them, eyes flaming, her body painted with the blood from her neck. Her foot came down on his arm, pinned it to the floor, his hand springing open and releasing the knife.

Then she stomped, heel first, on his wrist, once, twice, three times, until she crushed it with one final footfall, a splintering, crunching sound coming almost at the same moment as Brother Paul's high pitched scream.

Ali didn't stop.

Dropping to her knees, she grabbed his hair with both hands—directly over each ear—and smashed his head into the floor.

"You son of a bitch," she cried, smashing his head again, the crunching smack punctuated with a desperate sob.

"Ali." Cassie struggled, pulled herself free of the weight of his body. "Ali."

She didn't seem to hear. She smashed his head into the floor again.

"Ali." She crawled around Brother Paul's body. "Ali," she cried, touching her shoulder, closing her arms around her. "Come on. Stop." The floor was streaked with blood under the man's head, his hair wet and matted.

She smashed his head again.

"Come on." Cassie lifted her away, and Brother Paul's head dropped with a damp thud. "He can't hurt you. It's all right. It's all over."

Ali was a dead weight in her arms and Cassie couldn't hold her. They slumped together, sliding down the wall, coming to rest a short distance away from the heap of his body.

Cassie cradled Ali in her arms, stroking her shoulders, brushing back her hair.

"Shh," she said. "Shh. It's all right."

Ali was looking directly at Brother Paul. "Is he—"

Cassie studied him for a moment. "No, look. His chest." It was slight, but Brother Paul's chest rose and fell as he breathed.

"We should call the police," Ali said, her voice suddenly clear of any panic, any desperation. "And an ambulance."

But neither of them moved.

"Thank you," Ali said, and Cassie kissed her gently on the forehead. "I meant it, though." Her voice had softened, taken on a slow, dreamlike quality. "When I told you to run."

"I know," Cassie said, pulling her even closer. "But I'm not running anymore."

A cold wind seemed to blow through the bedroom, bringing the faint sound of sirens.

AFTER

The darkest of winter was the time of greatest light, when families gathered and friends embraced and enemies laid down their differences.

It was in the light that the Darkness found its home.

It moved unseen through the shopping malls and crowded sidewalks, in the Christmas carols and the coloured lights, between the candles and the shop windows.

It jumped from person to person, host to host. It knew that in the brightest of lights were the darkest of shadows.

The car screeched out of the parkade, deliberately cutting off the approaching driver.

The driver of the cut-off car shouted once, then let the anger settle in, speeding up to keep right on the bumper of the bastard who had cut him off, ignoring the yellow light of the intersection.

The mother pulled her child back from the edge of the road, screaming about being more careful as she lifted the child and threw her into the stroller.

The old man shouted at the young mother as she juggled her bags, as the toddler cried in the stroller.

The boys outside the shopping mall laughed at the shouting old man.

The security guard stepped out the front door, toward the boys.

The Darkness takes us all.

Every time the door swung open, every time someone came into the restaurant, Cassie would glance up, turning slightly, her body tensing, her heart racing.

Then Ali would squeeze her hand under the table, and she would remember to breathe again.

"Anytime now," Constable Farrow said, across the table. "Anytime."

The sidewalks outside the window were clotted with people, bright colours against the grey Boxing Day sky, everyone loaded down with packages, still smiling in the post-Christmas glow.

The restaurant was packed too, every table full, except the one next to the three women. Hong had let Ali put a *Reserved* sign on it, trying to look gruff, but failing utterly.

He had spent most of the past fifteen minutes at the bar watching them, pretending to be busy. Every time someone took even a sip out of their drink, he was there to refill, shushing Ali when she started to stand up, offering to help with the full house.

"We've got it under control," he said. "You've been through enough already."

"We should call the police," Cassie had said, still holding Ali as close as she could, both of them staring at Brother Paul's fallen body, both of them watching the slow, uncertain rise and fall of his chest.

"The kitchen," Ali had said. "The phone is in the kitchen."

They had held on to each other for support as they stumbled out of the bedroom, Ali's hand pressed against the cut on her throat, tiptoeing through the darkness, the strange cold until they reached the light switch on the wall outside the door. It took Ali two tries to flick the switch.

When the lights came on, Cassie had crumpled to the ground, her breath stuck deep inside her chest, building inside her like a muted roar of anguish and pain.

Constable Harrison was lying on the kitchen floor, still and silent. A pool of blood was dark, almost black on the tiles next to his left side, and as Cassie watched, the surface of the blood seemed to shimmer, creeping farther and farther away from him. Behind him, the door was wide open, snow swirling in the light from the kitchen.

He was holding the telephone in his right hand. A scratchy, distorted voice echoed in the silence. "Hold on, Constable. Hold on. Cars are en route."

Seconds later, red lights sprayed across the falling snow, and police officers were spilling through the door, guns drawn, voices shouting, "Get down, get down."

The fourth officer through the door, smaller than the others, dropped to her knees beside Harrison's body, her gun falling to the floor as she grabbed him by the shoulders of his heavy coat.

"Harrison!" Farrow had shouted. "Harrison!"

As if the sound of her voice could bring him back.

"He always was a prima donna," Farrow muttered, taking a sip of her coffee.

Hong refilled the cup the moment she set it down.

Cassie remembered a blinking Christmas tree in the corner of the emergency room. There was no one else there.

The nurses had let them stay together. Cassie had held Ali's hand as the doctor examined the cut on her throat.

"This should heal up just fine," he had said, as he applied butterfly closures to the wound. "It could have been a whole lot worse."

Cassie and Ali had just looked at each other.

"Now let's take a look at you," the doctor had said, turning to Cassie.

Cassie shook her head. "I'm all right," she said.

"How about you let me be the judge of that, okay?" The doctor's smile had been warm, friendly.

When they finally emerged from the warren of examining rooms behind the Restricted Access door, Farrow was in the waiting area, talking to the cop who had ridden in with them.

Farrow broke off in mid-sentence and crossed the floor to them in three steps. The front of her coat was wet; it took Cassie a moment to realize that it was Harrison's blood.

"Are you all right?" Farrow asked.

Ali had nodded, but Cassie asked, "Where's Constable Harrison? Where's Chris?"

Farrow flinched. "He's in surgery," she said, her voice shaking. She sniffed, and Cassie could see the wet of tears in the corners of her eyes. "The doctors don't know. They rushed him right in."

"Come here," Cassie said, touching her arm, guiding her toward the chairs in the waiting area. "Let's sit down."

"Actually . . ." The cop who had accompanied them in the ambulance had appeared on Farrow's other side. "We need to get you to the station. We need to get statements, and—"

"No," Cassie said, sitting down next to her. "We're not going anywhere."

"I've got orders."

"I don't care," Cassie said flatly. And then, turning to Farrow, "Cream and sugar, right?"

Farrow hesitated, then nodded.

Cassie looked pointedly at the cop. "Would you mind?"

The cop stared at her for a moment, then shook his head. "Sure," he said. "I need to call in anyway. Do you want anything while I'm at the machine?" He glanced between Cassie and Ali, who had sat down next to her.

"I'm all right," she had said.

The world outside the restaurant windows was slate grey, high clouds bright and cold. A crow alighted on the concrete rim of the planter across the sidewalk.

"Here he is," Cassie said, catching a glimpse of someone coming down the sidewalk.

Ali jumped up to hold the door open for him.

"I could get used to this," Harrison said, smiling at Ali, walking slowly toward the table.

Farrow had already pulled his chair out for him. "Don't," she warned.

Harrison was drawn and pale, and he looked weak, but the grey circles were gone from around his eyes, and there was a smile at the corner of his mouth.

"We were just talking about you," Farrow said.

"Conquering hero?"

"Prima donna."

He smiled. "That works too."

Cassie had no idea what to say, what words might even come close to doing justice to what she was feeling. As she looked at him, tears welled up in her eyes.

"You're doing okay?" he asked, as Ali sat back down and took her hand again.

She nodded. "Better than," she said.

"That's good."

"What about you? You're . . . ?"

"Apparently I'm a miracle," he said, shooting a glance at Farrow.

"You're just a crappy dresser."

"It could have been a lot worse," the surgeon had reported, hours later. The sun had come up on Christmas morning, and they could see the world whitening outside the emergency room windows.

Cassie wondered if doctors in emergency were required to say that.

"Your partner's going to be fine," the doctor had continued, and Cassie thought she saw Farrow shudder. "It appears that the blade got diverted by the layers of clothing he was wearing. An inch to the left . . ." He shook his head. "As it is, it's largely a flesh wound. We've cleaned it and double-checked it and stitched it up."

Cassie's ears had roared with relief.

"I resent that remark," Harrison said, as Hong slipped a cup of coffee in front of him.

"You were saved by a hoodie," Farrow said.

Watching the two of them talk, Cassie squeezed Ali's hand.

After the surgeon had left, the three of them had sat in the waiting area for a long time, not saying anything. The television high in the corner of the room provided a constant running hum of news, mostly footage of Christmas celebrations from around the world.

The cop who had accompanied them in the ambulance, who had been sitting silently across from them, cleared his throat pointedly.

"Jane," Cassie said quietly.

Farrow turned sharply at the sound of her first name.

"I think we have to go." She cocked her head in the direction of the waiting officer.

Farrow nodded slowly, like she should be saying something.

"Can you do me a favour?" Cassie asked, and her voice shook a little.

"Is it going to get me suspended?" Farrow smiled as she asked.

"I don't think so," Cassie said. "I was just . . . Can you call my mom, please?"

Ali's hand had been warm on her shoulder.

"So, are you gonna tell me what's in there?" Harrison asked, pointing at the file folders on the table in front of Farrow.

She raised an eyebrow. "You know our policy about not commenting on ongoing investigations. Last I heard, you were suspended."

Harrison nodded slowly. "There is that," he said.

Farrow looked at him for a long moment, then broke off, shaking her head.

She opened up the top file.

"Well, first," she started, glancing at Cassie, then looking away. "I already told Cassie. Her father was arrested last night, crossing into the US."

"Here?"

Farrow shook her head. "In the Okanagan. As far as we can tell, he never came to the island."

Harrison nodded. "Well, that's something." Cassie looked down at the table and didn't see Harrison turn to her. "Was there a warrant?" he asked.

"There was an alert," Farrow said slowly, carefully. "Investigators, after the fire . . ."

"They found pictures," Cassie said, without looking up. "In the basement. Pictures of me. And other girls." She squeezed Ali's hand, struggled to steady her breath. She didn't know how to react, what to feel.

It was over. The basement was gone.

In the silence, she realized that something had happened. Looking up, she met Harrison's eye.

"I'm sorry," he said. "I'm sorry I didn't—"

She shook her head to cut him off. "You tried," she said. "That was more than almost anyone else ever did."

He looked distraught, and like he wanted to speak, but no words came.

Farrow cleared her throat, moved the file to the bottom of the small pile.

"Paul James Corbett," she said. "A.k.a. Paul Corbett. A.k.a. Brother Paul. A.k.a. Brother James."

At the police station, they had separated Cassie and Ali, taking them into different interview rooms.

Cassie spent about forty-five minutes in the first interview, answering every question the heavy-set detective with the Italian name asked as best she could: where had she met Brother Paul, could she detail any encounters she had had with Brother Paul, what was the nature of her relationship with Brother Paul, what was the nature of her relationship with Sarah from Edmonton, what was the nature of her relationship with Laura Ensley . . .

"I'm just about done," he said, and the apology in his tone seemed genuine. "I just want to ask you about one more thing."

Reaching into a bag that had been out of sight under the edge of the table, he set a black book in front of Cassie.

"Do you recognize this?"

She had hesitated, then nodded. With the duct tape along the spine, it was unmistakable. "It was Brother Paul's."

"You saw him with it?"

She nodded. "Yes. He always had it with him."

The detective picked the book off the table and opened it to the first page. "Did you ever have any idea what was in it?"

Cassie had shaken her head, and the detective had begun to read in a flat monotone. "There are only two elements, eternally opposed, irreconcilable, irreducible. Light. And the Darkness. In the beginning God created the heaven and the earth. And the earth was without form, and void; and the Darkness was upon the face of the deep." He closed the book. "It goes on and on like that."

Across the sidewalk, another crow alighted on the edge of the planter.

"Well, we interviewed Cassie and Ali early on Christmas morning, and again later in the day." Farrow looked across the table at them, then returned to the folder. "And based on their statements we started making some calls. It turns out that Mr. Corbett had something of a secret life."

Harrison looked at Cassie, his gaze lingering as Farrow continued.

"He appears to have been living on quite a sizable inheritance following the death of his parents in a car accident about twelve years ago." She looked at Harrison. "And yes, we're looking pretty closely at that."

"I would assume."

"We've started to put together his travel records from the last decade or so. It appears that he would take lengthy trips every fall. Montreal. Halifax. St. John's. Edmonton." Cassie flinched. "These trips seem to coincide with the disappearances of young women in each of those cities."

She sighed heavily and closed the folder. "It appears that Mr. Corbett would travel to cities where young women were being reported missing. And he would add to that number. One or two victims at a time. Usually runaways. And he was always well gone and away before the bodies were found or any discrepancies between the killings were noticed." Farrow looked meaningfully at Harrison.

"He called them 'game preserves,'" Cassie said quietly. "The places that he made. The communities. They were his own private hunting reserves."

Farrow looked toward the bar, avoiding meeting Cassie's eye as she said, "He also . . . There was a book. At the crime scene."

Cassie flinched at the memory, then nodded. "He carried that with him everywhere. He used to hold it." She thought back to the circles at the camp, those nights next to Skylark, listening to Brother Paul talk about how they were all changing the world. "He never told us what it was. He just said that he had found all of the answers in it."

Farrow snorted. "Egotistical—" She muttered something that might have been "prick."

Turning back to Cassie, she leaned over the table. "It was a journal," she said. "Of his . . ." Farrow nodded. "Beliefs. And his activities."

Ali squeezed her hand as she shuddered.

Harrison cleared his throat. "And Mr. Corbett is now—" he started, changing the subject.

Farrow looked pointedly at Ali. "He's currently recovering from injuries sustained on Christmas Eve. The reports I have indicate head trauma, a broken wrist"—Ali began to blush, and Cassie smiled at her—"and a knife wound to the back of the leg. Oh, and he's also been charged with one count of murder, with a dozen or so others pending. And something about a charge of attempted murder?" She raised her eyebrows at Harrison, who just nodded. "You want to tell me what the hell you thought you were doing?"

The question seemed to take Harrison by surprise.

"I was—"

"You went in without backup, without a side arm. You could have gotten yourself killed. You just about did get yourself killed." Farrow's voice broke.

"I'm sorry," he said. "I couldn't just stand back and . . ." He shook his head. "I knew that Wolcott hadn't killed Laura Ensley. And when I thought back to it, I remembered something Cassie had said about Edmonton, about something Sarah had said, so I thought it might have something to do with the camp. So I figured I should . . ." His voice trailed off and he seemed to shrink into himself.

"You figured you should follow me," Cassie said.

He nodded slowly.

She reached her hand across the table, and he took it.

"Thank you for that," she said.

Farrow sighed heavily. "Don't encourage him," she said, in a voice of transparent bluster. "We have partners for a reason."

"I figured I was in enough trouble already. I didn't want to pull you down with me."

Farrow leaned toward him. "Next time?" she said. "Pull me down with you. Deal?"

He smiled. "Deal," he said. "Though, I kinda doubt there's going to be a next time. As you mentioned, there is that small matter of a suspension."

"I imagine," Farrow said. "a bit of stupid heroics goes a long way toward clearing your name."

He shifted uncomfortably in his chair. "Anyway." He looked around the restaurant, then down at his watch. "So what's the story?" he asked. "Are they—"

"Ferry," Farrow explained, before Cassie could say anything. "They'll—"

The door swung open with a bang, smashing into the wall behind the fish tank. The bell jingled.

Cassie started to stand, her face twisting in a mix of anguish and hope. "Mom. Heather."

Across the sidewalk, the crows watched as the girl rose to her feet, her arms widening, her face breaking into tears. They watched as she crossed the room toward the door.

They cocked their heads together, their black eyes glistening in the steel air.

Then, as one, the crows took wing, rising into the cold wind, their bodies shadows, arcing and soaring against the winter-grey sky.

ACKNOWLEDGEMENTS

If you had told me when I started *Black Feathers* where I would be when I finished, what my life would be like, I wouldn't have believed you. And yet, here I am. Life is funny that way.

It's been a long road. Thanks are due to the many people who helped me get here.

First off, I would like to both acknowledge the support of the British Columbia Arts Council for their faith in this project and express my deepest gratitude to them.

For everyone who followed this road along with me via social media: apologies and appreciation, as appropriate.

Thanks to Martha Good, who never fails to inspire.

Thanks to Colin Holt, Lindsay Williams and Clare Hitchens for their keen eyes and valuable feedback during their early readings of this manuscript.

Thanks to Lisa Tench for her feedback and her friendship.

Thanks, always, to James Grainger, the one and only Saint Jimmy, whose unique outlook and stern vision give rise to the questions that make my books better.

Thanks, of course, to Cori Dusmann, whose support of this book in its earliest stages, and likewise of my writing career, made an incalculable difference.

And thanks to Samantha Holmes and everyone at Bolen Books—I may no longer be a bookseller, but you're still family.

Thanks to Erik and Svetlana and everyone at Floathouse in Victoria, who help to keep me grounded and inspired by turns.

As always, deepest thanks to Chris Bucci, Martha Magor Webb, Monica Pacheco and, of course, Anne McDermid, without whom I would be . . . best not to think about it.

Hearty thanks to everyone at HarperCollins Canada, but especially my editor, Jennifer Lambert, who may have gotten more than she bargained for when she decided to take a chance on this book and this author, and my copy editor, Chandra Wohleber, who saved me from myself.

Always, all my heart to Lex, fifteen years old as I write this. I'm probably a so-so father, but I have a great kid, one who never fails to amaze and inspire me. To see the world through Lex's eyes is a wonder, and I am so grateful. So, so grateful. I love you, kiddo. And you'll always be kiddo, no matter how much taller than me you are.

And Athena.

Words fail me. Just how something so quite new can feel so timeless is one of those mysteries I am content to never try to solve. Thank you for coming into my life when you did. Thank you for everything you brought, everything you bring. Just . . . thank you.